LUBA

FANTAGRAPHICS BOOKS

LUBA: THREE DAUGHTERS

Fantagraphics Books . 7563 Lake City Way NE . Seattle WA 98115

Edited by Gary Groth . Published by Gary Groth and Kim Thompson
Art Direction by Jacob Covey . Production by Paul Baresh

This is Volume 23 in THE COMPLETE LOVE AND ROCKETS.

The stories in this book originally appeared in Luba's Comics and Stories #3, 4, 6, 8;
Measles #1; and LOVE AND ROCKETS Vol. II #6, 11-16. "The Petra Question," "Mystery
of the Sea Hog," "Message from an X," "For Art's Sake," "Who the Fuck is Hector?,"
"Sister, Thithter," "Something About Pipo," "Ms. Super Fit USA," "Hector's 2¢", "Day
Job," and "Genetically Predisposed" appear here for the first time.

Distributed in the U.S. by W.W. Norton and Company, Inc. (212-354-5500)

Distributed in Canada by Raincoast Books (800-663-5714)

Distributed in the United Kingdom by Turnaround Distribution (208-829-3009)

See the last page for information on ordering more LOVE AND ROCKETS work!

First edition: August, 2006 . ISBN10: 1-56097-769-8 ISBN13: 978-1-56097-769-8

Printed in China.

LUBA
LUBA
THREE DAUGHTERS
LUBA

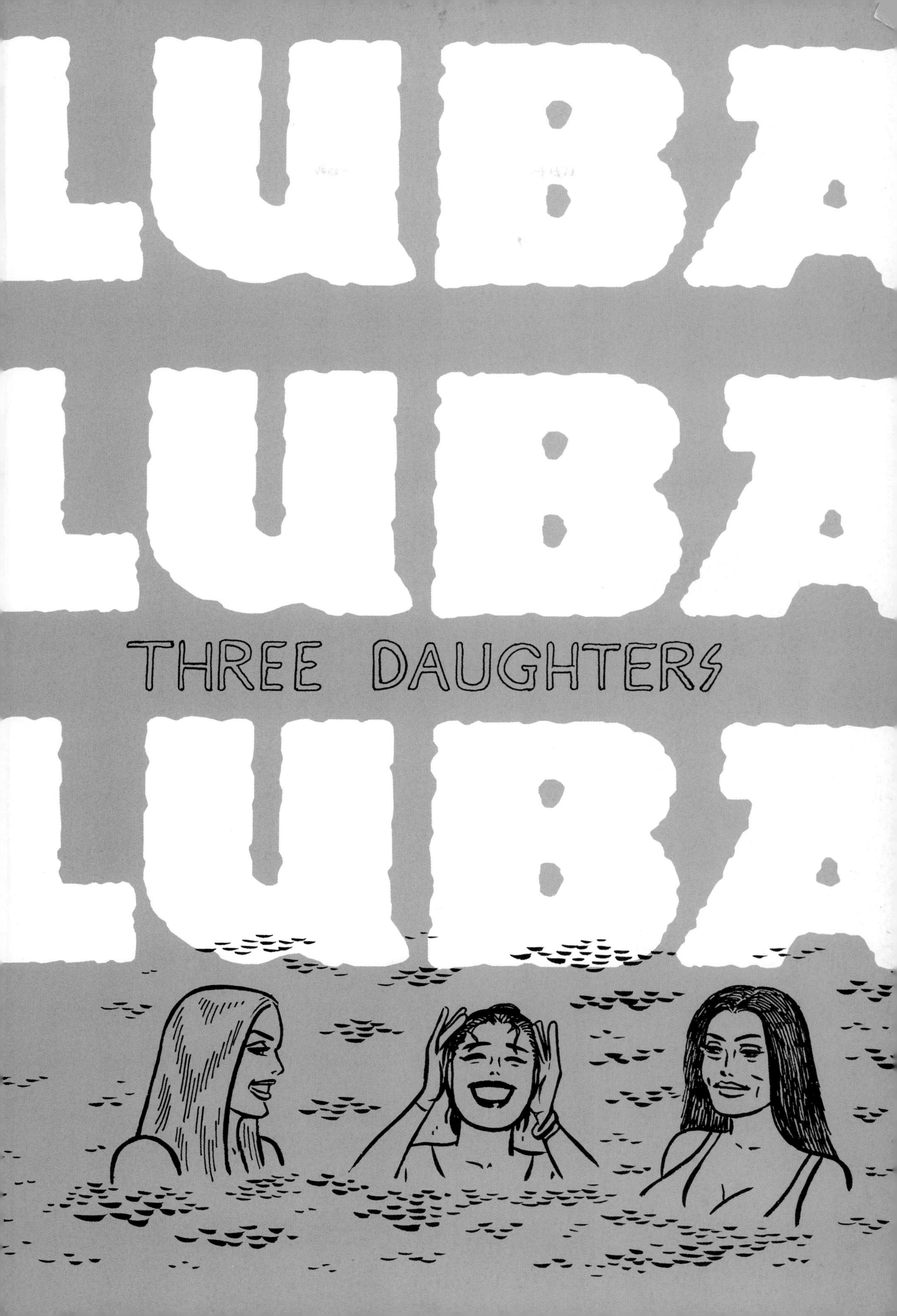

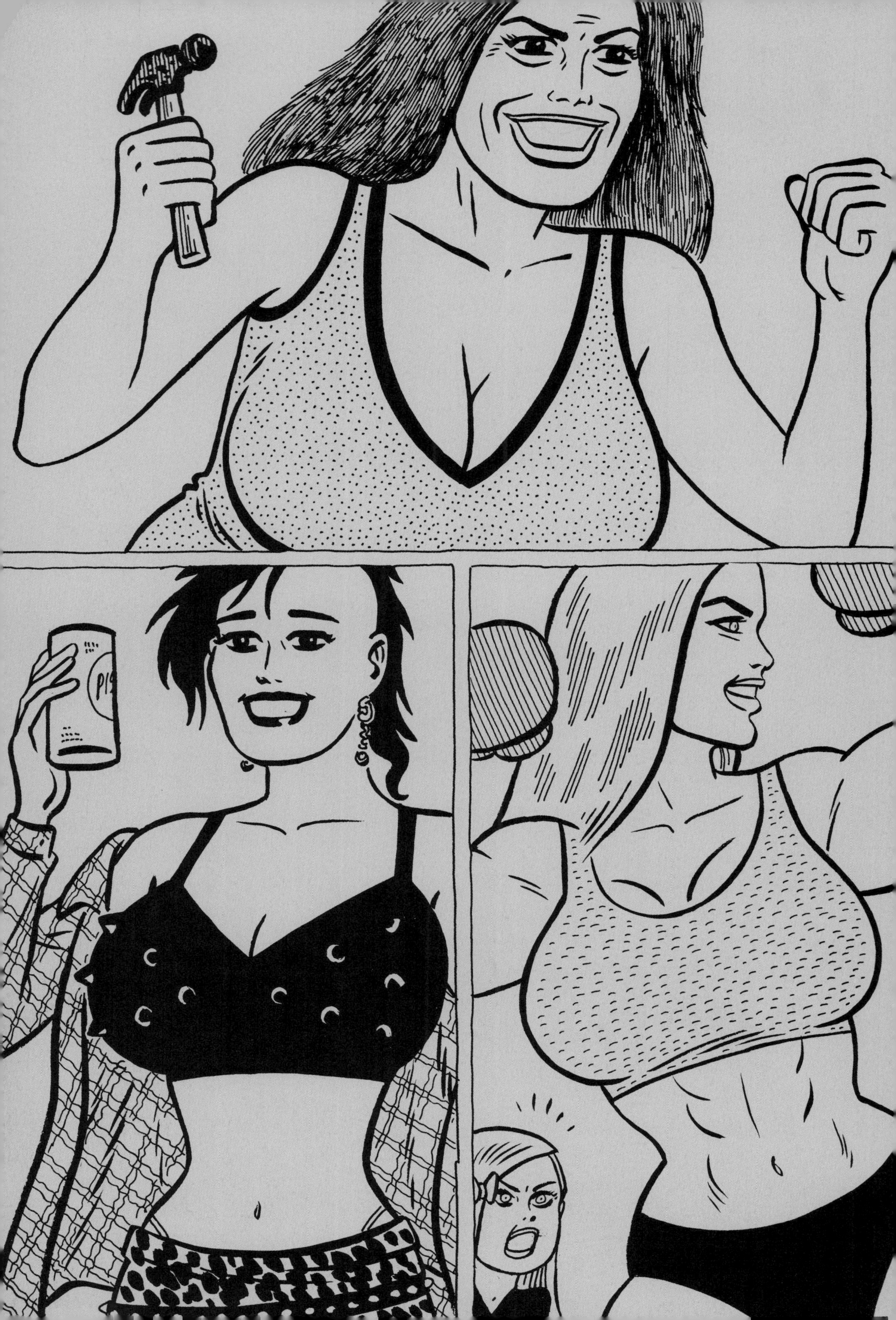

THREE DAUGHTERS

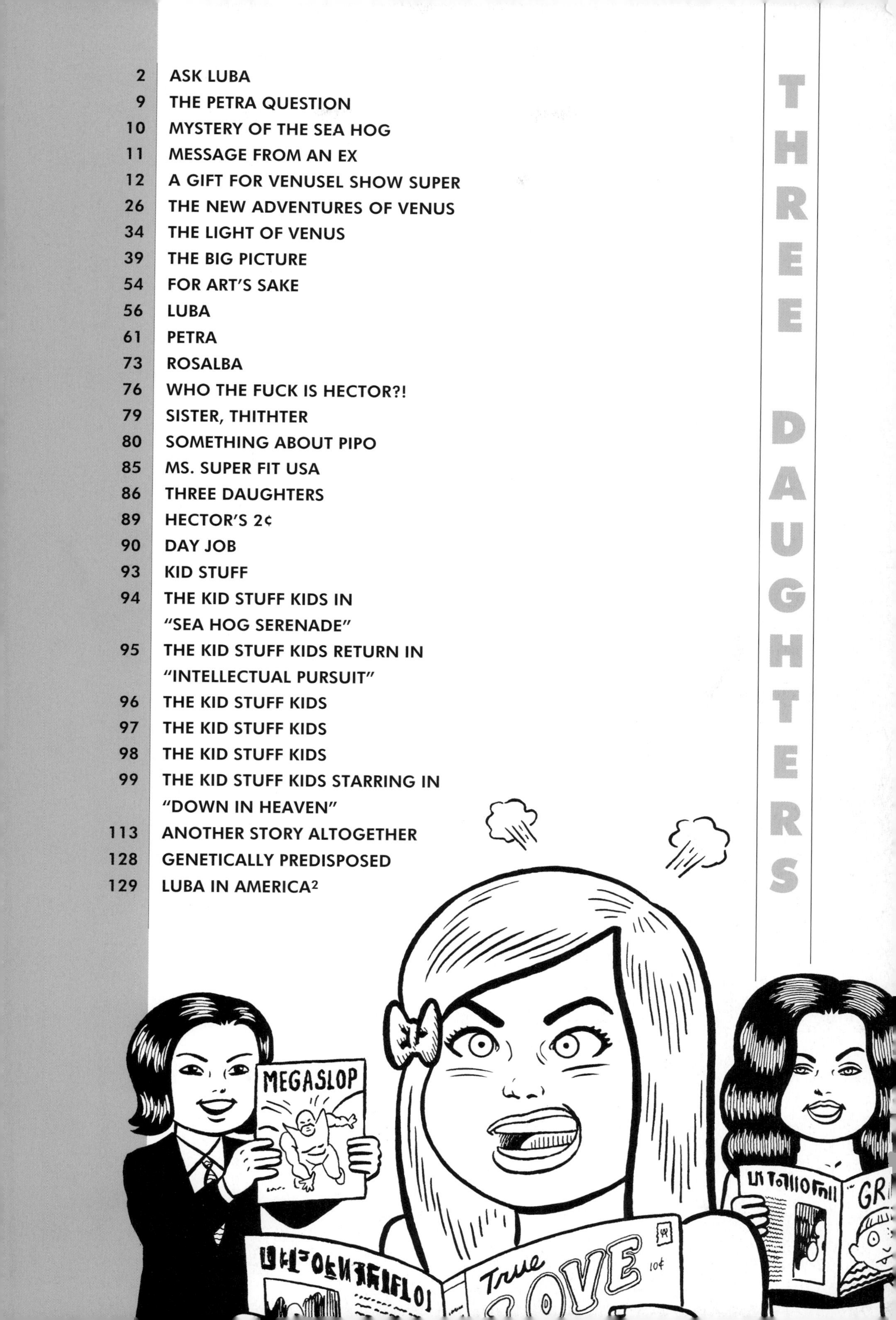

MEGASLOP
True LOVE
10¢

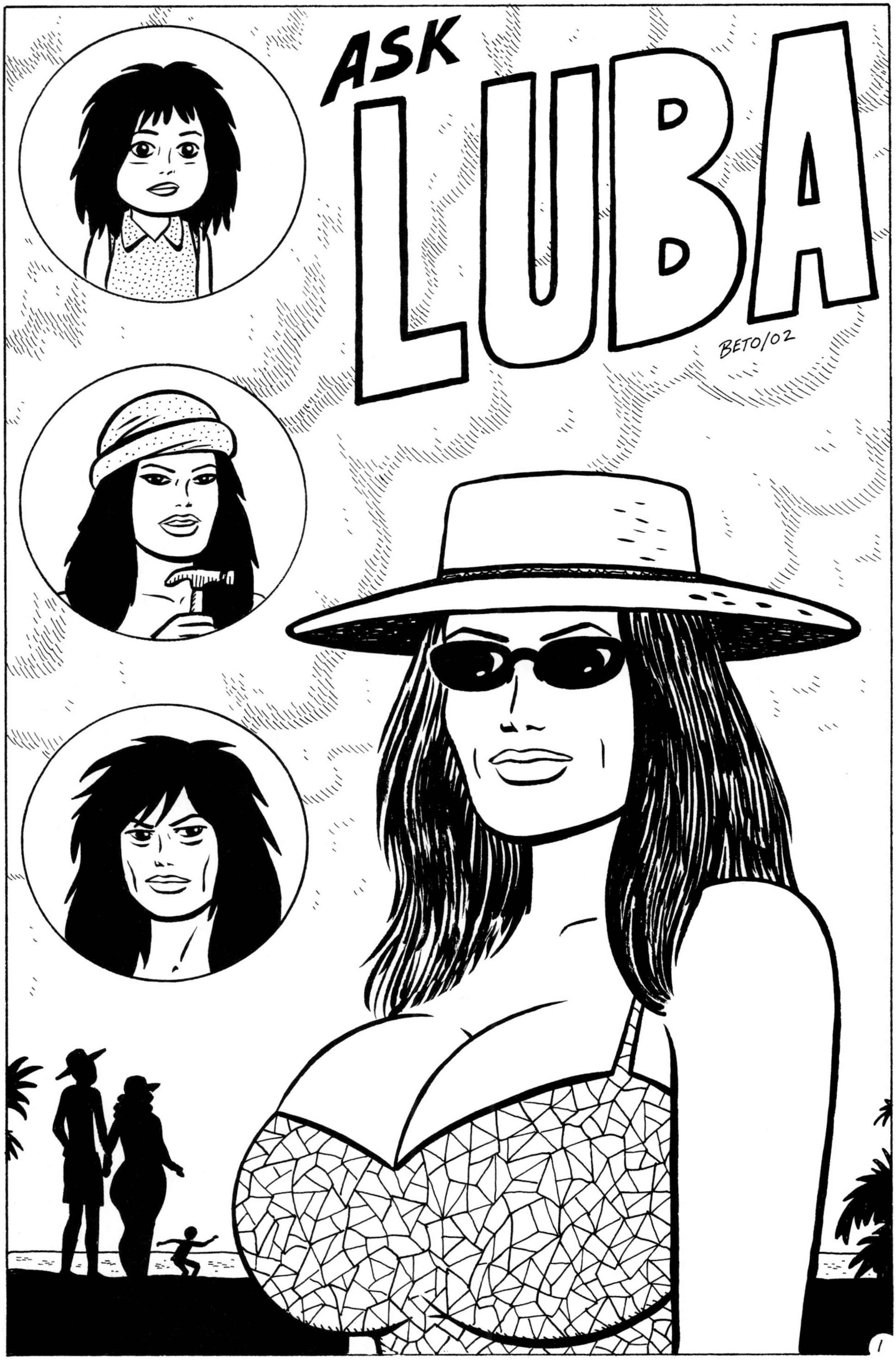
ASK
LUBA
BETO/02
1

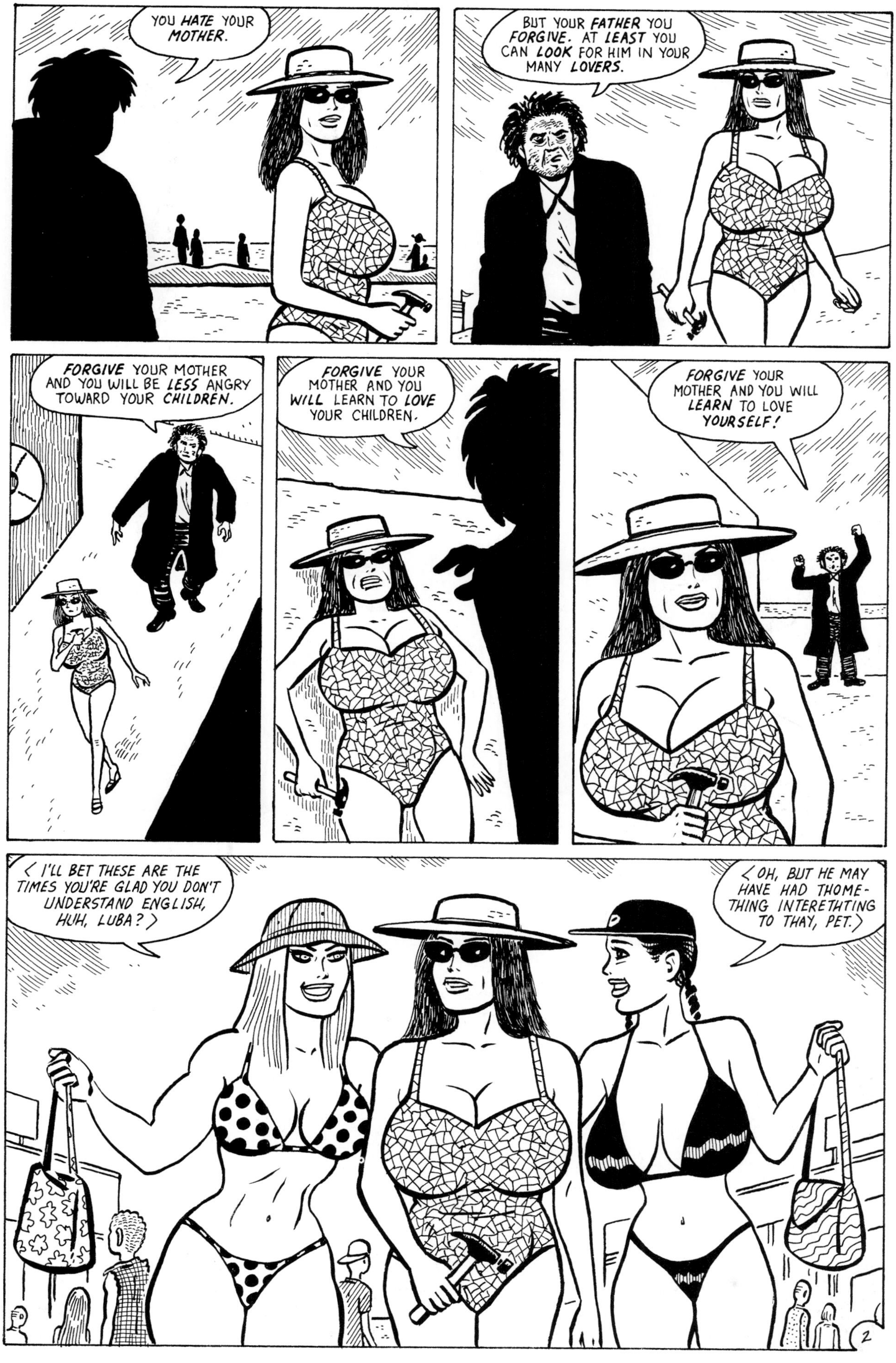
YOU HATE YOUR MOTHER.
BUT YOUR FATHER YOU FORGIVE. AT LEAST YOU CAN LOOK FOR HIM IN YOUR MANY LOVERS.
FORGIVE YOUR MOTHER AND YOU WILL BE LESS ANGRY TOWARD YOUR CHILDREN.
FORGIVE YOUR MOTHER AND YOU WILL LEARN TO LOVE YOUR CHILDREN.
FORGIVE YOUR MOTHER AND YOU WILL LEARN TO LOVE YOURSELF!
< I'LL BET THESE ARE THE TIMES YOU'RE GLAD YOU DON'T UNDERSTAND ENGLISH, HUH, LUBA? >
< OH, BUT HE MAY HAVE HAD THOME-THING INTERETHTING TO THAY, PET. >
2

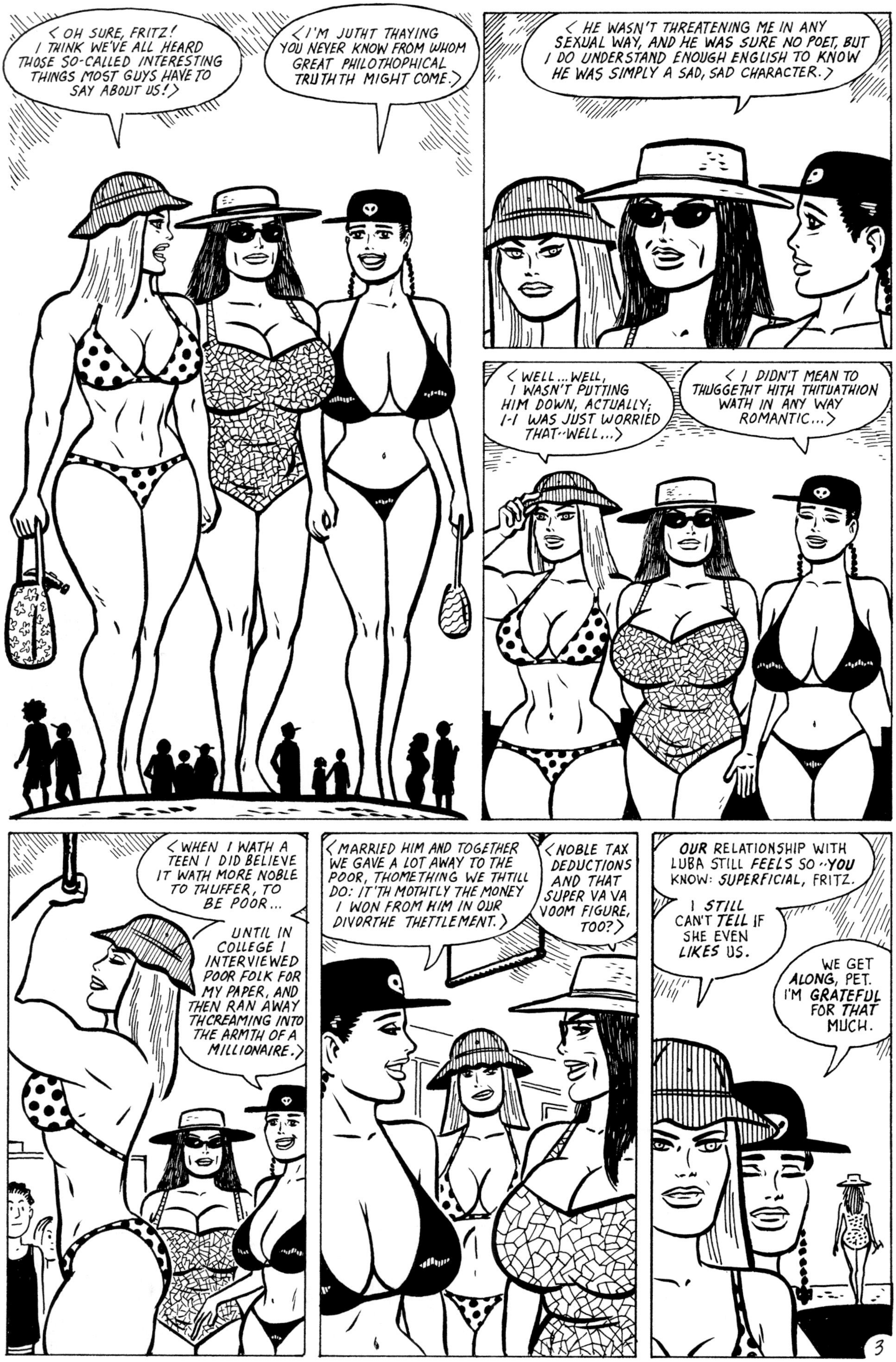
< OH SURE, FRITZ! I THINK WE'VE ALL HEARD THOSE SO-CALLED INTERESTING THINGS MOST GUYS HAVE TO SAY ABOUT US! >
< I'M JUTHT THAYING YOU NEVER KNOW FROM WHOM GREAT PHILOTHOPHICAL TRUTHTH MIGHT COME. >
< HE WASN'T THREATENING ME IN ANY SEXUAL WAY, AND HE WAS SURE NO POET, BUT I DO UNDERSTAND ENOUGH ENGLISH TO KNOW HE WAS SIMPLY A SAD, SAD CHARACTER. >
< WELL... WELL, I WASN'T PUTTING HIM DOWN, ACTUALLY; I-I WAS JUST WORRIED THAT·· WELL... >
< I DIDN'T MEAN TO THUGGETHT HITH THITUATHION WATH IN ANY WAY ROMANTIC... >
< WHEN I WATH A TEEN I DID BELIEVE IT WATH MORE NOBLE TO THUFFER, TO BE POOR...
UNTIL IN COLLEGE I INTERVIEWED POOR FOLK FOR MY PAPER, AND THEN RAN AWAY THCREAMING INTO THE ARMTH OF A MILLIONAIRE. >
< MARRIED HIM AND TOGETHER WE GAVE A LOT AWAY TO THE POOR, THOMETHING WE THTILL DO: IT'TH MOTHTLY THE MONEY I WON FROM HIM IN OUR DIVORTHE THETTLEMENT. >
< NOBLE TAX DEDUCTIONS AND THAT SUPER VA VA VOOM FIGURE, TOO? >
OUR RELATIONSHIP WITH LUBA STILL FEELS SO ·· YOU KNOW: SUPERFICIAL, FRITZ.
I STILL CAN'T TELL IF SHE EVEN LIKES US.
WE GET ALONG, PET. I'M GRATEFUL FOR THAT MUCH.
3

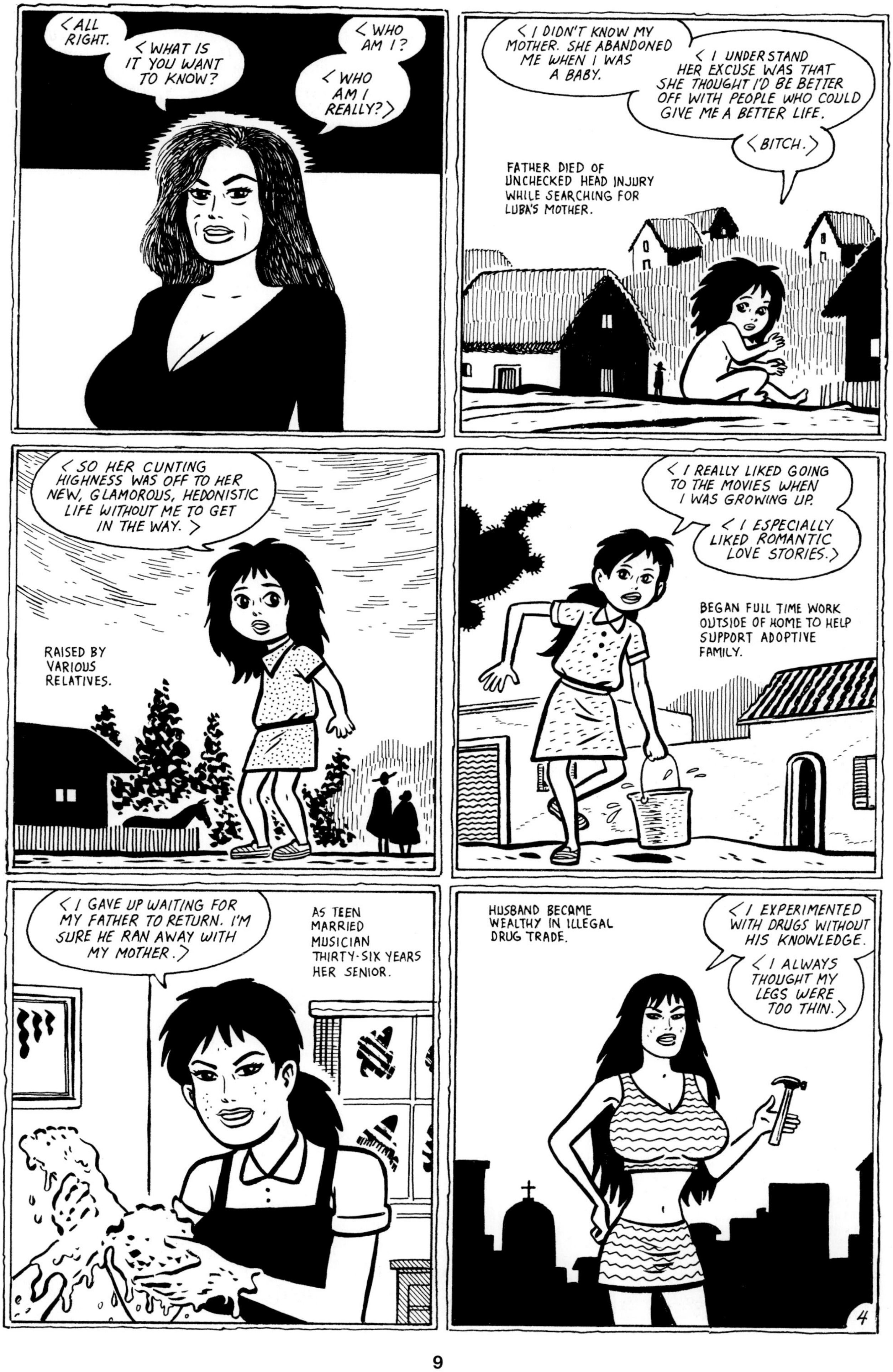

<ALL RIGHT.
<WHAT IS IT YOU WANT TO KNOW?
<WHO AM I?
<WHO AM I REALLY?>
<I DIDN'T KNOW MY MOTHER. SHE ABANDONED ME WHEN I WAS A BABY.
<I UNDERSTAND HER EXCUSE WAS THAT SHE THOUGHT I'D BE BETTER OFF WITH PEOPLE WHO COULD GIVE ME A BETTER LIFE.
<BITCH.>
FATHER DIED OF UNCHECKED HEAD INJURY WHILE SEARCHING FOR LUBA'S MOTHER.
<SO HER CUNTING HIGHNESS WAS OFF TO HER NEW, GLAMOROUS, HEDONISTIC LIFE WITHOUT ME TO GET IN THE WAY.>
RAISED BY VARIOUS RELATIVES.
<I REALLY LIKED GOING TO THE MOVIES WHEN I WAS GROWING UP.
<I ESPECIALLY LIKED ROMANTIC LOVE STORIES.>
BEGAN FULL TIME WORK OUTSIDE OF HOME TO HELP SUPPORT ADOPTIVE FAMILY.
<I GAVE UP WAITING FOR MY FATHER TO RETURN. I'M SURE HE RAN AWAY WITH MY MOTHER.>
AS TEEN MARRIED MUSICIAN THIRTY-SIX YEARS HER SENIOR.
HUSBAND BECAME WEALTHY IN ILLEGAL DRUG TRADE.
<I EXPERIMENTED WITH DRUGS WITHOUT HIS KNOWLEDGE.
<I ALWAYS THOUGHT MY LEGS WERE TOO THIN.>
4

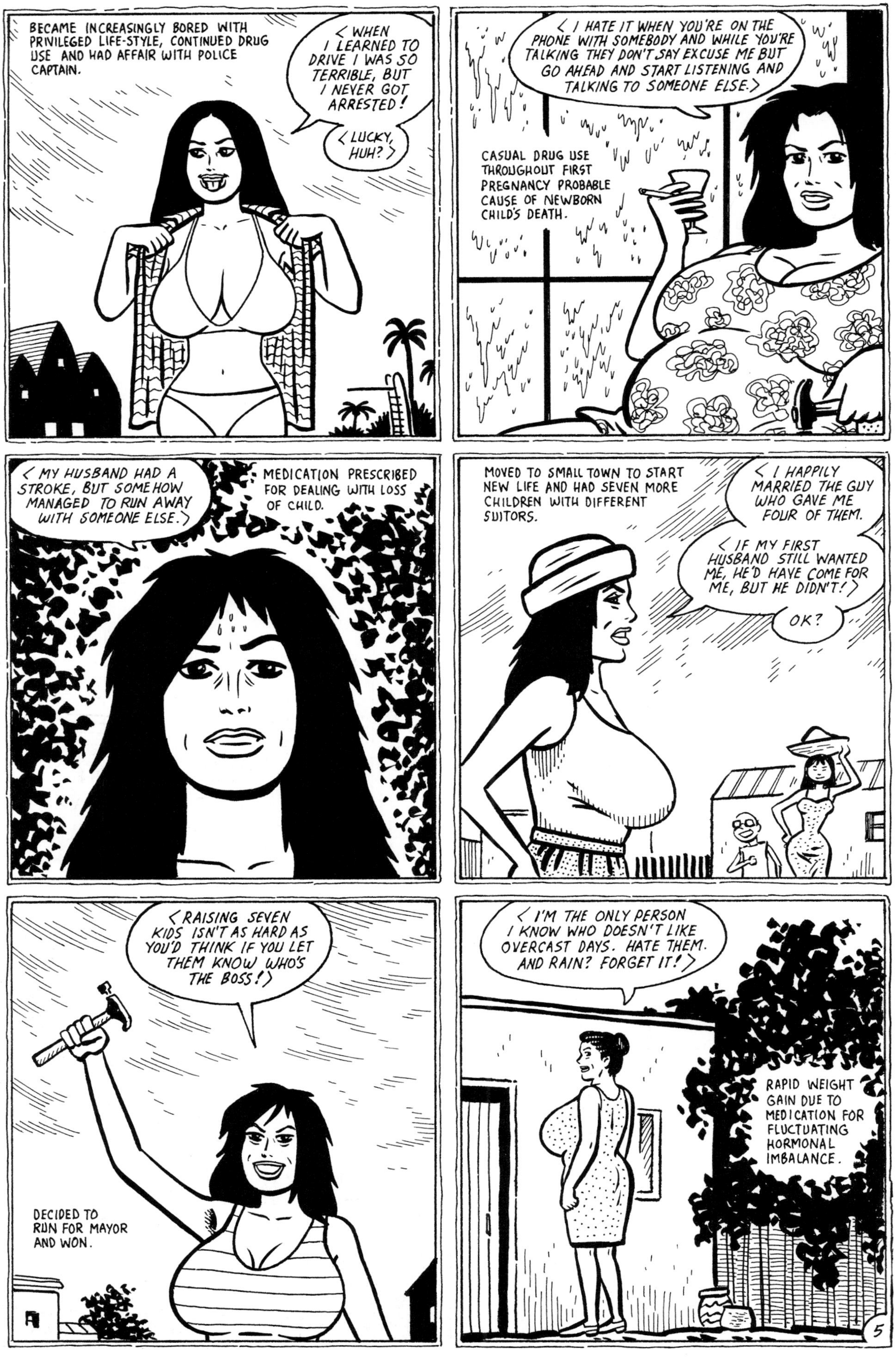
BECAME INCREASINGLY BORED WITH PRIVILEGED LIFE-STYLE, CONTINUED DRUG USE AND HAD AFFAIR WITH POLICE CAPTAIN.
< WHEN I LEARNED TO DRIVE I WAS SO TERRIBLE, BUT I NEVER GOT ARRESTED!
< LUCKY, HUH? >
< I HATE IT WHEN YOU'RE ON THE PHONE WITH SOMEBODY AND WHILE YOU'RE TALKING THEY DON'T SAY EXCUSE ME BUT GO AHEAD AND START LISTENING AND TALKING TO SOMEONE ELSE. >
CASUAL DRUG USE THROUGHOUT FIRST PREGNANCY PROBABLE CAUSE OF NEWBORN CHILD'S DEATH.
< MY HUSBAND HAD A STROKE, BUT SOMEHOW MANAGED TO RUN AWAY WITH SOMEONE ELSE. >
MEDICATION PRESCRIBED FOR DEALING WITH LOSS OF CHILD.
MOVED TO SMALL TOWN TO START NEW LIFE AND HAD SEVEN MORE CHILDREN WITH DIFFERENT SUITORS.
< I HAPPILY MARRIED THE GUY WHO GAVE ME FOUR OF THEM.
< IF MY FIRST HUSBAND STILL WANTED ME, HE'D HAVE COME FOR ME, BUT HE DIDN'T! >
OK?
< RAISING SEVEN KIDS ISN'T AS HARD AS YOU'D THINK IF YOU LET THEM KNOW WHO'S THE BOSS! >
DECIDED TO RUN FOR MAYOR AND WON.
< I'M THE ONLY PERSON I KNOW WHO DOESN'T LIKE OVERCAST DAYS. HATE THEM. AND RAIN? FORGET IT! >
RAPID WEIGHT GAIN DUE TO MEDICATION FOR FLUCTUATING HORMONAL IMBALANCE.
5

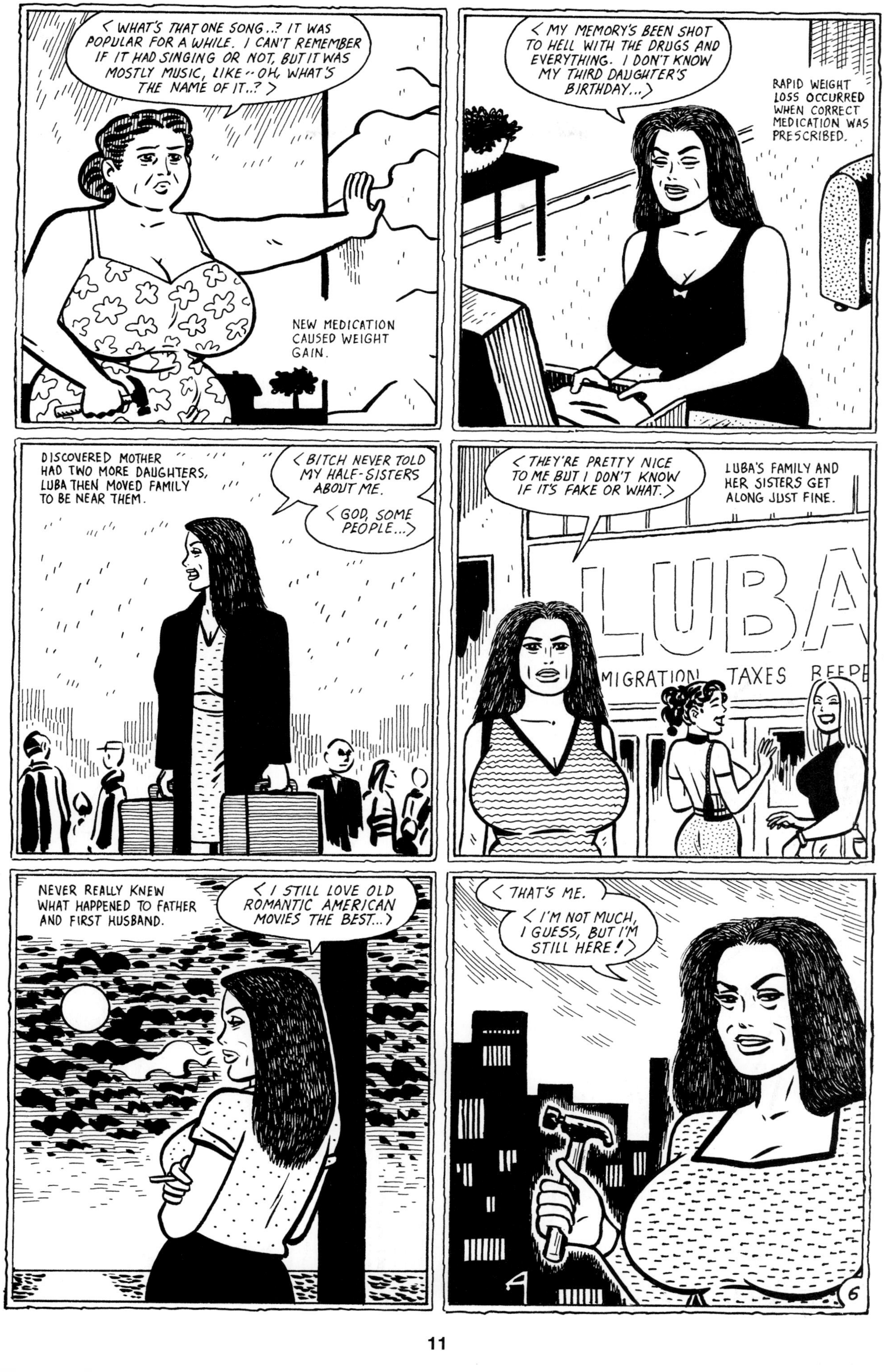
< WHAT'S THAT ONE SONG..? IT WAS POPULAR FOR A WHILE. I CAN'T REMEMBER IF IT HAD SINGING OR NOT, BUT IT WAS MOSTLY MUSIC, LIKE-- OH, WHAT'S THE NAME OF IT..? >
NEW MEDICATION CAUSED WEIGHT GAIN.
< MY MEMORY'S BEEN SHOT TO HELL WITH THE DRUGS AND EVERYTHING. I DON'T KNOW MY THIRD DAUGHTER'S BIRTHDAY...>
RAPID WEIGHT LOSS OCCURRED WHEN CORRECT MEDICATION WAS PRESCRIBED.
DISCOVERED MOTHER HAD TWO MORE DAUGHTERS, LUBA THEN MOVED FAMILY TO BE NEAR THEM.
< BITCH NEVER TOLD MY HALF-SISTERS ABOUT ME.
< GOD, SOME PEOPLE...>
< THEY'RE PRETTY NICE TO ME BUT I DON'T KNOW IF IT'S FAKE OR WHAT.>
LUBA'S FAMILY AND HER SISTERS GET ALONG JUST FINE.
LUBA
MIGRATION TAXES
NEVER REALLY KNEW WHAT HAPPENED TO FATHER AND FIRST HUSBAND.
< I STILL LOVE OLD ROMANTIC AMERICAN MOVIES THE BEST...>
< THAT'S ME.
< I'M NOT MUCH, I GUESS, BUT I'M STILL HERE! >
6

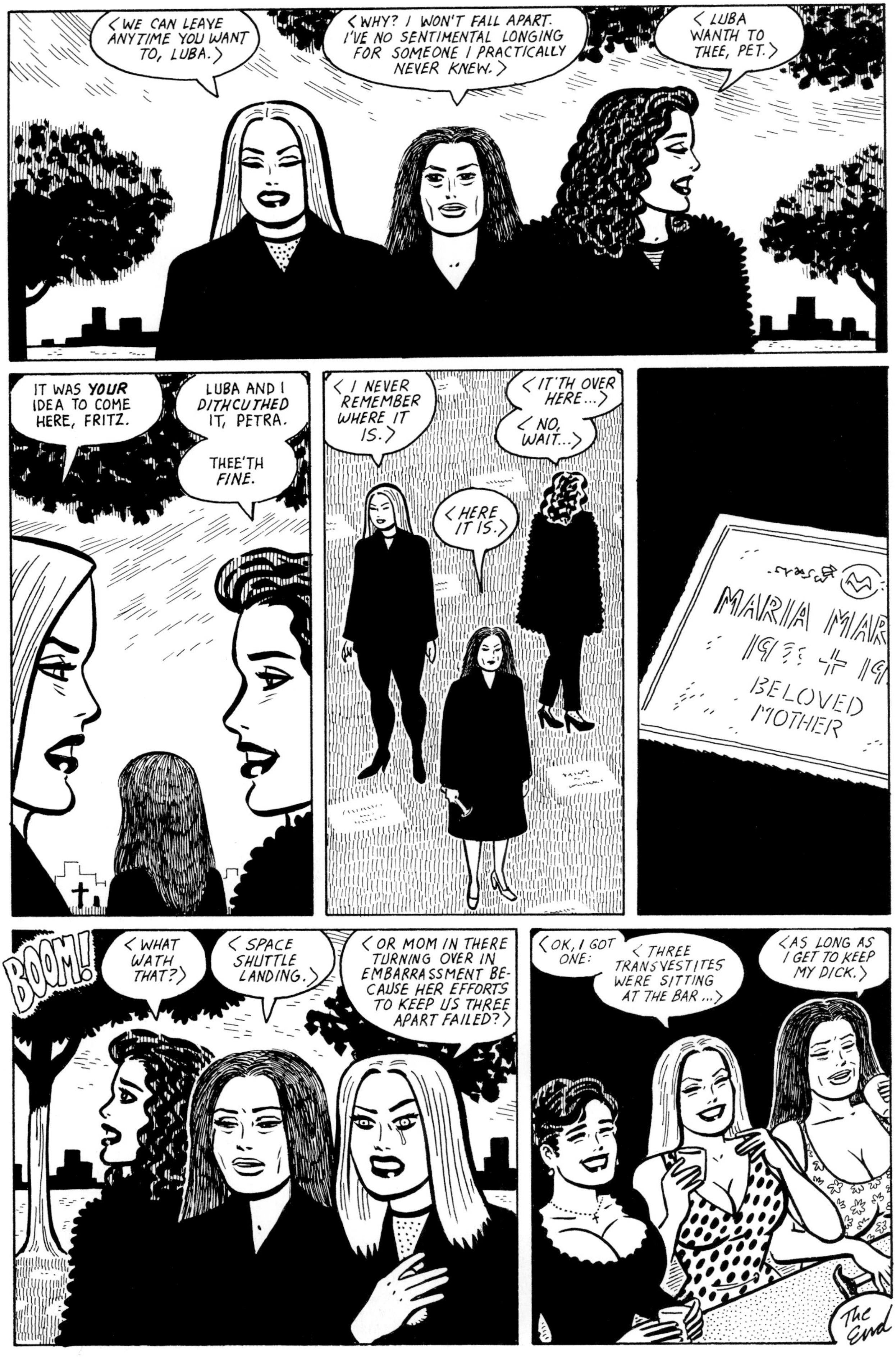
< WE CAN LEAVE ANYTIME YOU WANT TO, LUBA. >
< WHY? I WON'T FALL APART. I'VE NO SENTIMENTAL LONGING FOR SOMEONE I PRACTICALLY NEVER KNEW. >
< LUBA WANTH TO THEE, PET. >
IT WAS YOUR IDEA TO COME HERE, FRITZ.
LUBA AND I DITHCUTHED IT, PETRA.
THEE'TH FINE.
< I NEVER REMEMBER WHERE IT IS. >
< IT'TH OVER HERE... >
< NO, WAIT... >
< HERE IT IS. >
MARIA MAR
BELOVED MOTHER
BOOM!
< WHAT WATH THAT? >
< SPACE SHUTTLE LANDING. >
< OR MOM IN THERE TURNING OVER IN EMBARRASSMENT BECAUSE HER EFFORTS TO KEEP US THREE APART FAILED? >
< OK, I GOT ONE:
< THREE TRANSVESTITES WERE SITTING AT THE BAR ... >
< AS LONG AS I GET TO KEEP MY DICK. >
The End

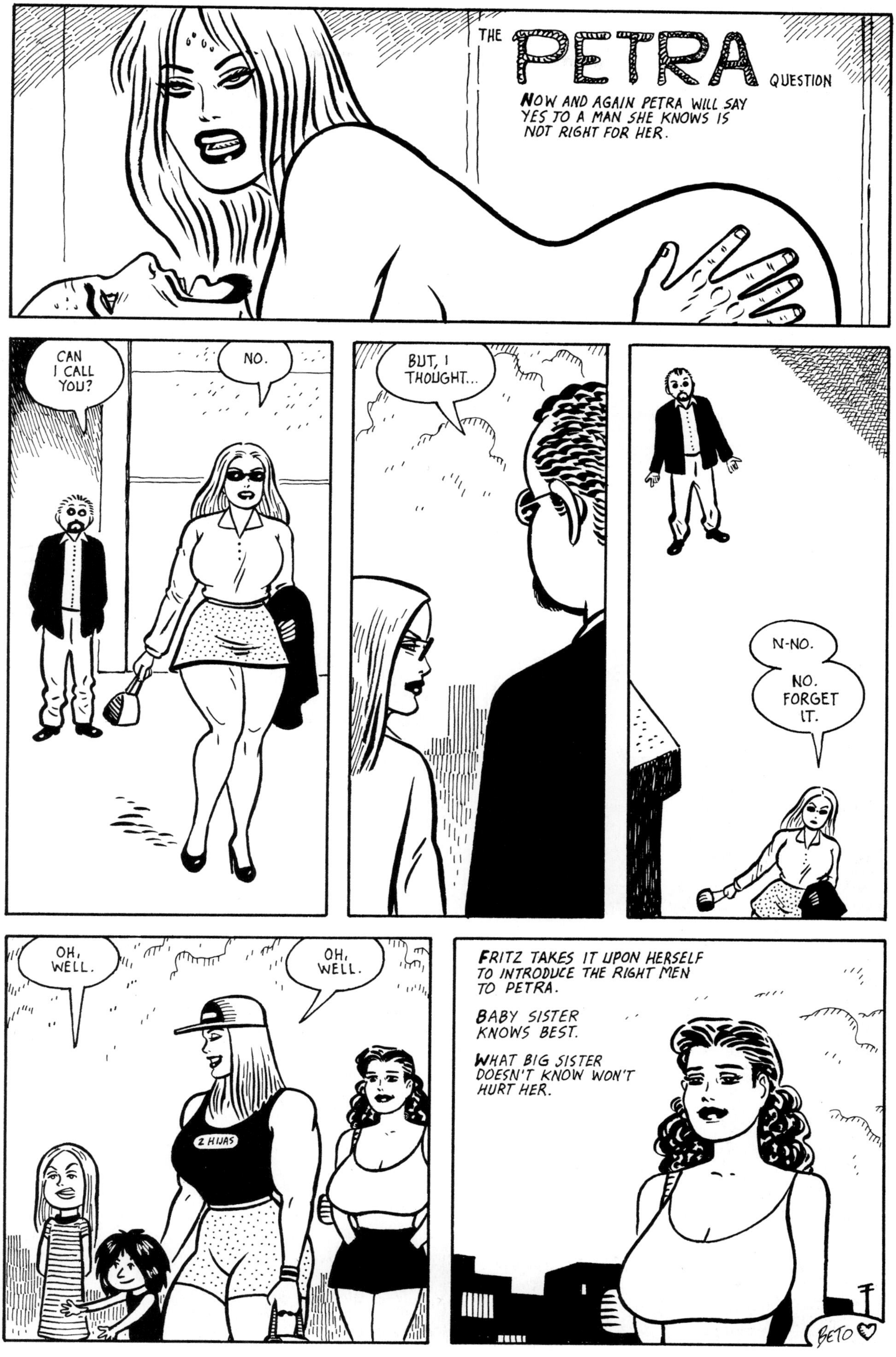

THE PETRA QUESTION
NOW AND AGAIN PETRA WILL SAY YES TO A MAN SHE KNOWS IS NOT RIGHT FOR HER.
CAN I CALL YOU?
NO.
BUT, I THOUGHT...
N-NO.
NO. FORGET IT.
OH, WELL.
OH, WELL.
2 HIJAS
FRITZ TAKES IT UPON HERSELF TO INTRODUCE THE RIGHT MEN TO PETRA.
BABY SISTER KNOWS BEST.
WHAT BIG SISTER DOESN'T KNOW WON'T HURT HER.
BETO

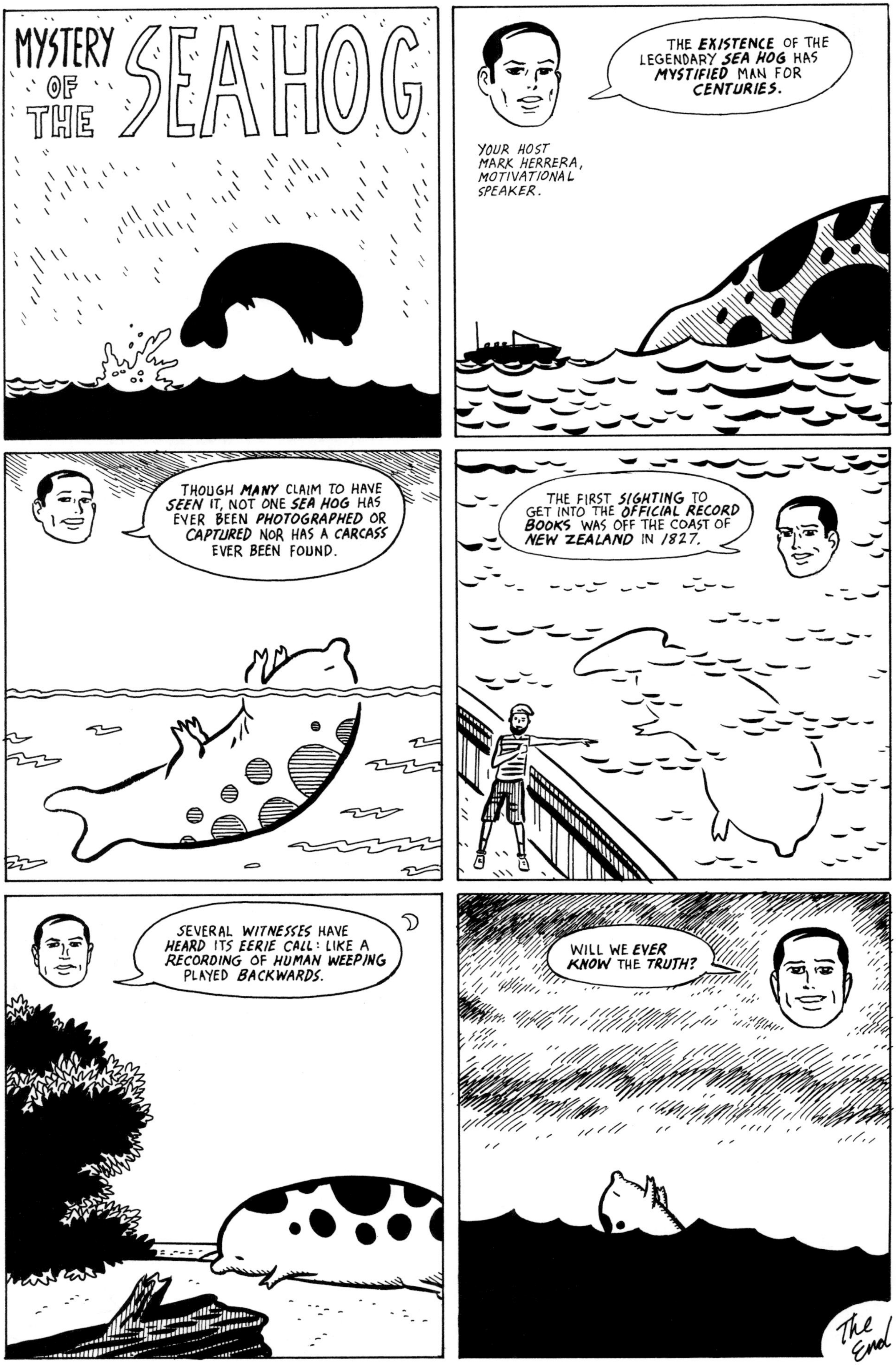
MYSTERY OF THE SEA HOG
THE EXISTENCE OF THE LEGENDARY SEA HOG HAS MYSTIFIED MAN FOR CENTURIES.
YOUR HOST MARK HERRERA, MOTIVATIONAL SPEAKER.
THOUGH MANY CLAIM TO HAVE SEEN IT, NOT ONE SEA HOG HAS EVER BEEN PHOTOGRAPHED OR CAPTURED NOR HAS A CARCASS EVER BEEN FOUND.
THE FIRST SIGHTING TO GET INTO THE OFFICIAL RECORD BOOKS WAS OFF THE COAST OF NEW ZEALAND IN 1827.
SEVERAL WITNESSES HAVE HEARD ITS EERIE CALL: LIKE A RECORDING OF HUMAN WEEPING PLAYED BACKWARDS.
WILL WE EVER KNOW THE TRUTH?
The End

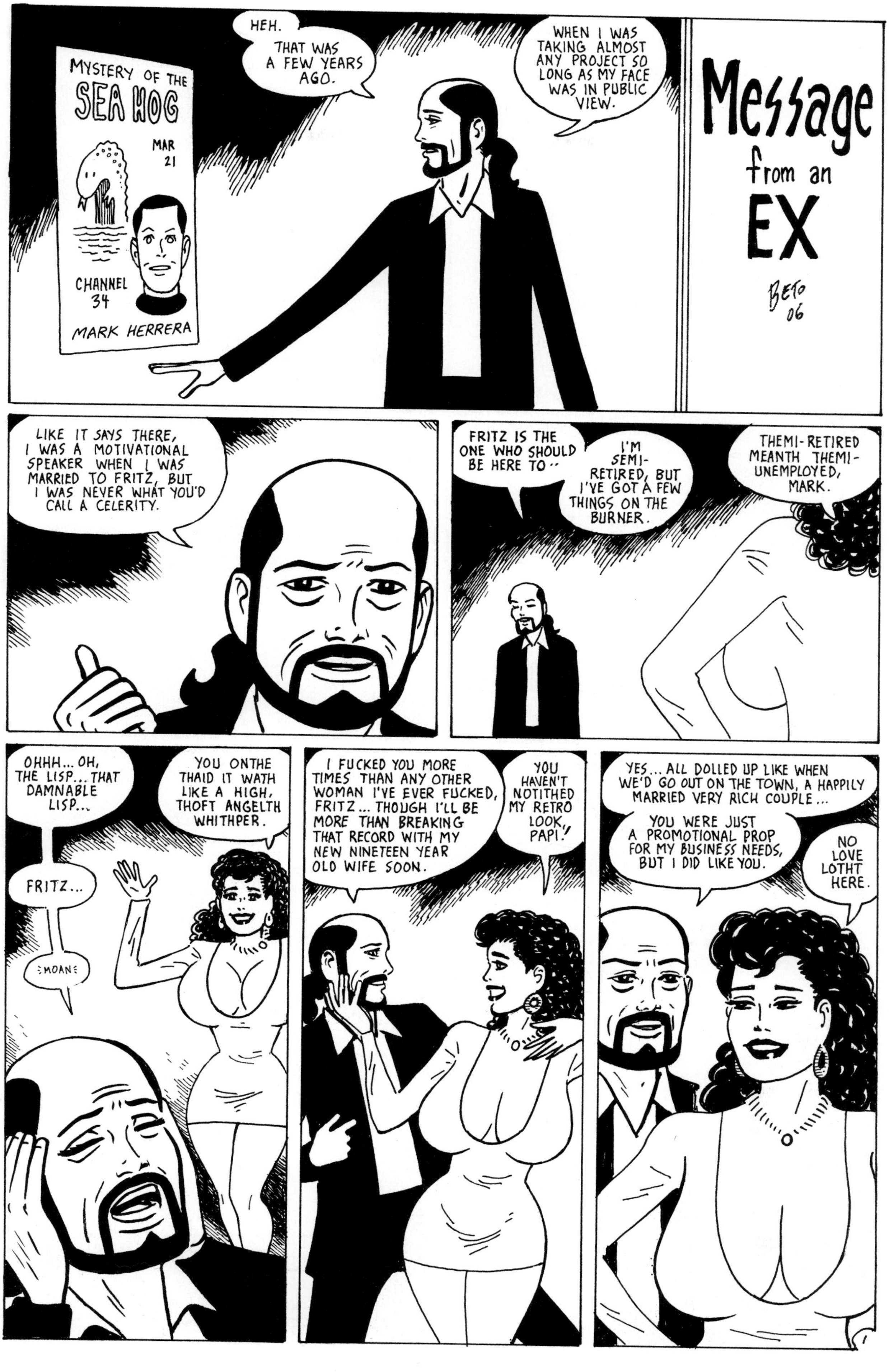
MYSTERY OF THE SEA HOG
MAR 21
CHANNEL 34
MARK HERRERA
HEH.
THAT WAS A FEW YEARS AGO.
WHEN I WAS TAKING ALMOST ANY PROJECT SO LONG AS MY FACE WAS IN PUBLIC VIEW.
Message from an EX
BETO 06
LIKE IT SAYS THERE, I WAS A MOTIVATIONAL SPEAKER WHEN I WAS MARRIED TO FRITZ, BUT I WAS NEVER WHAT YOU'D CALL A CELERITY.
FRITZ IS THE ONE WHO SHOULD BE HERE TO··
I'M SEMI-RETIRED, BUT I'VE GOT A FEW THINGS ON THE BURNER.
THEMI-RETIRED MEANTH THEMI-UNEMPLOYED, MARK.
OHHH... OH, THE LISP... THAT DAMNABLE LISP...
FRITZ...
MOAN
YOU ONTHE THAID IT WATH LIKE A HIGH, THOFT ANGELTH WHITHPER.
I FUCKED YOU MORE TIMES THAN ANY OTHER WOMAN I'VE EVER FUCKED, FRITZ... THOUGH I'LL BE MORE THAN BREAKING THAT RECORD WITH MY NEW NINETEEN YEAR OLD WIFE SOON.
YOU HAVEN'T NOTITHED MY RETRO LOOK, PAPI!
YES... ALL DOLLED UP LIKE WHEN WE'D GO OUT ON THE TOWN, A HAPPILY MARRIED VERY RICH COUPLE...
YOU WERE JUST A PROMOTIONAL PROP FOR MY BUSINESS NEEDS, BUT I DID LIKE YOU.
NO LOVE LOTHT HERE.

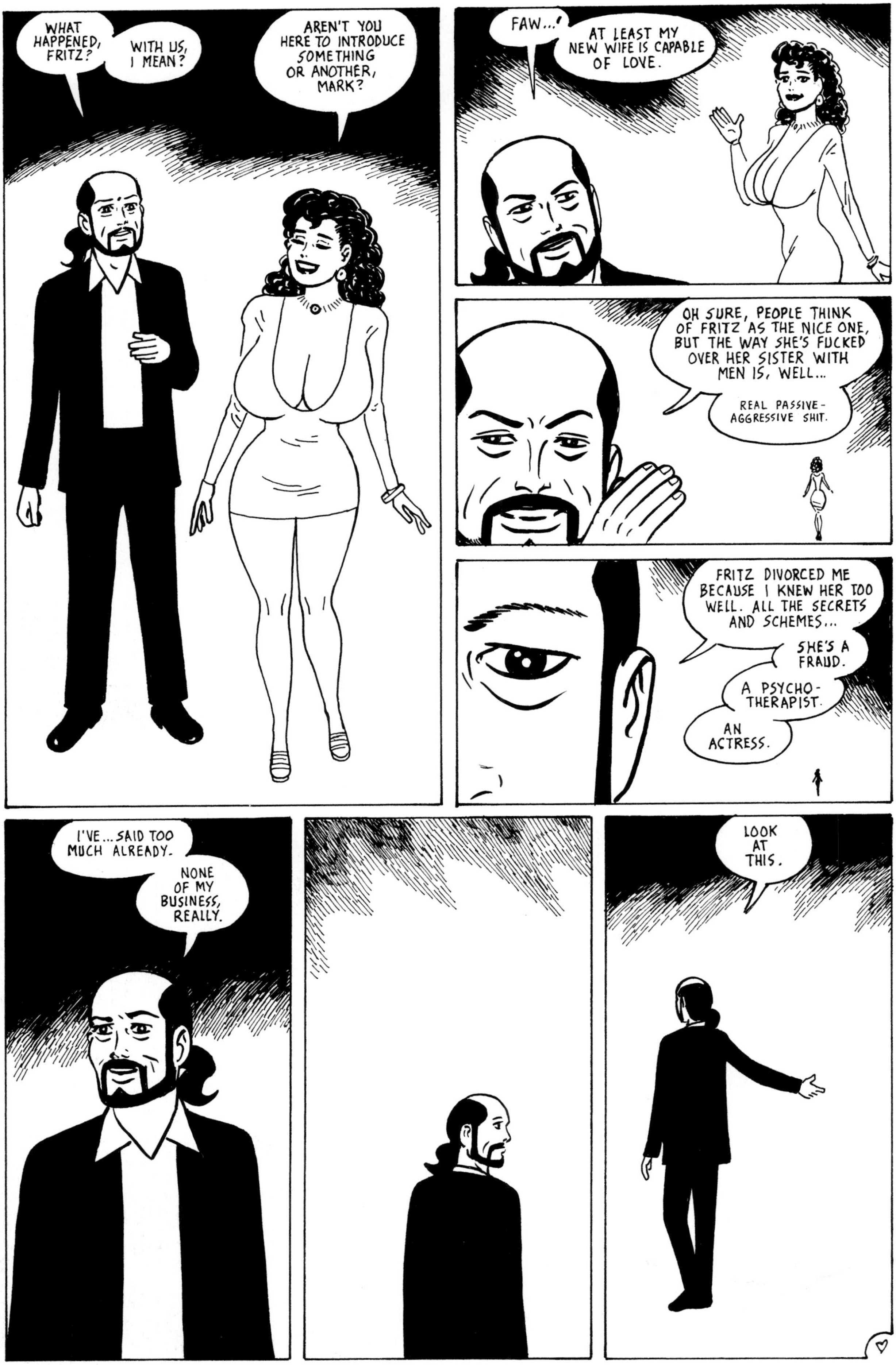
WHAT HAPPENED, FRITZ?
WITH US, I MEAN?
AREN'T YOU HERE TO INTRODUCE SOMETHING OR ANOTHER, MARK?
FAW...!
AT LEAST MY NEW WIFE IS CAPABLE OF LOVE.
OH SURE, PEOPLE THINK OF FRITZ AS THE NICE ONE, BUT THE WAY SHE'S FUCKED OVER HER SISTER WITH MEN IS, WELL...
REAL PASSIVE-AGGRESSIVE SHIT.
FRITZ DIVORCED ME BECAUSE I KNEW HER TOO WELL. ALL THE SECRETS AND SCHEMES...
SHE'S A FRAUD.
A PSYCHO-THERAPIST.
AN ACTRESS.
I'VE... SAID TOO MUCH ALREADY.
NONE OF MY BUSINESS, REALLY.
LOOK AT THIS.
2.

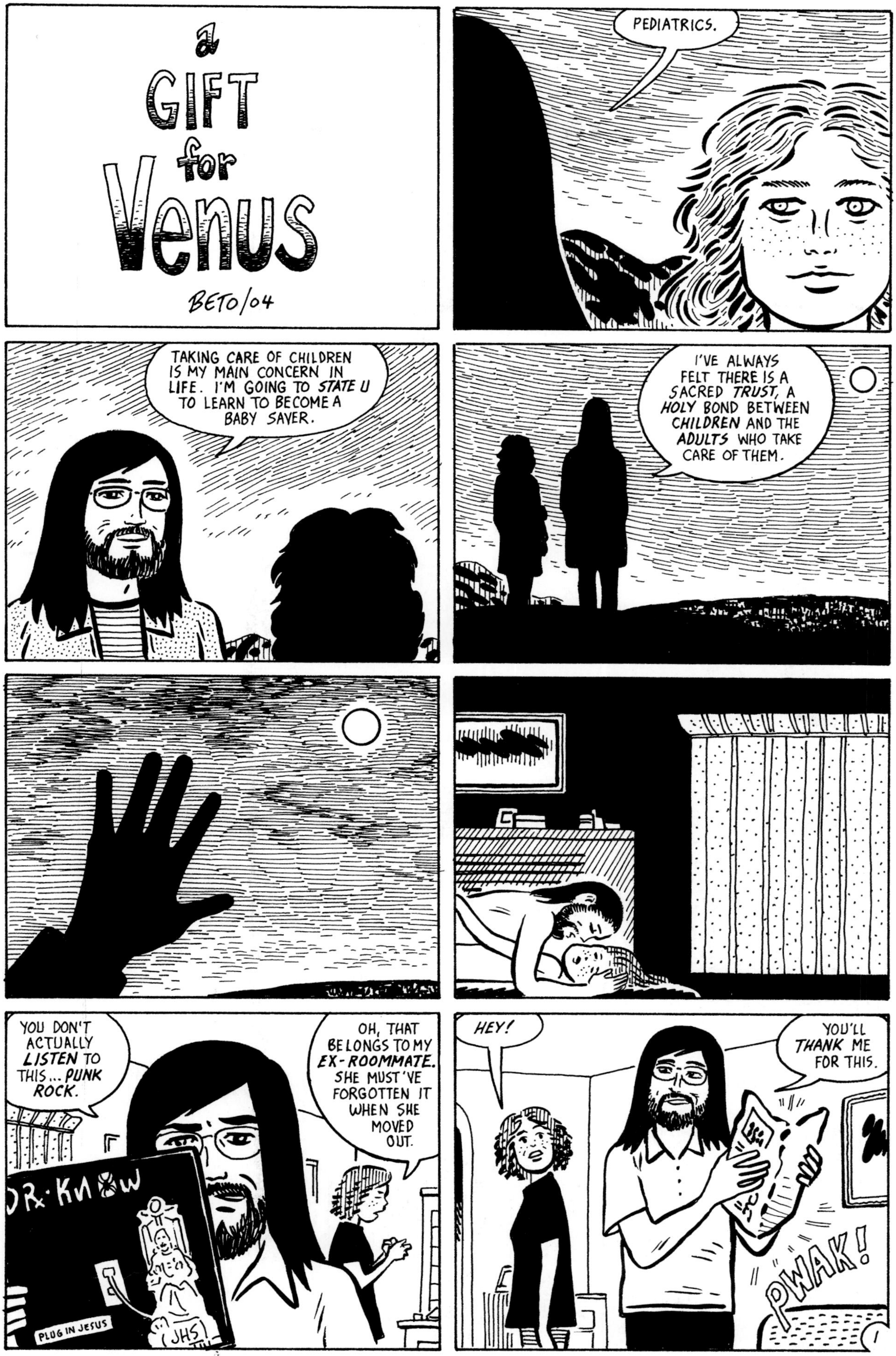
a GIFT for Venus
BETO/04
PEDIATRICS.
TAKING CARE OF CHILDREN IS MY MAIN CONCERN IN LIFE. I'M GOING TO STATE U TO LEARN TO BECOME A BABY SAVER.
I'VE ALWAYS FELT THERE IS A SACRED TRUST, A HOLY BOND BETWEEN CHILDREN AND THE ADULTS WHO TAKE CARE OF THEM.
YOU DON'T ACTUALLY LISTEN TO THIS... PUNK ROCK.
OH, THAT BELONGS TO MY EX-ROOMMATE. SHE MUST'VE FORGOTTEN IT WHEN SHE MOVED OUT.
DR. KNOW
PLUG IN JESUS
JHS
HEY!
YOU'LL THANK ME FOR THIS.
PWAK!

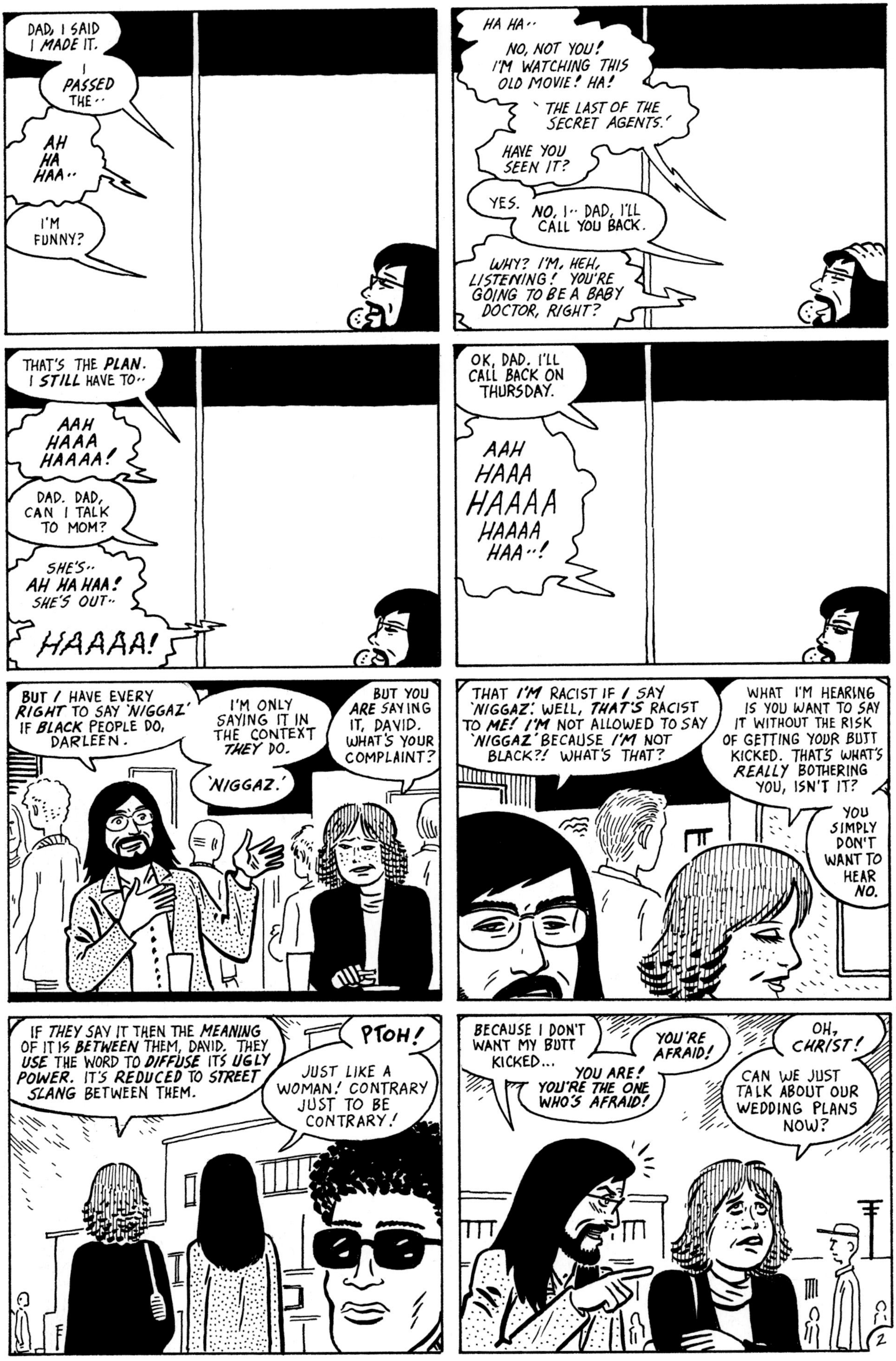
DAD, I SAID I MADE IT.
I PASSED THE··
AH HA HAA··
I'M FUNNY?
HA HA··
NO, NOT YOU! I'M WATCHING THIS OLD MOVIE! HA!
'THE LAST OF THE SECRET AGENTS.'
HAVE YOU SEEN IT?
YES.
NO, I·· DAD, I'LL CALL YOU BACK.
WHY? I'M, HEH, LISTENING! YOU'RE GOING TO BE A BABY DOCTOR, RIGHT?
THAT'S THE PLAN. I STILL HAVE TO··
AAH HAAA HAAAA!
DAD. DAD, CAN I TALK TO MOM?
SHE'S·· AH HA HAA! SHE'S OUT··
HAAAA!
OK, DAD. I'LL CALL BACK ON THURSDAY.
AAH HAAA HAAAA HAAAA, HAA··!
BUT I HAVE EVERY RIGHT TO SAY 'NIGGAZ' IF BLACK PEOPLE DO, DARLEEN.
I'M ONLY SAYING IT IN THE CONTEXT THEY DO.
'NIGGAZ.'
BUT YOU ARE SAYING IT, DAVID. WHAT'S YOUR COMPLAINT?
THAT I'M RACIST IF I SAY 'NIGGAZ.' WELL, THAT'S RACIST TO ME! I'M NOT ALLOWED TO SAY 'NIGGAZ' BECAUSE I'M NOT BLACK?! WHAT'S THAT?
WHAT I'M HEARING IS YOU WANT TO SAY IT WITHOUT THE RISK OF GETTING YOUR BUTT KICKED. THAT'S WHAT'S REALLY BOTHERING YOU, ISN'T IT?
YOU SIMPLY DON'T WANT TO HEAR NO.
IF THEY SAY IT THEN THE MEANING OF IT IS BETWEEN THEM, DAVID. THEY USE THE WORD TO DIFFUSE ITS UGLY POWER. IT'S REDUCED TO STREET SLANG BETWEEN THEM.
PTOH!
JUST LIKE A WOMAN! CONTRARY JUST TO BE CONTRARY!
BECAUSE I DON'T WANT MY BUTT KICKED...
YOU'RE AFRAID!
YOU ARE! YOU'RE THE ONE WHO'S AFRAID!
OH, CHRIST!
CAN WE JUST TALK ABOUT OUR WEDDING PLANS NOW?

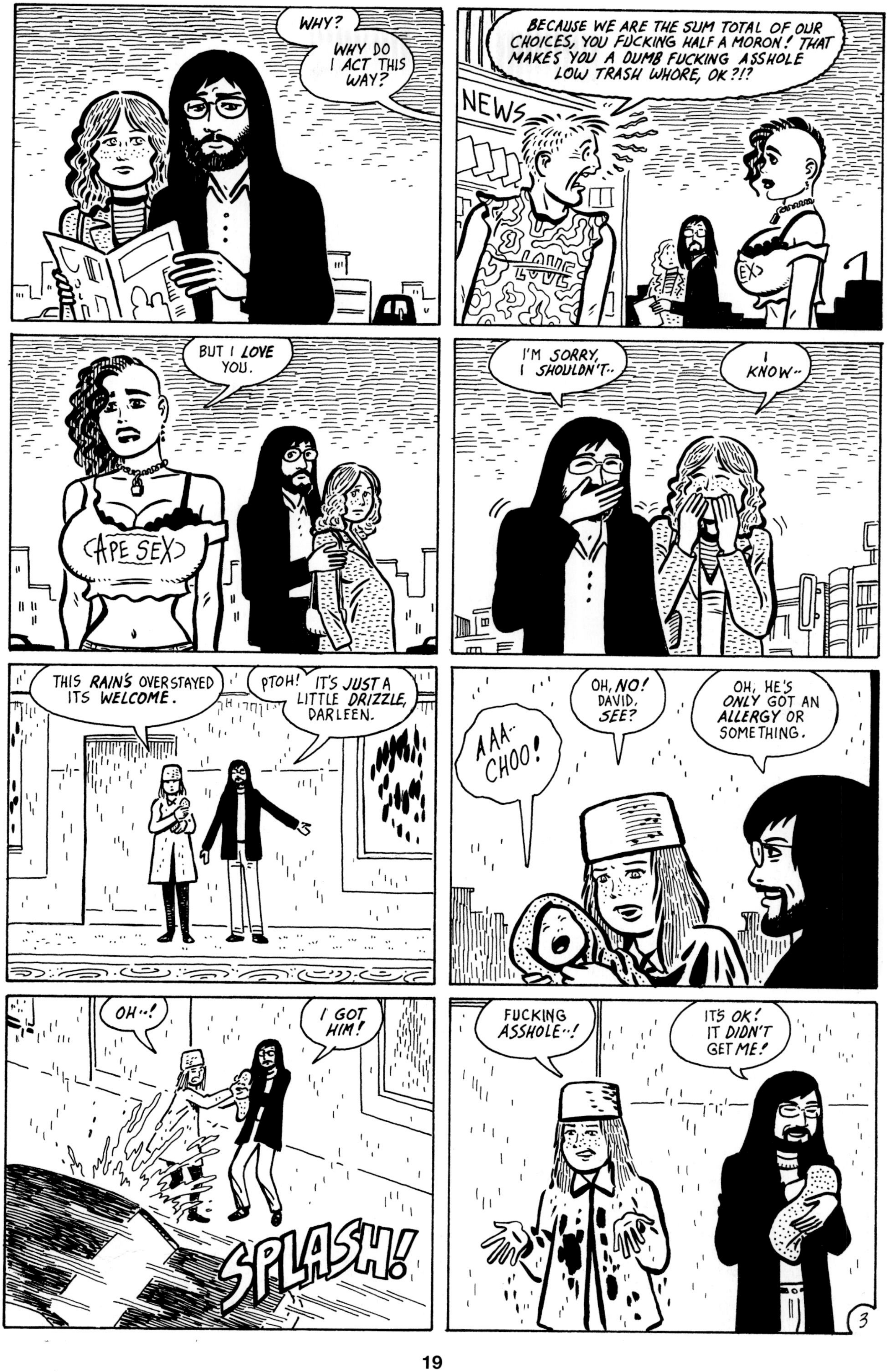
WHY?
WHY DO I ACT THIS WAY?
BECAUSE WE ARE THE SUM TOTAL OF OUR CHOICES, YOU FUCKING HALF A MORON! THAT MAKES YOU A DUMB FUCKING ASSHOLE LOW TRASH WHORE, OK?!?
NEWS
LOVE
EX
BUT I LOVE YOU.
APE SEX
I'M SORRY, I SHOULDN'T..
I KNOW..
THIS RAIN'S OVERSTAYED ITS WELCOME.
PTOH! IT'S JUST A LITTLE DRIZZLE, DARLEEN.
AAA-CHOO!
OH, NO! DAVID, SEE?
OH, HE'S ONLY GOT AN ALLERGY OR SOMETHING.
OH..!
I GOT HIM!
SPLASH!
FUCKING ASSHOLE..!
IT'S OK! IT DIDN'T GET ME!
3

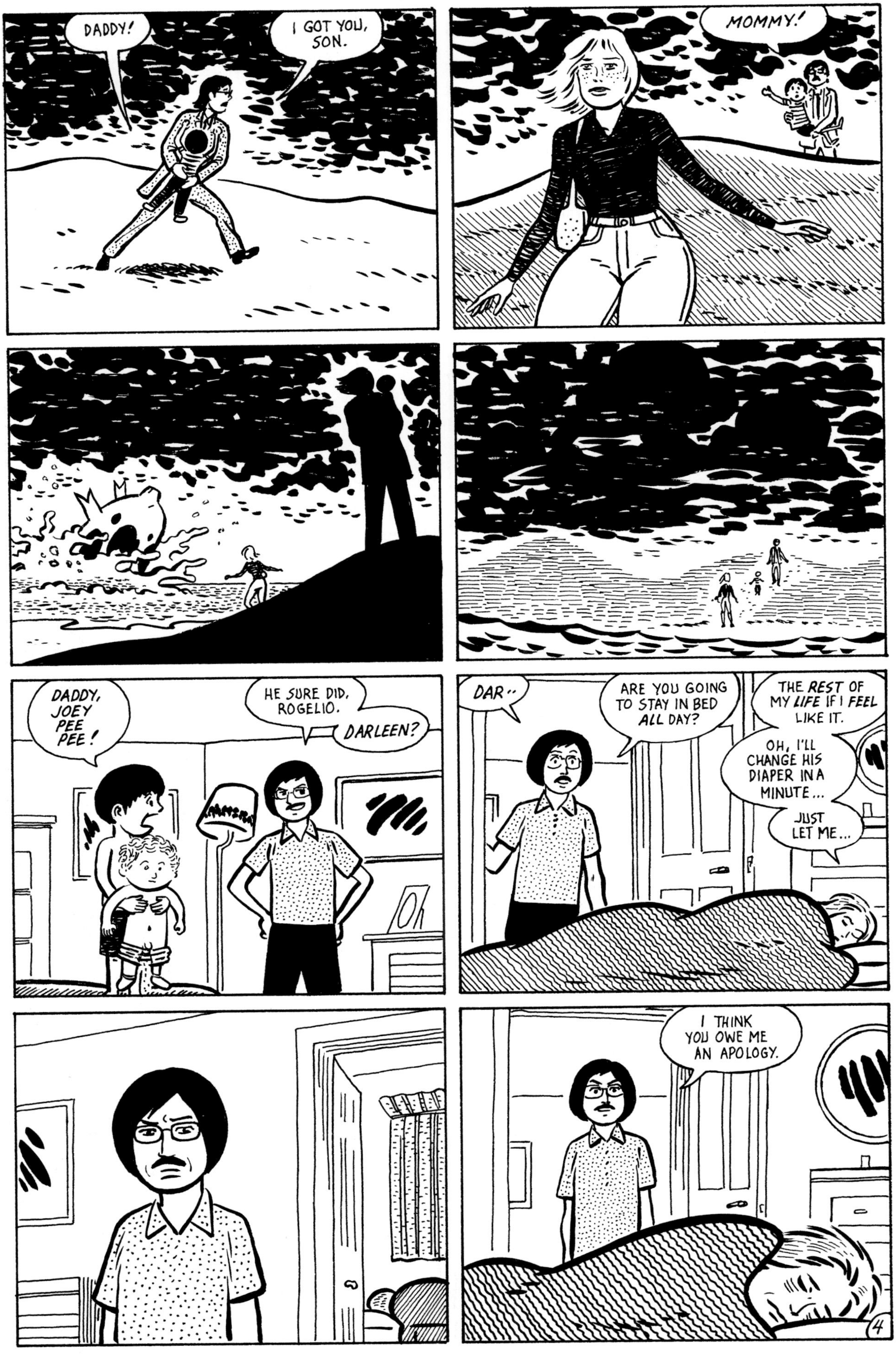
DADDY!
I GOT YOU, SON.
MOMMY!
DADDY, JOEY PEE PEE!
HE SURE DID, ROGELIO.
DARLEEN?
DAR..
ARE YOU GOING TO STAY IN BED ALL DAY?
THE REST OF MY LIFE IF I FEEL LIKE IT.
OH, I'LL CHANGE HIS DIAPER IN A MINUTE...
JUST LET ME...
I THINK YOU OWE ME AN APOLOGY.
4

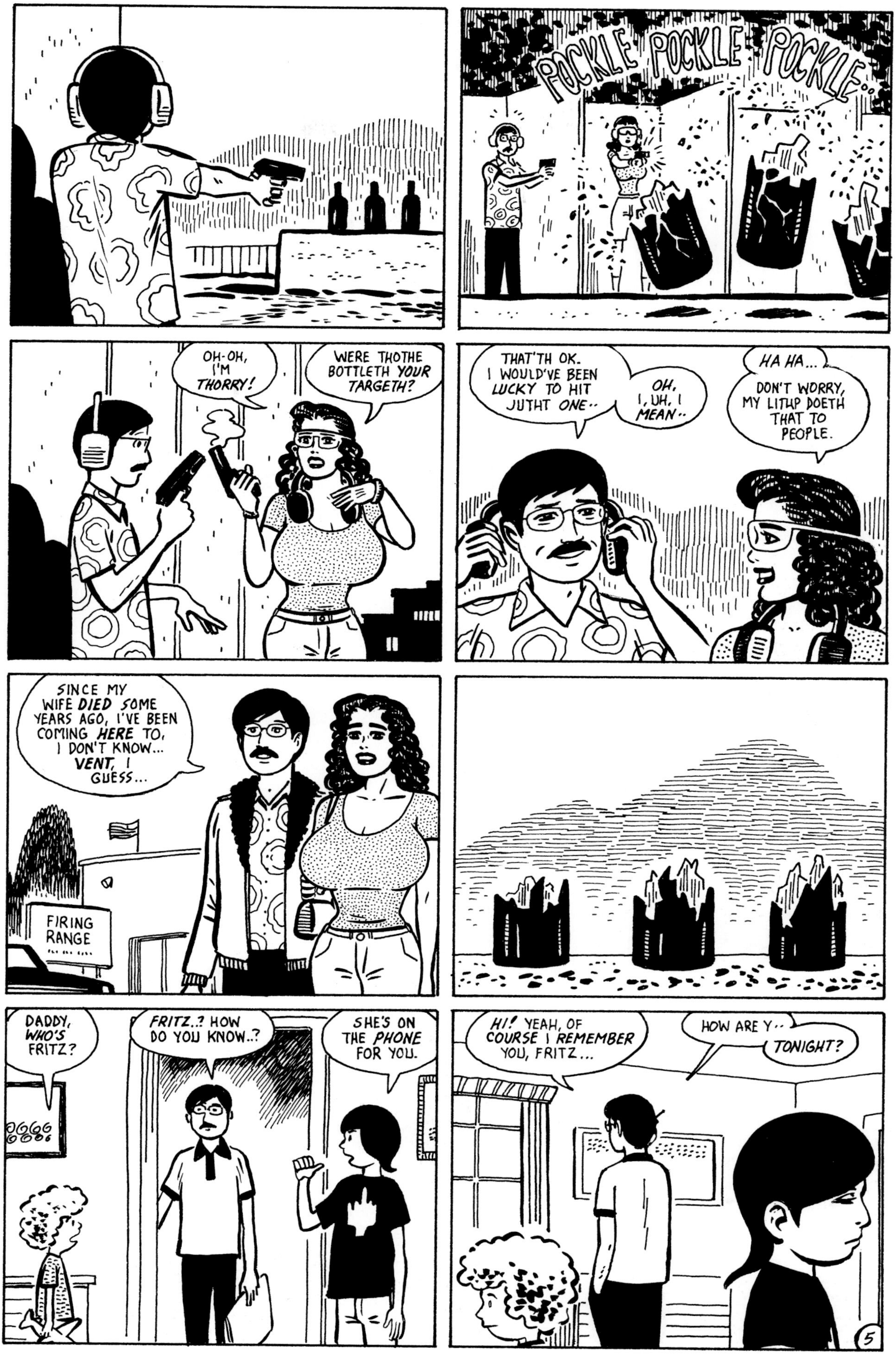

POCKLE POCKLE POCKLE..
OH-OH, I'M THORRY!
WERE THOTHE BOTTLETH YOUR TARGETH?
THAT'TH OK. I WOULD'VE BEEN LUCKY TO HIT JUTHT ONE..
OH, I, UH, I MEAN..
HA HA...
DON'T WORRY, MY LITHP DOETH THAT TO PEOPLE.
SINCE MY WIFE DIED SOME YEARS AGO, I'VE BEEN COMING HERE TO, I DON'T KNOW... VENT, I GUESS...
FIRING RANGE
DADDY, WHO'S FRITZ?
FRITZ..? HOW DO YOU KNOW..?
SHE'S ON THE PHONE FOR YOU.
HI! YEAH, OF COURSE I REMEMBER YOU, FRITZ...
HOW ARE Y..
TONIGHT?
5

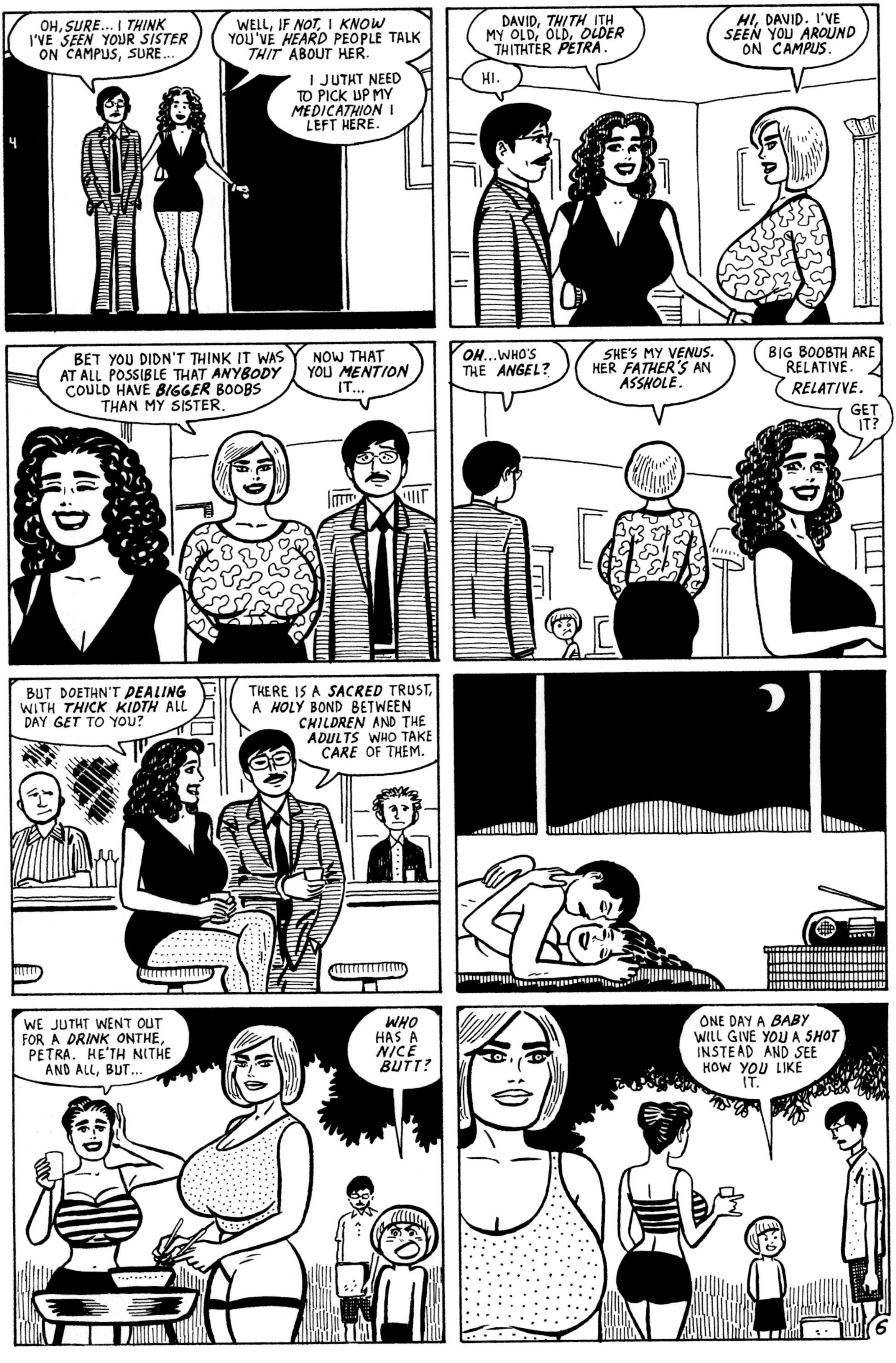
OH, SURE... I THINK I'VE SEEN YOUR SISTER ON CAMPUS, SURE...
WELL, IF NOT, I KNOW YOU'VE HEARD PEOPLE TALK THIT ABOUT HER.
I JUTHT NEED TO PICK UP MY MEDICATHION I LEFT HERE.
4
DAVID, THITH ITH MY OLD, OLD, OLDER THITHTER PETRA.
HI.
HI, DAVID. I'VE SEEN YOU AROUND ON CAMPUS.
BET YOU DIDN'T THINK IT WAS AT ALL POSSIBLE THAT ANYBODY COULD HAVE BIGGER BOOBS THAN MY SISTER.
NOW THAT YOU MENTION IT...
OH...WHO'S THE ANGEL?
SHE'S MY VENUS. HER FATHER'S AN ASSHOLE.
BIG BOOBTH ARE RELATIVE.
RELATIVE.
GET IT?
BUT DOETHN'T DEALING WITH THICK KIDTH ALL DAY GET TO YOU?
THERE IS A SACRED TRUST, A HOLY BOND BETWEEN CHILDREN AND THE ADULTS WHO TAKE CARE OF THEM.
WE JUTHT WENT OUT FOR A DRINK ONTHE, PETRA. HE'TH NITHE AND ALL, BUT...
WHO HAS A NICE BUTT?
ONE DAY A BABY WILL GIVE YOU A SHOT INSTEAD AND SEE HOW YOU LIKE IT.
6

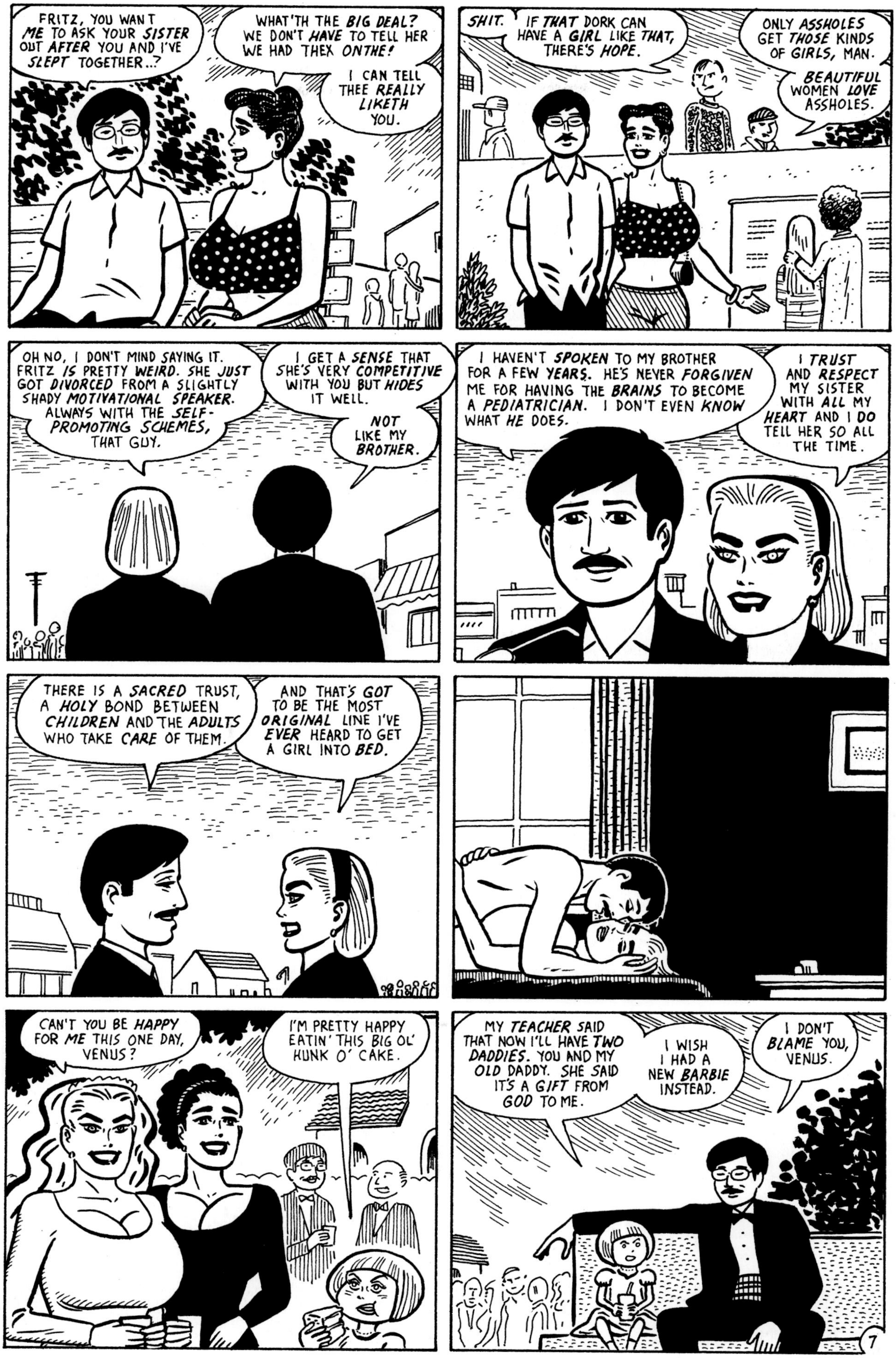
FRITZ, YOU WANT ME TO ASK YOUR SISTER OUT AFTER YOU AND I'VE SLEPT TOGETHER..?
WHAT'TH THE BIG DEAL? WE DON'T HAVE TO TELL HER WE HAD THEX ONTHE!
I CAN TELL THEE REALLY LIKETH YOU.
SHIT. IF THAT DORK CAN HAVE A GIRL LIKE THAT, THERE'S HOPE.
ONLY ASSHOLES GET THOSE KINDS OF GIRLS, MAN.
BEAUTIFUL WOMEN LOVE ASSHOLES.
OH NO, I DON'T MIND SAYING IT. FRITZ IS PRETTY WEIRD. SHE JUST GOT DIVORCED FROM A SLIGHTLY SHADY MOTIVATIONAL SPEAKER. ALWAYS WITH THE SELF-PROMOTING SCHEMES, THAT GUY.
I GET A SENSE THAT SHE'S VERY COMPETITIVE WITH YOU BUT HIDES IT WELL.
NOT LIKE MY BROTHER.
I HAVEN'T SPOKEN TO MY BROTHER FOR A FEW YEARS. HE'S NEVER FORGIVEN ME FOR HAVING THE BRAINS TO BECOME A PEDIATRICIAN. I DON'T EVEN KNOW WHAT HE DOES.
I TRUST AND RESPECT MY SISTER WITH ALL MY HEART AND I DO TELL HER SO ALL THE TIME.
THERE IS A SACRED TRUST, A HOLY BOND BETWEEN CHILDREN AND THE ADULTS WHO TAKE CARE OF THEM.
AND THAT'S GOT TO BE THE MOST ORIGINAL LINE I'VE EVER HEARD TO GET A GIRL INTO BED.
CAN'T YOU BE HAPPY FOR ME THIS ONE DAY, VENUS?
I'M PRETTY HAPPY EATIN' THIS BIG OL' HUNK O' CAKE.
MY TEACHER SAID THAT NOW I'LL HAVE TWO DADDIES. YOU AND MY OLD DADDY. SHE SAID IT'S A GIFT FROM GOD TO ME.
I WISH I HAD A NEW BARBIE INSTEAD.
I DON'T BLAME YOU, VENUS.
7

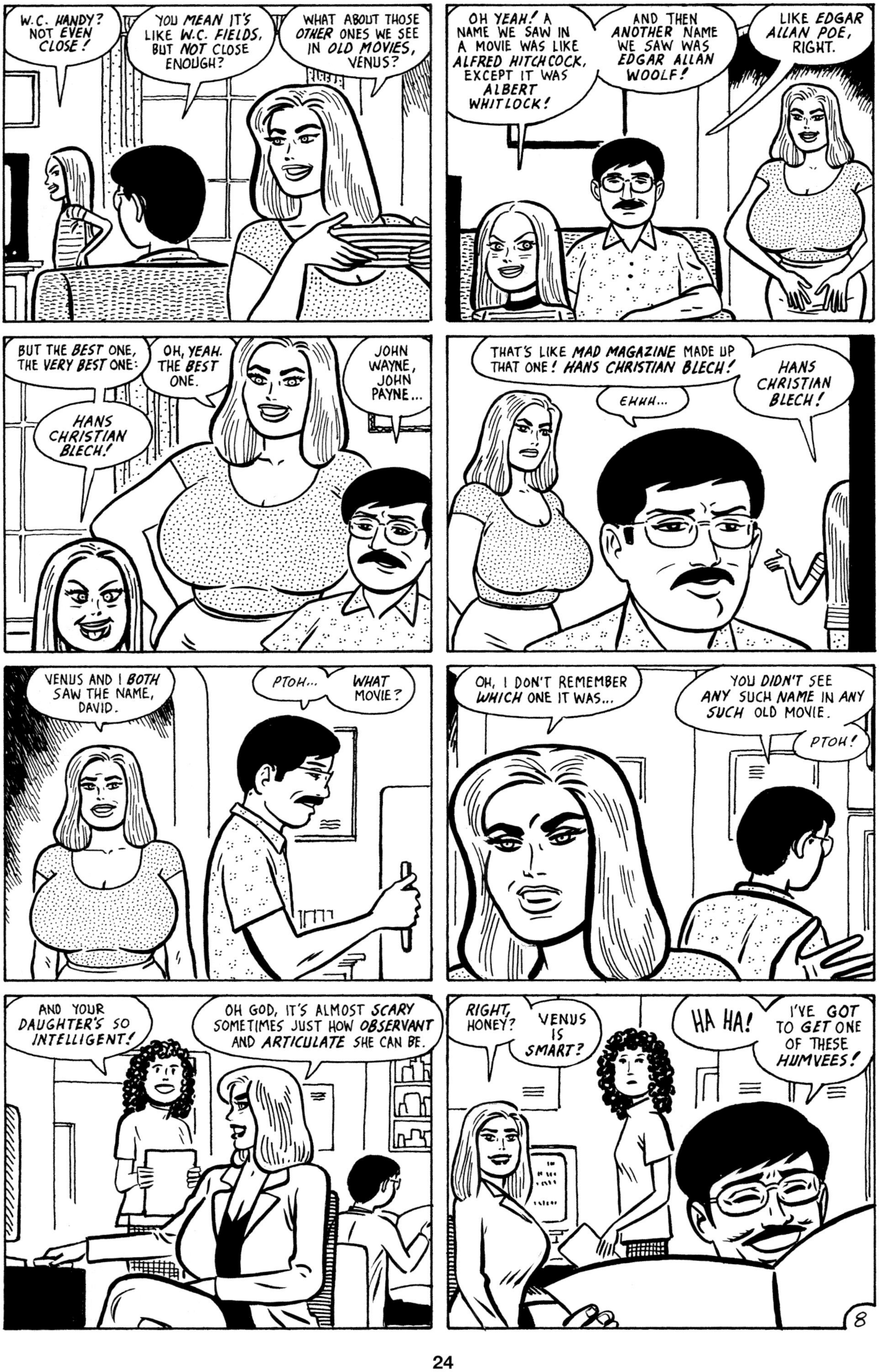
W.C. HANDY? NOT EVEN CLOSE!
YOU MEAN IT'S LIKE W.C. FIELDS, BUT NOT CLOSE ENOUGH?
WHAT ABOUT THOSE OTHER ONES WE SEE IN OLD MOVIES, VENUS?
OH YEAH! A NAME WE SAW IN A MOVIE WAS LIKE ALFRED HITCHCOCK, EXCEPT IT WAS ALBERT WHITLOCK!
AND THEN ANOTHER NAME WE SAW WAS EDGAR ALLAN WOOLF!
LIKE EDGAR ALLAN POE, RIGHT.
BUT THE BEST ONE, THE VERY BEST ONE:
OH, YEAH. THE BEST ONE.
JOHN WAYNE, JOHN PAYNE...
HANS CHRISTIAN BLECH!
THAT'S LIKE MAD MAGAZINE MADE UP THAT ONE! HANS CHRISTIAN BLECH!
EHHH...
HANS CHRISTIAN BLECH!
VENUS AND I BOTH SAW THE NAME, DAVID.
PTOH...
WHAT MOVIE?
OH, I DON'T REMEMBER WHICH ONE IT WAS...
YOU DIDN'T SEE ANY SUCH NAME IN ANY SUCH OLD MOVIE.
PTOH!
AND YOUR DAUGHTER'S SO INTELLIGENT!
OH GOD, IT'S ALMOST SCARY SOMETIMES JUST HOW OBSERVANT AND ARTICULATE SHE CAN BE.
RIGHT, HONEY?
VENUS IS SMART?
HA HA!
I'VE GOT TO GET ONE OF THESE HUMVEES!
8

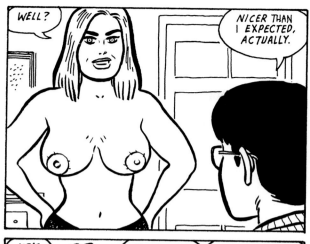

WELL?

NICER THAN I EXPECTED, ACTUALLY.

YOWCH...!

YEAH, THE DOCTOR *WARNED* ME: *NO MORE KIDS* OR THEY'LL PROBABLY GROW BACK.

MY *BOOBS*, THAT IS.

HE'S *STILL* GOT IT!

WHOO!

YOU DIDN'T *SEE* IT WHEN IT *FIRST* CAME OUT?

A GUY TOOK ME ON A *DATE* TO SEE IT.

SOME *DATE* MOVIE.

AT LEAST IT WAS *BETTER* THAN THAT STUPID `THE SHINING` SHIT.

OH, I LOVE *EVERYTHING* KUBRICK DOES, BUT I GUESS I'LL HAVE TO WAIT ANOTHER *TEN* YEARS FOR HIS NEXT ONE.

THAT ONE PART WITH THE SOLDIERS *CLUBBING* THE FAT GUY WITH BARS OF *SOAP* WRAPPED IN TOWELS?

WELL, I HEARD..

HAW HAW HAW..

THAT WAS GREAT!

WELL, THE GUY I DATED WAS AN EX-*MARINE*, AND HE SAID THEY DID THAT TO A GUY, BUT THEY USED THEIR *GUN CLIPS* IN THE TOWELS *INSTEAD* OF SOAP.

PTOH!

THAT *JAR HEAD IDIOT* WAS *LYING!* THEY *DIDN'T* USE THEIR GUN CLIPS!

WHAT A BUNCH OF *BULLSHIT!*

PTOH!

PTOH!

USED THEIR GUN CLIPS...

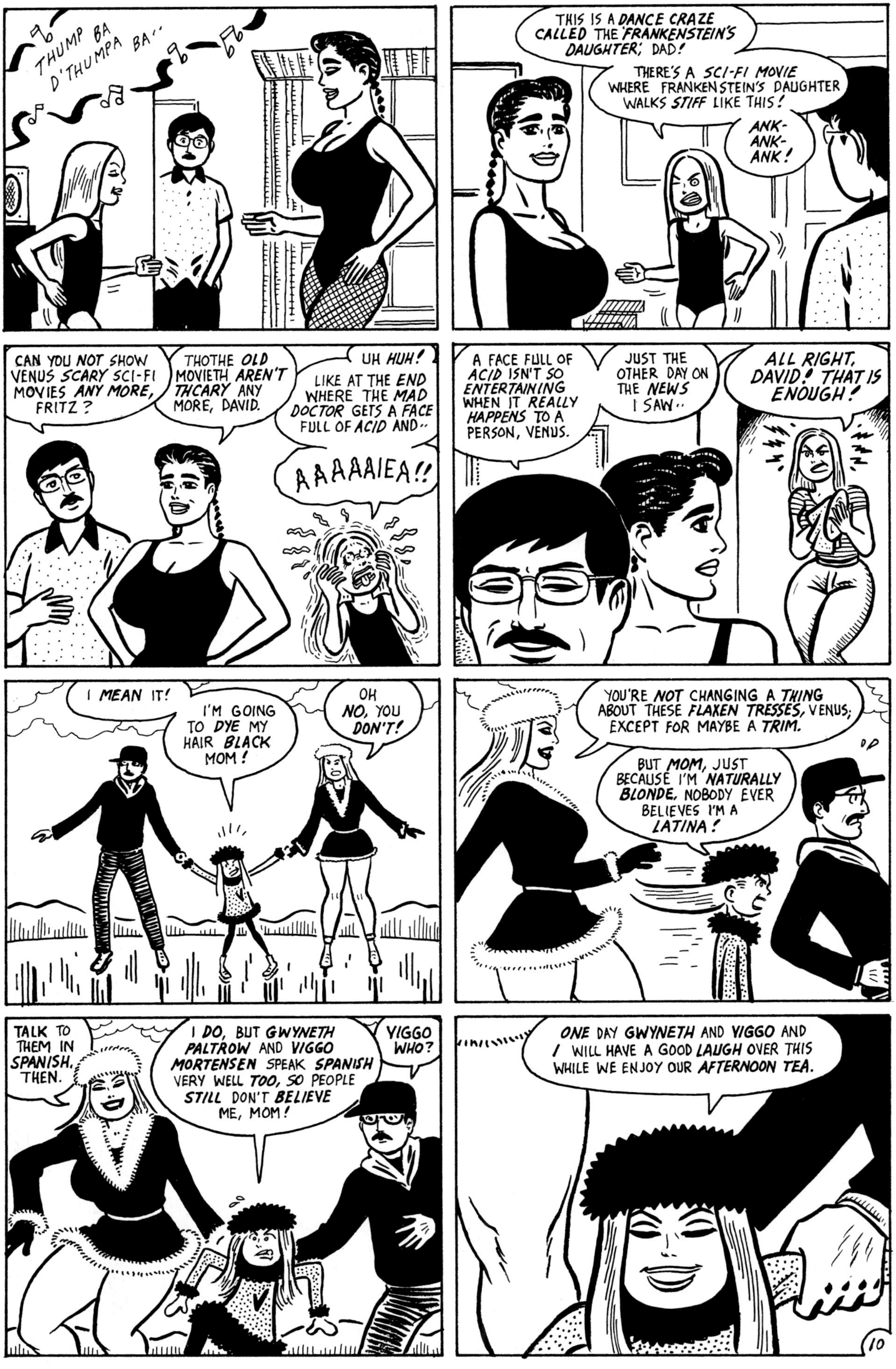
THUMP BA D'THUMPA BA..
THIS IS A DANCE CRAZE CALLED THE 'FRANKENSTEIN'S DAUGHTER,' DAD!
THERE'S A SCI-FI MOVIE WHERE FRANKENSTEIN'S DAUGHTER WALKS STIFF LIKE THIS!
ANK-ANK-ANK!
CAN YOU NOT SHOW VENUS SCARY SCI-FI MOVIES ANY MORE, FRITZ?
THOTHE OLD MOVIETH AREN'T THCARY ANY MORE, DAVID.
UH HUH!
LIKE AT THE END WHERE THE MAD DOCTOR GETS A FACE FULL OF ACID AND..
AAAAAIEA!!
A FACE FULL OF ACID ISN'T SO ENTERTAINING WHEN IT REALLY HAPPENS TO A PERSON, VENUS.
JUST THE OTHER DAY ON THE NEWS I SAW..
ALL RIGHT, DAVID! THAT IS ENOUGH!
I MEAN IT!
I'M GOING TO DYE MY HAIR BLACK MOM!
OH NO, YOU DON'T!
YOU'RE NOT CHANGING A THING ABOUT THESE FLAXEN TRESSES, VENUS; EXCEPT FOR MAYBE A TRIM.
BUT MOM, JUST BECAUSE I'M NATURALLY BLONDE, NOBODY EVER BELIEVES I'M A LATINA!
TALK TO THEM IN SPANISH, THEN.
I DO, BUT GWYNETH PALTROW AND VIGGO MORTENSEN SPEAK SPANISH VERY WELL TOO, SO PEOPLE STILL DON'T BELIEVE ME, MOM!
VIGGO WHO?
ONE DAY GWYNETH AND VIGGO AND I WILL HAVE A GOOD LAUGH OVER THIS WHILE WE ENJOY OUR AFTERNOON TEA.
10

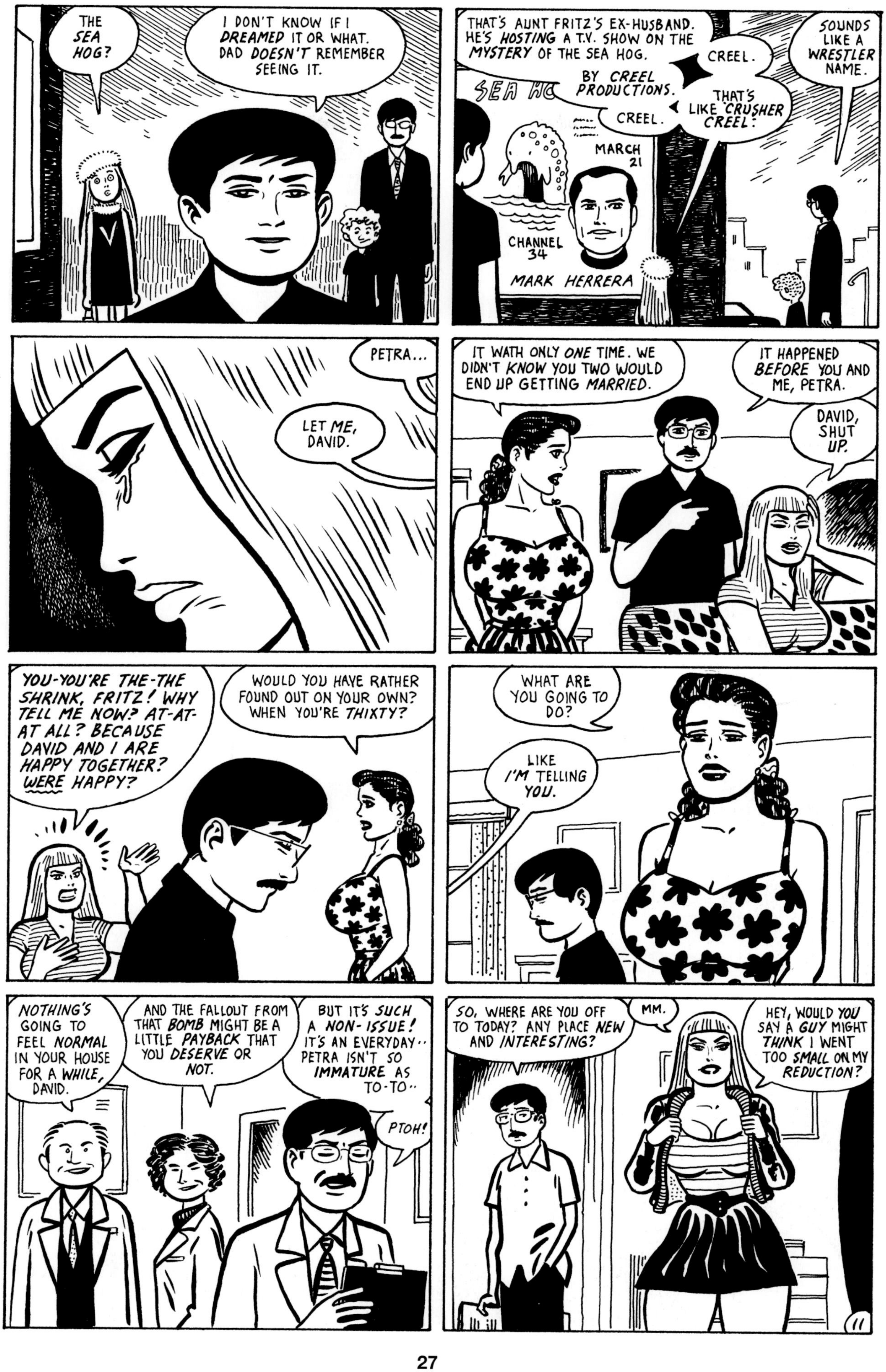
THE SEA HOG?
I DON'T KNOW IF I DREAMED IT OR WHAT. DAD DOESN'T REMEMBER SEEING IT.
THAT'S AUNT FRITZ'S EX-HUSBAND. HE'S HOSTING A T.V. SHOW ON THE MYSTERY OF THE SEA HOG.
SEA HO
BY CREEL PRODUCTIONS.
CREEL.
CREEL.
MARCH 21
CHANNEL 34
MARK HERRERA
THAT'S LIKE 'CRUSHER CREEL.'
SOUNDS LIKE A WRESTLER NAME.
PETRA...
LET ME, DAVID.
IT WATH ONLY ONE TIME. WE DIDN'T KNOW YOU TWO WOULD END UP GETTING MARRIED.
IT HAPPENED BEFORE YOU AND ME, PETRA.
DAVID, SHUT UP.
YOU-YOU'RE THE-THE SHRINK, FRITZ! WHY TELL ME NOW? AT-AT-AT ALL? BECAUSE DAVID AND I ARE HAPPY TOGETHER? WERE HAPPY?
WOULD YOU HAVE RATHER FOUND OUT ON YOUR OWN? WHEN YOU'RE THIXTY?
WHAT ARE YOU GOING TO DO?
LIKE I'M TELLING YOU.
NOTHING'S GOING TO FEEL NORMAL IN YOUR HOUSE FOR A WHILE, DAVID.
AND THE FALLOUT FROM THAT BOMB MIGHT BE A LITTLE PAYBACK THAT YOU DESERVE OR NOT.
BUT IT'S SUCH A NON-ISSUE! IT'S AN EVERYDAY.. PETRA ISN'T SO IMMATURE AS TO-TO..
PTOH!
SO, WHERE ARE YOU OFF TO TODAY? ANY PLACE NEW AND INTERESTING?
MM.
HEY, WOULD YOU SAY A GUY MIGHT THINK I WENT TOO SMALL ON MY REDUCTION?
11

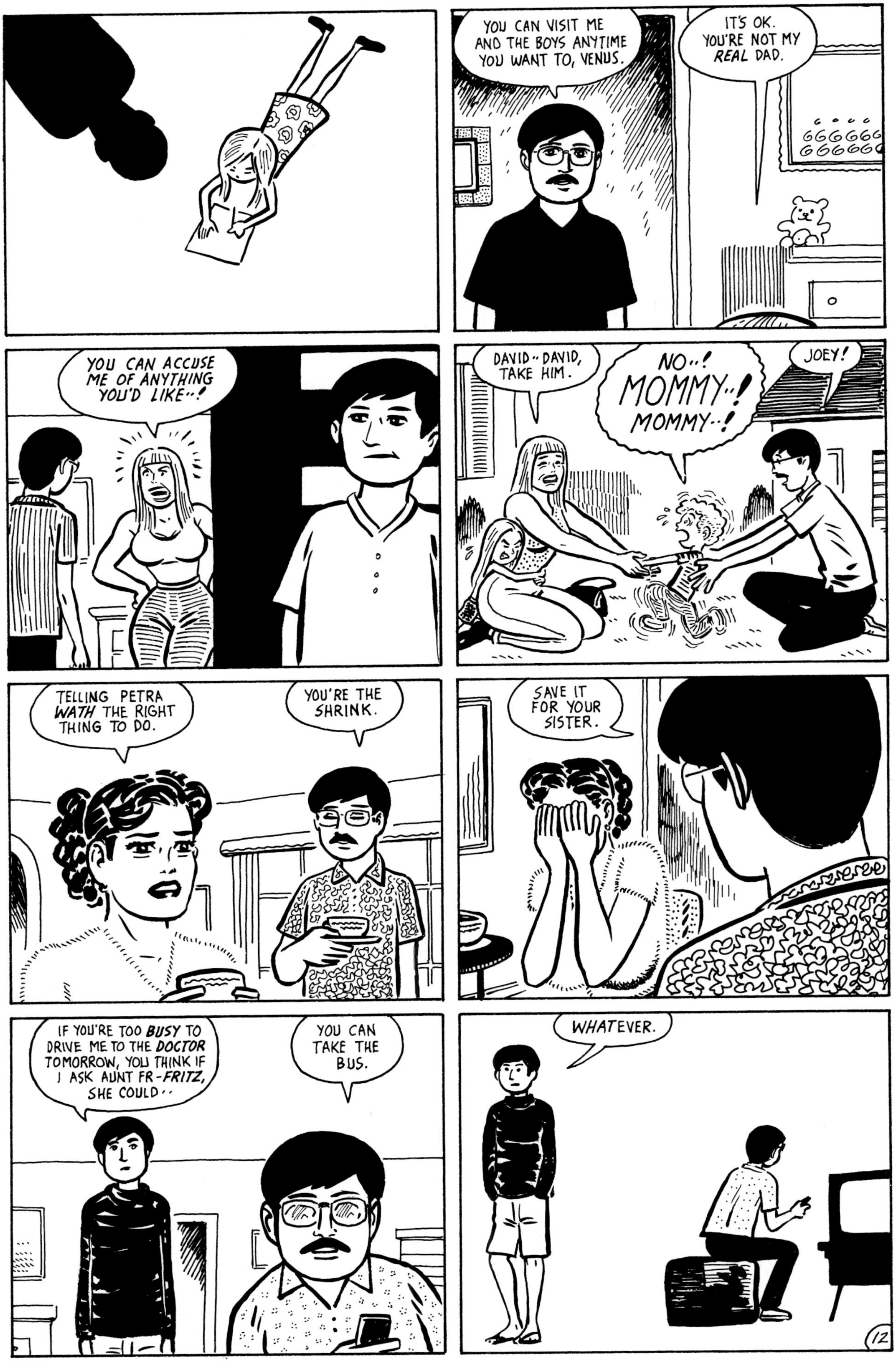
YOU CAN VISIT ME AND THE BOYS ANYTIME YOU WANT TO, VENUS.
IT'S OK. YOU'RE NOT MY *REAL* DAD.
YOU CAN ACCUSE ME OF ANYTHING YOU'D LIKE..!
DAVID.. DAVID, TAKE HIM.
NO..! MOMMY..! MOMMY..!
JOEY!
TELLING PETRA *WATH* THE RIGHT THING TO DO.
YOU'RE THE SHRINK.
SAVE IT FOR YOUR SISTER.
IF YOU'RE TOO *BUSY* TO DRIVE ME TO THE *DOCTOR* TOMORROW, YOU THINK IF I ASK AUNT FR-*FRITZ*, SHE COULD..
YOU CAN TAKE THE BUS.
*WHAT*EVER.
12

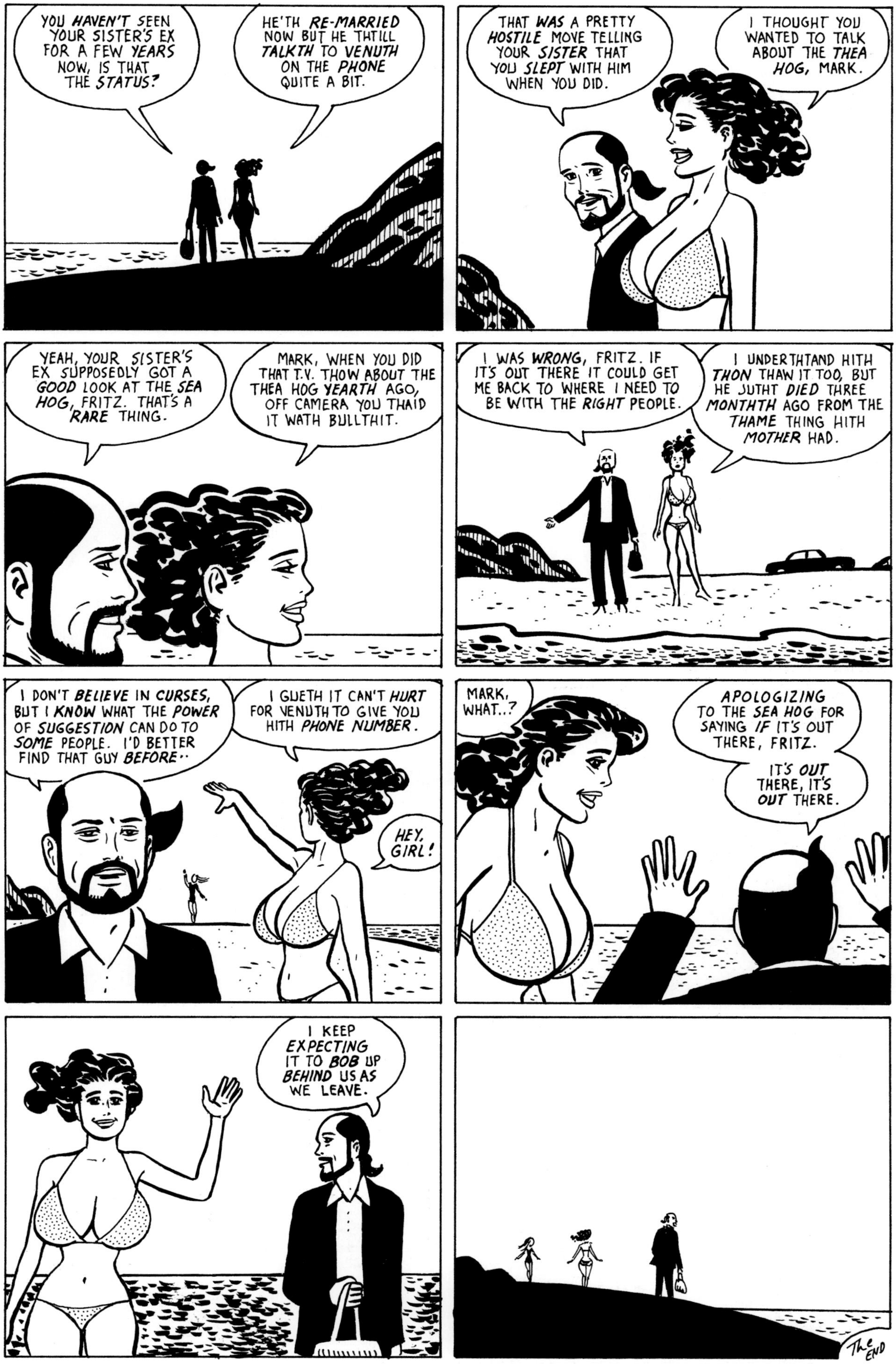
YOU HAVEN'T SEEN YOUR SISTER'S EX FOR A FEW YEARS NOW, IS THAT THE STATUS?
HE'TH RE-MARRIED NOW BUT HE THTILL TALKTH TO VENUTH ON THE PHONE QUITE A BIT.
THAT WAS A PRETTY HOSTILE MOVE TELLING YOUR SISTER THAT YOU SLEPT WITH HIM WHEN YOU DID.
I THOUGHT YOU WANTED TO TALK ABOUT THE THEA HOG, MARK.
YEAH, YOUR SISTER'S EX SUPPOSEDLY GOT A GOOD LOOK AT THE SEA HOG, FRITZ. THAT'S A RARE THING.
MARK, WHEN YOU DID THAT T.V. THOW ABOUT THE THEA HOG YEARTH AGO, OFF CAMERA YOU THAID IT WATH BULLTHIT.
I WAS WRONG, FRITZ. IF IT'S OUT THERE IT COULD GET ME BACK TO WHERE I NEED TO BE WITH THE RIGHT PEOPLE.
I UNDERTHTAND HITH THON THAW IT TOO, BUT HE JUTHT DIED THREE MONTHTH AGO FROM THE THAME THING HITH MOTHER HAD.
I DON'T BELIEVE IN CURSES, BUT I KNOW WHAT THE POWER OF SUGGESTION CAN DO TO SOME PEOPLE. I'D BETTER FIND THAT GUY BEFORE··
I GUETH IT CAN'T HURT FOR VENUTH TO GIVE YOU HITH PHONE NUMBER.
HEY, GIRL!
MARK, WHAT..?
APOLOGIZING TO THE SEA HOG FOR SAYING IF IT'S OUT THERE, FRITZ.
IT'S OUT THERE, IT'S OUT THERE.
I KEEP EXPECTING IT TO BOB UP BEHIND US AS WE LEAVE.
The END

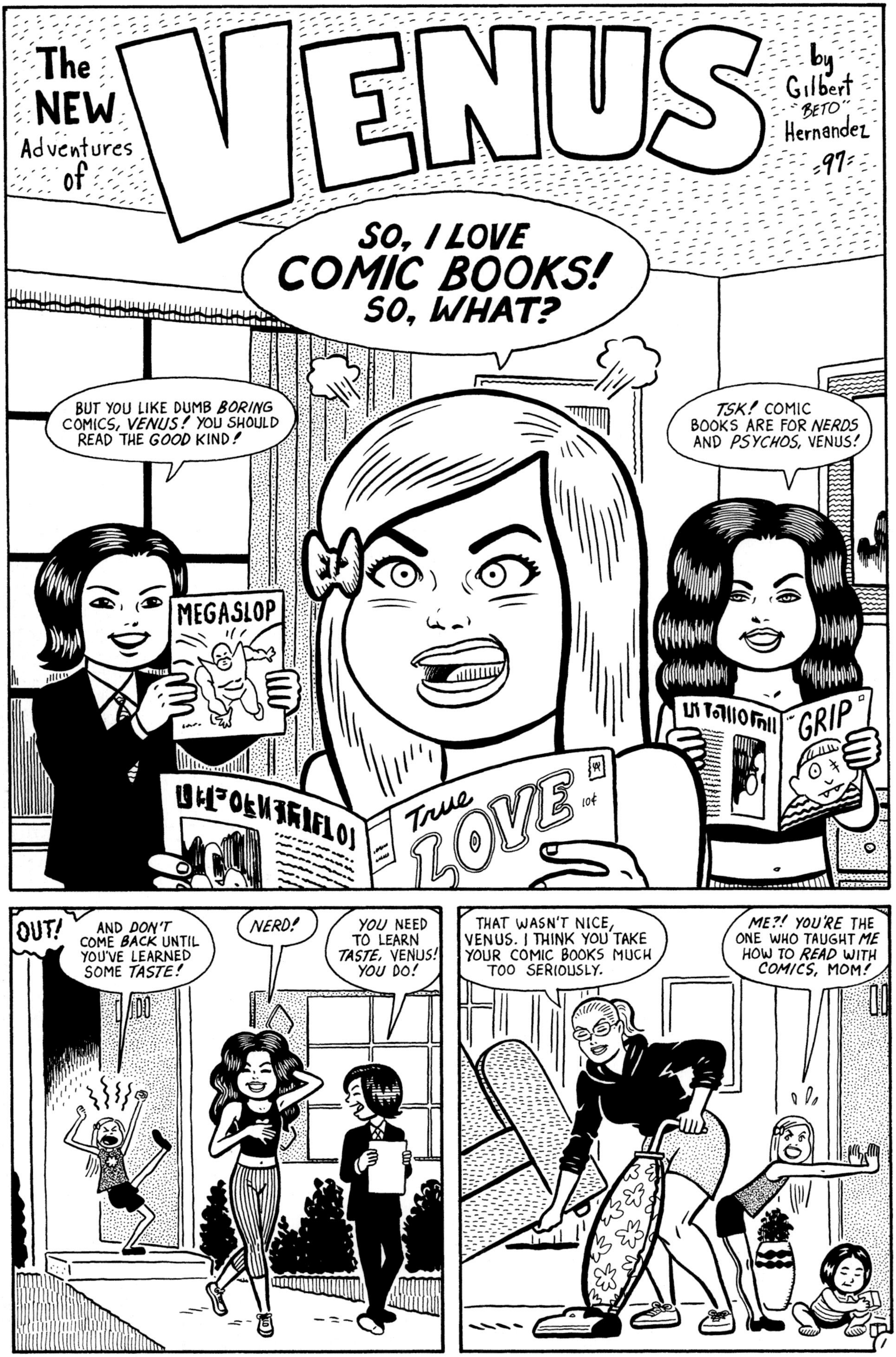
The NEW Adventures of VENUS
by Gilbert "BETO" Hernandez -97-
SO, I LOVE COMIC BOOKS! SO, WHAT?
BUT YOU LIKE DUMB BORING COMICS, VENUS! YOU SHOULD READ THE GOOD KIND!
TSK! COMIC BOOKS ARE FOR NERDS AND PSYCHOS, VENUS!
MEGASLOP
True LOVE
10¢
GRIP
OUT!
AND DON'T COME BACK UNTIL YOU'VE LEARNED SOME TASTE!
NERD!
YOU NEED TO LEARN TASTE, VENUS! YOU DO!
THAT WASN'T NICE, VENUS. I THINK YOU TAKE YOUR COMIC BOOKS MUCH TOO SERIOUSLY.
ME?! YOU'RE THE ONE WHO TAUGHT ME HOW TO READ WITH COMICS, MOM!

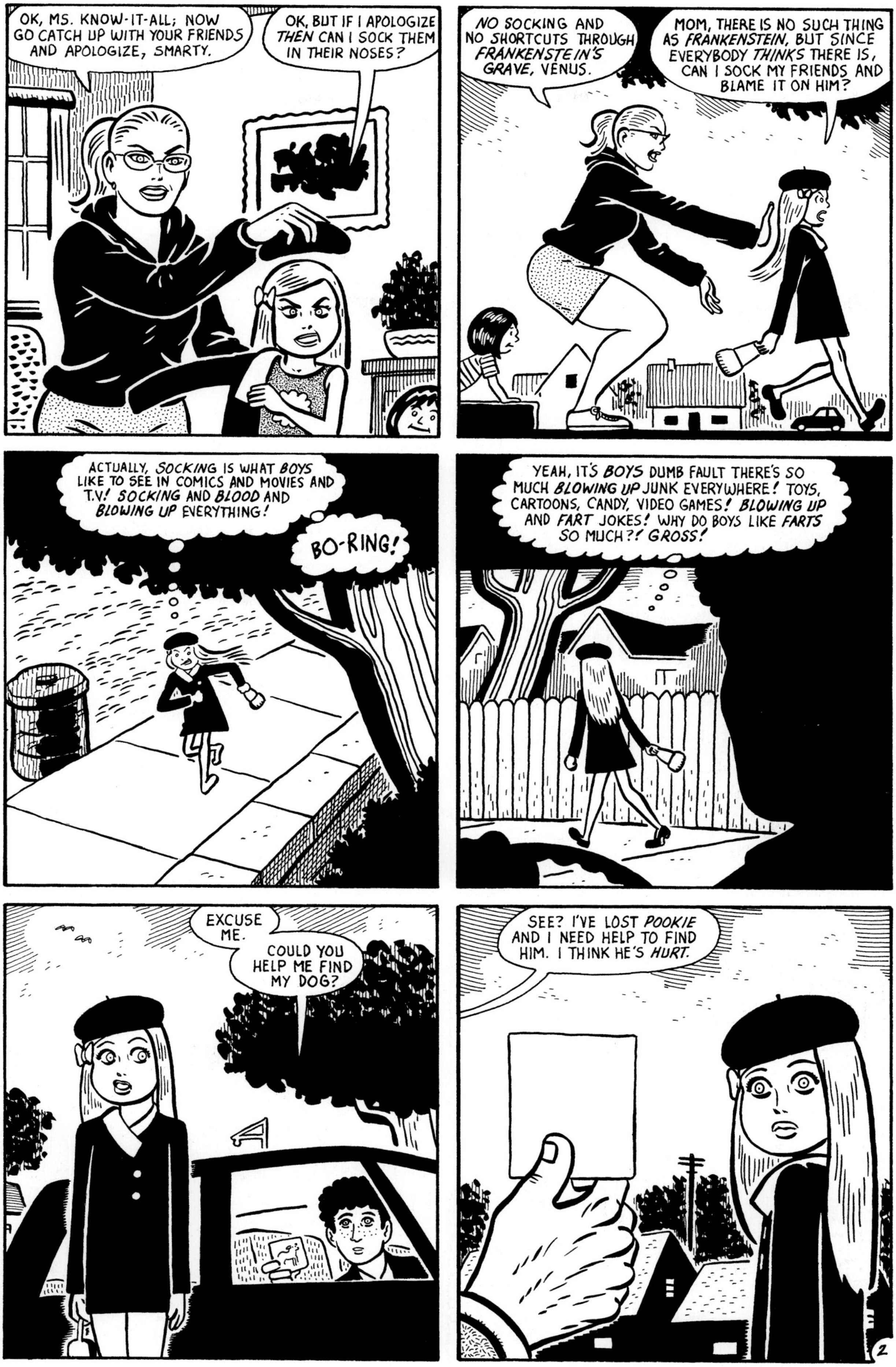
OK, MS. KNOW-IT-ALL; NOW GO CATCH UP WITH YOUR FRIENDS AND APOLOGIZE, SMARTY.
OK, BUT IF I APOLOGIZE THEN CAN I SOCK THEM IN THEIR NOSES?
NO SOCKING AND NO SHORTCUTS THROUGH FRANKENSTEIN'S GRAVE, VENUS.
MOM, THERE IS NO SUCH THING AS FRANKENSTEIN, BUT SINCE EVERYBODY THINKS THERE IS, CAN I SOCK MY FRIENDS AND BLAME IT ON HIM?
ACTUALLY, SOCKING IS WHAT BOYS LIKE TO SEE IN COMICS AND MOVIES AND T.V.! SOCKING AND BLOOD AND BLOWING UP EVERYTHING!
BO-RING!
YEAH, IT'S BOYS DUMB FAULT THERE'S SO MUCH BLOWING UP JUNK EVERYWHERE! TOYS, CARTOONS, CANDY, VIDEO GAMES! BLOWING UP AND FART JOKES! WHY DO BOYS LIKE FARTS SO MUCH?! GROSS!
EXCUSE ME.
COULD YOU HELP ME FIND MY DOG?
SEE? I'VE LOST POOKIE AND I NEED HELP TO FIND HIM. I THINK HE'S HURT.
2

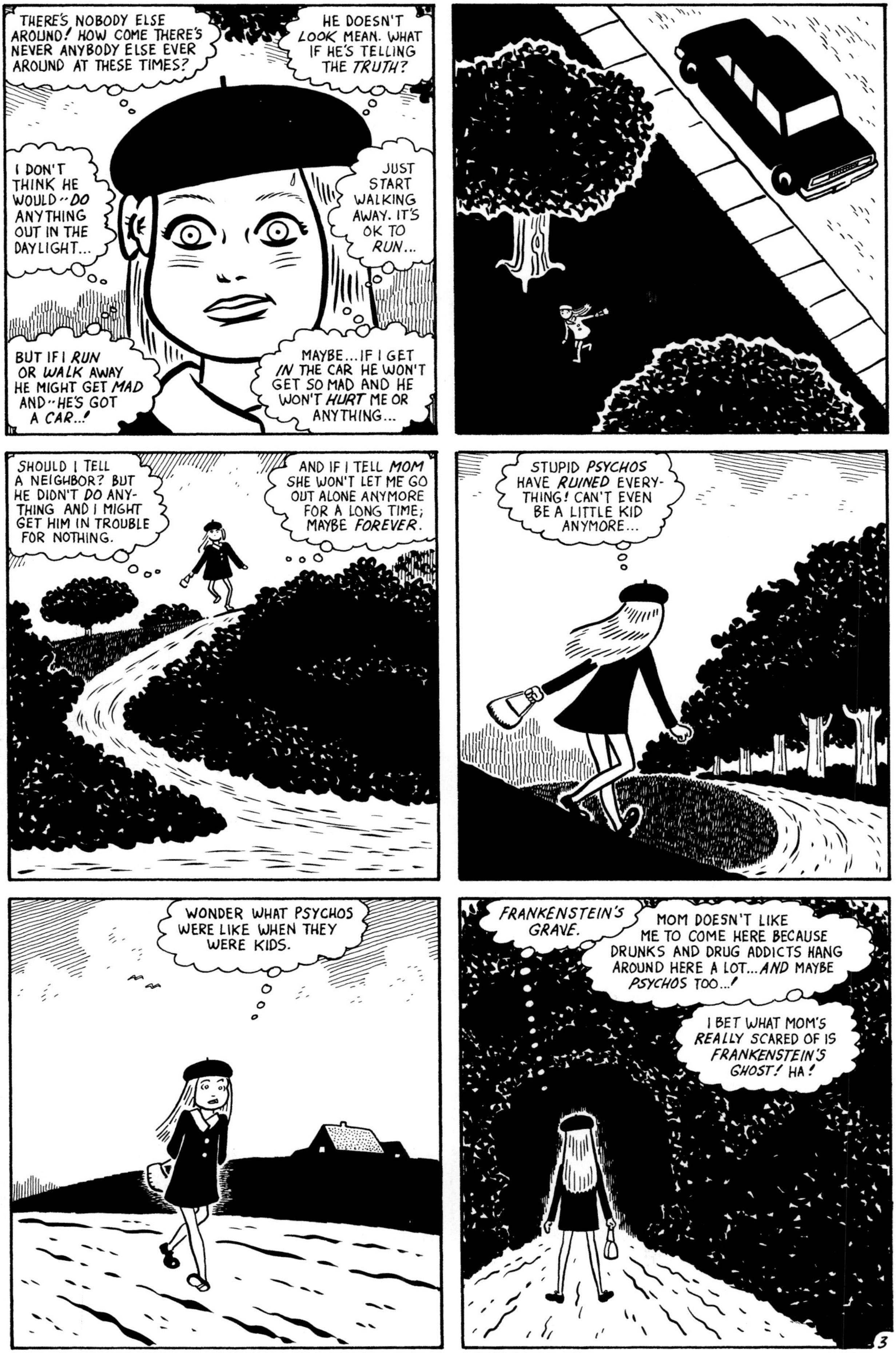
THERE'S NOBODY ELSE AROUND! HOW COME THERE'S NEVER ANYBODY ELSE EVER AROUND AT THESE TIMES?
HE DOESN'T LOOK MEAN. WHAT IF HE'S TELLING THE TRUTH?
I DON'T THINK HE WOULD--DO ANYTHING OUT IN THE DAYLIGHT...
JUST START WALKING AWAY. IT'S OK TO RUN...
BUT IF I RUN OR WALK AWAY HE MIGHT GET MAD AND--HE'S GOT A CAR..!
MAYBE...IF I GET IN THE CAR HE WON'T GET SO MAD AND HE WON'T HURT ME OR ANYTHING...
SHOULD I TELL A NEIGHBOR? BUT HE DIDN'T DO ANYTHING AND I MIGHT GET HIM IN TROUBLE FOR NOTHING.
AND IF I TELL MOM SHE WON'T LET ME GO OUT ALONE ANYMORE FOR A LONG TIME; MAYBE FOREVER.
STUPID PSYCHOS HAVE RUINED EVERYTHING! CAN'T EVEN BE A LITTLE KID ANYMORE...
WONDER WHAT PSYCHOS WERE LIKE WHEN THEY WERE KIDS.
FRANKENSTEIN'S GRAVE.
MOM DOESN'T LIKE ME TO COME HERE BECAUSE DRUNKS AND DRUG ADDICTS HANG AROUND HERE A LOT...AND MAYBE PSYCHOS TOO...!
I BET WHAT MOM'S REALLY SCARED OF IS FRANKENSTEIN'S GHOST! HA!
3

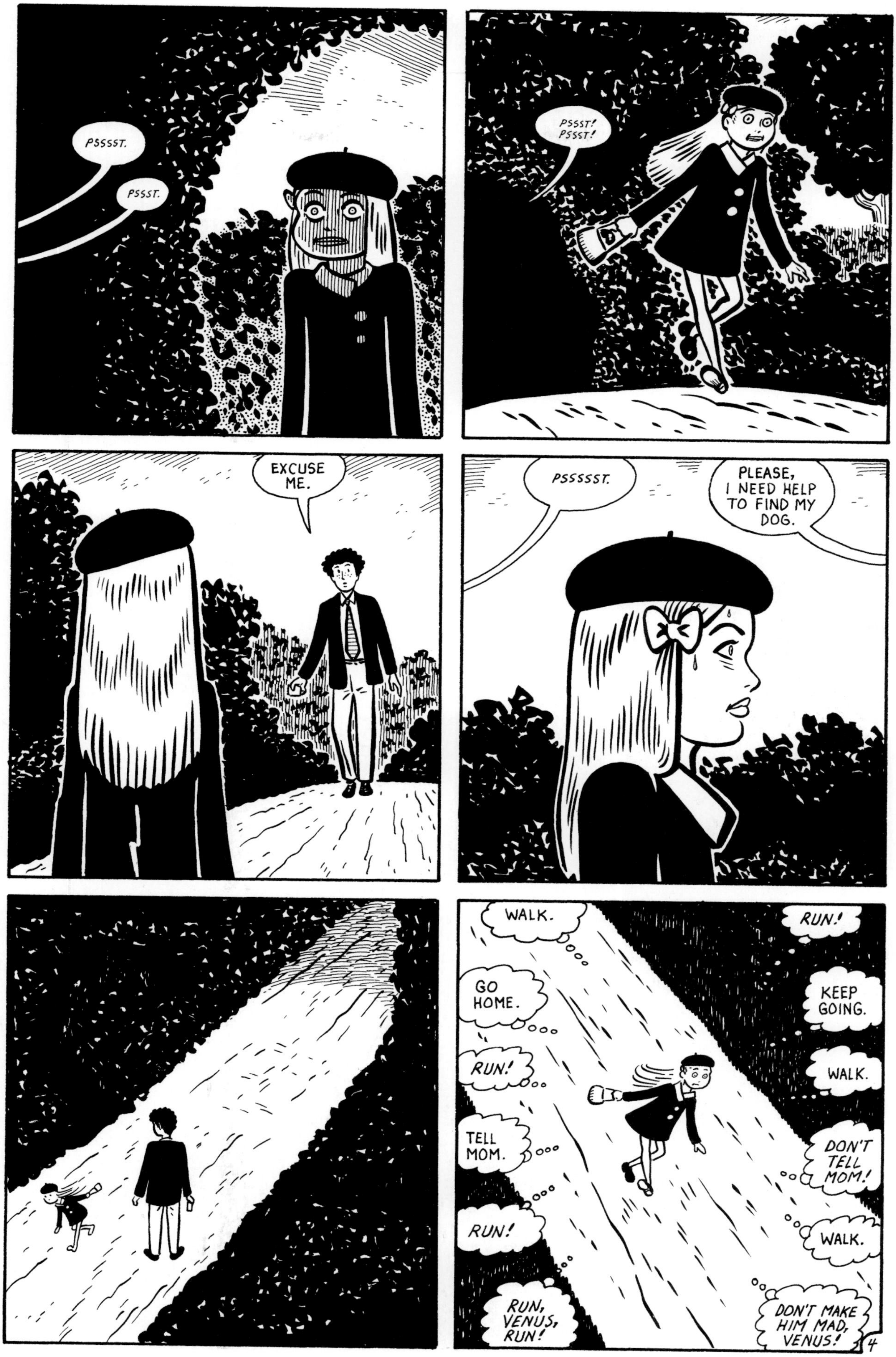
PSSSST.
PSSST.
PSSST! PSSST!
EXCUSE ME.
PSSSSST.
PLEASE, I NEED HELP TO FIND MY DOG.
WALK.
RUN!
GO HOME.
KEEP GOING.
RUN!
WALK.
TELL MOM.
DON'T TELL MOM!
RUN!
WALK.
RUN, VENUS, RUN!
DON'T MAKE HIM MAD, VENUS!
4

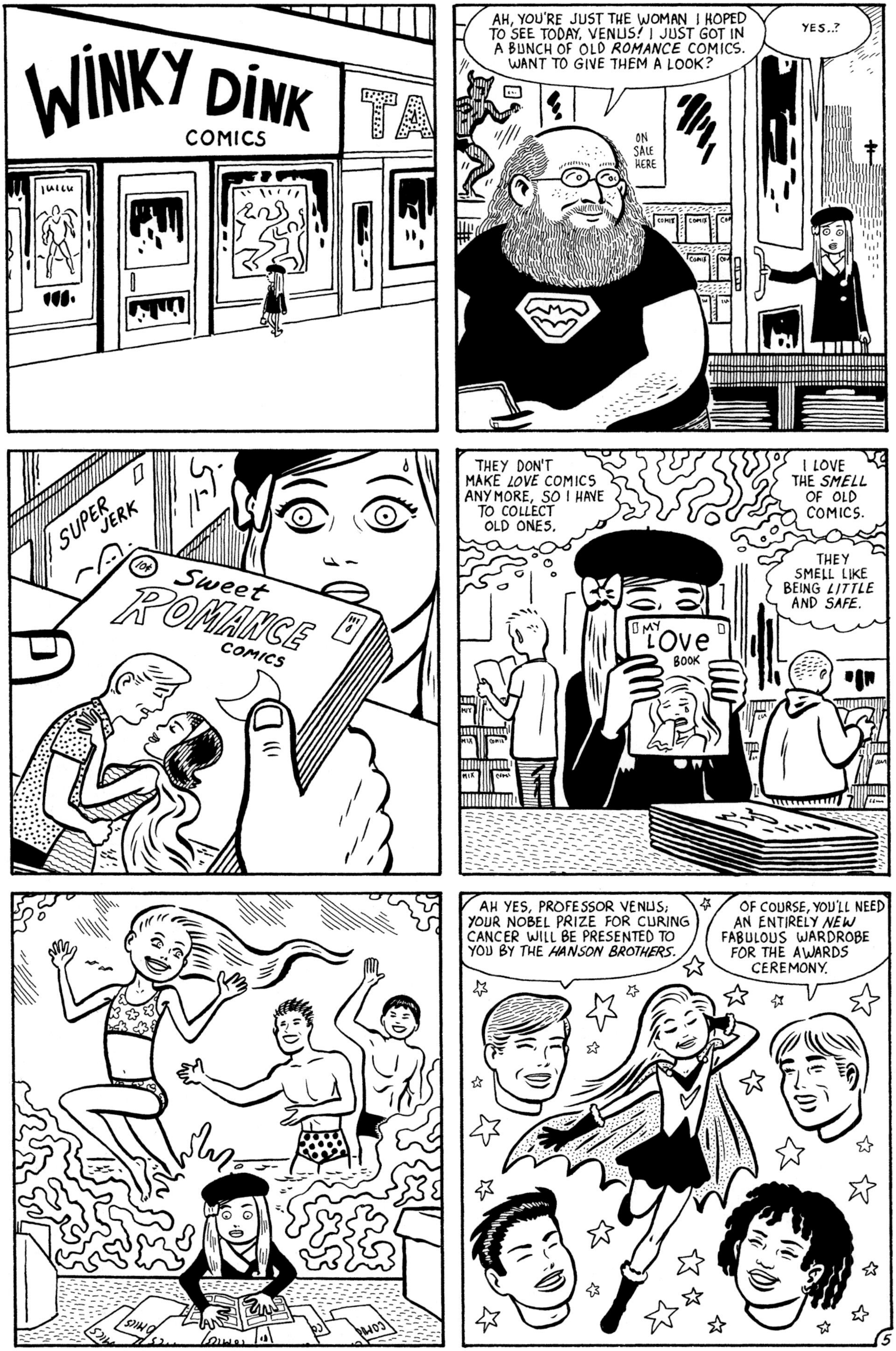
WINKY DINK
COMICS
AH, YOU'RE JUST THE WOMAN I HOPED TO SEE TODAY, VENUS! I JUST GOT IN A BUNCH OF OLD ROMANCE COMICS. WANT TO GIVE THEM A LOOK?
YES..?
ON SALE HERE
SUPER JERK
10¢
Sweet ROMANCE COMICS
THEY DON'T MAKE LOVE COMICS ANYMORE, SO I HAVE TO COLLECT OLD ONES.
I LOVE THE SMELL OF OLD COMICS.
THEY SMELL LIKE BEING LITTLE AND SAFE.
MY LOVE BOOK
AH YES, PROFESSOR VENUS; YOUR NOBEL PRIZE FOR CURING CANCER WILL BE PRESENTED TO YOU BY THE HANSON BROTHERS.
OF COURSE, YOU'LL NEED AN ENTIRELY NEW FABULOUS WARDROBE FOR THE AWARDS CEREMONY.
5

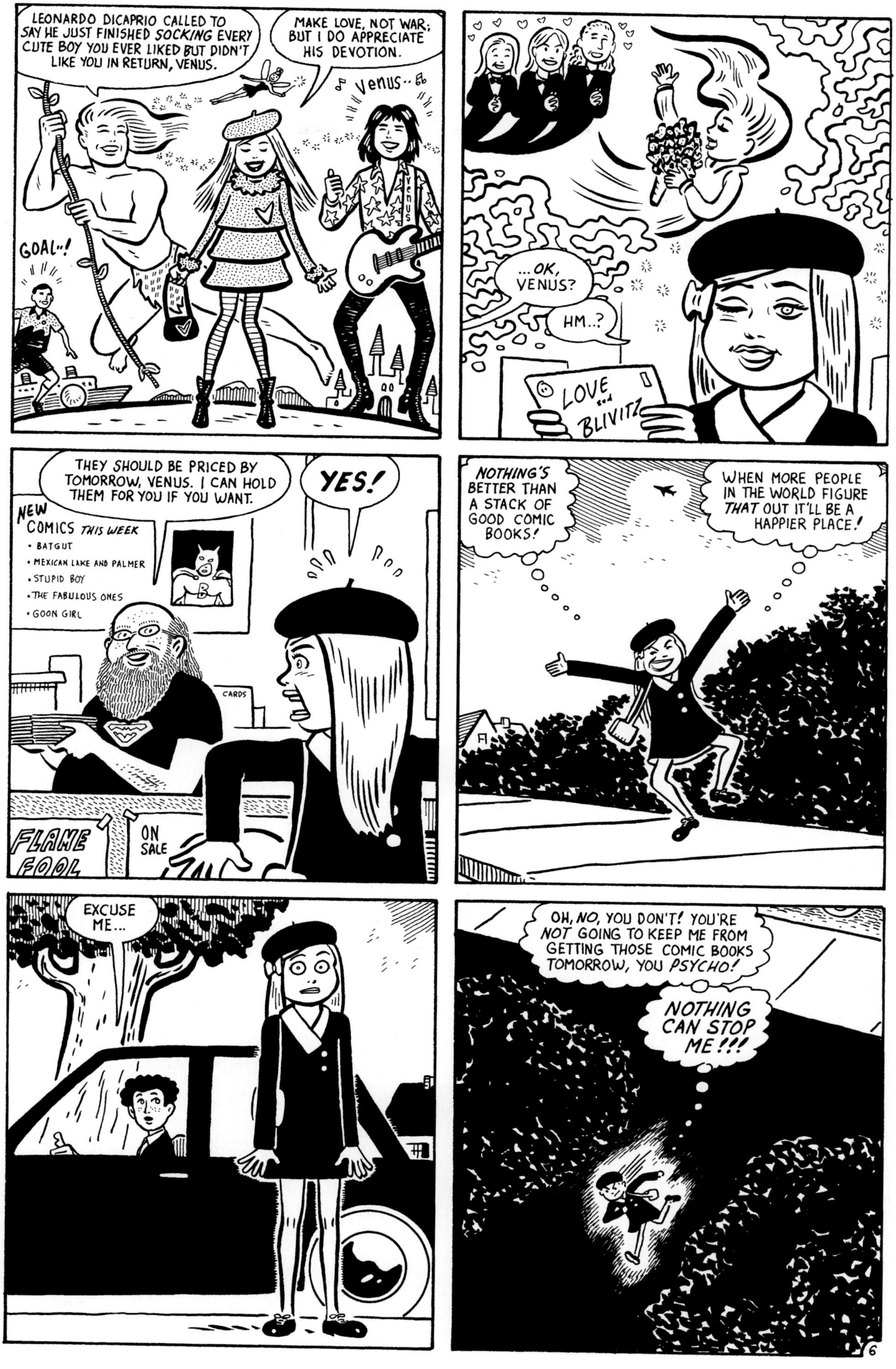
LEONARDO DICAPRIO CALLED TO SAY HE JUST FINISHED SOCKING EVERY CUTE BOY YOU EVER LIKED BUT DIDN'T LIKE YOU IN RETURN, VENUS.
MAKE LOVE, NOT WAR; BUT I DO APPRECIATE HIS DEVOTION.
Venus..
GOAL..!
...OK, VENUS?
HM..?
LOVE and BLIVITZ
THEY SHOULD BE PRICED BY TOMORROW, VENUS. I CAN HOLD THEM FOR YOU IF YOU WANT.
YES!
NEW COMICS THIS WEEK
• BATGUT
• MEXICAN LAKE AND PALMER
• STUPID BOY
• THE FABULOUS ONES
• GOON GIRL
CARDS
FLAME FOOL
ON SALE
NOTHING'S BETTER THAN A STACK OF GOOD COMIC BOOKS!
WHEN MORE PEOPLE IN THE WORLD FIGURE THAT OUT IT'LL BE A HAPPIER PLACE!
EXCUSE ME...
OH, NO, YOU DON'T! YOU'RE NOT GOING TO KEEP ME FROM GETTING THOSE COMIC BOOKS TOMORROW, YOU PSYCHO!
NOTHING CAN STOP ME!!!
6

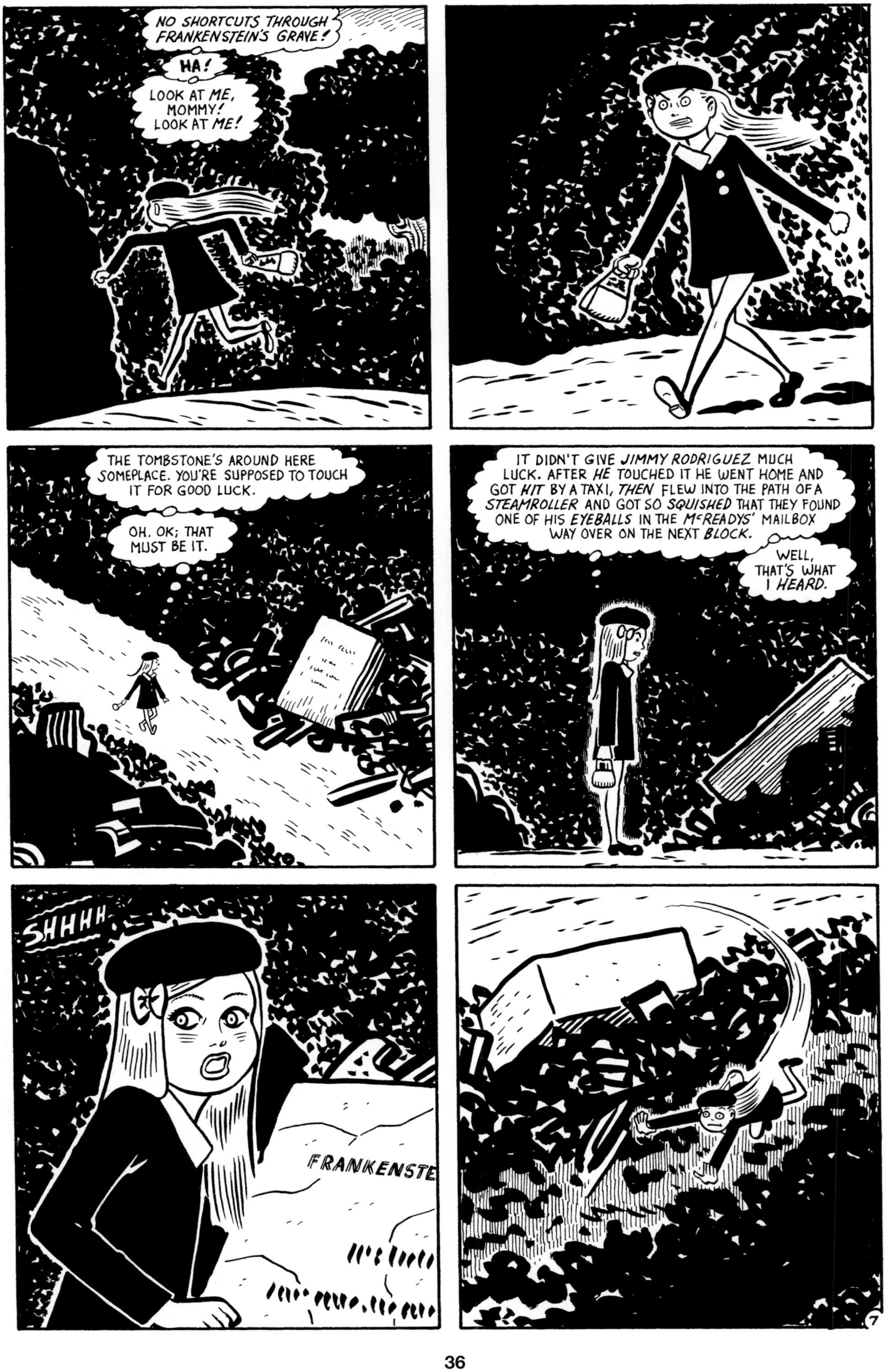
NO SHORTCUTS THROUGH FRANKENSTEIN'S GRAVE!
HA!
LOOK AT ME, MOMMY! LOOK AT ME!
THE TOMBSTONE'S AROUND HERE SOMEPLACE. YOU'RE SUPPOSED TO TOUCH IT FOR GOOD LUCK.
OH. OK; THAT MUST BE IT.
IT DIDN'T GIVE JIMMY RODRIGUEZ MUCH LUCK. AFTER HE TOUCHED IT HE WENT HOME AND GOT HIT BY A TAXI, THEN FLEW INTO THE PATH OF A STEAMROLLER AND GOT SO SQUISHED THAT THEY FOUND ONE OF HIS EYEBALLS IN THE McREADYS' MAILBOX WAY OVER ON THE NEXT BLOCK.
WELL, THAT'S WHAT I HEARD.
SHHHH
FRANKENSTE
7

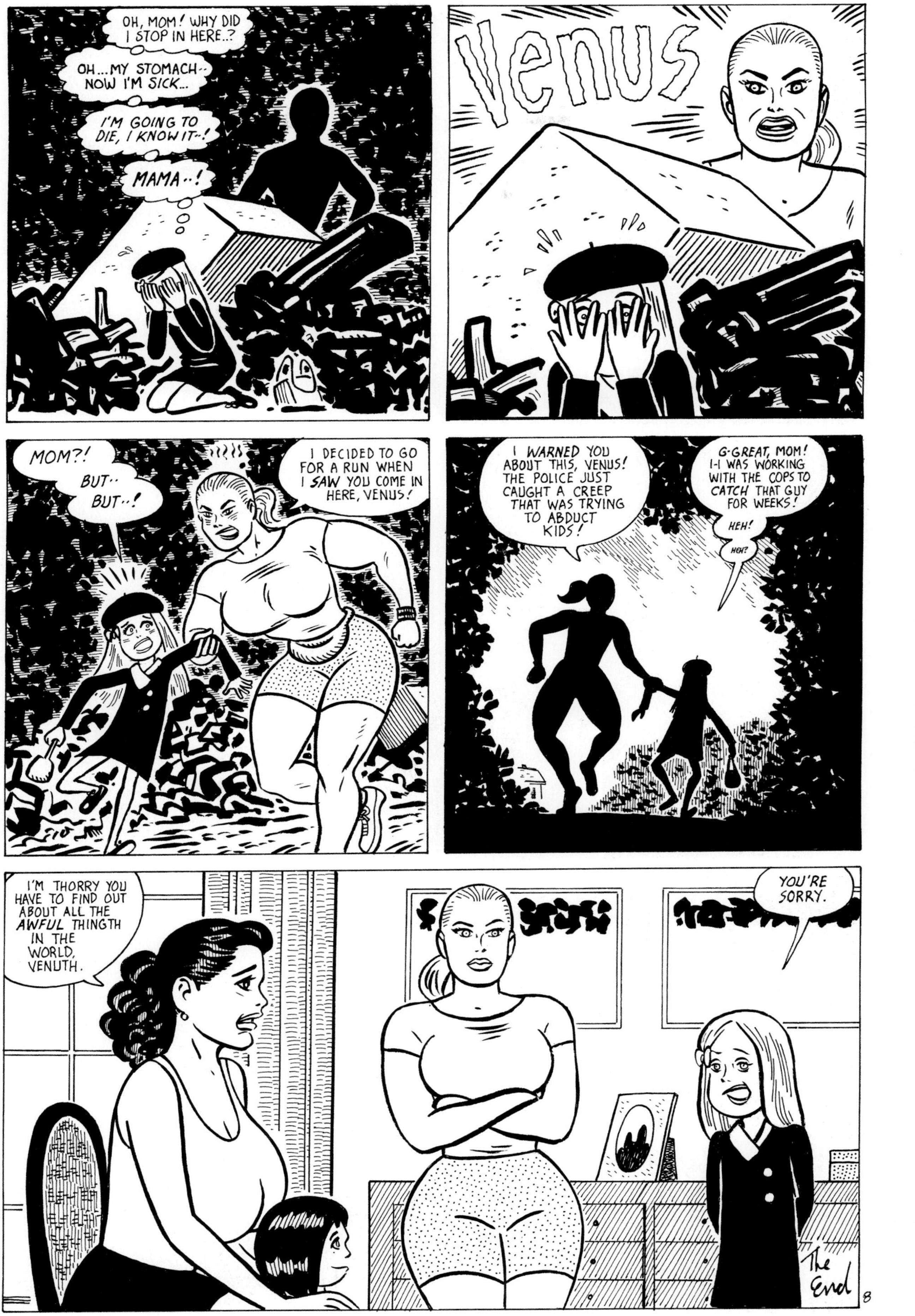
OH, MOM! WHY DID I STOP IN HERE..?
OH...MY STOMACH-- NOW I'M SICK...
I'M GOING TO DIE, I KNOW IT--!
MAMA--!
VENUS
MOM?!
BUT--
BUT--!
I DECIDED TO GO FOR A RUN WHEN I SAW YOU COME IN HERE, VENUS!
I WARNED YOU ABOUT THIS, VENUS! THE POLICE JUST CAUGHT A CREEP THAT WAS TRYING TO ABDUCT KIDS!
G-GREAT, MOM! I-I WAS WORKING WITH THE COPS TO CATCH THAT GUY FOR WEEKS!
HEH!
HEH?
I'M THORRY YOU HAVE TO FIND OUT ABOUT ALL THE AWFUL THINGTH IN THE WORLD, VENUTH.
YOU'RE SORRY.
The End
8

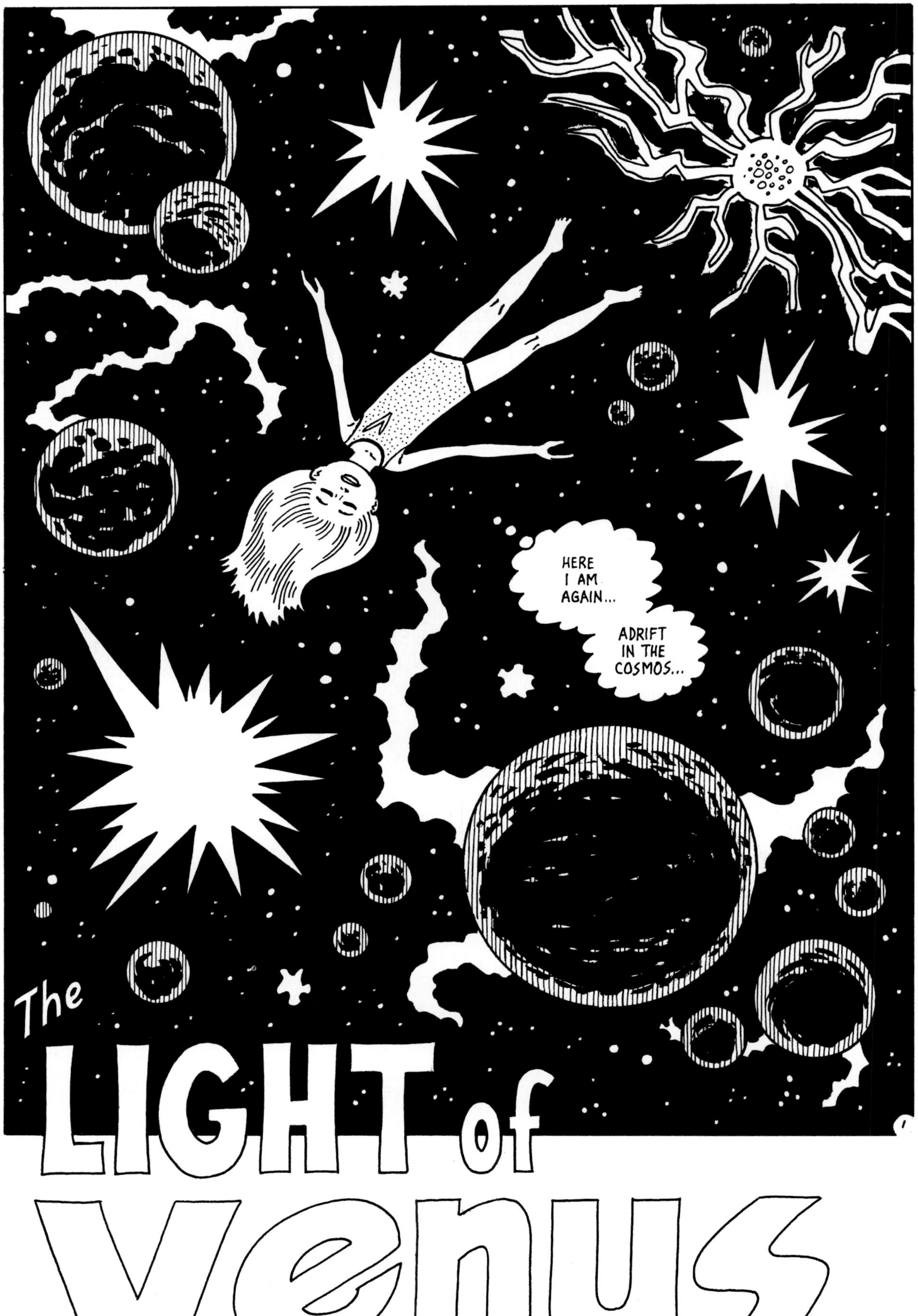
HERE I AM AGAIN...
ADRIFT IN THE COSMOS...
The LIGHT of Venus
BETO '04

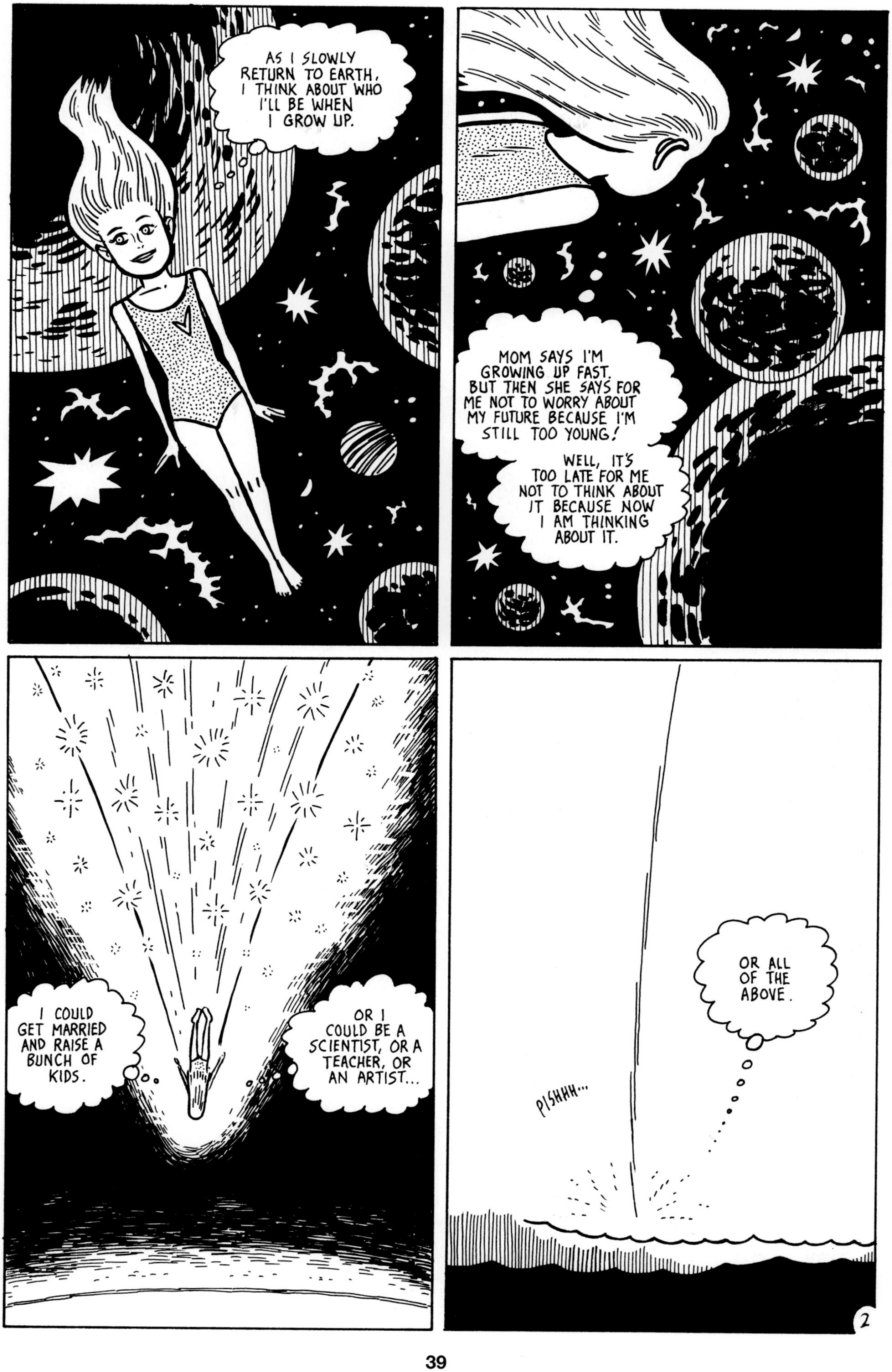
AS I SLOWLY RETURN TO EARTH, I THINK ABOUT WHO I'LL BE WHEN I GROW UP.
MOM SAYS I'M GROWING UP FAST. BUT THEN SHE SAYS FOR ME NOT TO WORRY ABOUT MY FUTURE BECAUSE I'M STILL TOO YOUNG!
WELL, IT'S TOO LATE FOR ME NOT TO THINK ABOUT IT BECAUSE NOW I AM THINKING ABOUT IT.
I COULD GET MARRIED AND RAISE A BUNCH OF KIDS.
OR I COULD BE A SCIENTIST, OR A TEACHER, OR AN ARTIST...
OR ALL OF THE ABOVE.
PISHHH...
2

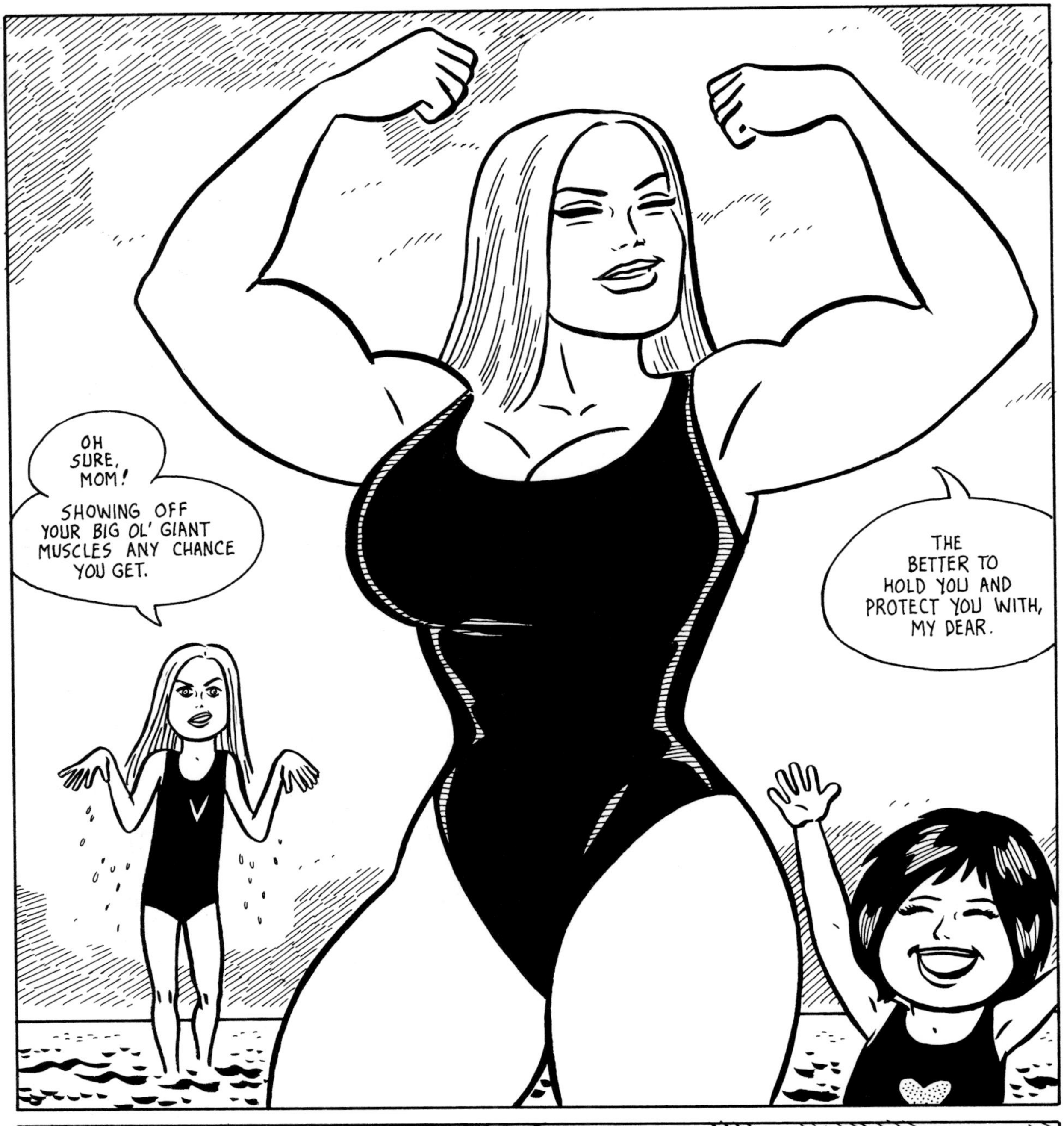
OH SURE, MOM!
SHOWING OFF YOUR BIG OL' GIANT MUSCLES ANY CHANCE YOU GET.
THE BETTER TO HOLD YOU AND PROTECT YOU WITH, MY DEAR.

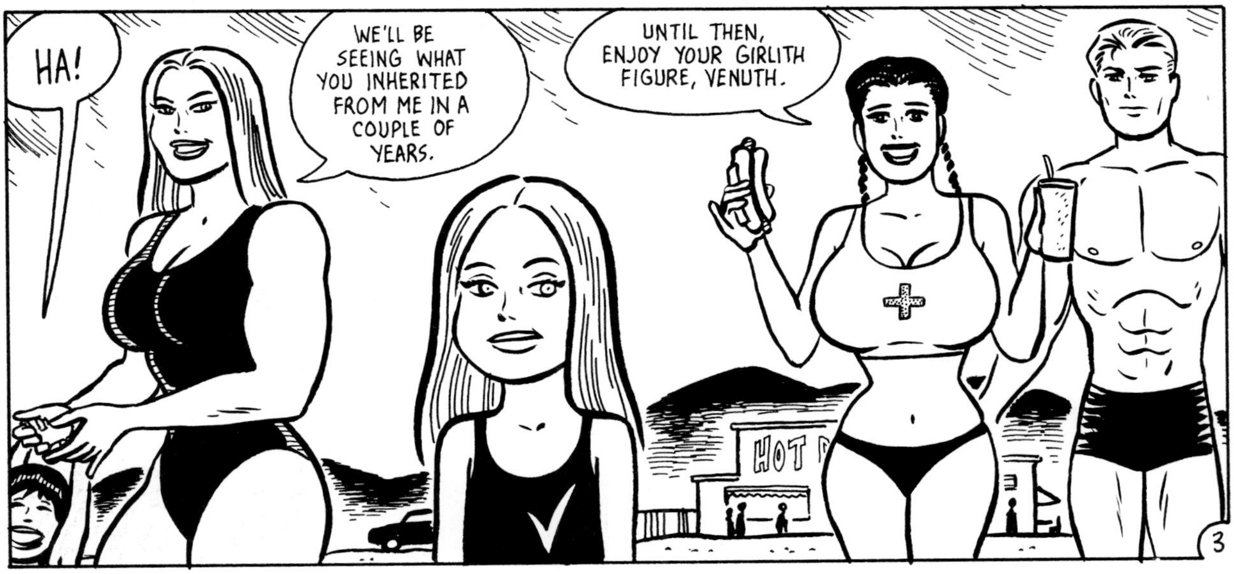
HA!
WE'LL BE SEEING WHAT YOU INHERITED FROM ME IN A COUPLE OF YEARS.
UNTIL THEN, ENJOY YOUR GIRLITH FIGURE, VENUTH.
HOT D
3

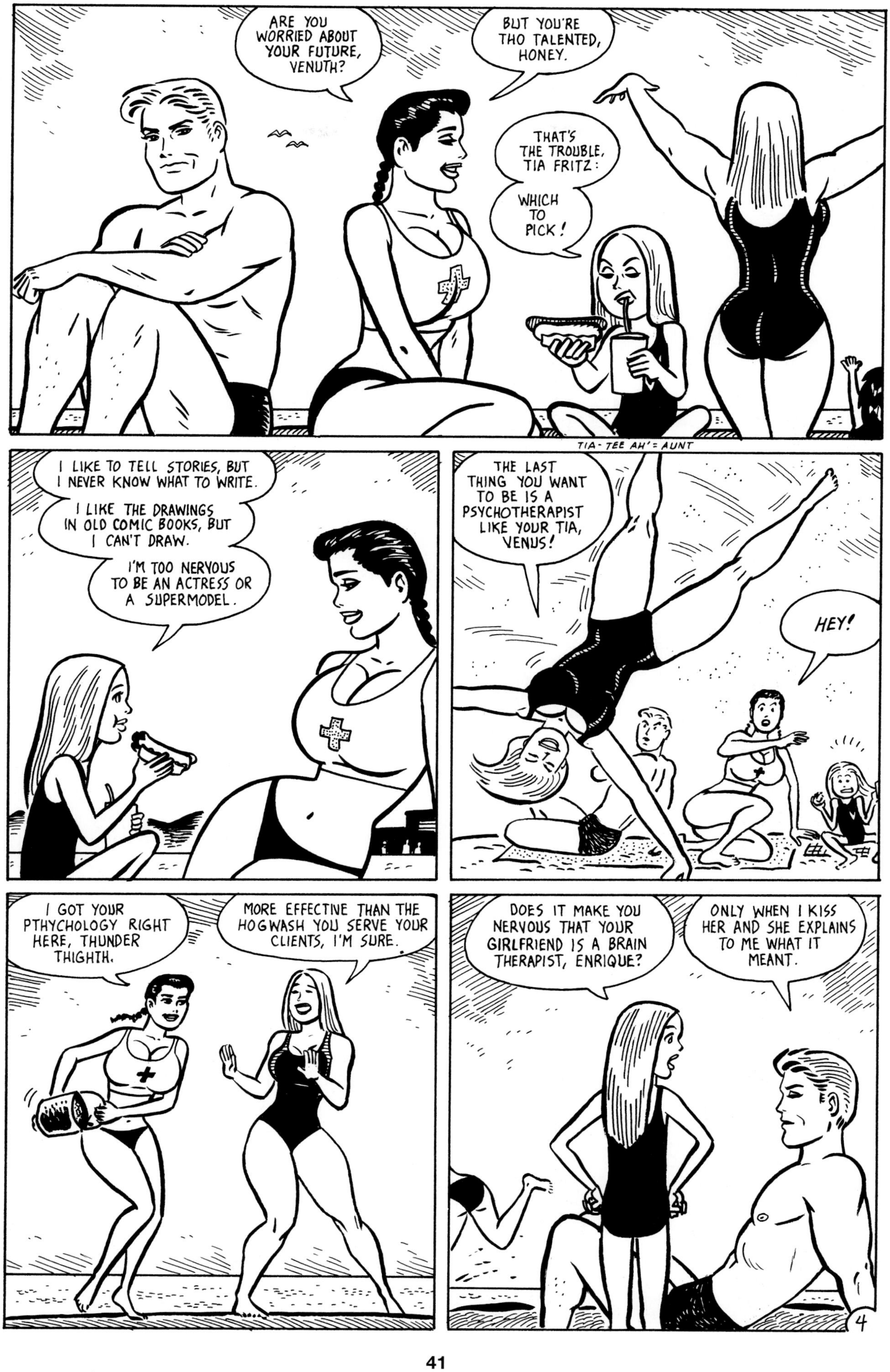
ARE YOU WORRIED ABOUT YOUR FUTURE, VENUTH?
BUT YOU'RE THO TALENTED, HONEY.
THAT'S THE TROUBLE, TIA FRITZ:
WHICH TO PICK!
TIA- TEE AH' = AUNT
I LIKE TO TELL STORIES, BUT I NEVER KNOW WHAT TO WRITE.
I LIKE THE DRAWINGS IN OLD COMIC BOOKS, BUT I CAN'T DRAW.
I'M TOO NERVOUS TO BE AN ACTRESS OR A SUPERMODEL.
THE LAST THING YOU WANT TO BE IS A PSYCHOTHERAPIST LIKE YOUR TIA, VENUS!
HEY!
I GOT YOUR PTHYCHOLOGY RIGHT HERE, THUNDER THIGHTH.
MORE EFFECTIVE THAN THE HOGWASH YOU SERVE YOUR CLIENTS, I'M SURE.
DOES IT MAKE YOU NERVOUS THAT YOUR GIRLFRIEND IS A BRAIN THERAPIST, ENRIQUE?
ONLY WHEN I KISS HER AND SHE EXPLAINS TO ME WHAT IT MEANT.
4

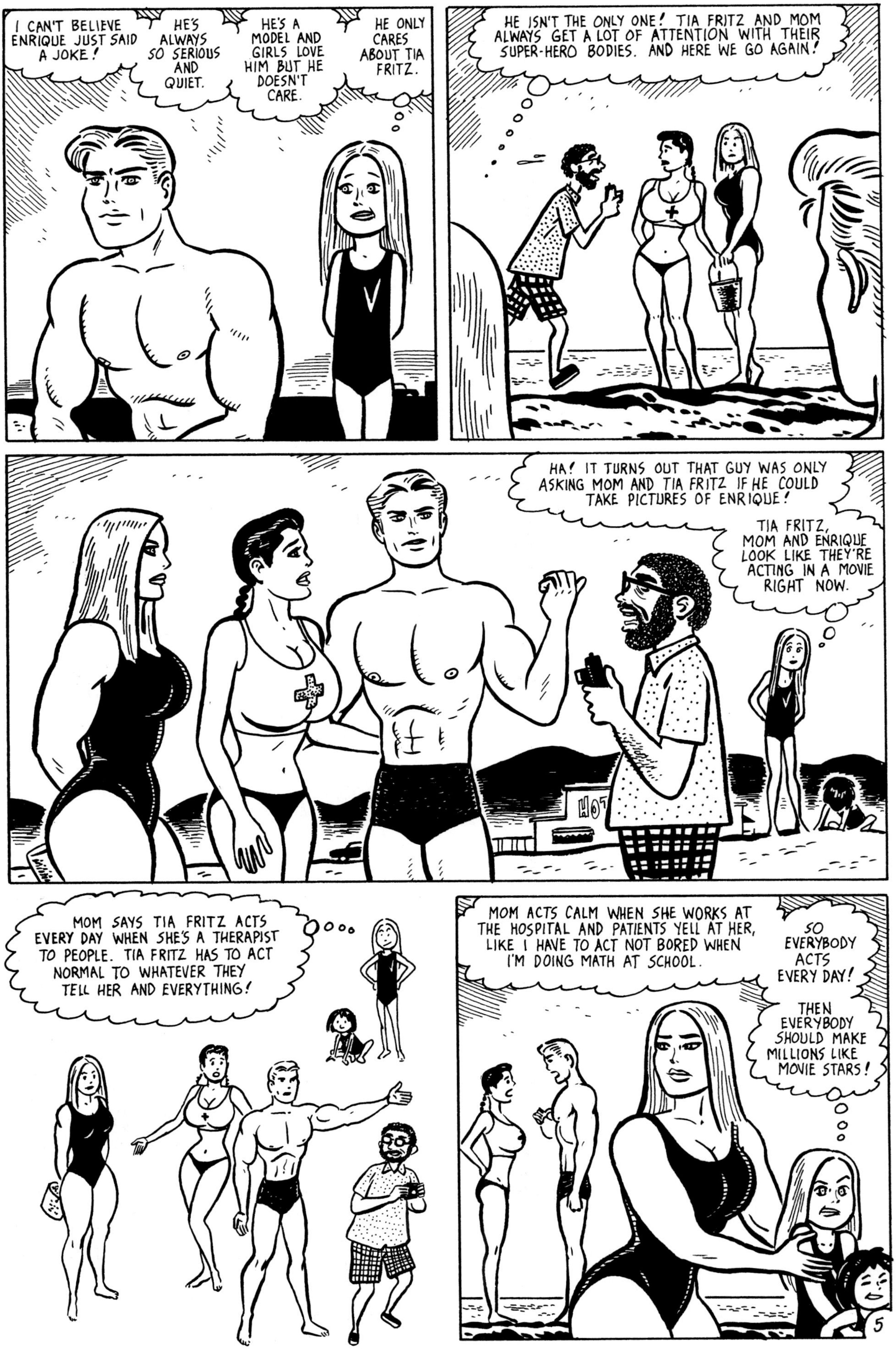
I CAN'T BELIEVE ENRIQUE JUST SAID A JOKE!
HE'S ALWAYS SO SERIOUS AND QUIET.
HE'S A MODEL AND GIRLS LOVE HIM BUT HE DOESN'T CARE.
HE ONLY CARES ABOUT TIA FRITZ.
HE ISN'T THE ONLY ONE! TIA FRITZ AND MOM ALWAYS GET A LOT OF ATTENTION WITH THEIR SUPER-HERO BODIES. AND HERE WE GO AGAIN!
HA! IT TURNS OUT THAT GUY WAS ONLY ASKING MOM AND TIA FRITZ IF HE COULD TAKE PICTURES OF ENRIQUE!
TIA FRITZ, MOM AND ENRIQUE LOOK LIKE THEY'RE ACTING IN A MOVIE RIGHT NOW.
HOT
MOM SAYS TIA FRITZ ACTS EVERY DAY WHEN SHE'S A THERAPIST TO PEOPLE. TIA FRITZ HAS TO ACT NORMAL TO WHATEVER THEY TELL HER AND EVERYTHING!
MOM ACTS CALM WHEN SHE WORKS AT THE HOSPITAL AND PATIENTS YELL AT HER, LIKE I HAVE TO ACT NOT BORED WHEN I'M DOING MATH AT SCHOOL.
SO EVERYBODY ACTS EVERY DAY!
THEN EVERYBODY SHOULD MAKE MILLIONS LIKE MOVIE STARS!
5

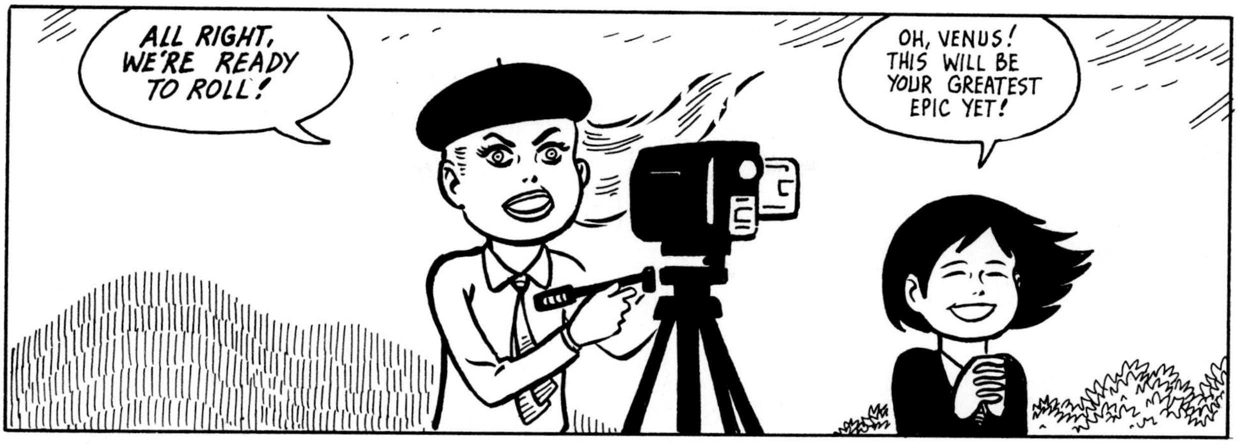
ALL RIGHT, WE'RE READY TO ROLL!
OH, VENUS! THIS WILL BE YOUR GREATEST EPIC YET!

The BIG·PICTURE

BETO 04

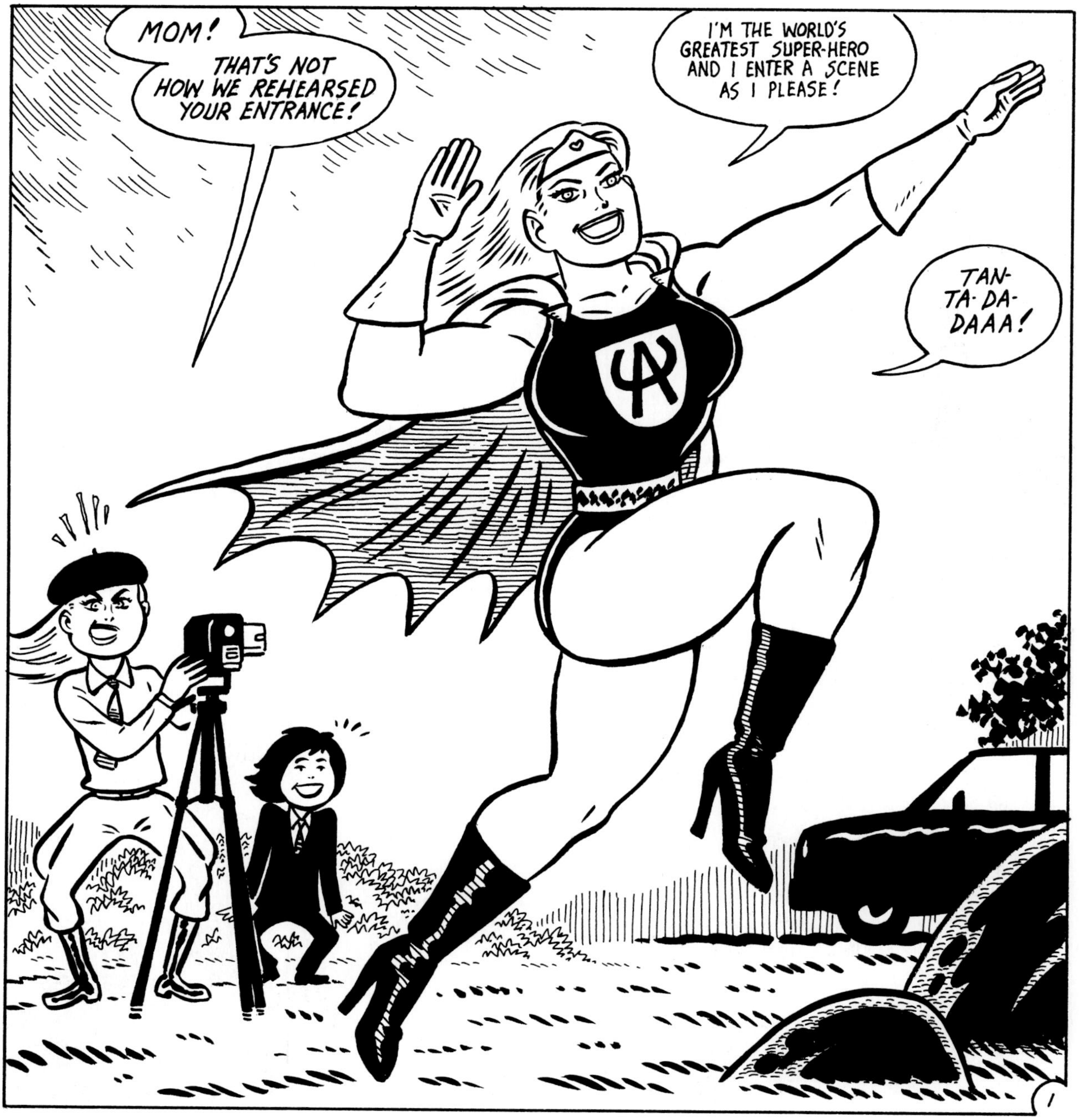
MOM!
THAT'S NOT HOW WE REHEARSED YOUR ENTRANCE!
I'M THE WORLD'S GREATEST SUPER-HERO AND I ENTER A SCENE AS I PLEASE!
TAN-TA-DA-DAAA!
1

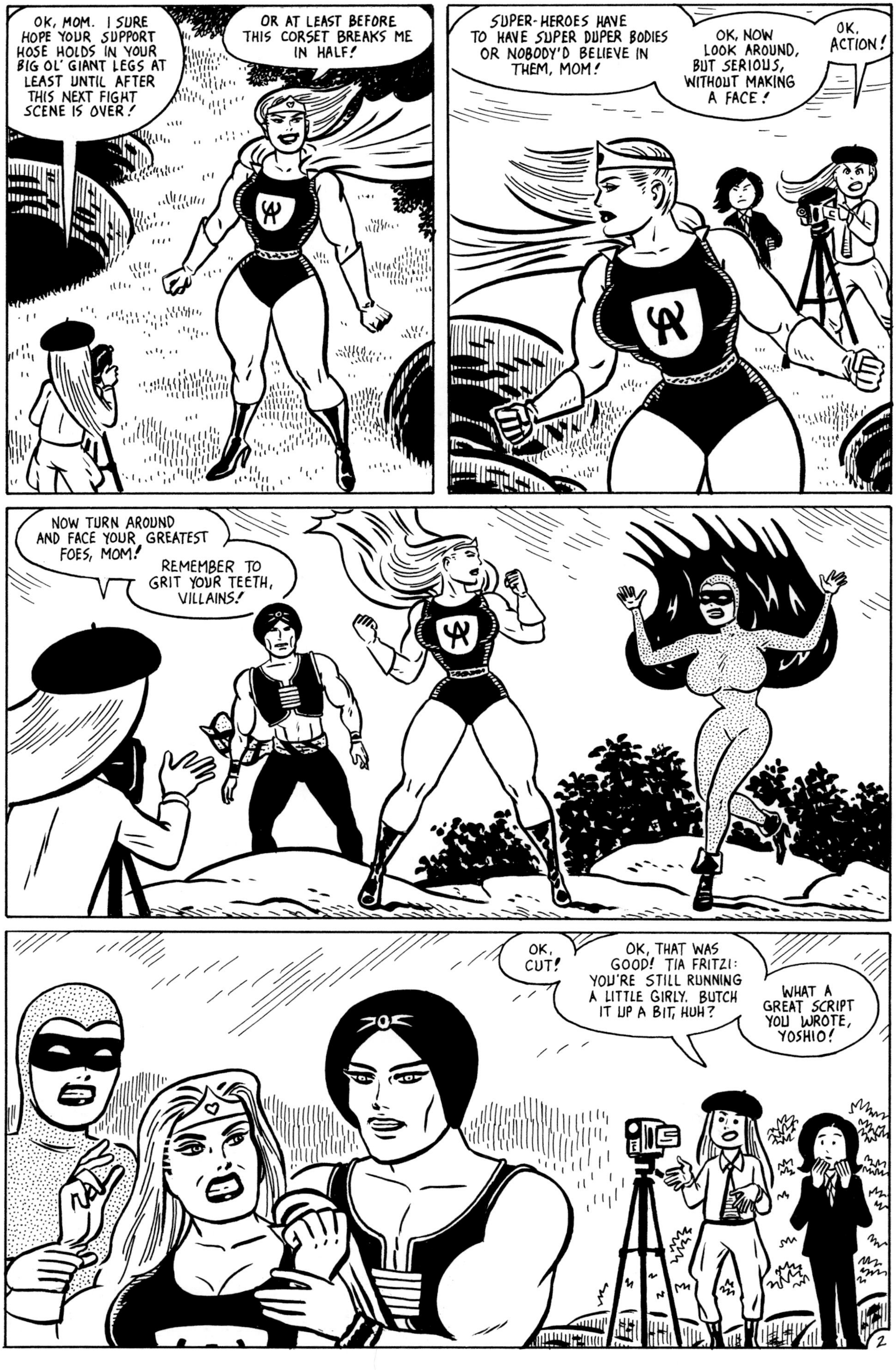
OK, MOM. I SURE HOPE YOUR SUPPORT HOSE HOLDS IN YOUR BIG OL' GIANT LEGS AT LEAST UNTIL AFTER THIS NEXT FIGHT SCENE IS OVER!
OR AT LEAST BEFORE THIS CORSET BREAKS ME IN HALF!
SUPER-HEROES HAVE TO HAVE SUPER DUPER BODIES OR NOBODY'D BELIEVE IN THEM, MOM!
OK, NOW LOOK AROUND, BUT SERIOUS, WITHOUT MAKING A FACE!
OK, ACTION!
NOW TURN AROUND AND FACE YOUR GREATEST FOES, MOM!
REMEMBER TO GRIT YOUR TEETH, VILLAINS!
OK, CUT!
OK, THAT WAS GOOD! TIA FRITZI: YOU'RE STILL RUNNING A LITTLE GIRLY. BUTCH IT UP A BIT, HUH?
WHAT A GREAT SCRIPT YOU WROTE, YOSHIO!
2

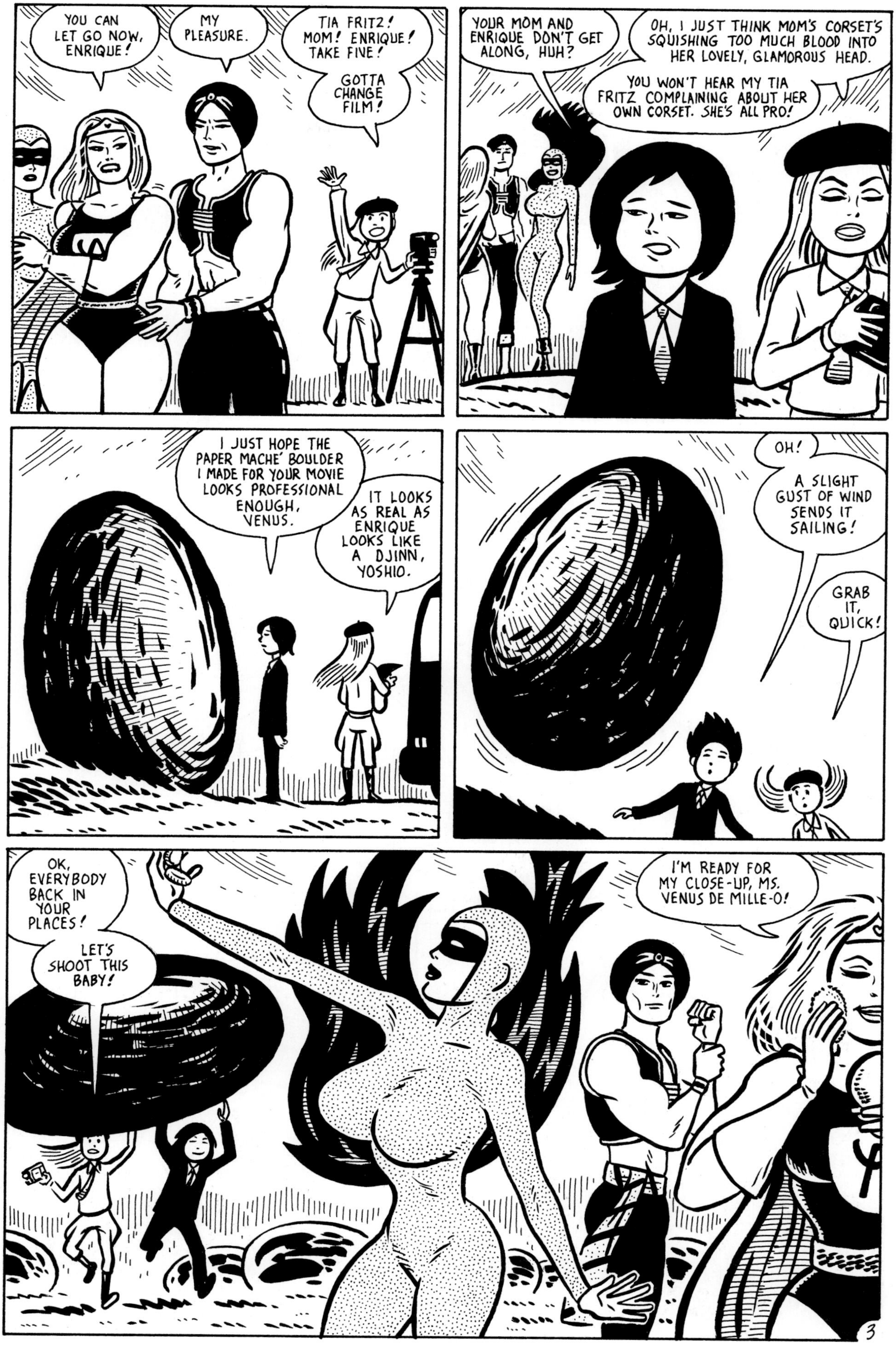
YOU CAN LET GO NOW, ENRIQUE!
MY PLEASURE.
TIA FRITZ! MOM! ENRIQUE! TAKE FIVE!
GOTTA CHANGE FILM!
YOUR MOM AND ENRIQUE DON'T GET ALONG, HUH?
OH, I JUST THINK MOM'S CORSET'S SQUISHING TOO MUCH BLOOD INTO HER LOVELY, GLAMOROUS HEAD.
YOU WON'T HEAR MY TIA FRITZ COMPLAINING ABOUT HER OWN CORSET. SHE'S ALL PRO!
I JUST HOPE THE PAPER MACHE' BOULDER I MADE FOR YOUR MOVIE LOOKS PROFESSIONAL ENOUGH, VENUS.
IT LOOKS AS REAL AS ENRIQUE LOOKS LIKE A DJINN, YOSHIO.
OH!
A SLIGHT GUST OF WIND SENDS IT SAILING!
GRAB IT, QUICK!
OK, EVERYBODY BACK IN YOUR PLACES!
LET'S SHOOT THIS BABY!
I'M READY FOR MY CLOSE-UP, MS. VENUS DE MILLE-O!
3

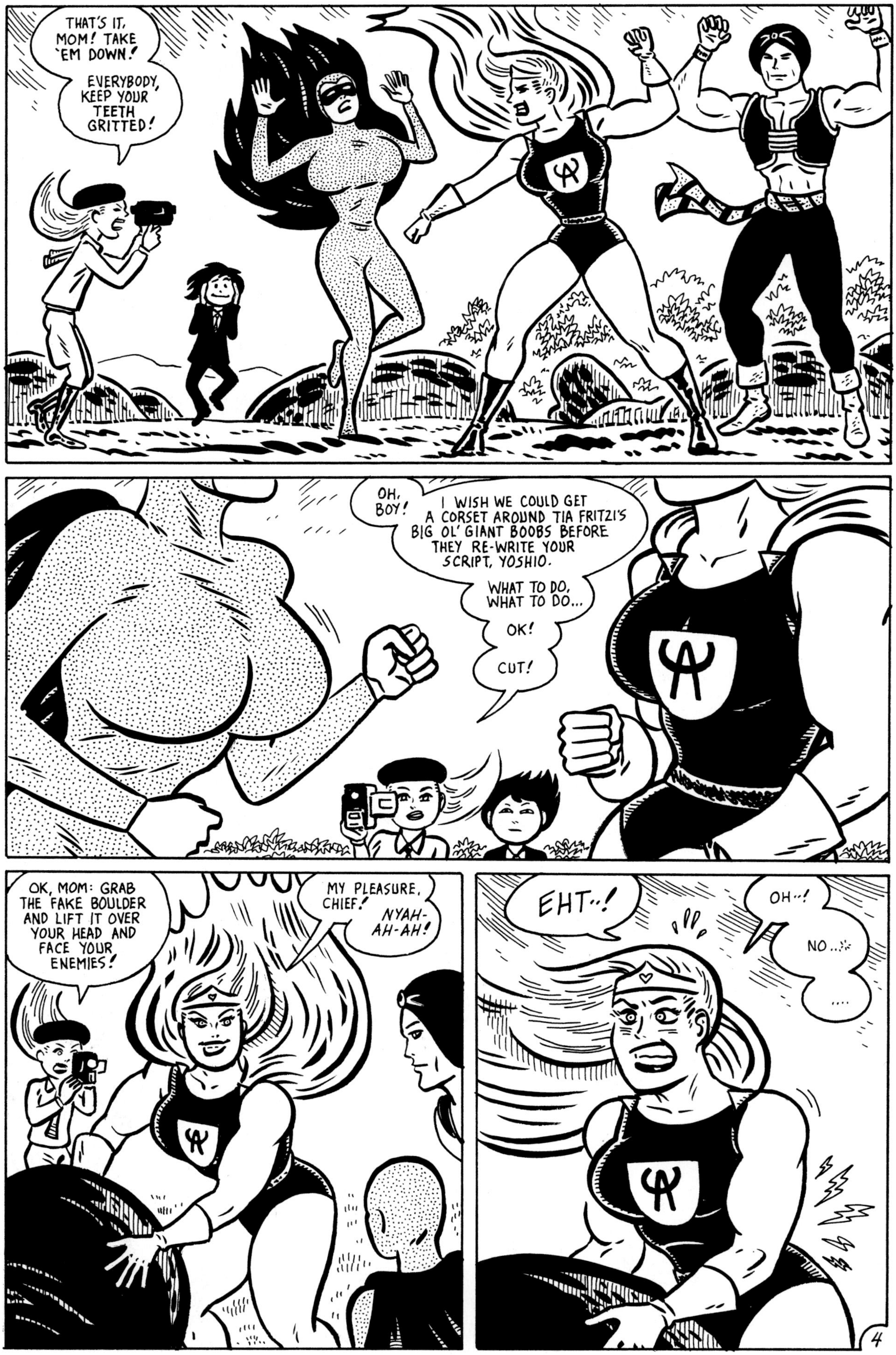

THAT'S IT, MOM! TAKE 'EM DOWN!
EVERYBODY, KEEP YOUR TEETH GRITTED!
OH, BOY!
I WISH WE COULD GET A CORSET AROUND TIA FRITZI'S BIG OL' GIANT BOOBS BEFORE THEY RE-WRITE YOUR SCRIPT, YOSHIO.
WHAT TO DO, WHAT TO DO...
OK!
CUT!
OK, MOM: GRAB THE FAKE BOULDER AND LIFT IT OVER YOUR HEAD AND FACE YOUR ENEMIES!
MY PLEASURE, CHIEF!
NYAH-AH-AH!
EHT..!
OH..!
NO...
....
4

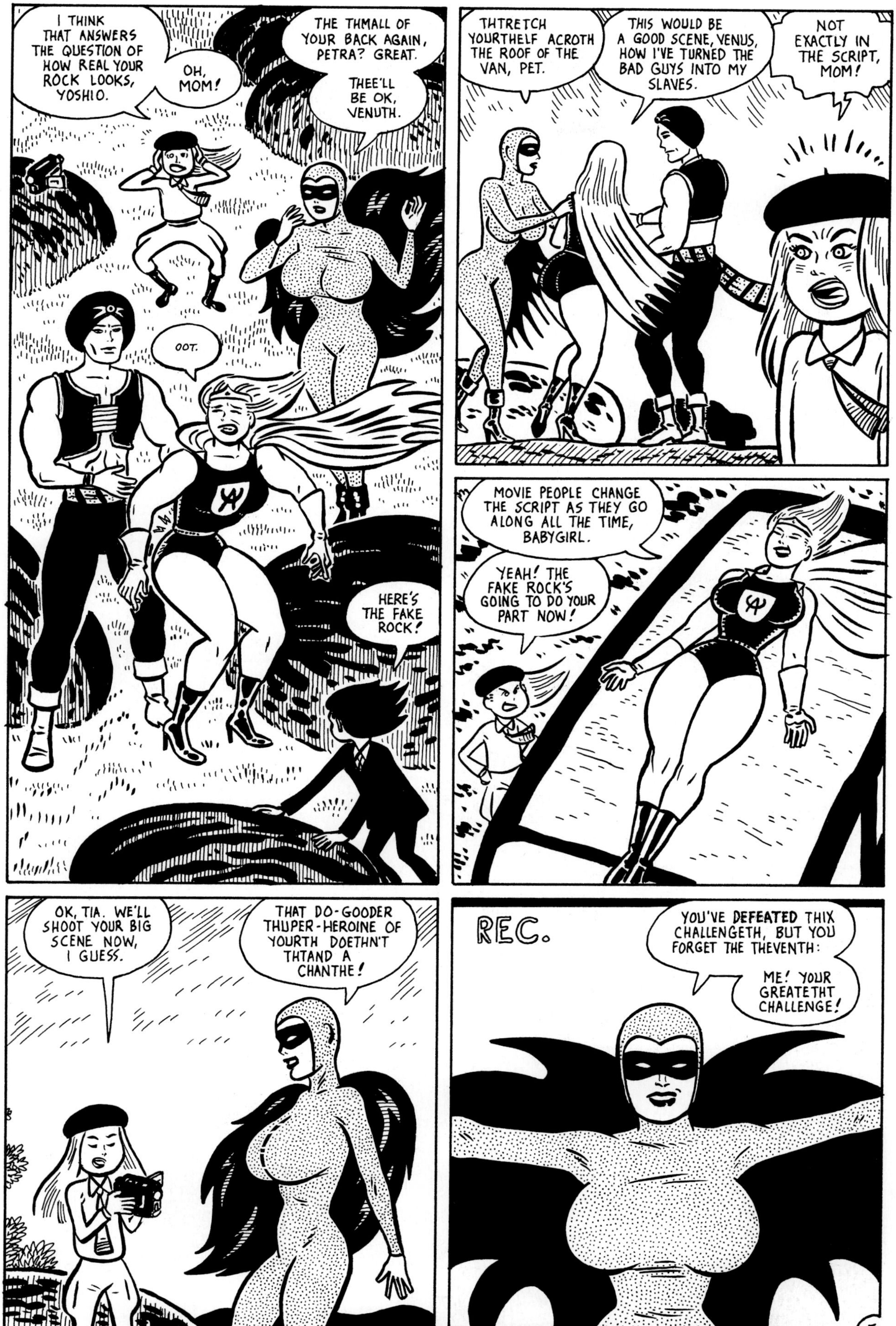
I THINK THAT ANSWERS THE QUESTION OF HOW REAL YOUR ROCK LOOKS, YOSHIO.
OH, MOM!
THE THMALL OF YOUR BACK AGAIN, PETRA? GREAT.
THEE'LL BE OK, VENUTH.
OOT.
HERE'S THE FAKE ROCK!
THTRETCH YOURTHELF ACROTH THE ROOF OF THE VAN, PET.
THIS WOULD BE A GOOD SCENE, VENUS, HOW I'VE TURNED THE BAD GUYS INTO MY SLAVES.
NOT EXACTLY IN THE SCRIPT, MOM!
MOVIE PEOPLE CHANGE THE SCRIPT AS THEY GO ALONG ALL THE TIME, BABYGIRL.
YEAH! THE FAKE ROCK'S GOING TO DO YOUR PART NOW!
OK, TIA. WE'LL SHOOT YOUR BIG SCENE NOW, I GUESS.
THAT DO-GOODER THUPER-HEROINE OF YOURTH DOETHN'T THTAND A CHANTHE!
REC.
YOU'VE DEFEATED THIX CHALLENGETH, BUT YOU FORGET THE THEVENTH:
ME! YOUR GREATETHT CHALLENGE!
5

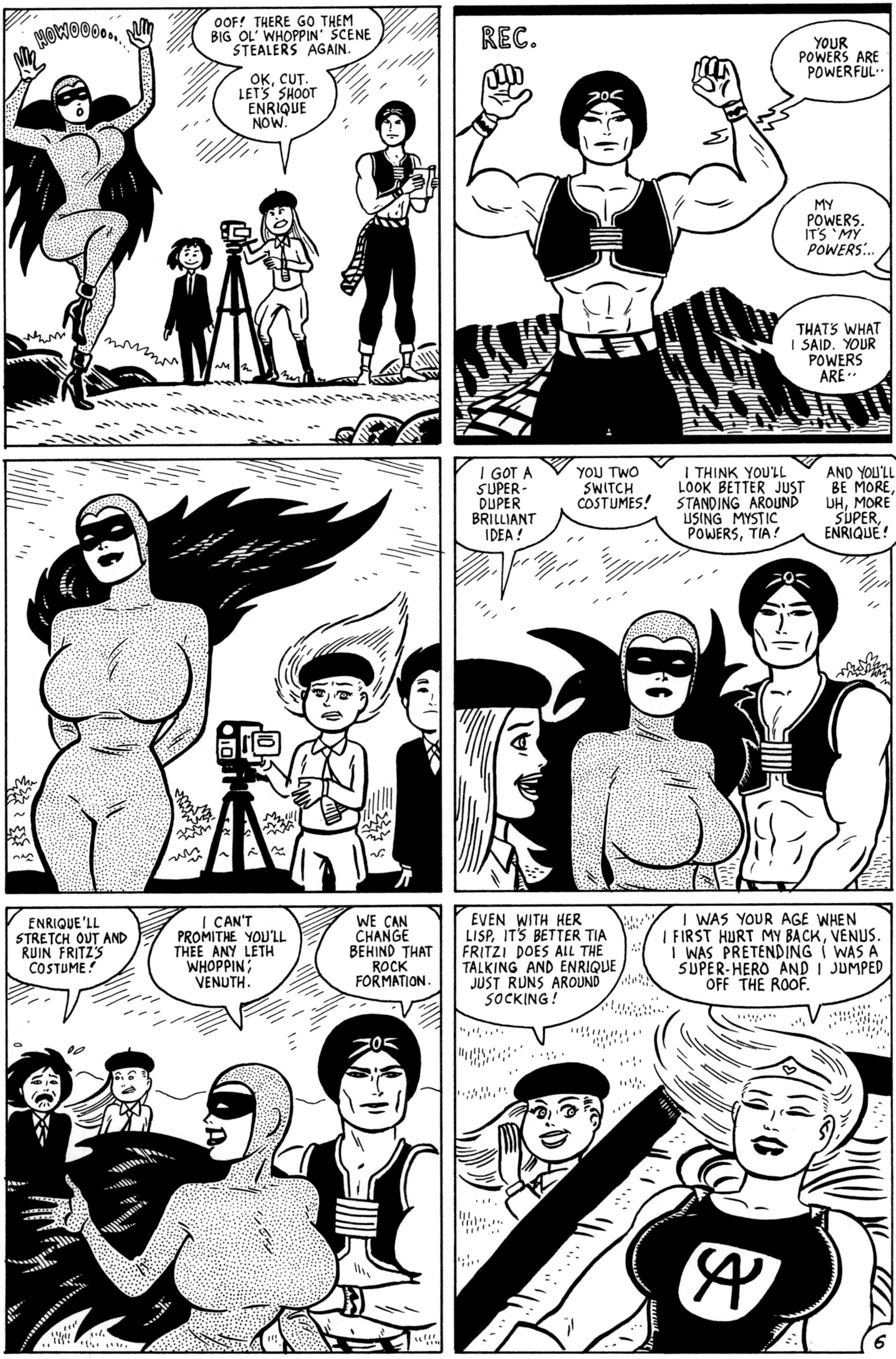
HOWOOOo...
OOF! THERE GO THEM BIG OL' WHOPPIN' SCENE STEALERS AGAIN.
OK, CUT. LET'S SHOOT ENRIQUE NOW.
REC.
YOUR POWERS ARE POWERFUL..
MY POWERS. IT'S 'MY POWERS'...
THAT'S WHAT I SAID. YOUR POWERS ARE..
I GOT A SUPER-DUPER BRILLIANT IDEA!
YOU TWO SWITCH COSTUMES!
I THINK YOU'LL LOOK BETTER JUST STANDING AROUND USING MYSTIC POWERS, TIA!
AND YOU'LL BE MORE, UH, MORE SUPER, ENRIQUE!
ENRIQUE'LL STRETCH OUT AND RUIN FRITZ'S COSTUME!
I CAN'T PROMITHE YOU'LL THEE ANY LETH WHOPPIN', VENUTH.
WE CAN CHANGE BEHIND THAT ROCK FORMATION.
EVEN WITH HER LISP, IT'S BETTER TIA FRITZI DOES ALL THE TALKING AND ENRIQUE JUST RUNS AROUND SOCKING!
I WAS YOUR AGE WHEN I FIRST HURT MY BACK, VENUS. I WAS PRETENDING I WAS A SUPER-HERO AND I JUMPED OFF THE ROOF.
6

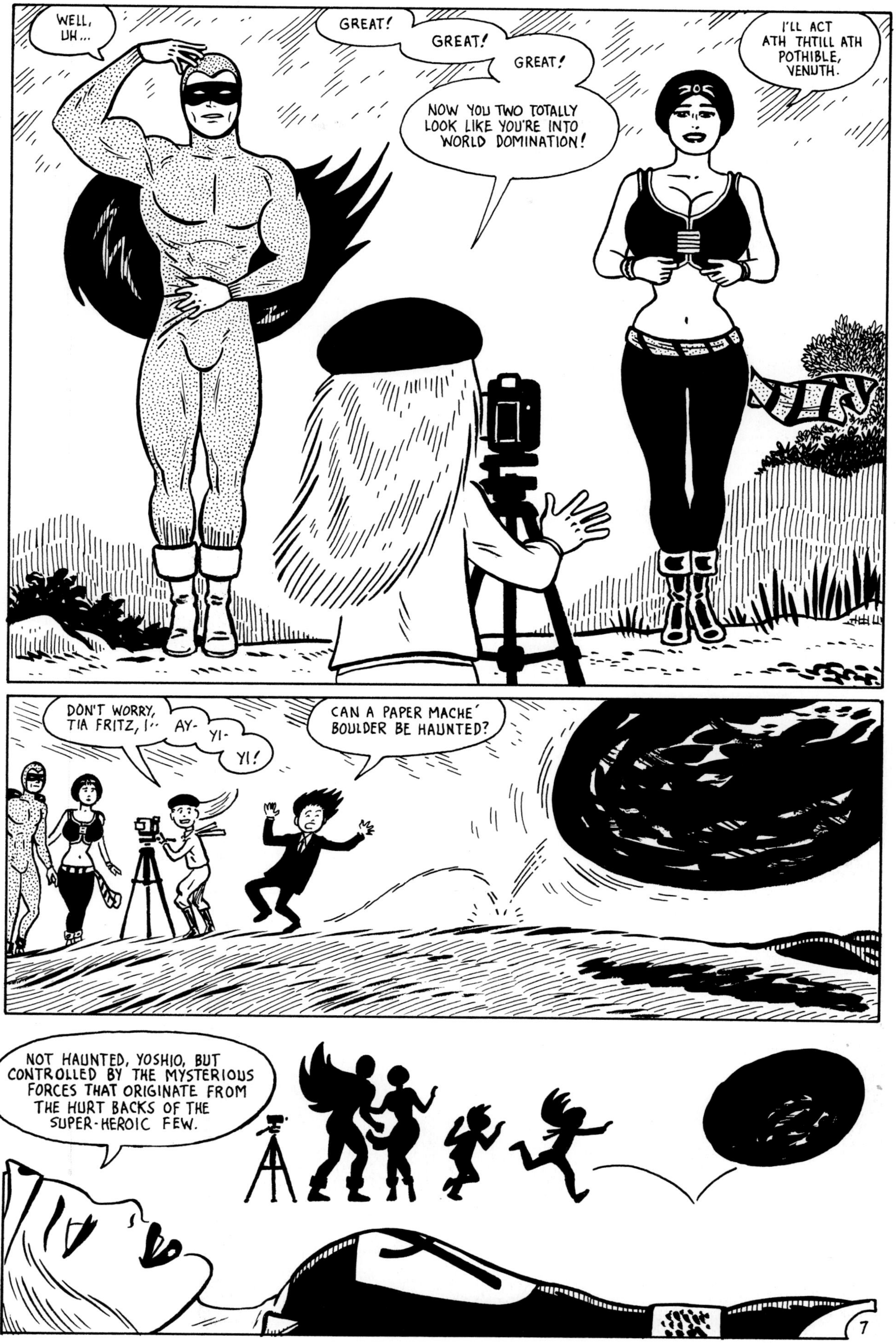

WELL, UH...
GREAT!
GREAT!
GREAT!
NOW YOU TWO TOTALLY LOOK LIKE YOU'RE INTO WORLD DOMINATION!
I'LL ACT ATH THTILL ATH POTHIBLE, VENUTH.
DON'T WORRY, TIA FRITZ, I··
AY-YI-YI!
CAN A PAPER MACHE´ BOULDER BE HAUNTED?
NOT HAUNTED, YOSHIO, BUT CONTROLLED BY THE MYSTERIOUS FORCES THAT ORIGINATE FROM THE HURT BACKS OF THE SUPER-HEROIC FEW.
7

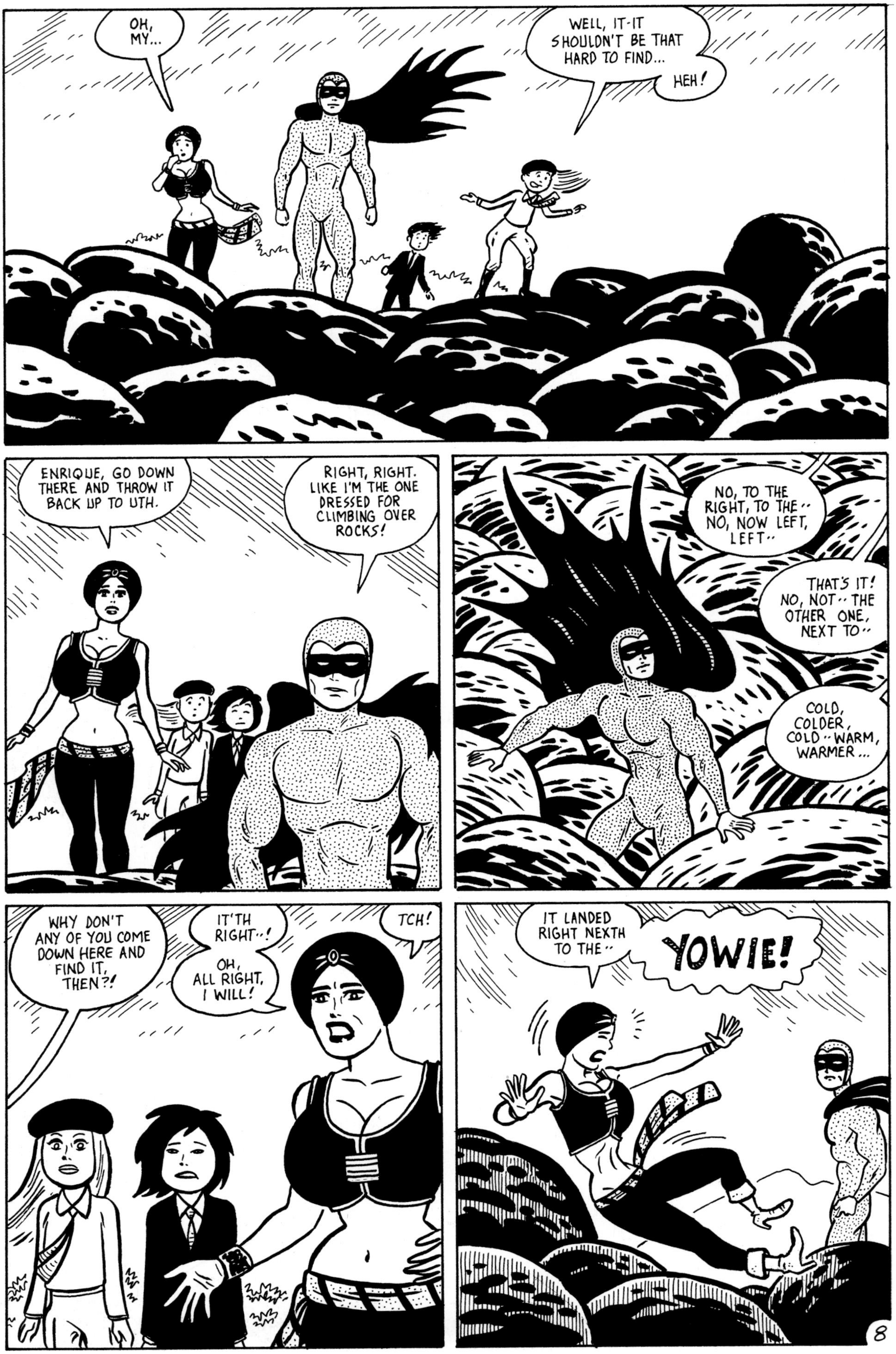
OH, MY...
WELL, IT-IT SHOULDN'T BE THAT HARD TO FIND...
HEH!
ENRIQUE, GO DOWN THERE AND THROW IT BACK UP TO UTH.
RIGHT, RIGHT. LIKE I'M THE ONE DRESSED FOR CLIMBING OVER ROCKS!
NO, TO THE RIGHT, TO THE·· NO, NOW LEFT, LEFT··
THAT'S IT! NO, NOT·· THE OTHER ONE, NEXT TO··
COLD, COLDER, COLD·· WARM, WARMER...
WHY DON'T ANY OF YOU COME DOWN HERE AND FIND IT, THEN?!
IT'TH RIGHT··!
OH, ALL RIGHT, I WILL!
TCH!
IT LANDED RIGHT NEXTH TO THE··
YOWIE!
8

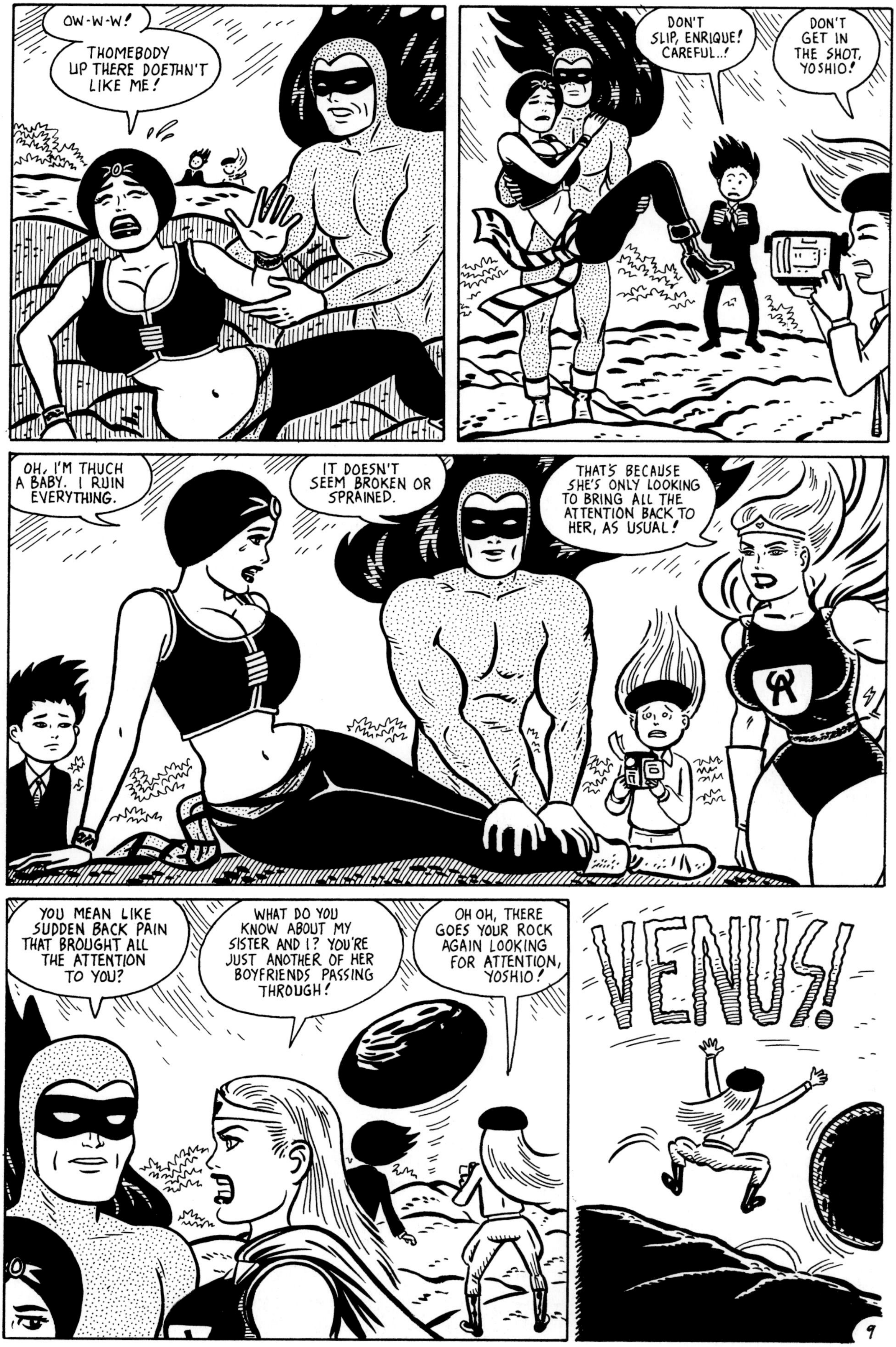
OW-W-W!
THOMEBODY UP THERE DOETHN'T LIKE ME!
DON'T SLIP, ENRIQUE! CAREFUL..!
DON'T GET IN THE SHOT, YOSHIO!
OH, I'M THUCH A BABY. I RUIN EVERYTHING.
IT DOESN'T SEEM BROKEN OR SPRAINED.
THAT'S BECAUSE SHE'S ONLY LOOKING TO BRING ALL THE ATTENTION BACK TO HER, AS USUAL!
YOU MEAN LIKE SUDDEN BACK PAIN THAT BROUGHT ALL THE ATTENTION TO YOU?
WHAT DO YOU KNOW ABOUT MY SISTER AND I? YOU'RE JUST ANOTHER OF HER BOYFRIENDS PASSING THROUGH!
OH OH, THERE GOES YOUR ROCK AGAIN LOOKING FOR ATTENTION, YOSHIO!
VENUS!
9

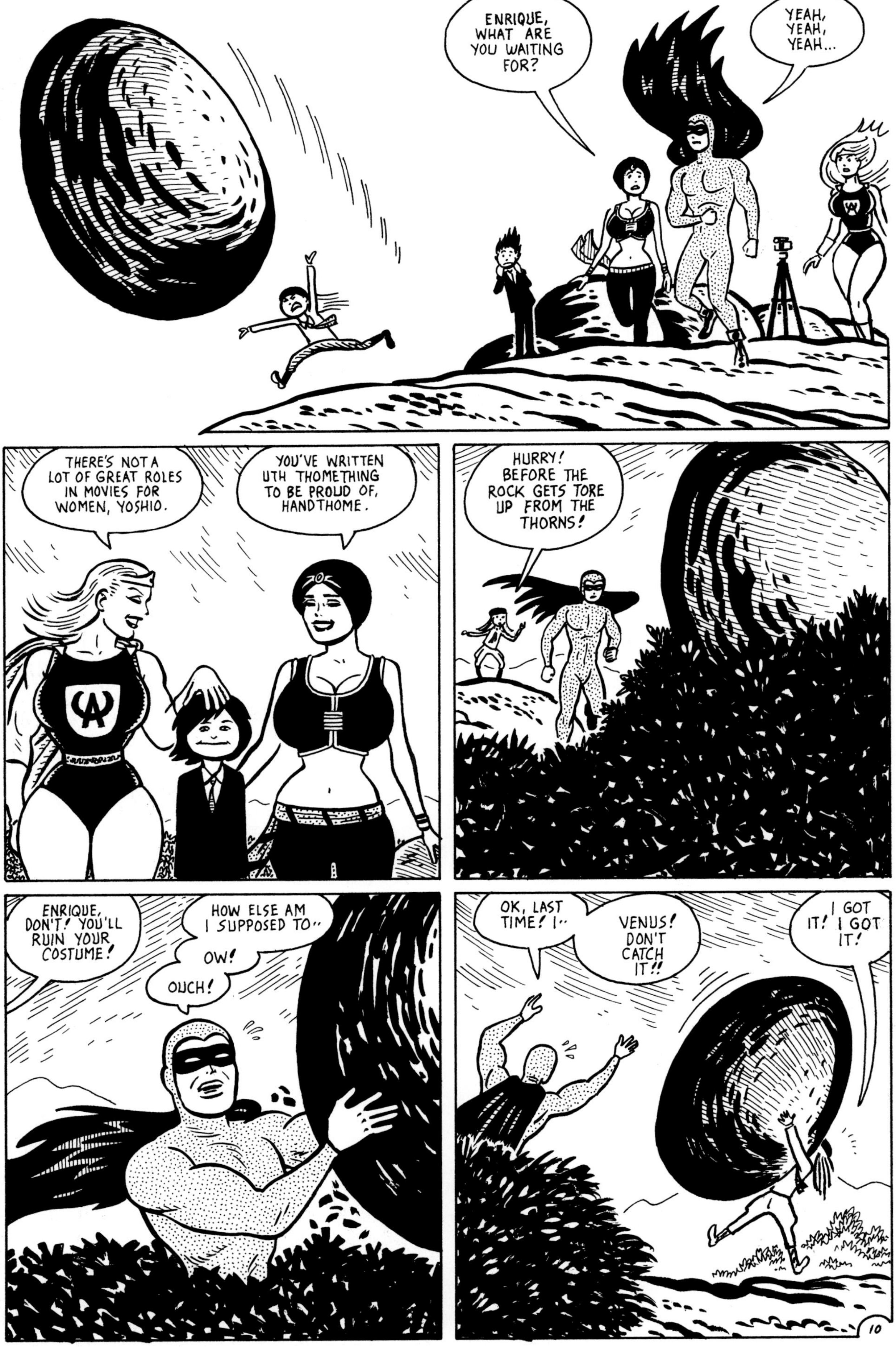
ENRIQUE, WHAT ARE YOU WAITING FOR?
YEAH, YEAH, YEAH...
THERE'S NOT A LOT OF GREAT ROLES IN MOVIES FOR WOMEN, YOSHIO.
YOU'VE WRITTEN UTH THOMETHING TO BE PROUD OF, HANDTHOME.
HURRY! BEFORE THE ROCK GETS TORE UP FROM THE THORNS!
ENRIQUE, DON'T! YOU'LL RUIN YOUR COSTUME!
HOW ELSE AM I SUPPOSED TO..
OW!
OUCH!
OK, LAST TIME! I..
VENUS! DON'T CATCH IT!!
I GOT IT! I GOT IT!
10

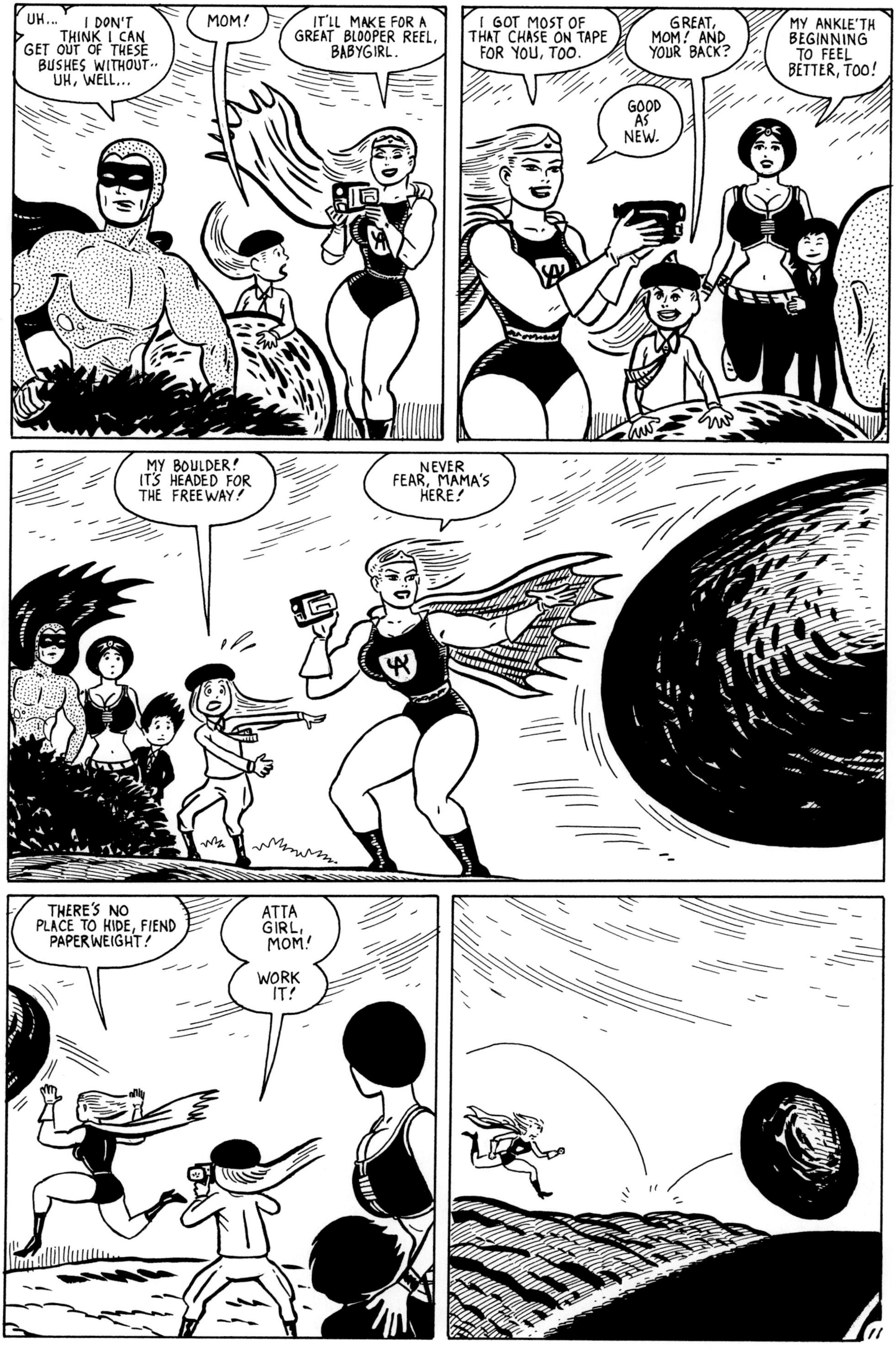
UH... I DON'T THINK I CAN GET OUT OF THESE BUSHES WITHOUT.. UH, WELL...
MOM!
IT'LL MAKE FOR A GREAT BLOOPER REEL, BABYGIRL.
I GOT MOST OF THAT CHASE ON TAPE FOR YOU, TOO.
GREAT, MOM! AND YOUR BACK?
GOOD AS NEW.
MY ANKLE'TH BEGINNING TO FEEL BETTER, TOO!
MY BOULDER! IT'S HEADED FOR THE FREEWAY!
NEVER FEAR, MAMA'S HERE!
THERE'S NO PLACE TO HIDE, FIEND PAPERWEIGHT!
ATTA GIRL, MOM!
WORK IT!

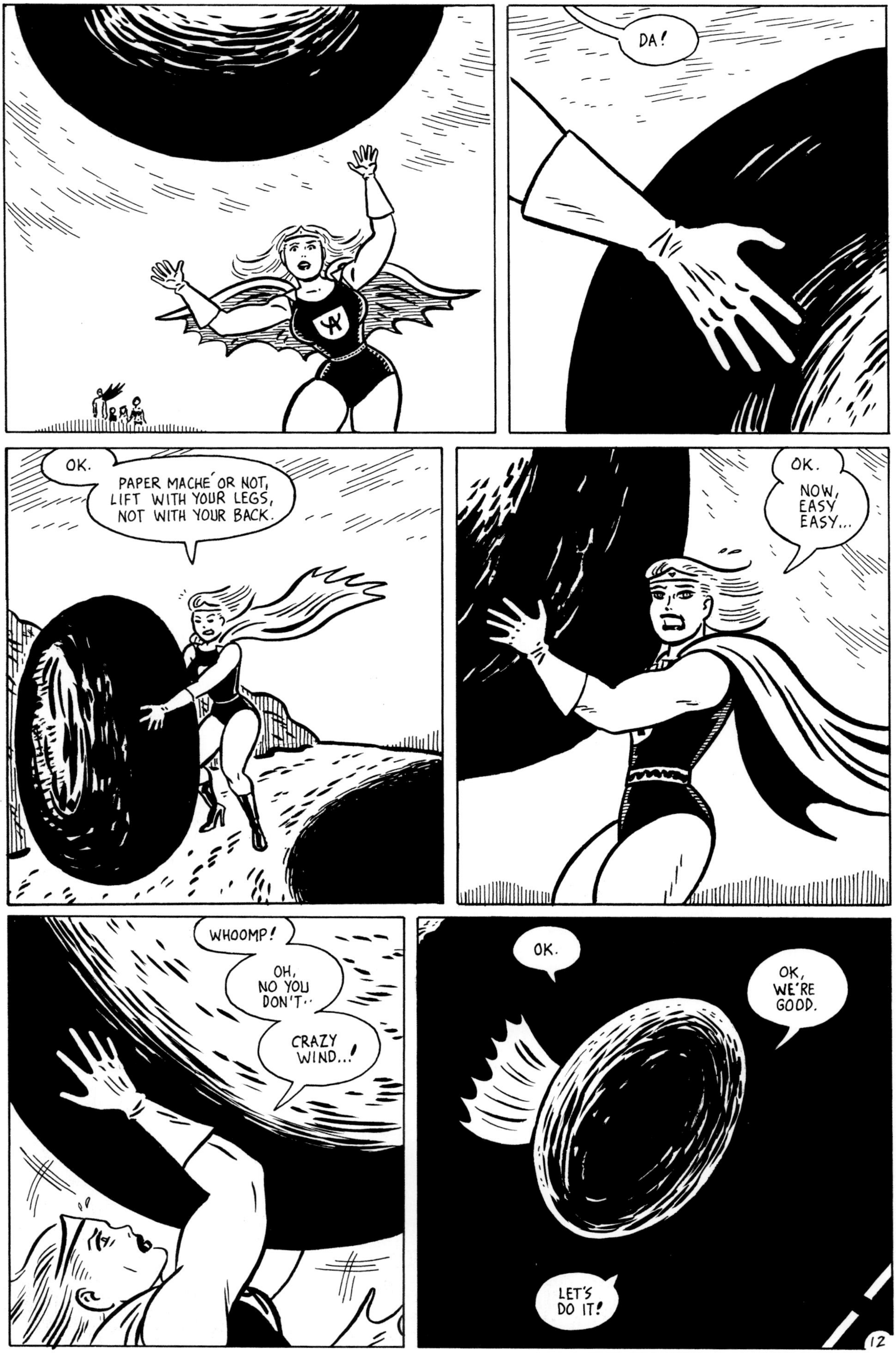
DA!
OK.
PAPER MACHÉ OR NOT, LIFT WITH YOUR LEGS, NOT WITH YOUR BACK.
OK.
NOW, EASY EASY...
WHOOMP!
OH, NO YOU DON'T..
CRAZY WIND...!
OK.
OK, WE'RE GOOD.
LET'S DO IT!
12

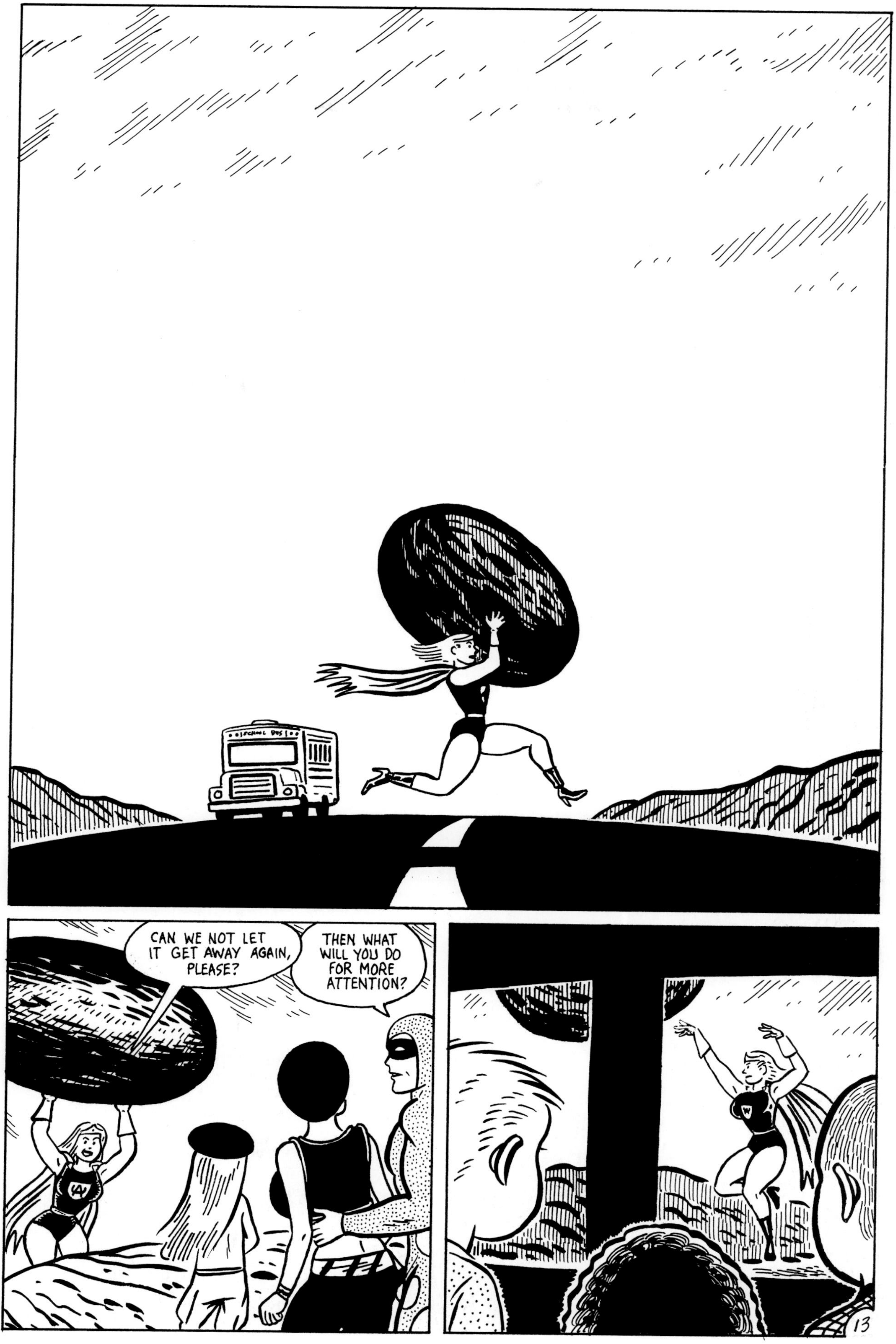
CAN WE NOT LET IT GET AWAY AGAIN, PLEASE?
THEN WHAT WILL YOU DO FOR MORE ATTENTION?
13

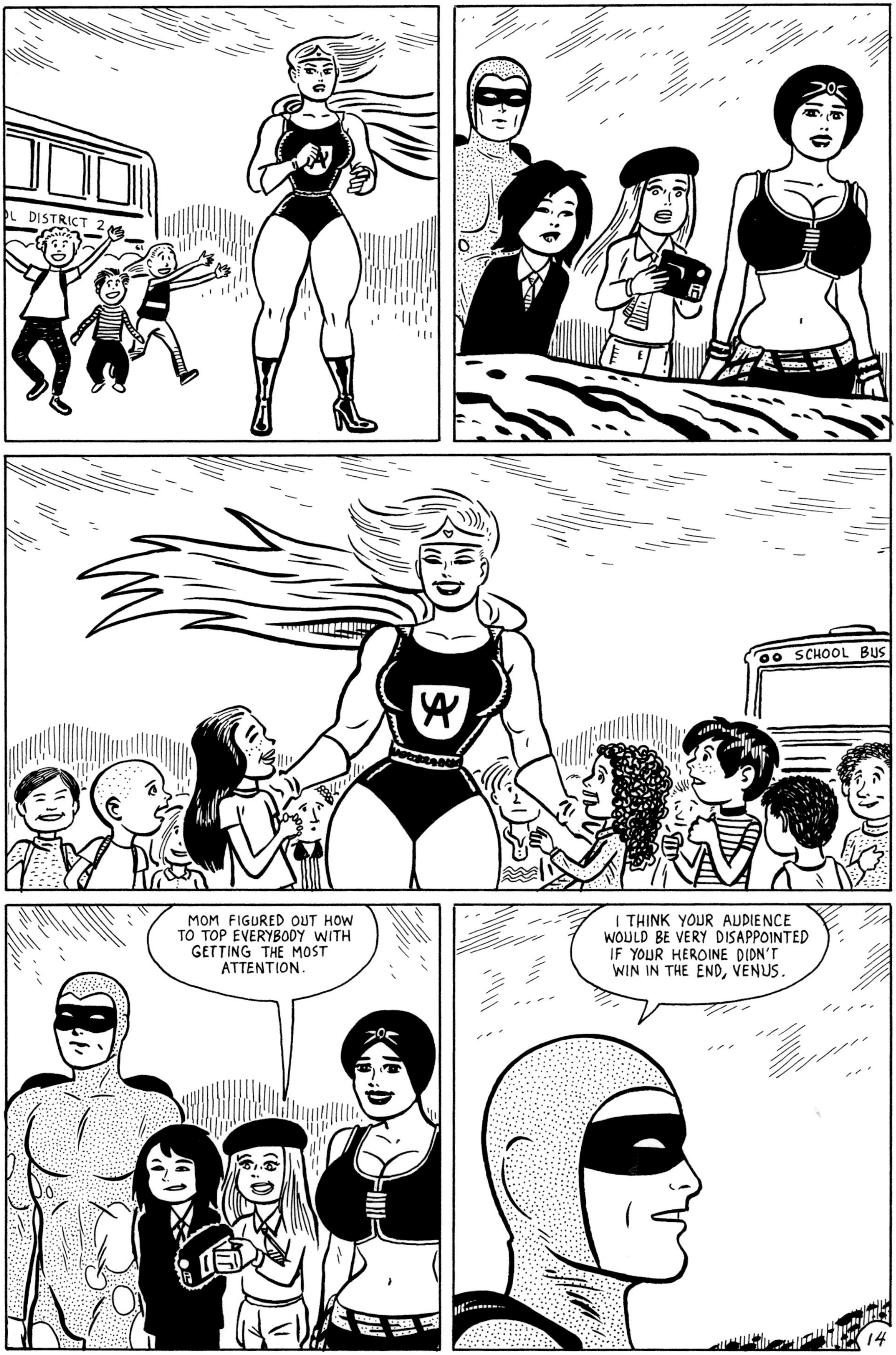

OL DISTRICT 2
SCHOOL BUS
MOM FIGURED OUT HOW TO TOP EVERYBODY WITH GETTING THE MOST ATTENTION.
I THINK YOUR AUDIENCE WOULD BE VERY DISAPPOINTED IF YOUR HEROINE DIDN'T WIN IN THE END, VENUS.
14

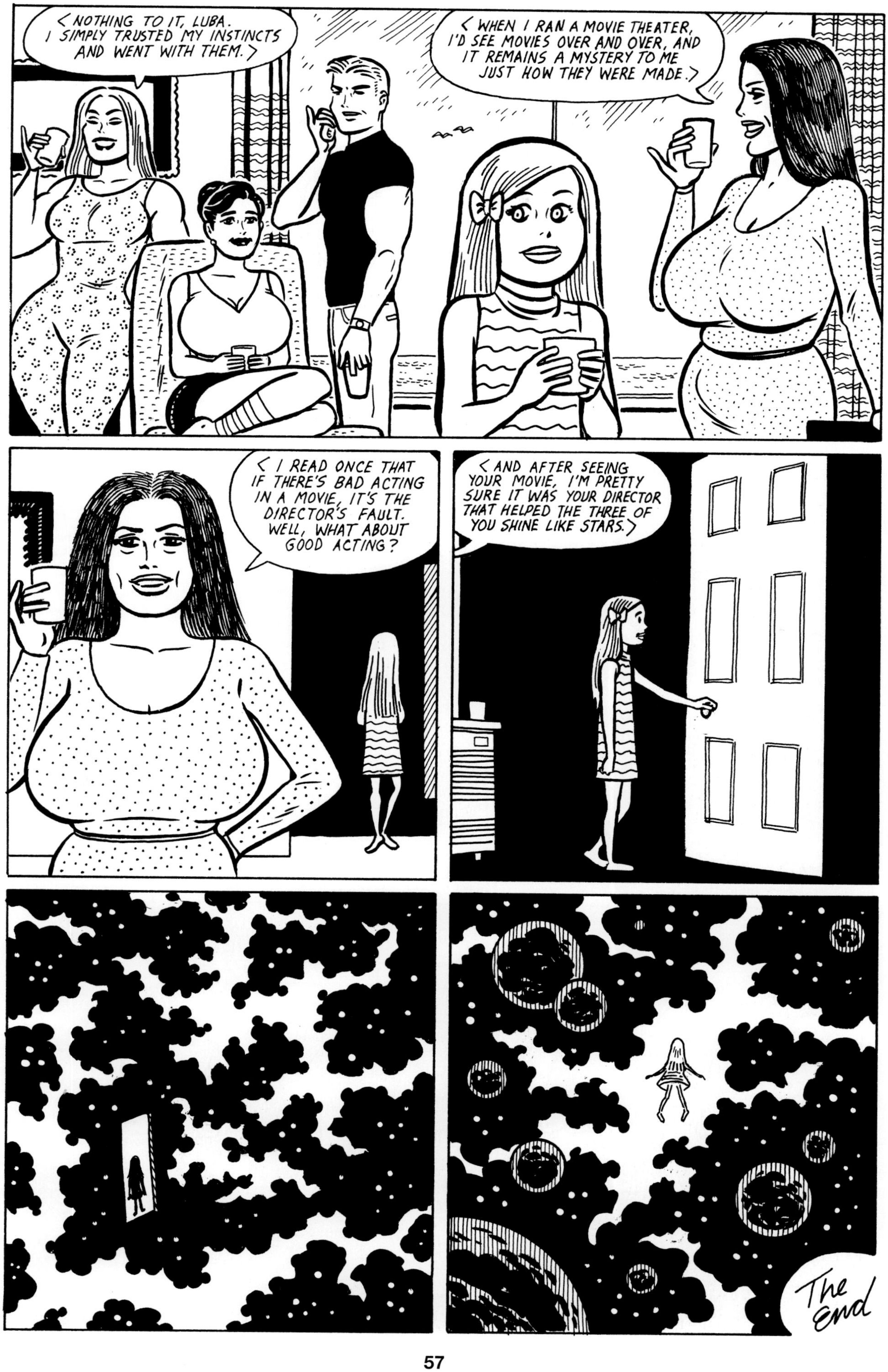

< NOTHING TO IT, LUBA. I SIMPLY TRUSTED MY INSTINCTS AND WENT WITH THEM. >
< WHEN I RAN A MOVIE THEATER, I'D SEE MOVIES OVER AND OVER, AND IT REMAINS A MYSTERY TO ME JUST HOW THEY WERE MADE. >
< I READ ONCE THAT IF THERE'S BAD ACTING IN A MOVIE, IT'S THE DIRECTOR'S FAULT. WELL, WHAT ABOUT GOOD ACTING?
< AND AFTER SEEING YOUR MOVIE, I'M PRETTY SURE IT WAS YOUR DIRECTOR THAT HELPED THE THREE OF YOU SHINE LIKE STARS. >
The End

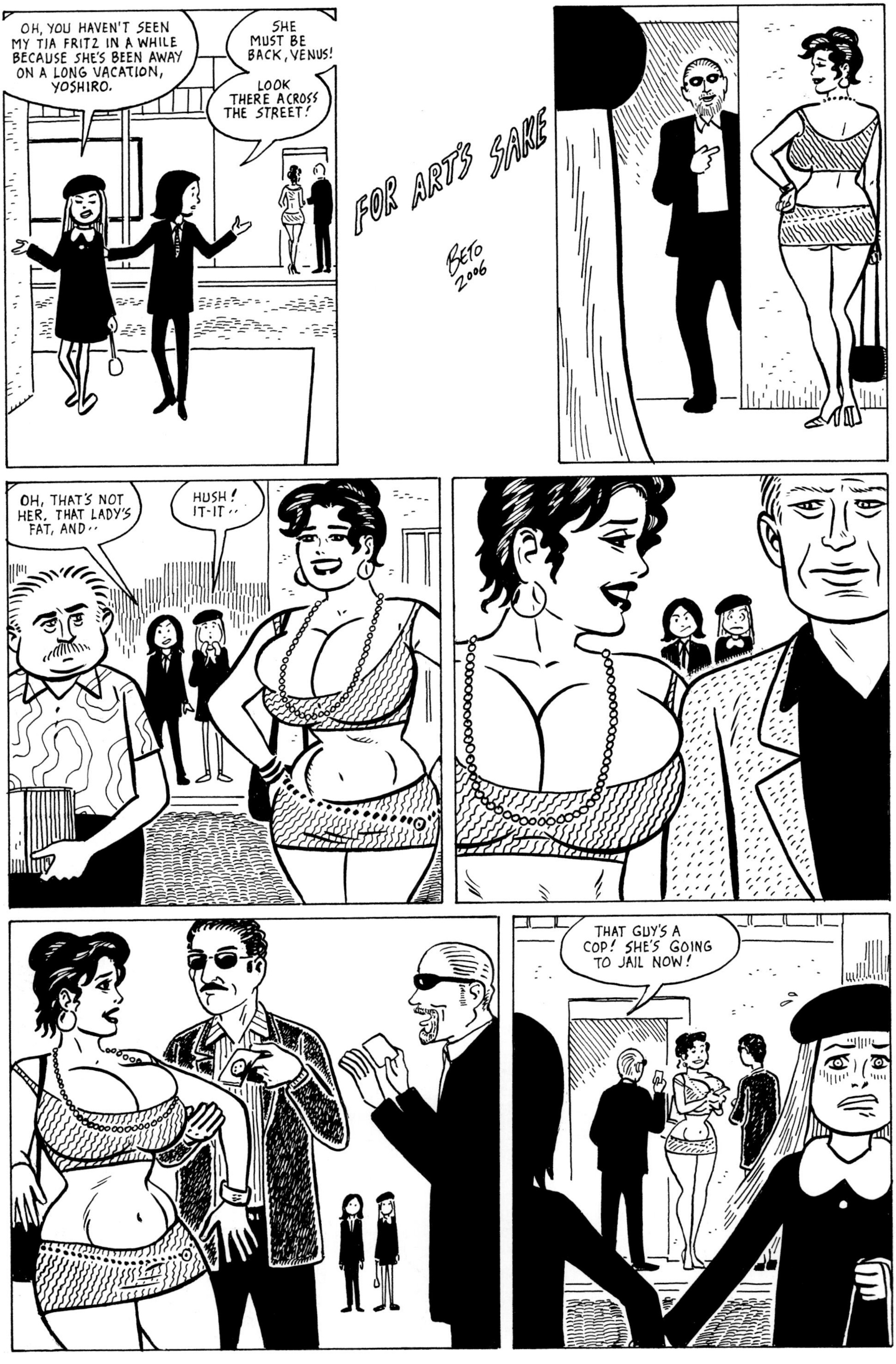

OH, YOU HAVEN'T SEEN MY TIA FRITZ IN A WHILE BECAUSE SHE'S BEEN AWAY ON A LONG VACATION, YOSHIRO.
SHE MUST BE BACK, VENUS!
LOOK THERE ACROSS THE STREET!
FOR ART'S SAKE
BETO 2006
OH, THAT'S NOT HER, THAT LADY'S FAT, AND..
HUSH! IT-IT..
THAT GUY'S A COP! SHE'S GOING TO JAIL NOW!

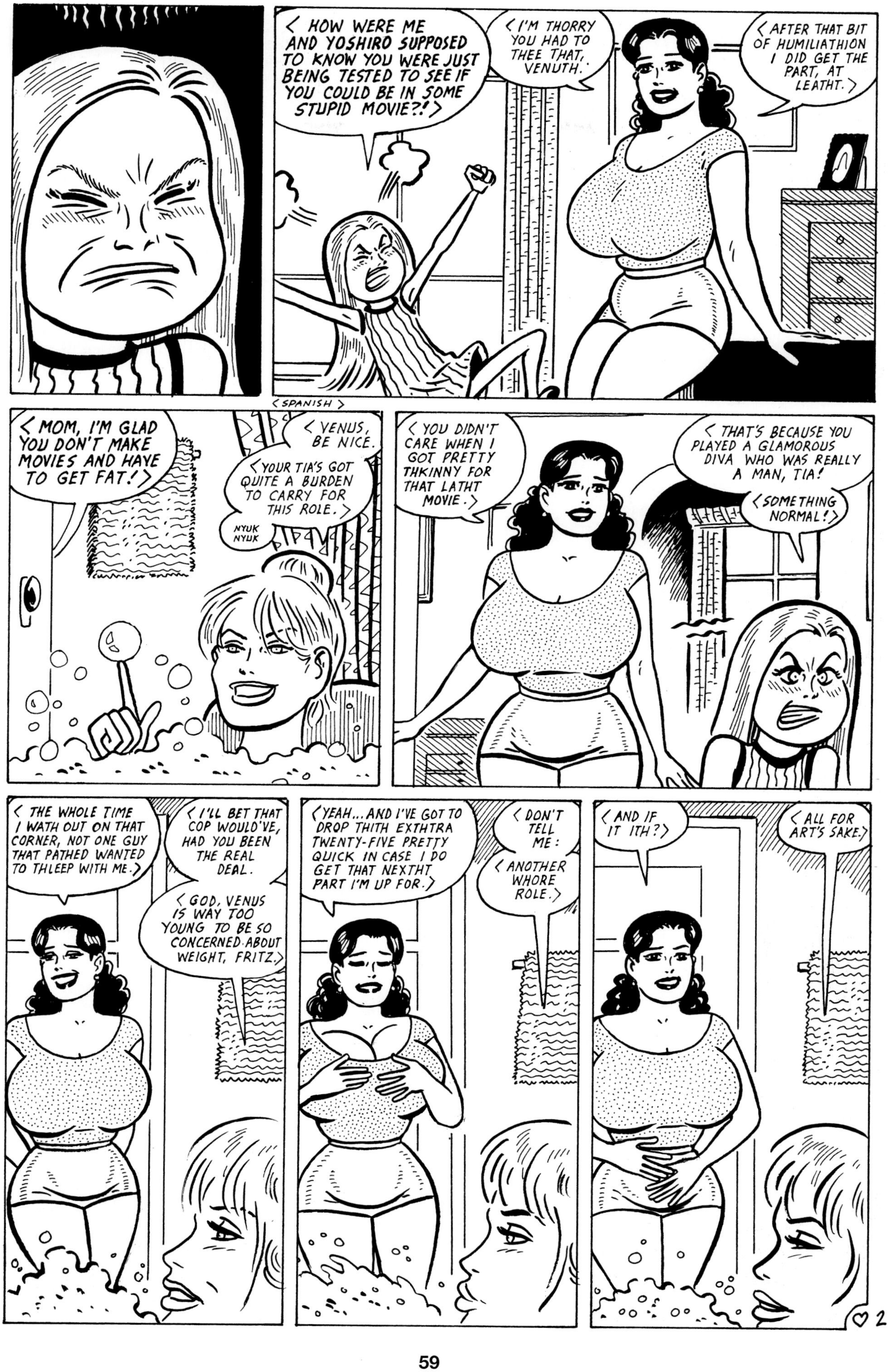

< HOW WERE ME AND YOSHIRO SUPPOSED TO KNOW YOU WERE JUST BEING TESTED TO SEE IF YOU COULD BE IN SOME STUPID MOVIE?!>
< I'M THORRY YOU HAD TO THEE THAT, VENUTH.
< AFTER THAT BIT OF HUMILIATHION I DID GET THE PART, AT LEATHT.>
< SPANISH >
< MOM, I'M GLAD YOU DON'T MAKE MOVIES AND HAVE TO GET FAT!>
< VENUS, BE NICE.
< YOUR TIA'S GOT QUITE A BURDEN TO CARRY FOR THIS ROLE.>
NYUK NYUK
< YOU DIDN'T CARE WHEN I GOT PRETTY THKINNY FOR THAT LATHT MOVIE.>
< THAT'S BECAUSE YOU PLAYED A GLAMOROUS DIVA WHO WAS REALLY A MAN, TIA!
< SOMETHING NORMAL!>
< THE WHOLE TIME I WATH OUT ON THAT CORNER, NOT ONE GUY THAT PATHED WANTED TO THLEEP WITH ME.>
< I'LL BET THAT COP WOULD'VE, HAD YOU BEEN THE REAL DEAL.
< GOD, VENUS IS WAY TOO YOUNG TO BE SO CONCERNED ABOUT WEIGHT, FRITZ.>
< YEAH... AND I'VE GOT TO DROP THITH EXTHTRA TWENTY-FIVE PRETTY QUICK IN CASE I DO GET THAT NEXTHT PART I'M UP FOR.>
< DON'T TELL ME:
< ANOTHER WHORE ROLE.>
< AND IF IT ITH?>
< ALL FOR ART'S SAKE.>
♡ 2

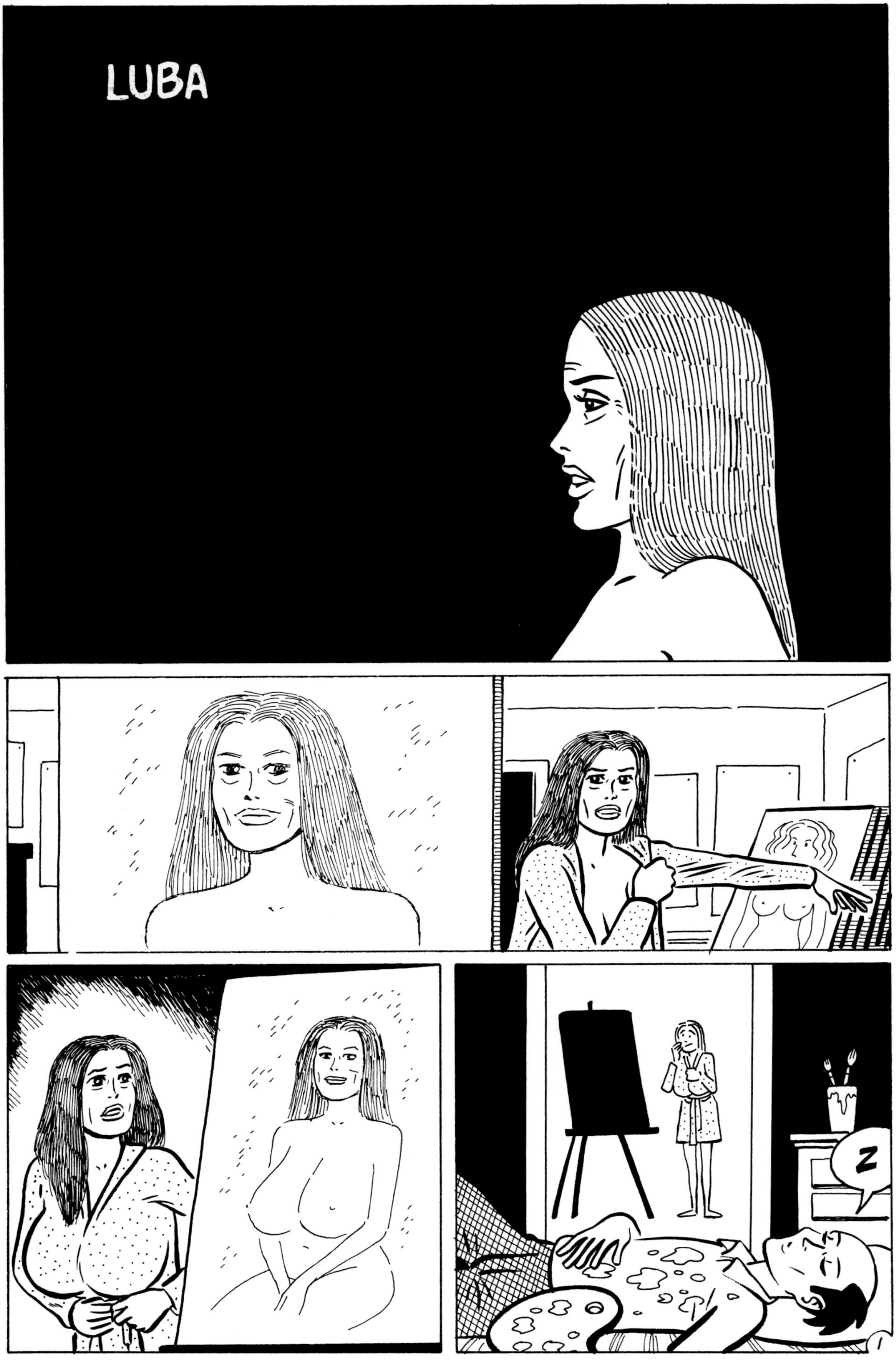
LUBA
Z

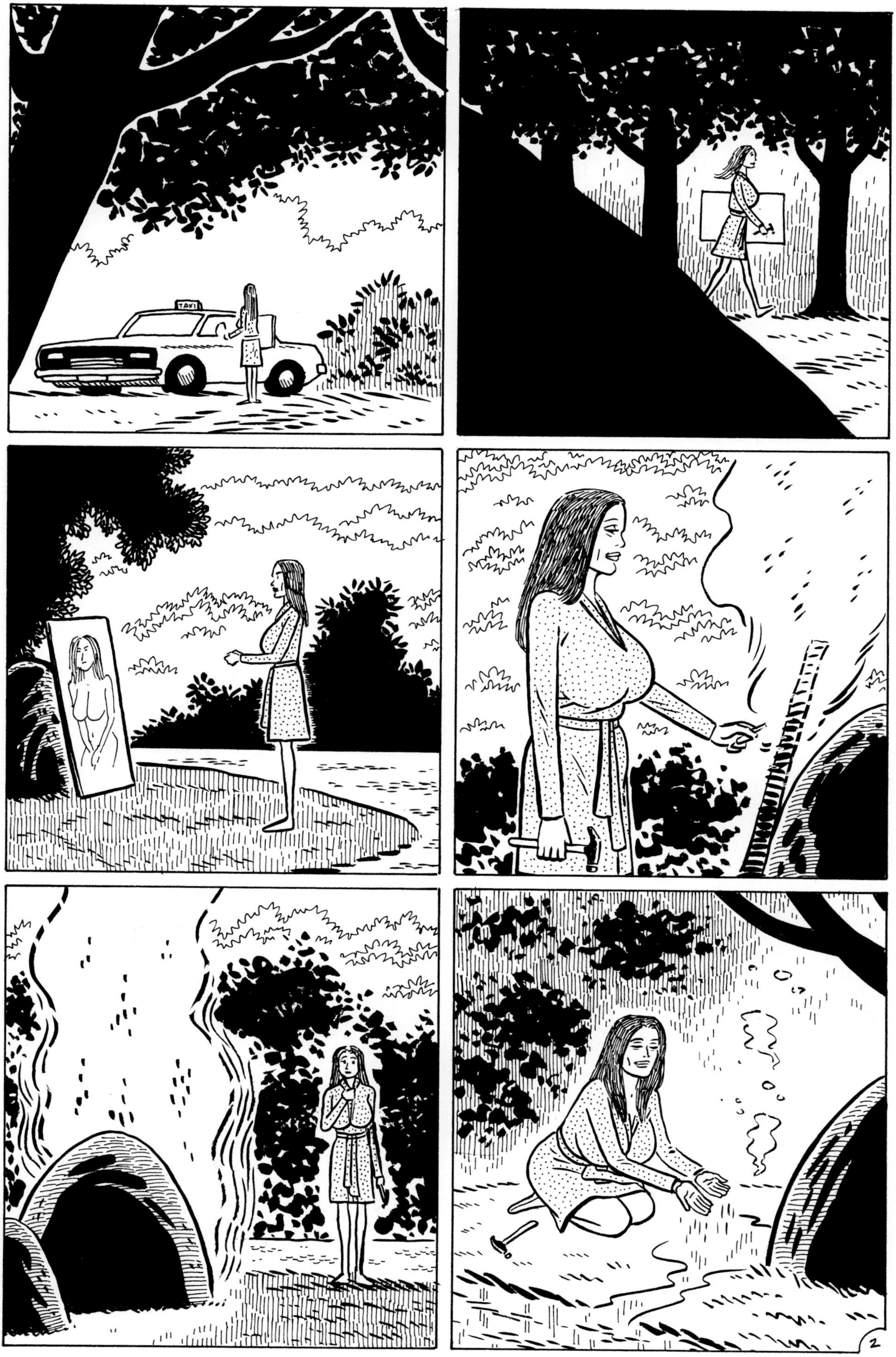
TAXI

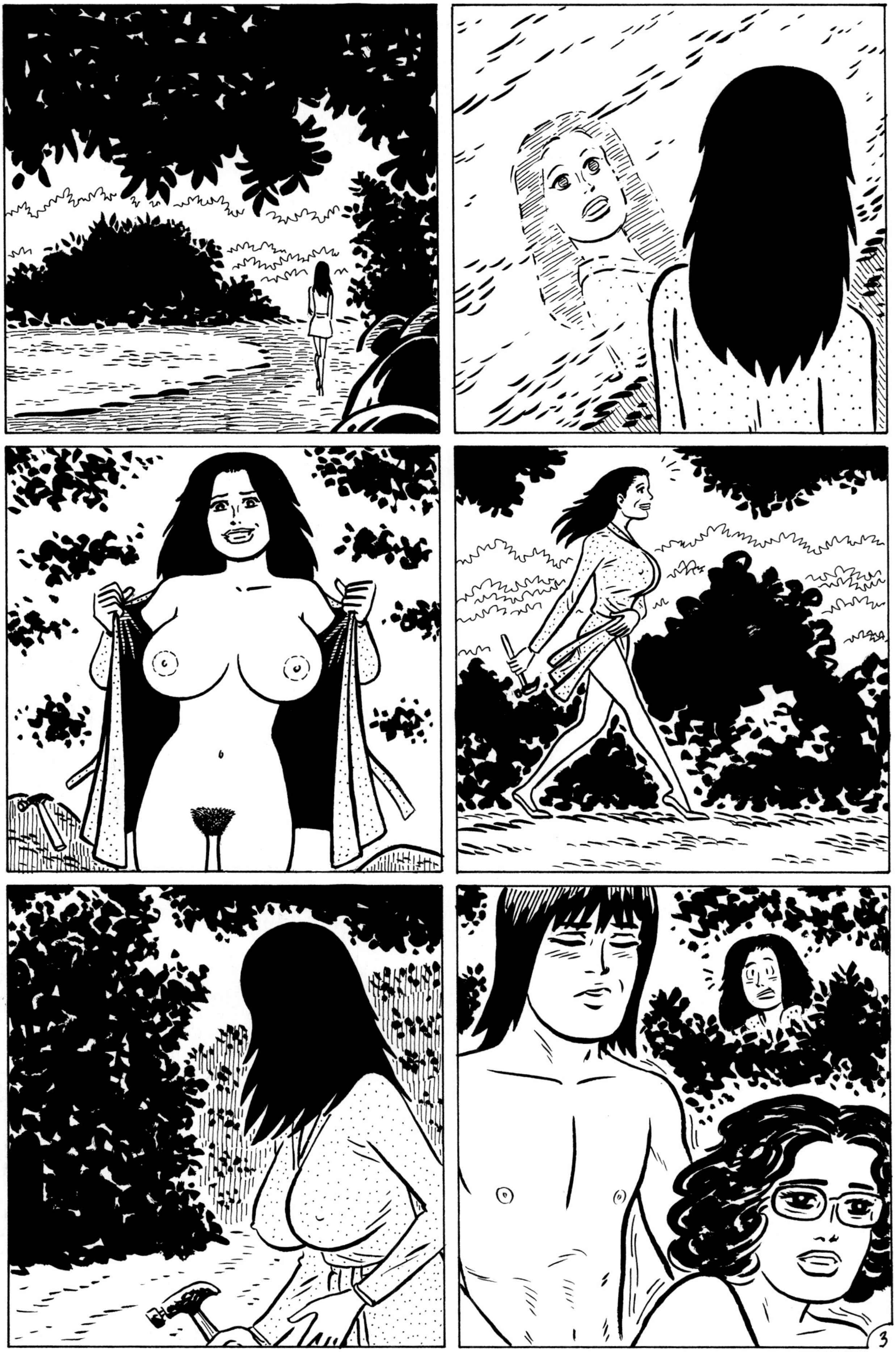
3

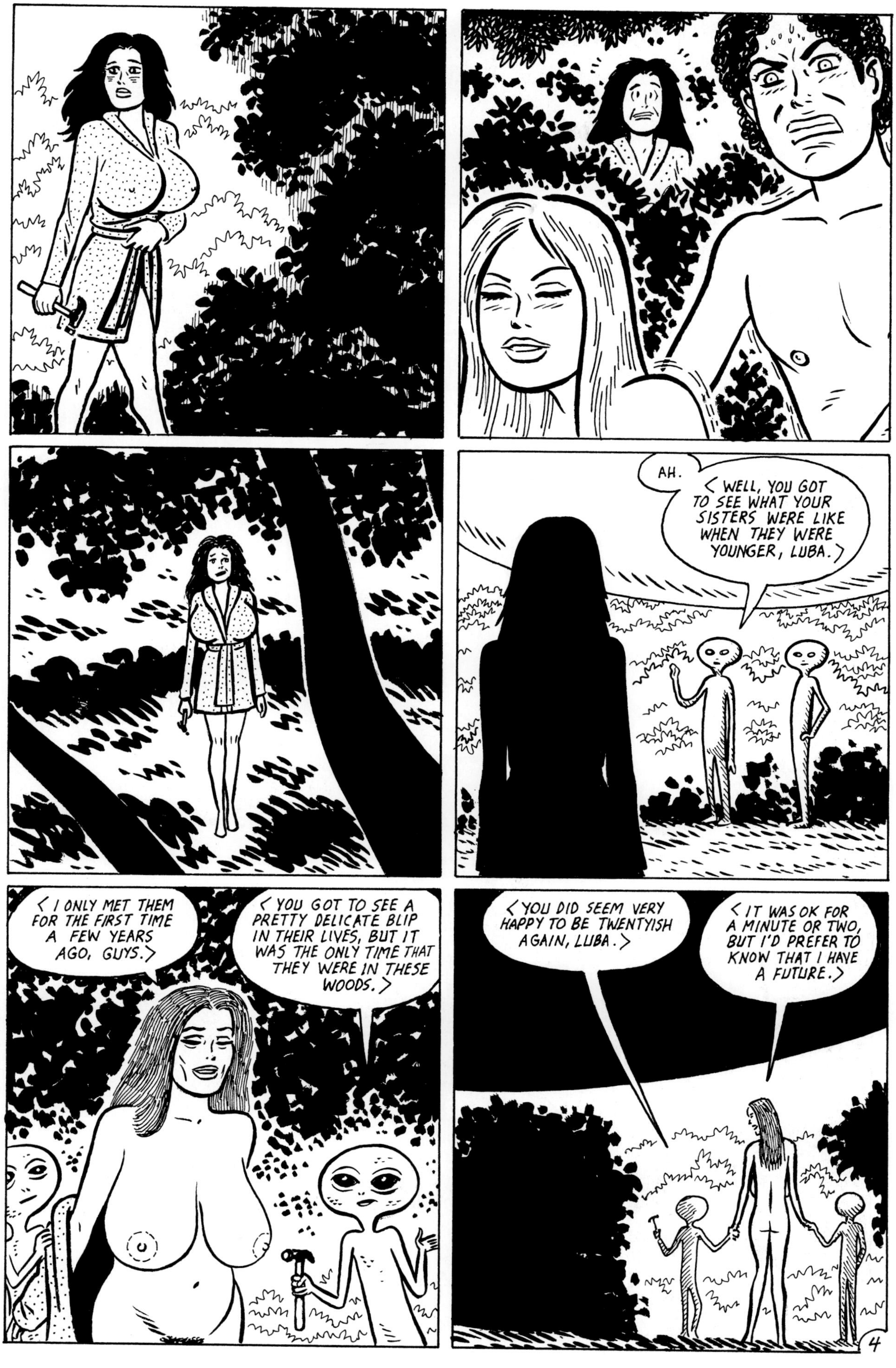

AH.
< WELL, YOU GOT TO SEE WHAT YOUR SISTERS WERE LIKE WHEN THEY WERE YOUNGER, LUBA. >
< I ONLY MET THEM FOR THE FIRST TIME A FEW YEARS AGO, GUYS. >
< YOU GOT TO SEE A PRETTY DELICATE BLIP IN THEIR LIVES, BUT IT WAS THE ONLY TIME THAT THEY WERE IN THESE WOODS. >
< YOU DID SEEM VERY HAPPY TO BE TWENTYISH AGAIN, LUBA. >
< IT WAS OK FOR A MINUTE OR TWO, BUT I'D PREFER TO KNOW THAT I HAVE A FUTURE. >
4

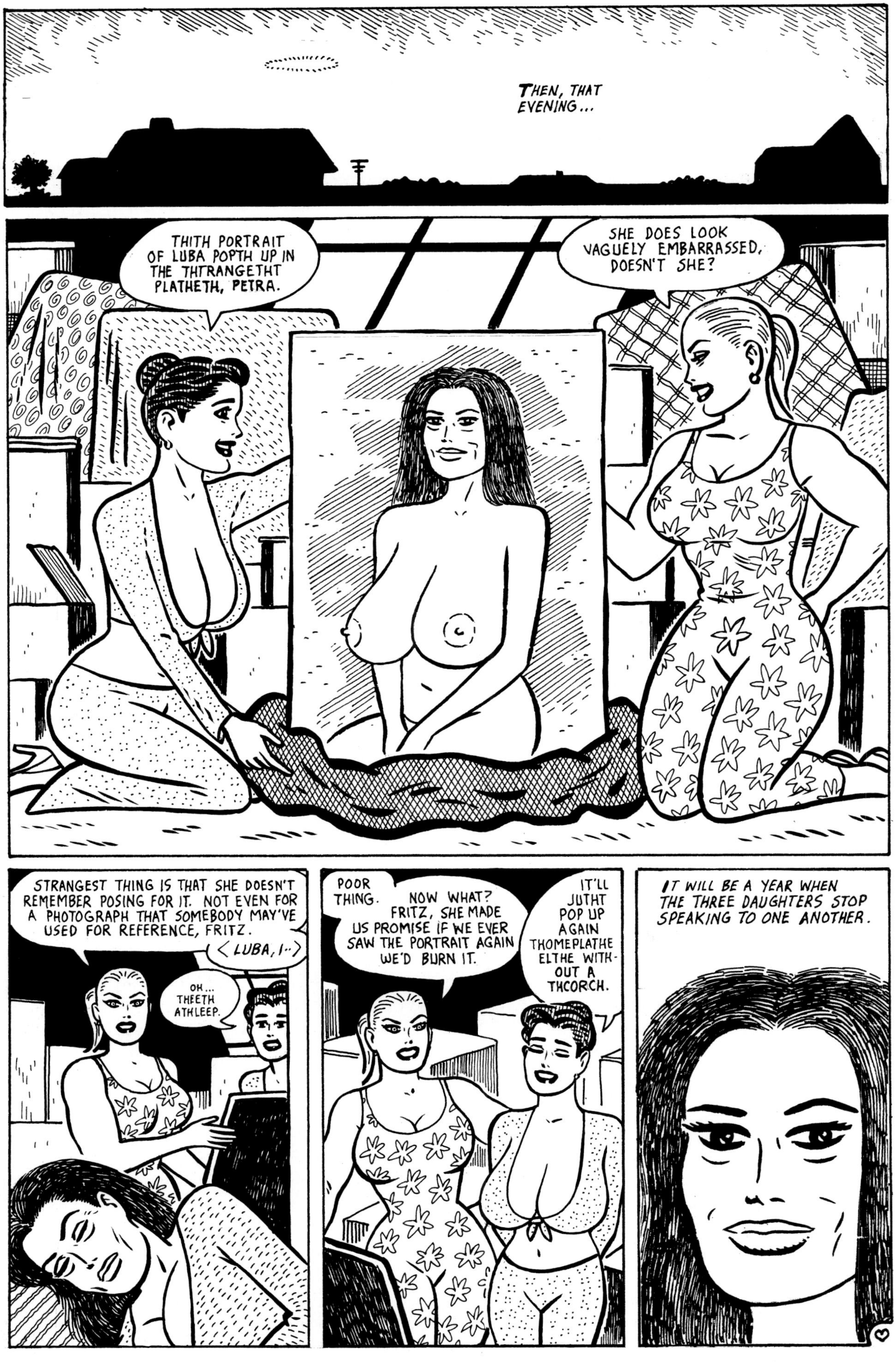
THEN, THAT EVENING...
THITH PORTRAIT OF LUBA POPTH UP IN THE THTRANGETHT PLATHETH, PETRA.
SHE DOES LOOK VAGUELY EMBARRASSED, DOESN'T SHE?
STRANGEST THING IS THAT SHE DOESN'T REMEMBER POSING FOR IT. NOT EVEN FOR A PHOTOGRAPH THAT SOMEBODY MAY'VE USED FOR REFERENCE, FRITZ.
< LUBA, I.. >
OH... THEETH ATHLEEP.
POOR THING.
NOW WHAT? FRITZ, SHE MADE US PROMISE IF WE EVER SAW THE PORTRAIT AGAIN WE'D BURN IT.
IT'LL JUTHT POP UP AGAIN THOMEPLATHE ELTHE WITH-OUT A THCORCH.
IT WILL BE A YEAR WHEN THE THREE DAUGHTERS STOP SPEAKING TO ONE ANOTHER.
5

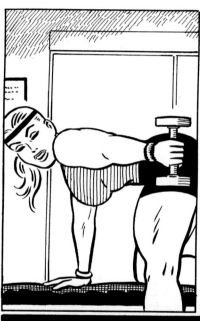

PETRA

I'M *NOT* BEING A *BRAT*, MOM! YOU'RE JUST *WAY* TOO SUPER DUPER *BUFF* SO PEOPLE THINK YOU'RE A *MAN* WITH LOVELY, SILKY HAIR!

VENUS, SHOULD I HAVE TO *APOLOGIZE* FOR HAVING MY SH··*LIFE* TOGETHER?

YOU DON'T EVEN *REMEMBER* BEING A *GIRL*, I BET!

I'LL *BET* YOUR SUPER DUPER *GIANT* MUSCLES HAVE *TAKEN* OVER YOUR *GIRL* MEMORY!

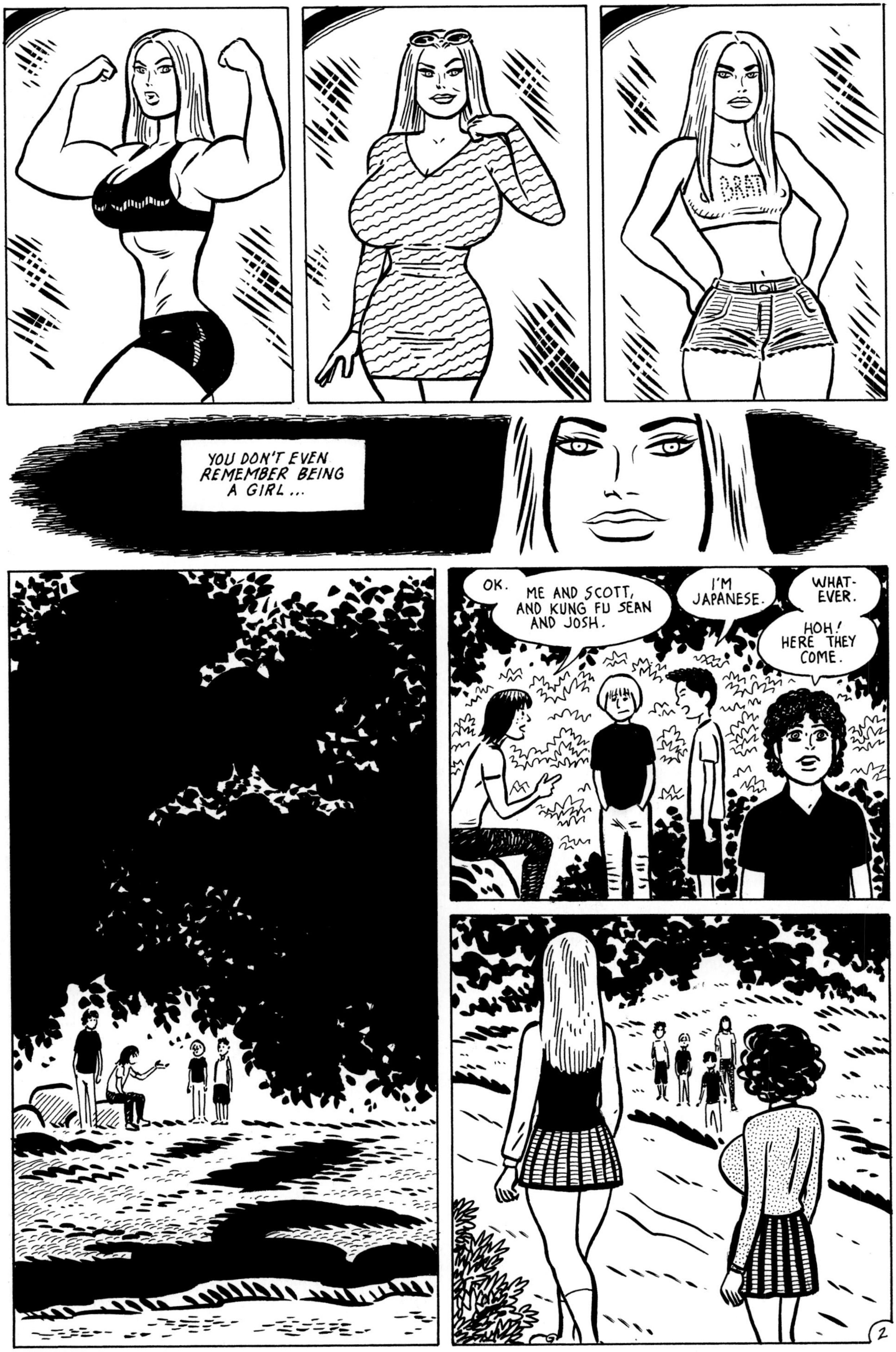

BRAT
YOU DON'T EVEN REMEMBER BEING A GIRL...
OK.
ME AND SCOTT, AND KUNG FU SEAN AND JOSH.
I'M JAPANESE.
WHAT-EVER.
HOH! HERE THEY COME.
2

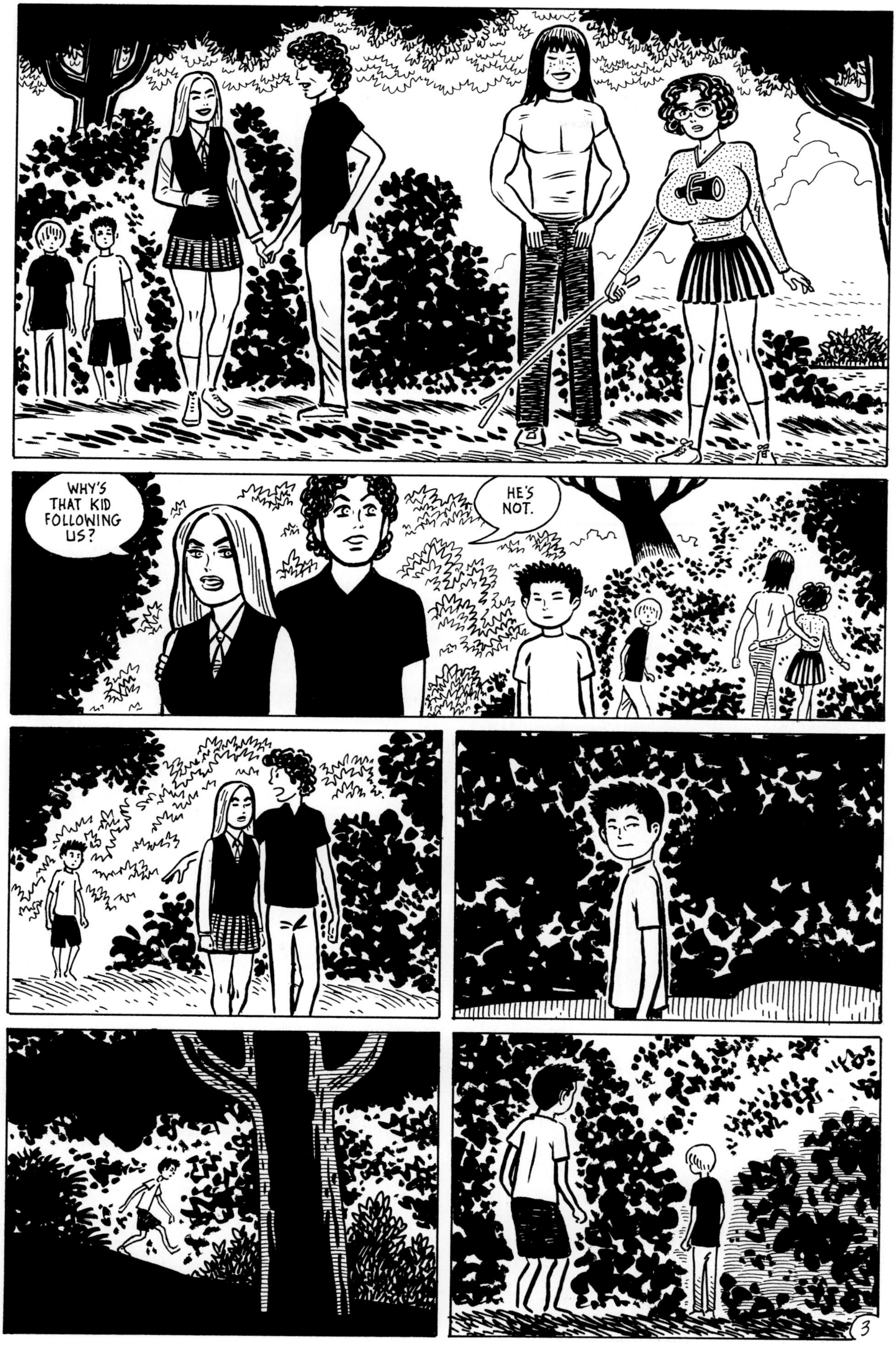
WHY'S THAT KID FOLLOWING US?
HE'S NOT.
3

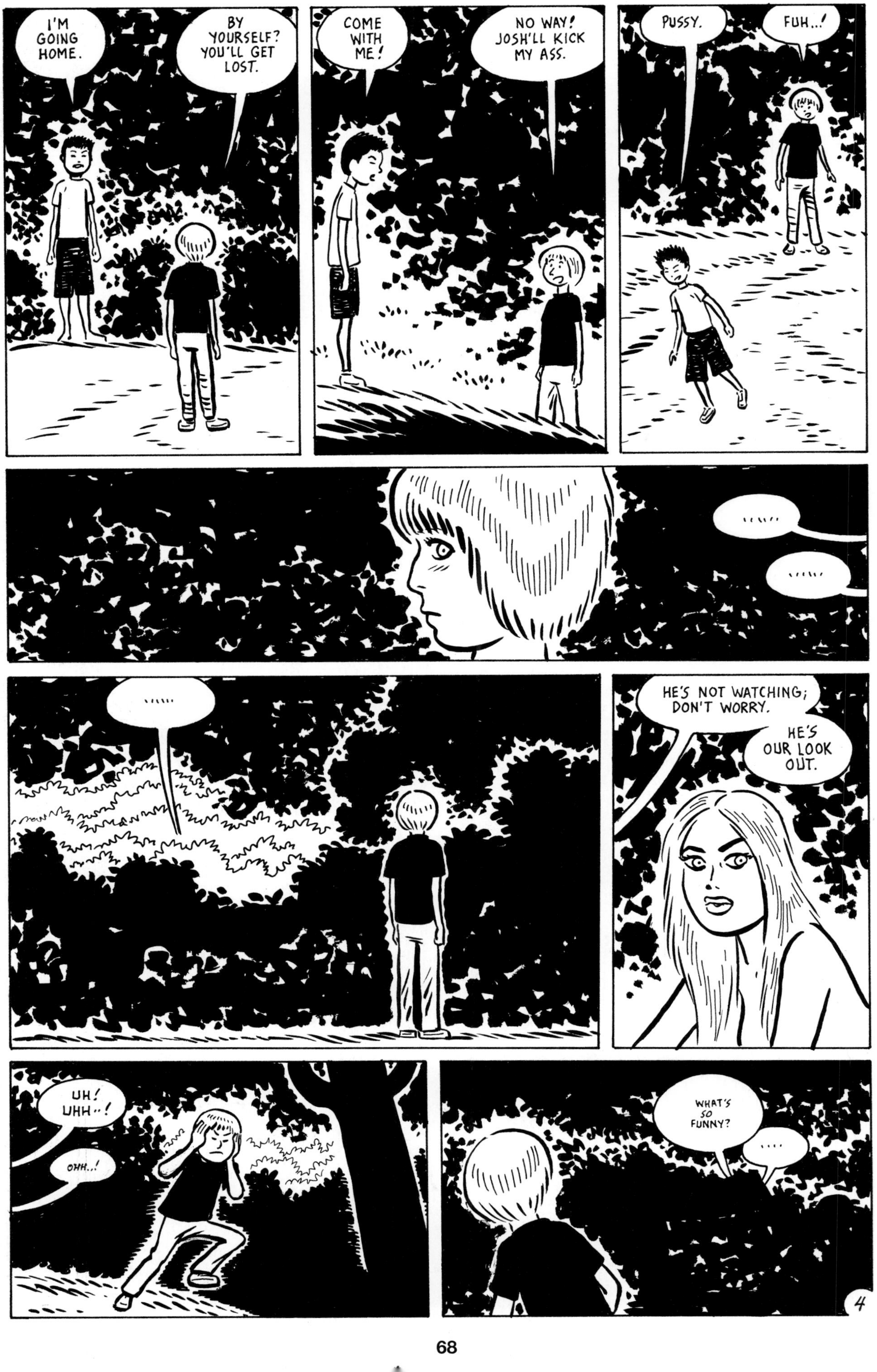
I'M GOING HOME.
BY YOURSELF? YOU'LL GET LOST.
COME WITH ME!
NO WAY! JOSH'LL KICK MY ASS.
PUSSY.
FUH...!
.....
.....
.....
HE'S NOT WATCHING; DON'T WORRY.
HE'S OUR LOOK OUT.
UH! UHH..!
OHH..!
WHAT'S SO FUNNY?
....

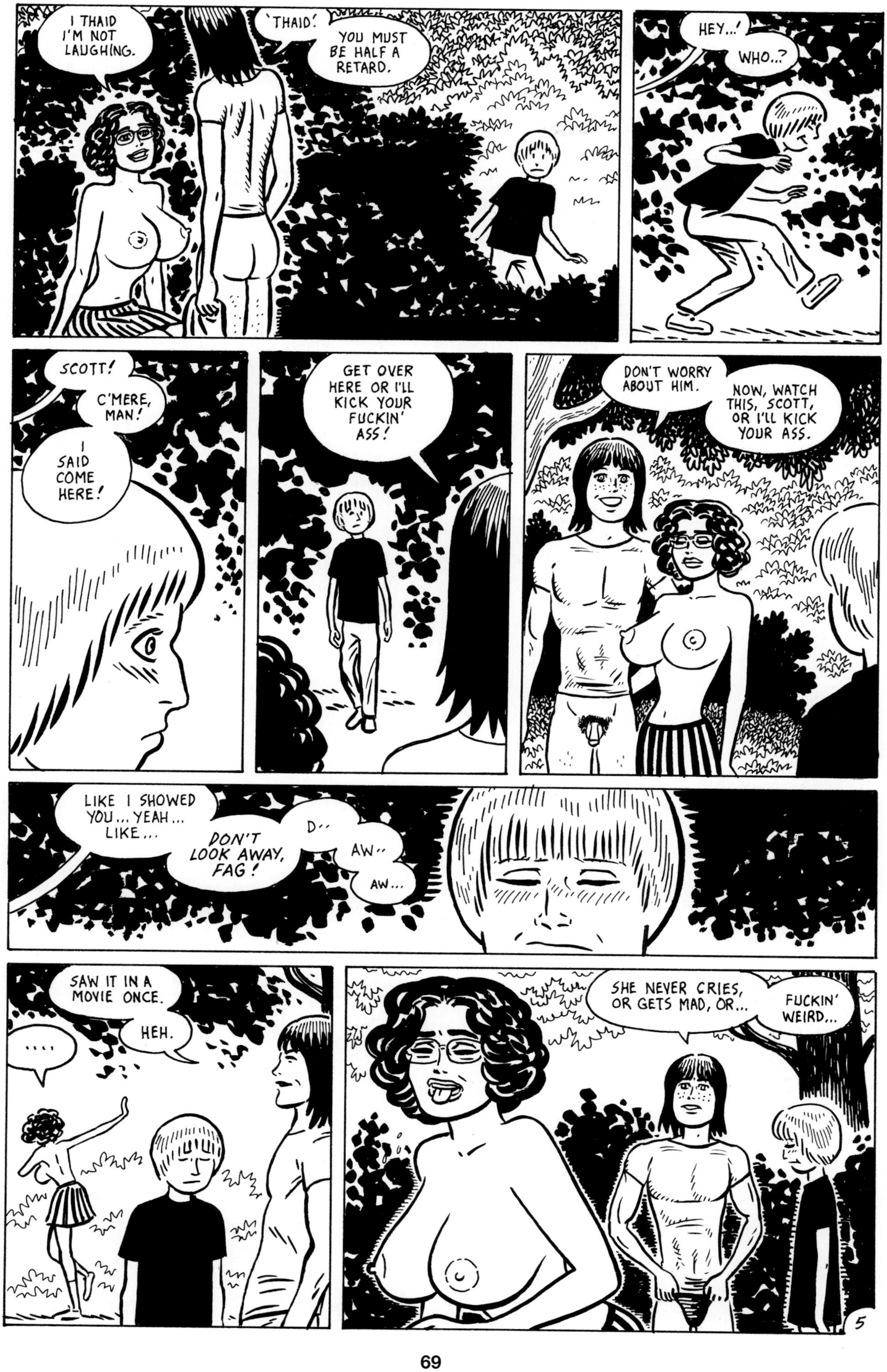
I THAID I'M NOT LAUGHING.
`THAID'.
YOU MUST BE HALF A RETARD.
HEY..!
WHO..?
SCOTT!
C'MERE, MAN!
I SAID COME HERE!
GET OVER HERE OR I'LL KICK YOUR FUCKIN' ASS!
DON'T WORRY ABOUT HIM.
NOW, WATCH THIS, SCOTT, OR I'LL KICK YOUR ASS.
LIKE I SHOWED YOU... YEAH... LIKE...
DON'T LOOK AWAY, FAG!
D..
AW..
AW...
SAW IT IN A MOVIE ONCE.
HEH.
....
SHE NEVER CRIES, OR GETS MAD, OR...
FUCKIN' WEIRD...
5

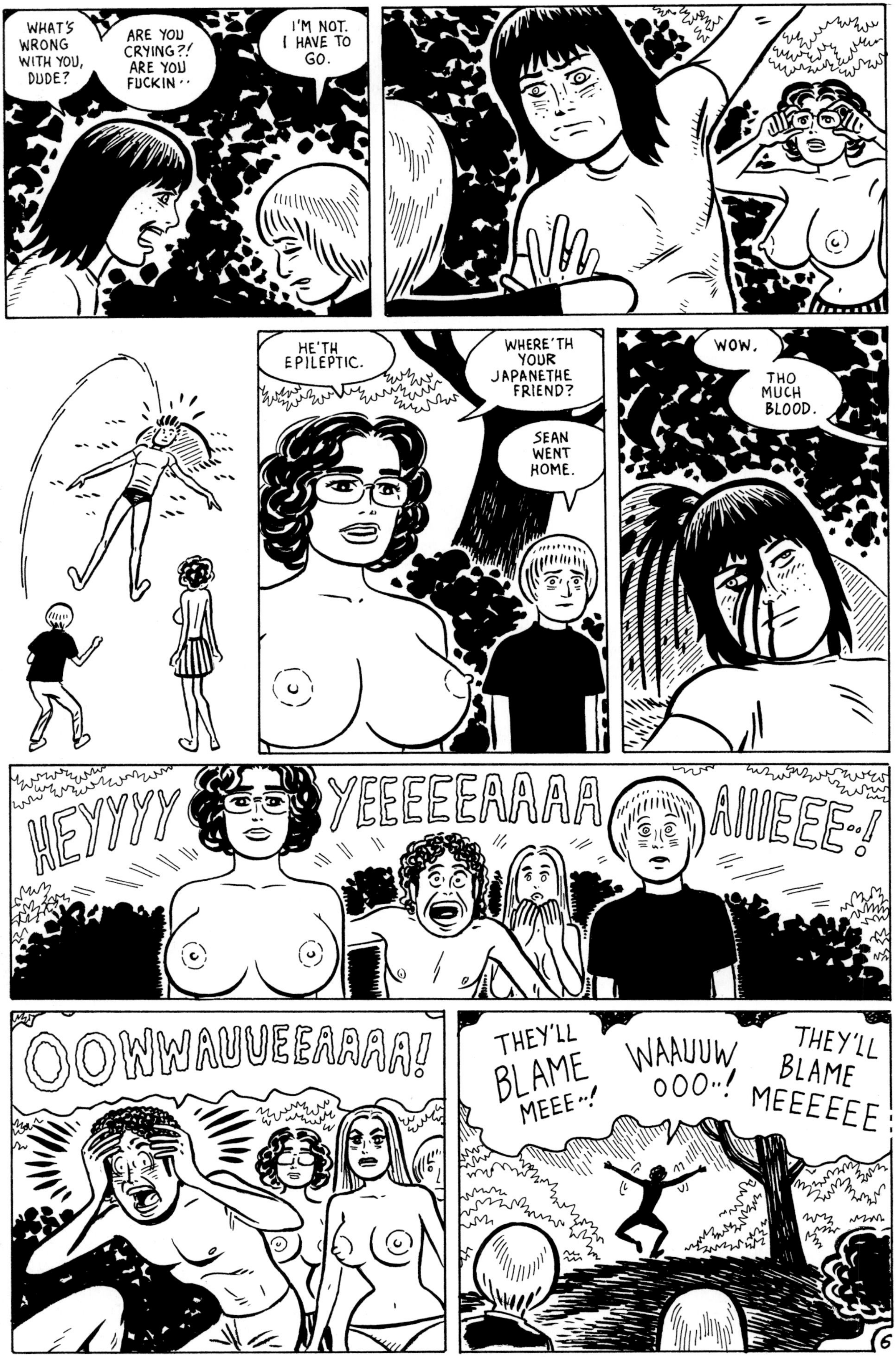

WHAT'S WRONG WITH YOU, DUDE?
ARE YOU CRYING?! ARE YOU FUCKIN··
I'M NOT. I HAVE TO GO.
HE'TH EPILEPTIC.
WHERE'TH YOUR JAPANETHE FRIEND?
SEAN WENT HOME.
WOW.
THO MUCH BLOOD.
HEYYYY YEEEEEAAAA AIIIEEE··!
OOWWAUUEEAAAA!
THEY'LL BLAME MEEE··!
WAAUUW OOO··!
THEY'LL BLAME MEEEEEE
6

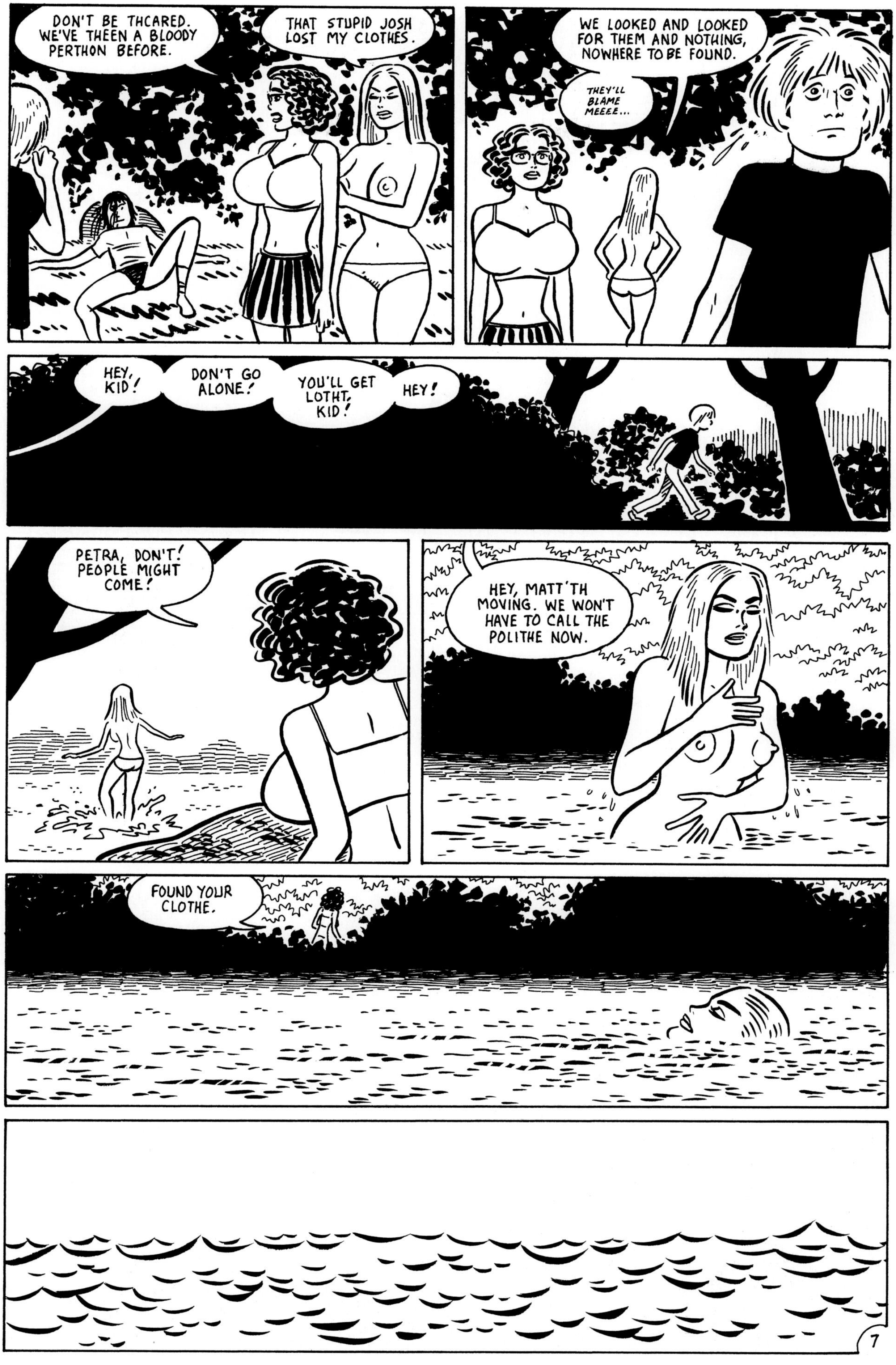
DON'T BE THCARED. WE'VE THEEN A BLOODY PERTHON BEFORE.
THAT STUPID JOSH LOST MY CLOTHES.
WE LOOKED AND LOOKED FOR THEM AND NOTHING, NOWHERE TO BE FOUND.
THEY'LL BLAME MEEEE...
HEY, KID!
DON'T GO ALONE!
YOU'LL GET LOTHT, KID!
HEY!
PETRA, DON'T! PEOPLE MIGHT COME!
HEY, MATT'TH MOVING. WE WON'T HAVE TO CALL THE POLITHE NOW.
FOUND YOUR CLOTHE.
7

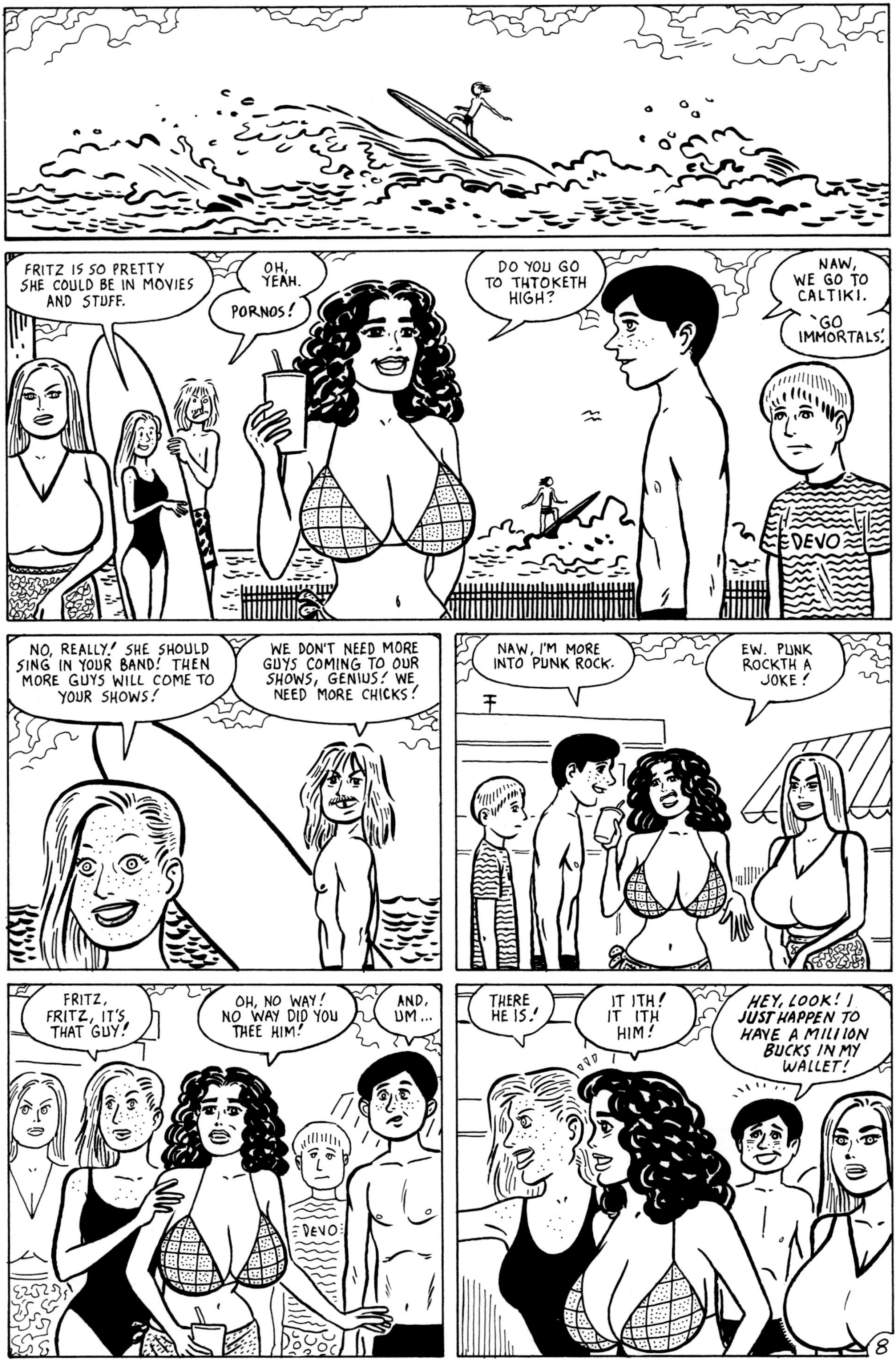

FRITZ IS SO PRETTY SHE COULD BE IN MOVIES AND STUFF.
OH, YEAH.
PORNOS!
DO YOU GO TO THTOKETH HIGH?
NAW, WE GO TO CALTIKI.
'GO IMMORTALS!
NO, REALLY! SHE SHOULD SING IN YOUR BAND! THEN MORE GUYS WILL COME TO YOUR SHOWS!
WE DON'T NEED MORE GUYS COMING TO OUR SHOWS, GENIUS! WE NEED MORE CHICKS!
NAW, I'M MORE INTO PUNK ROCK.
EW. PUNK ROCKTH A JOKE!
DEVO
FRITZ, FRITZ, IT'S THAT GUY!
OH, NO WAY! NO WAY DID YOU THEE HIM!
AND, UM...
DEVO
THERE HE IS!
IT ITH! IT ITH HIM!
HEY, LOOK! I JUST HAPPEN TO HAVE A MILLION BUCKS IN MY WALLET!
8

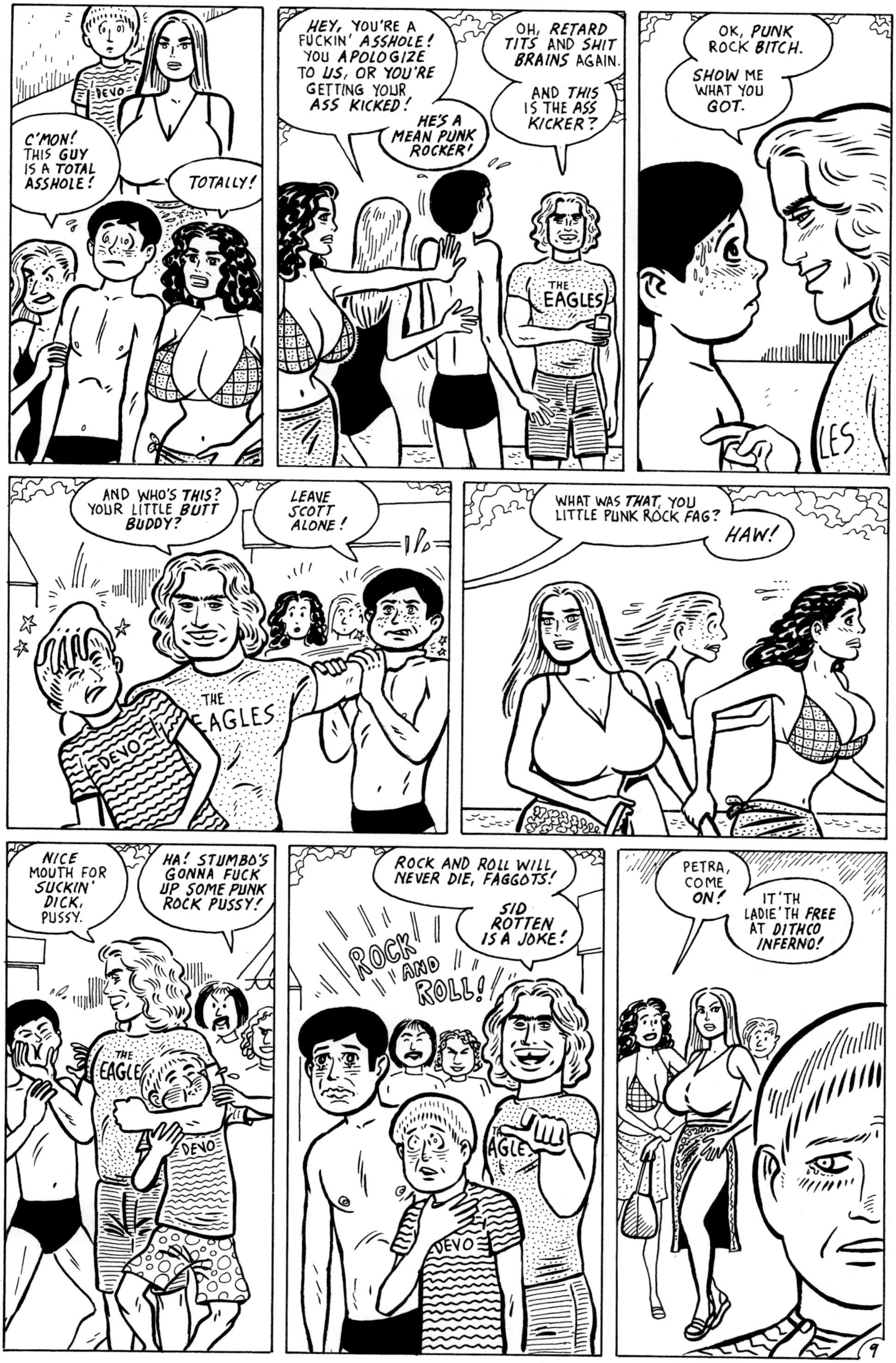
DEVO
C'MON! THIS GUY IS A TOTAL ASSHOLE!
TOTALLY!
HEY, YOU'RE A FUCKIN' ASSHOLE! YOU APOLOGIZE TO US, OR YOU'RE GETTING YOUR ASS KICKED!
HE'S A MEAN PUNK ROCKER!
OH, RETARD TITS AND SHIT BRAINS AGAIN.
AND THIS IS THE ASS KICKER?
THE EAGLES
OK, PUNK ROCK BITCH.
SHOW ME WHAT YOU GOT.
LES
AND WHO'S THIS? YOUR LITTLE BUTT BUDDY?
LEAVE SCOTT ALONE!
THE EAGLES
DEVO
WHAT WAS THAT, YOU LITTLE PUNK ROCK FAG?
HAW!
NICE MOUTH FOR SUCKIN' DICK, PUSSY.
HA! STUMBO'S GONNA FUCK UP SOME PUNK ROCK PUSSY!
THE EAGLE
DEVO
ROCK AND ROLL WILL NEVER DIE, FAGGOTS!
SID ROTTEN IS A JOKE!
ROCK AND ROLL!
AGLE
DEVO
PETRA, COME ON!
IT'TH LADIE'TH FREE AT DITHCO INFERNO!
9

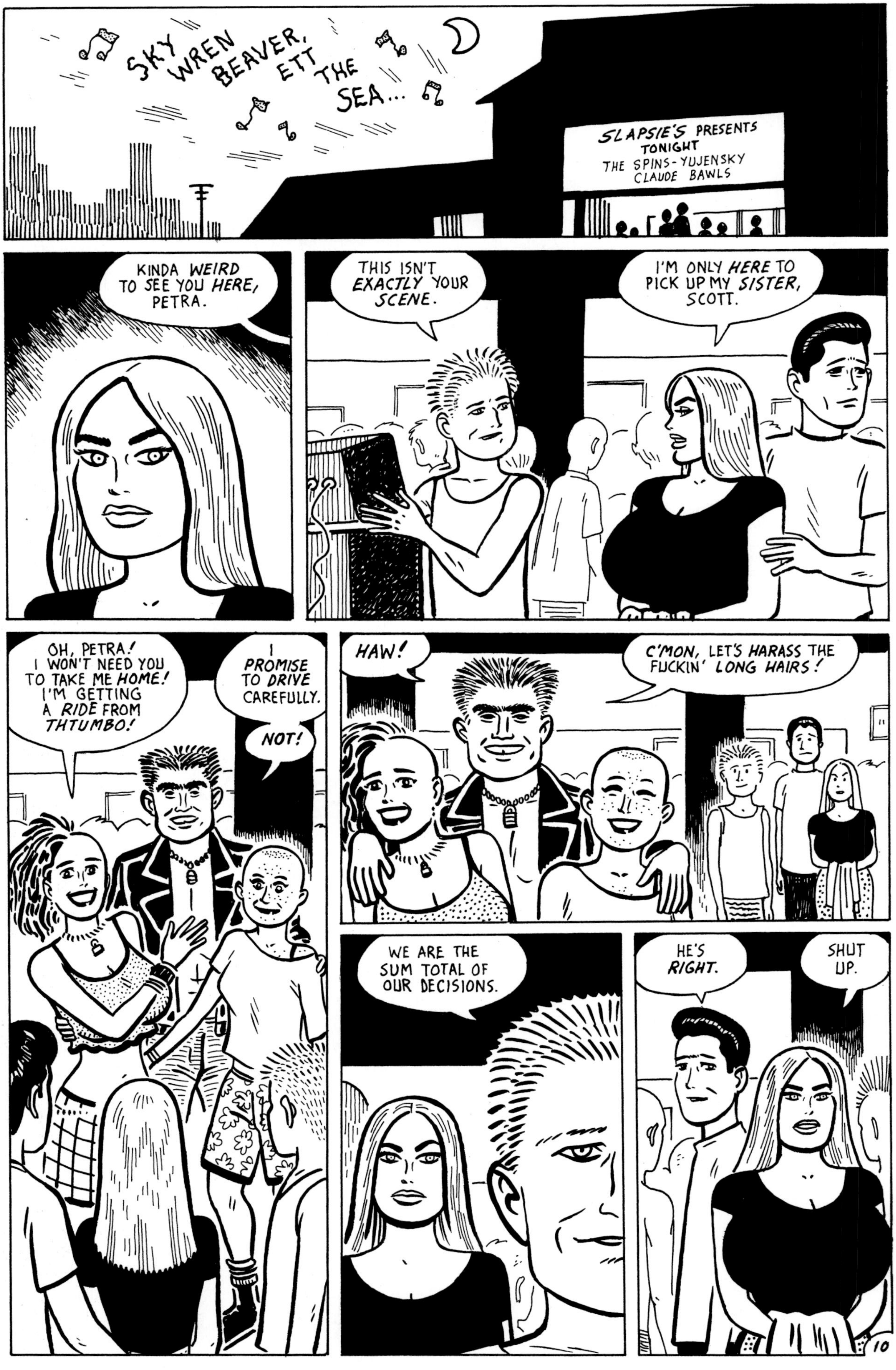
SKY WREN BEAVER, ETT THE SEA...
SLAPSIE'S PRESENTS TONIGHT THE SPINS-YUJENSKY CLAUDE BAWLS
KINDA WEIRD TO SEE YOU HERE, PETRA.
THIS ISN'T EXACTLY YOUR SCENE.
I'M ONLY HERE TO PICK UP MY SISTER, SCOTT.
OH, PETRA! I WON'T NEED YOU TO TAKE ME HOME! I'M GETTING A RIDE FROM THTUMBO!
I PROMISE TO DRIVE CAREFULLY.
NOT!
HAW!
C'MON, LET'S HARASS THE FUCKIN' LONG HAIRS!
WE ARE THE SUM TOTAL OF OUR DECISIONS.
HE'S RIGHT.
SHUT UP.
10

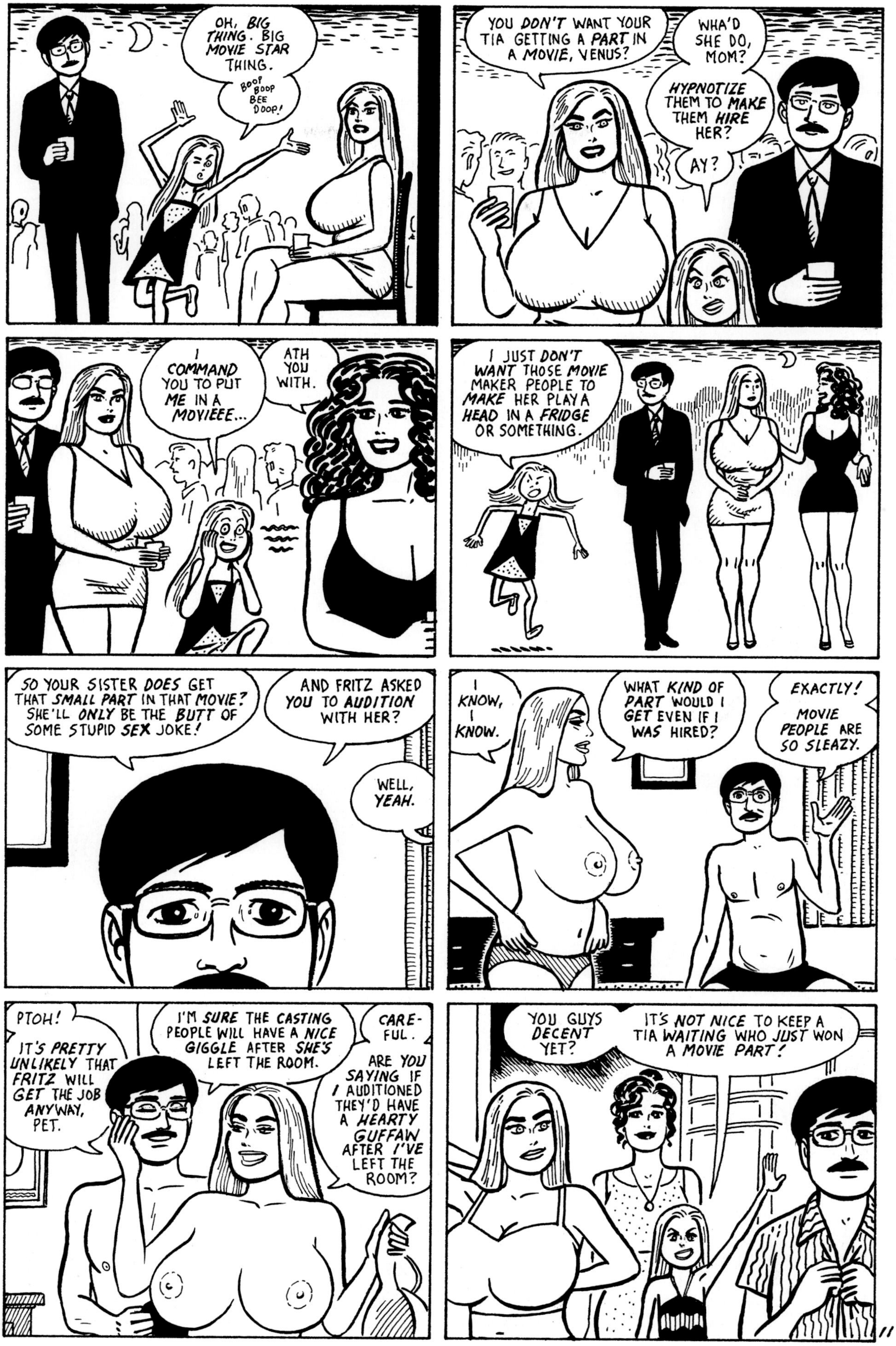

OH, BIG THING. BIG MOVIE STAR THING.
BOOP BOOP BEE DOOP!
YOU DON'T WANT YOUR TIA GETTING A PART IN A MOVIE, VENUS?
WHA'D SHE DO, MOM?
HYPNOTIZE THEM TO MAKE THEM HIRE HER?
AY?
I COMMAND YOU TO PUT ME IN A MOVIEEE...
ATH YOU WITH.
I JUST DON'T WANT THOSE MOVIE MAKER PEOPLE TO MAKE HER PLAY A HEAD IN A FRIDGE OR SOMETHING.
SO YOUR SISTER DOES GET THAT SMALL PART IN THAT MOVIE? SHE'LL ONLY BE THE BUTT OF SOME STUPID SEX JOKE!
AND FRITZ ASKED YOU TO AUDITION WITH HER?
WELL, YEAH.
I KNOW, I KNOW.
WHAT KIND OF PART WOULD I GET EVEN IF I WAS HIRED?
EXACTLY! MOVIE PEOPLE ARE SO SLEAZY.
PTOH!
IT'S PRETTY UNLIKELY THAT FRITZ WILL GET THE JOB ANYWAY, PET.
I'M SURE THE CASTING PEOPLE WILL HAVE A NICE GIGGLE AFTER SHE'S LEFT THE ROOM.
CARE-FUL.
ARE YOU SAYING IF I AUDITIONED THEY'D HAVE A HEARTY GUFFAW AFTER I'VE LEFT THE ROOM?
YOU GUYS DECENT YET?
IT'S NOT NICE TO KEEP A TIA WAITING WHO JUST WON A MOVIE PART!
11

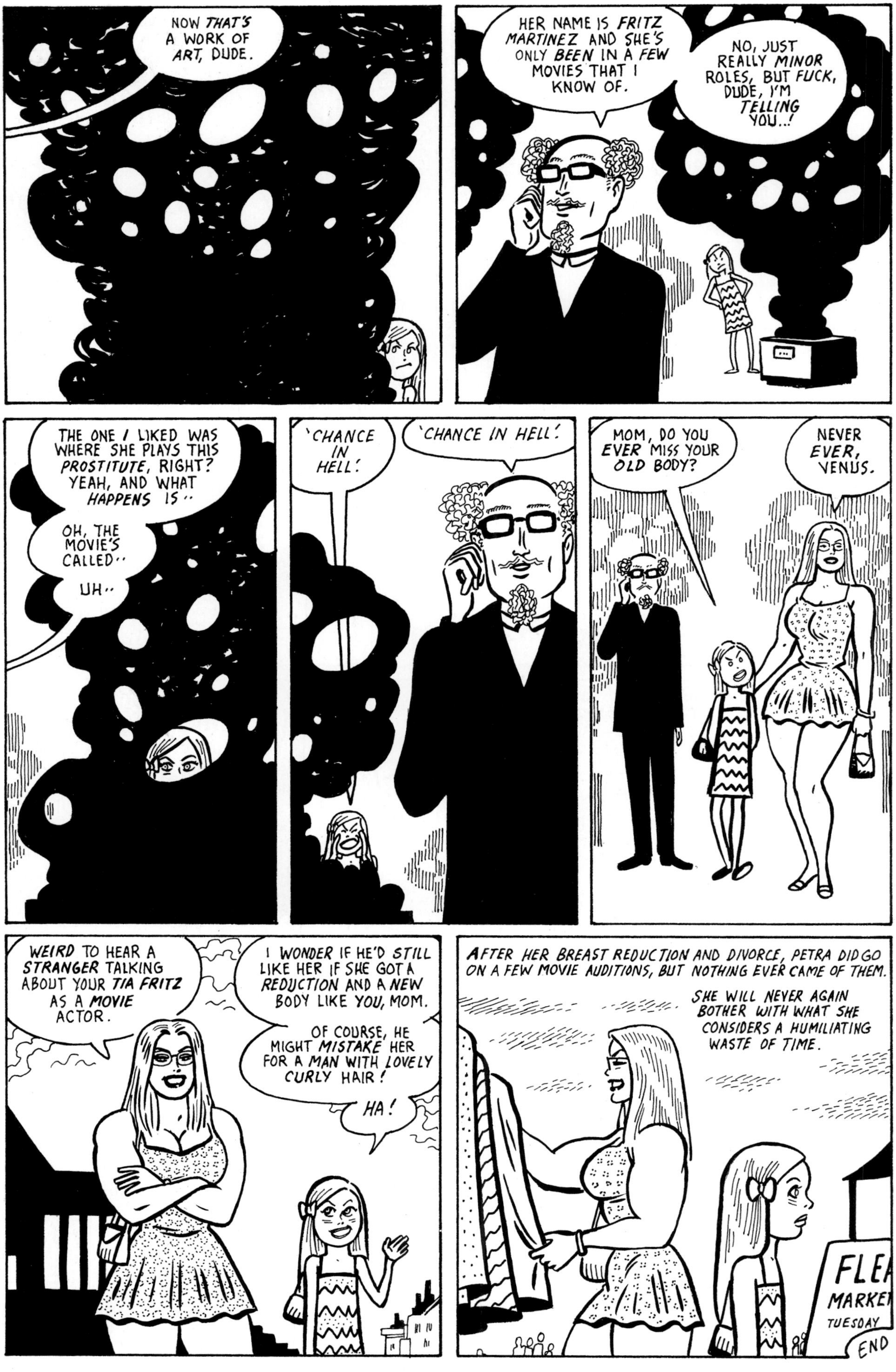
NOW THAT'S A WORK OF ART, DUDE.
HER NAME IS FRITZ MARTINEZ AND SHE'S ONLY BEEN IN A FEW MOVIES THAT I KNOW OF.
NO, JUST REALLY MINOR ROLES, BUT FUCK, DUDE, I'M TELLING YOU..!
THE ONE I LIKED WAS WHERE SHE PLAYS THIS PROSTITUTE, RIGHT? YEAH, AND WHAT HAPPENS IS..
OH, THE MOVIE'S CALLED..
UH..
'CHANCE IN HELL.'
'CHANCE IN HELL.'
MOM, DO YOU EVER MISS YOUR OLD BODY?
NEVER EVER, VENUS.
WEIRD TO HEAR A STRANGER TALKING ABOUT YOUR TIA FRITZ AS A MOVIE ACTOR.
I WONDER IF HE'D STILL LIKE HER IF SHE GOT A REDUCTION AND A NEW BODY LIKE YOU, MOM.
OF COURSE, HE MIGHT MISTAKE HER FOR A MAN WITH LOVELY CURLY HAIR!
HA!
AFTER HER BREAST REDUCTION AND DIVORCE, PETRA DID GO ON A FEW MOVIE AUDITIONS, BUT NOTHING EVER CAME OF THEM.
SHE WILL NEVER AGAIN BOTHER WITH WHAT SHE CONSIDERS A HUMILIATING WASTE OF TIME.
FLEA MARKET TUESDAY
12
END

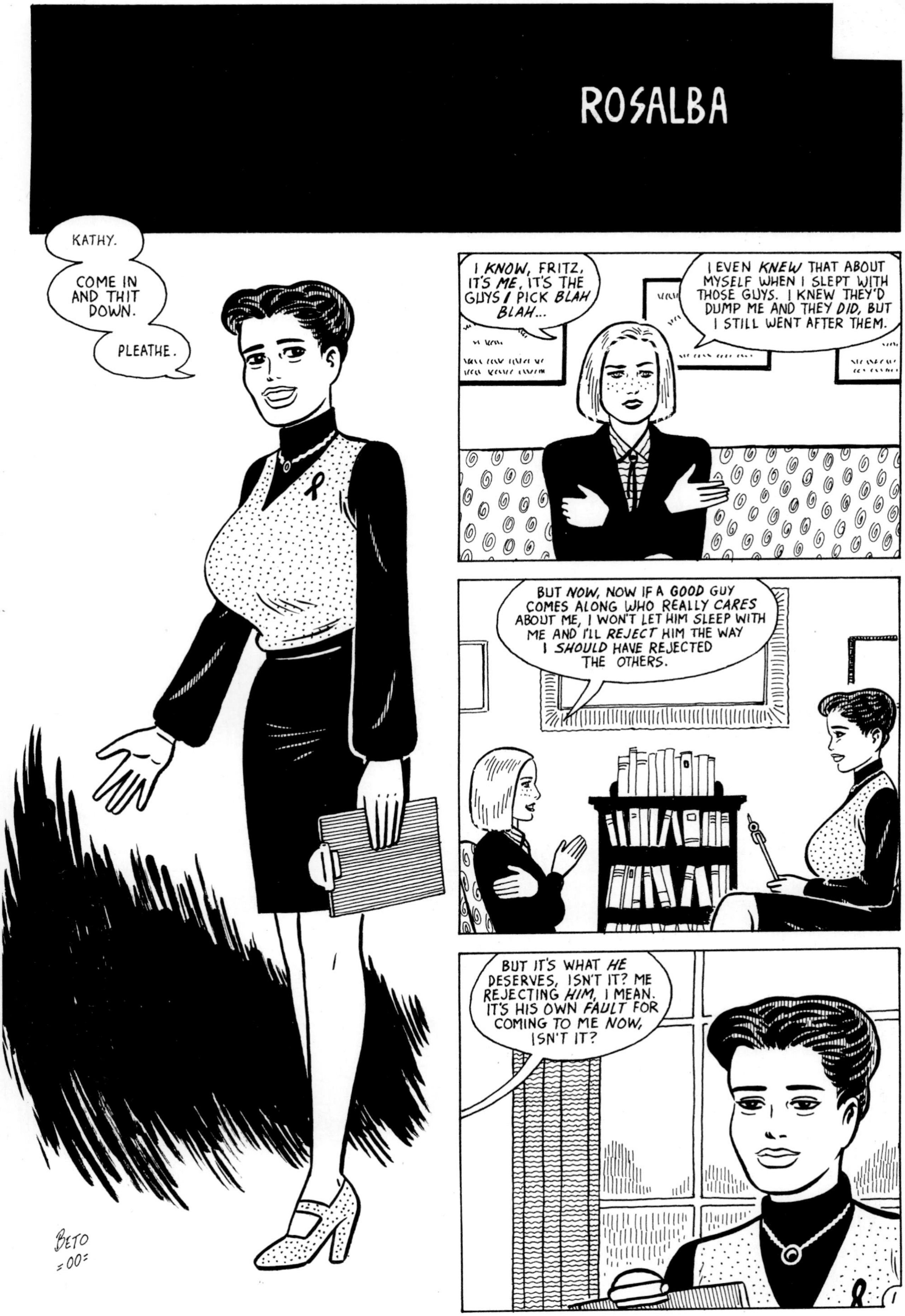
ROSALBA
KATHY.
COME IN AND THIT DOWN.
PLEATHE.
I KNOW, FRITZ, IT'S ME, IT'S THE GUYS I PICK BLAH BLAH...
I EVEN KNEW THAT ABOUT MYSELF WHEN I SLEPT WITH THOSE GUYS. I KNEW THEY'D DUMP ME AND THEY DID, BUT I STILL WENT AFTER THEM.
BUT NOW, NOW IF A GOOD GUY COMES ALONG WHO REALLY CARES ABOUT ME, I WON'T LET HIM SLEEP WITH ME AND I'LL REJECT HIM THE WAY I SHOULD HAVE REJECTED THE OTHERS.
BUT IT'S WHAT HE DESERVES, ISN'T IT? ME REJECTING HIM, I MEAN. IT'S HIS OWN FAULT FOR COMING TO ME NOW, ISN'T IT?
BETO =00=

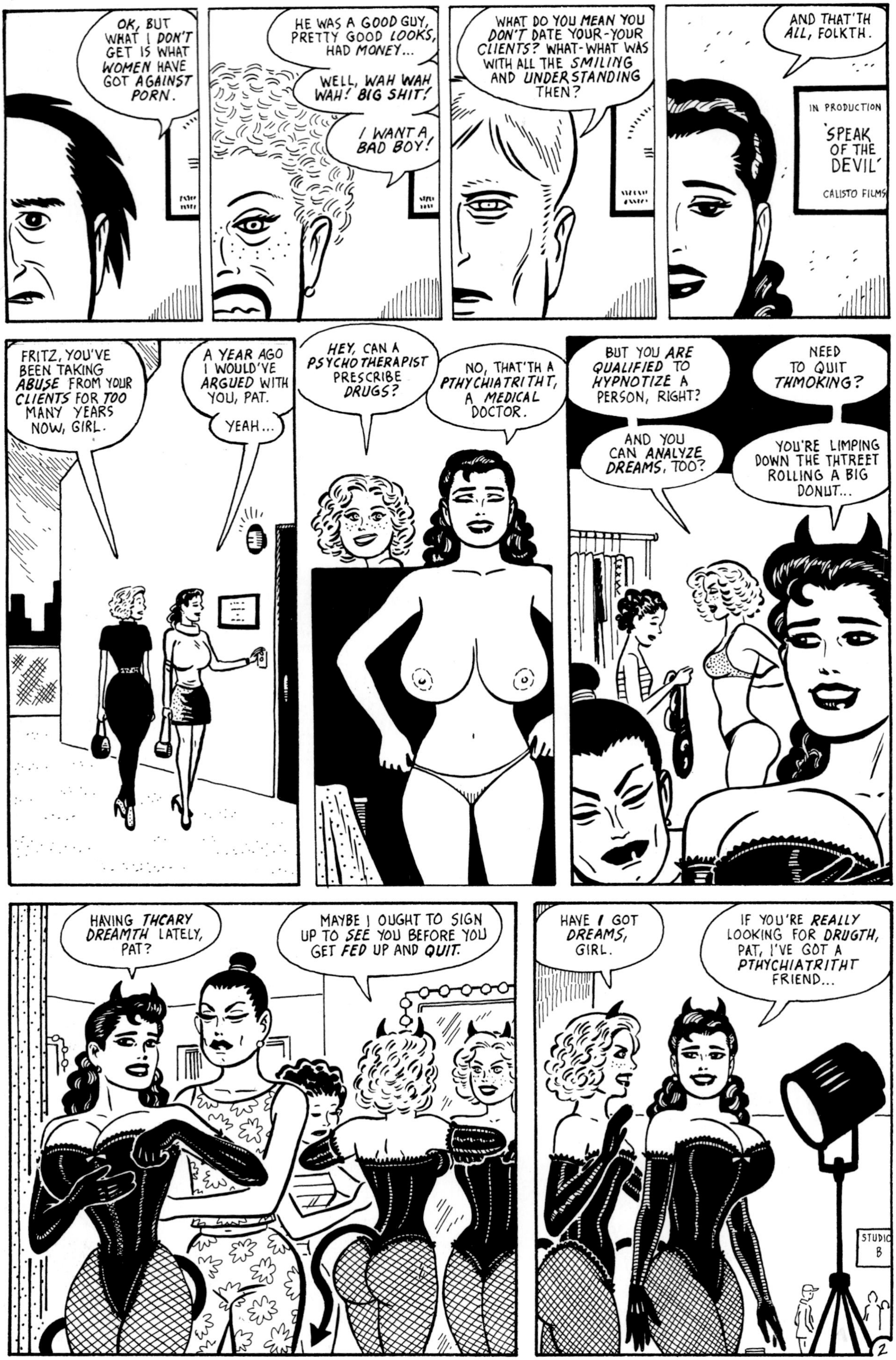
OK, BUT WHAT I DON'T GET IS WHAT WOMEN HAVE GOT AGAINST PORN.
HE WAS A GOOD GUY, PRETTY GOOD LOOKS, HAD MONEY...
WELL, WAH WAH WAH! BIG SHIT!
I WANT A BAD BOY!
WHAT DO YOU MEAN YOU DON'T DATE YOUR-YOUR CLIENTS? WHAT-WHAT WAS WITH ALL THE SMILING AND UNDERSTANDING THEN?
AND THAT'TH ALL, FOLKTH.
IN PRODUCTION
'SPEAK OF THE DEVIL'
CALISTO FILMS
FRITZ, YOU'VE BEEN TAKING ABUSE FROM YOUR CLIENTS FOR TOO MANY YEARS NOW, GIRL.
A YEAR AGO I WOULD'VE ARGUED WITH YOU, PAT.
YEAH...
HEY, CAN A PSYCHOTHERAPIST PRESCRIBE DRUGS?
NO, THAT'TH A PTHYCHIATRITHT, A MEDICAL DOCTOR.
BUT YOU ARE QUALIFIED TO HYPNOTIZE A PERSON, RIGHT?
AND YOU CAN ANALYZE DREAMS, TOO?
NEED TO QUIT THMOKING?
YOU'RE LIMPING DOWN THE THTREET ROLLING A BIG DONUT...
HAVING THCARY DREAMTH LATELY, PAT?
MAYBE I OUGHT TO SIGN UP TO SEE YOU BEFORE YOU GET FED UP AND QUIT.
HAVE I GOT DREAMS, GIRL.
IF YOU'RE REALLY LOOKING FOR DRUGTH, PAT, I'VE GOT A PTHYCHIATRITHT FRIEND...
STUDIO B
2

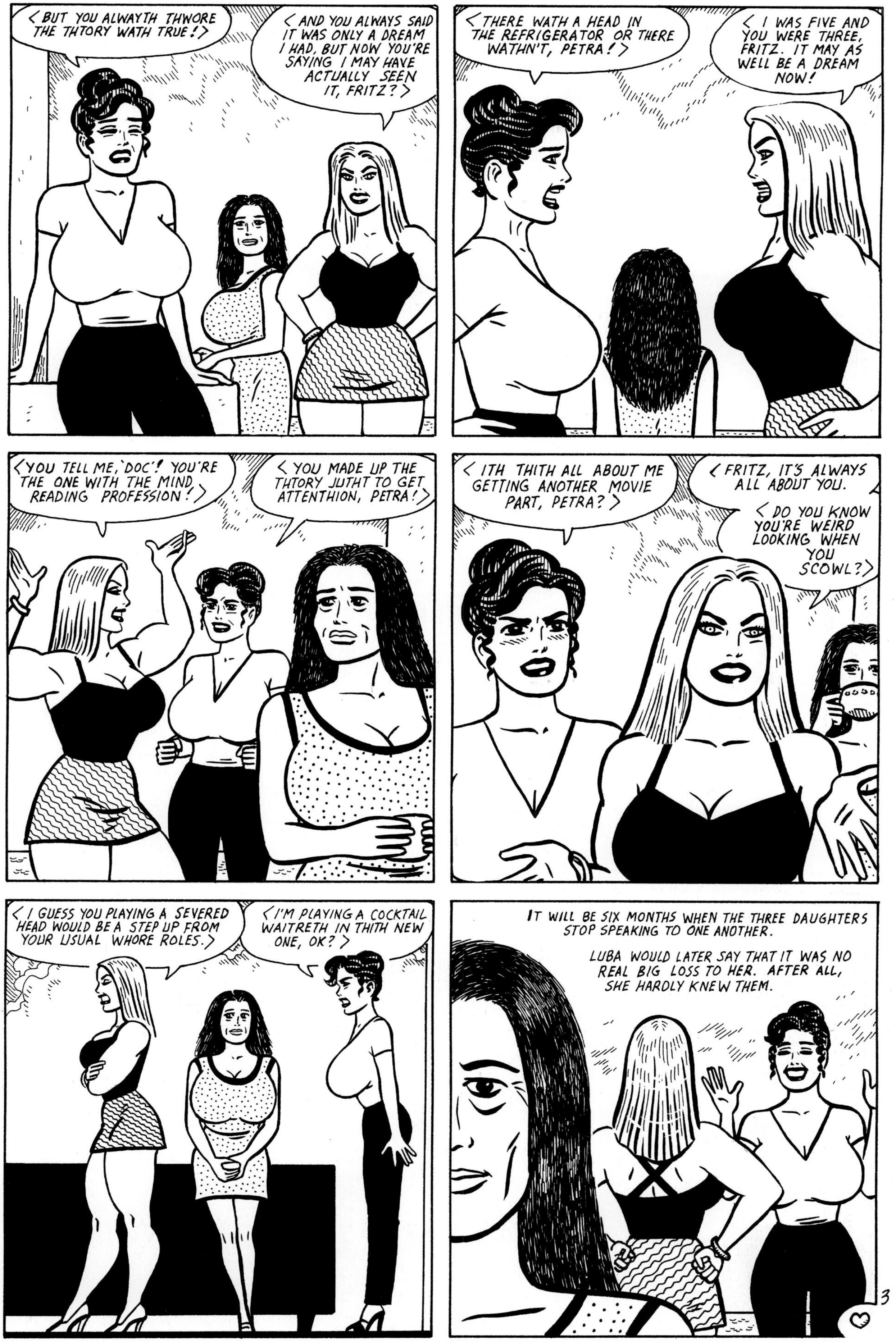
< BUT YOU ALWAYTH THWORE THE THTORY WATH TRUE! >
< AND YOU ALWAYS SAID IT WAS ONLY A DREAM I HAD, BUT NOW YOU'RE SAYING I MAY HAVE ACTUALLY SEEN IT, FRITZ? >
< THERE WATH A HEAD IN THE REFRIGERATOR OR THERE WATHN'T, PETRA! >
< I WAS FIVE AND YOU WERE THREE, FRITZ. IT MAY AS WELL BE A DREAM NOW! >
< YOU TELL ME, 'DOC'! YOU'RE THE ONE WITH THE MIND READING PROFESSION! >
< YOU MADE UP THE THTORY JUTHT TO GET ATTENTHION, PETRA! >
< ITH THITH ALL ABOUT ME GETTING ANOTHER MOVIE PART, PETRA? >
< FRITZ, IT'S ALWAYS ALL ABOUT YOU.
< DO YOU KNOW YOU'RE WEIRD LOOKING WHEN YOU SCOWL? >
< I GUESS YOU PLAYING A SEVERED HEAD WOULD BE A STEP UP FROM YOUR USUAL WHORE ROLES. >
< I'M PLAYING A COCKTAIL WAITRETH IN THITH NEW ONE, OK? >
IT WILL BE SIX MONTHS WHEN THE THREE DAUGHTERS STOP SPEAKING TO ONE ANOTHER.
LUBA WOULD LATER SAY THAT IT WAS NO REAL BIG LOSS TO HER. AFTER ALL, SHE HARDLY KNEW THEM.
3

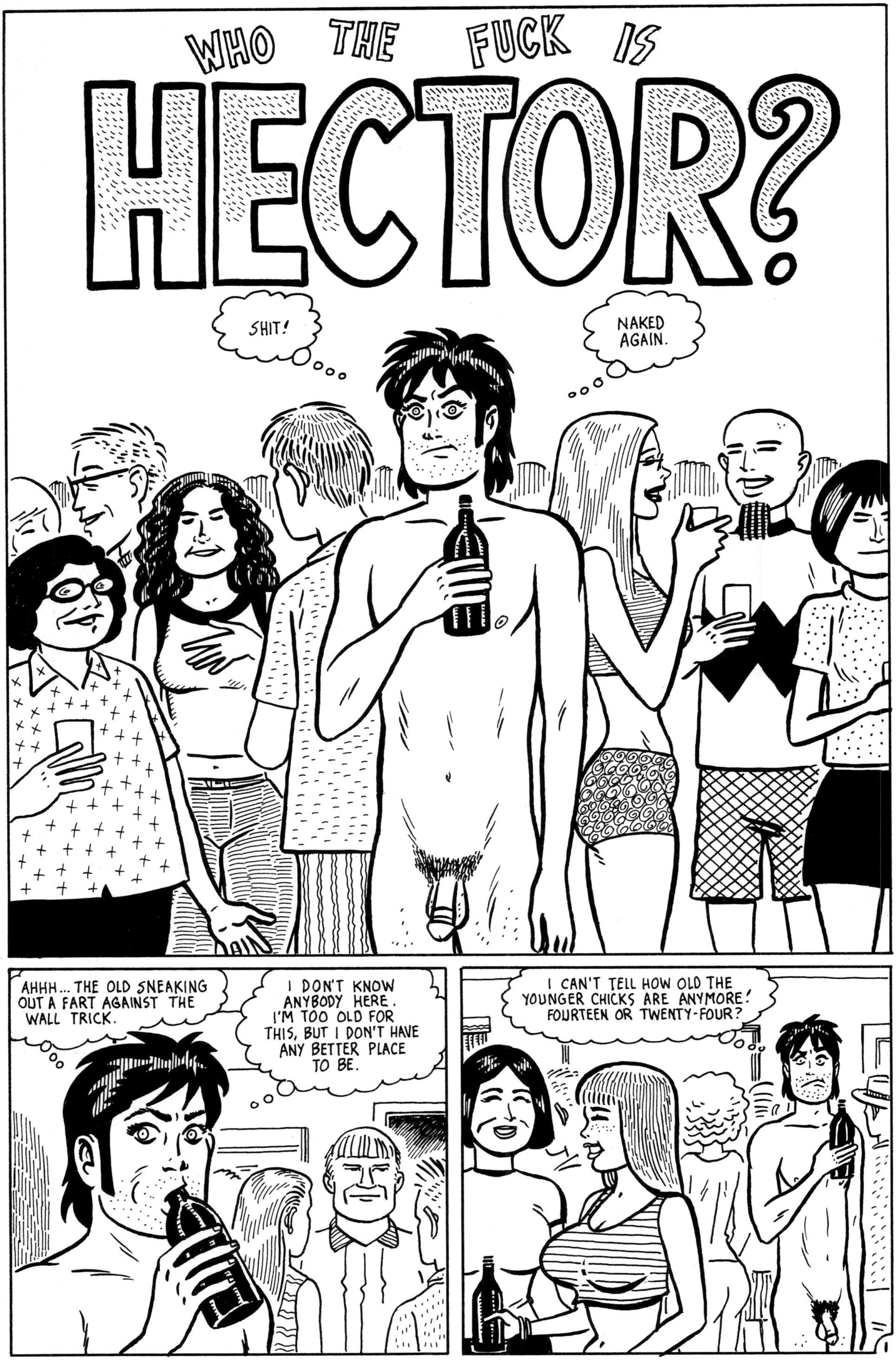
WHO THE FUCK IS
HECTOR?
SHIT!
NAKED AGAIN.
AHHH... THE OLD SNEAKING OUT A FART AGAINST THE WALL TRICK.
I DON'T KNOW ANYBODY HERE. I'M TOO OLD FOR THIS, BUT I DON'T HAVE ANY BETTER PLACE TO BE.
I CAN'T TELL HOW OLD THE YOUNGER CHICKS ARE ANYMORE! FOURTEEN OR TWENTY-FOUR?

I USED TO BE SHY AT PARTIES AND THOUGHT THAT WHEN I GOT OLDER I'D BE THE COOL, SMARTER GUY THAT EVERYBODY LOOKS UP TO.

WELL, THAT SURE THE FUCK NEVER HAPPENED.

IF I DIDN'T HAVE A GIRLFRIEND, I'D REALLY BE FEELING WORTHLESS.

SHE'S OUT OF TOWN, SO I'M FREE TO GIRL WATCH ALL I WANT.

OUT OF TOWN FOR A WEEK.

I'M SO LONELY I MUST FUCK THE WALL.

TROUBLE IS, I PREFER MY AMAZON GIRLFRIEND TO ANY OF THESE YOUNGER HOTTIES.

I GUESS A GUY COULD HAVE WORSE TROUBLE.

LIKE THAT URINARY TRACT INFECTION I GOT LAST YEAR.

OOF.

AS IF ANY BABE HERE WOULD BE INTERESTED. SURE, I MIGHT THINK OF MYSELF AS PERMANENTLY THIRTY-THREE EVEN AS I GET OLDER, BUT THE YOUNGER GALS ARE SEEING SOMETHING ELSE.

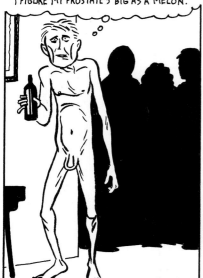

GETTIN' OLDER BY THE SECOND, ALL OF US. A URINARY TRACT INFECTION IS ONLY THE BEGINNING. I HAVE TO PEE SEVERAL TIMES WHEN I'M TRYING TO SLEEP AT NIGHT. I FIGURE MY PROSTATE'S BIG AS A MELON.

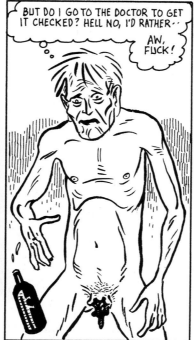

BUT DO I GO TO THE DOCTOR TO GET IT CHECKED? HELL NO, I'D RATHER--

AW, FUCK!

EVEN MY DICK AND BALLS ARE TIRED OF ME. OR MAYBE THEY'RE JUST MAKING THEIR GETAWAY IN CASE I DO HAVE PROSTATE CANCER.

2

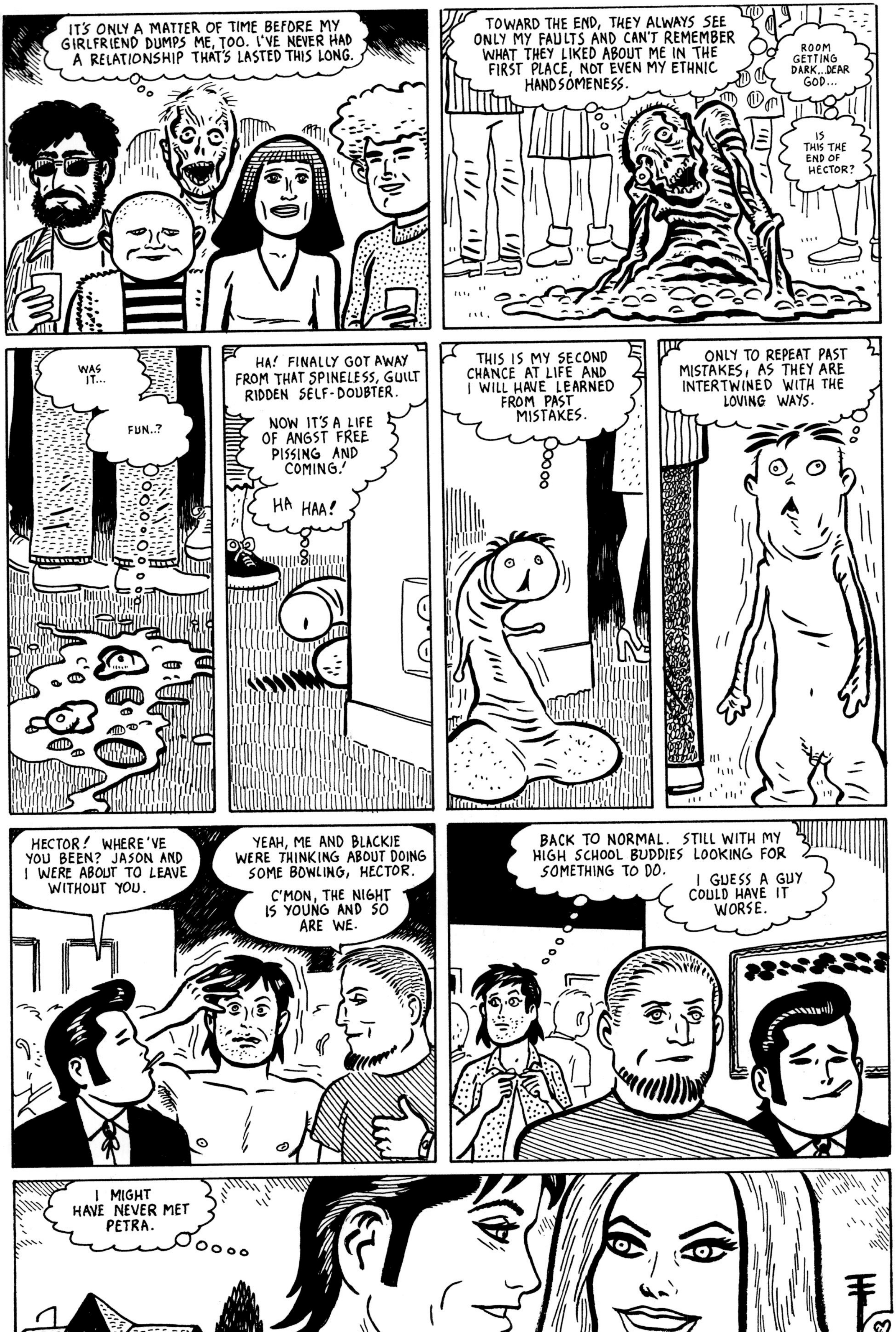
IT'S ONLY A MATTER OF TIME BEFORE MY GIRLFRIEND DUMPS ME, TOO. I'VE NEVER HAD A RELATIONSHIP THAT'S LASTED THIS LONG.
TOWARD THE END, THEY ALWAYS SEE ONLY MY FAULTS AND CAN'T REMEMBER WHAT THEY LIKED ABOUT ME IN THE FIRST PLACE, NOT EVEN MY ETHNIC HANDSOMENESS.
ROOM GETTING DARK...DEAR GOD...
IS THIS THE END OF HECTOR?
WAS IT...
FUN..?
HA! FINALLY GOT AWAY FROM THAT SPINELESS, GUILT RIDDEN SELF-DOUBTER.
NOW IT'S A LIFE OF ANGST FREE PISSING AND COMING!
HA HAA!
THIS IS MY SECOND CHANCE AT LIFE AND I WILL HAVE LEARNED FROM PAST MISTAKES.
ONLY TO REPEAT PAST MISTAKES, AS THEY ARE INTERTWINED WITH THE LOVING WAYS.
HECTOR! WHERE'VE YOU BEEN? JASON AND I WERE ABOUT TO LEAVE WITHOUT YOU.
YEAH, ME AND BLACKIE WERE THINKING ABOUT DOING SOME BOWLING, HECTOR.
C'MON, THE NIGHT IS YOUNG AND SO ARE WE.
BACK TO NORMAL. STILL WITH MY HIGH SCHOOL BUDDIES LOOKING FOR SOMETHING TO DO.
I GUESS A GUY COULD HAVE IT WORSE.
I MIGHT HAVE NEVER MET PETRA.
3

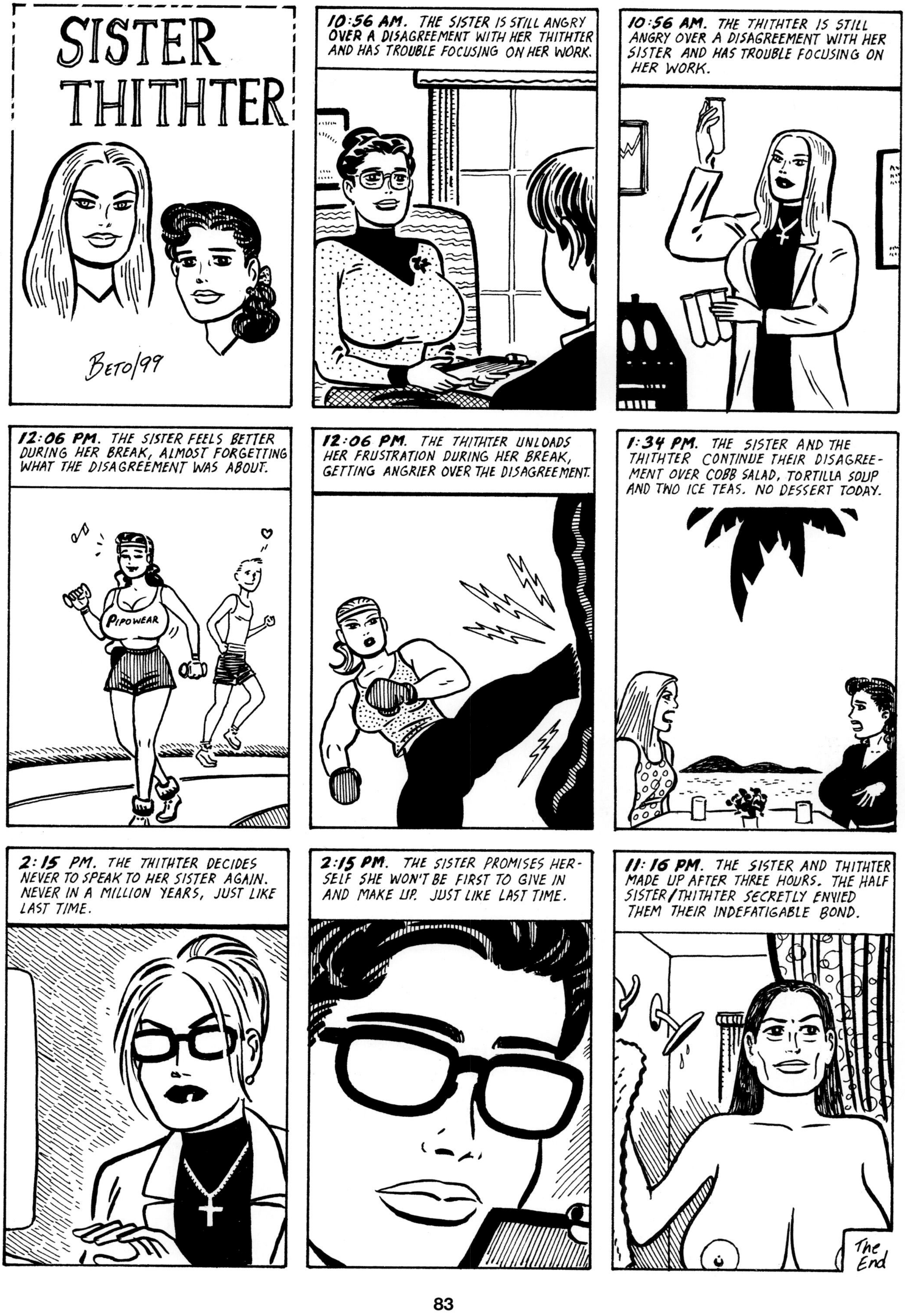
SISTER THITHTER
BETO/99
10:56 AM. THE SISTER IS STILL ANGRY OVER A DISAGREEMENT WITH HER THITHTER AND HAS TROUBLE FOCUSING ON HER WORK.
10:56 AM. THE THITHTER IS STILL ANGRY OVER A DISAGREEMENT WITH HER SISTER AND HAS TROUBLE FOCUSING ON HER WORK.
12:06 PM. THE SISTER FEELS BETTER DURING HER BREAK, ALMOST FORGETTING WHAT THE DISAGREEMENT WAS ABOUT.
PIPOWEAR
12:06 PM. THE THITHTER UNLOADS HER FRUSTRATION DURING HER BREAK, GETTING ANGRIER OVER THE DISAGREEMENT.
1:34 PM. THE SISTER AND THE THITHTER CONTINUE THEIR DISAGREEMENT OVER COBB SALAD, TORTILLA SOUP AND TWO ICE TEAS. NO DESSERT TODAY.
2:15 PM. THE THITHTER DECIDES NEVER TO SPEAK TO HER SISTER AGAIN. NEVER IN A MILLION YEARS, JUST LIKE LAST TIME.
2:15 PM. THE SISTER PROMISES HERSELF SHE WON'T BE FIRST TO GIVE IN AND MAKE UP. JUST LIKE LAST TIME.
11:16 PM. THE SISTER AND THITHTER MADE UP AFTER THREE HOURS. THE HALF SISTER/THITHTER SECRETLY ENVIED THEM THEIR INDEFATIGABLE BOND.
The End

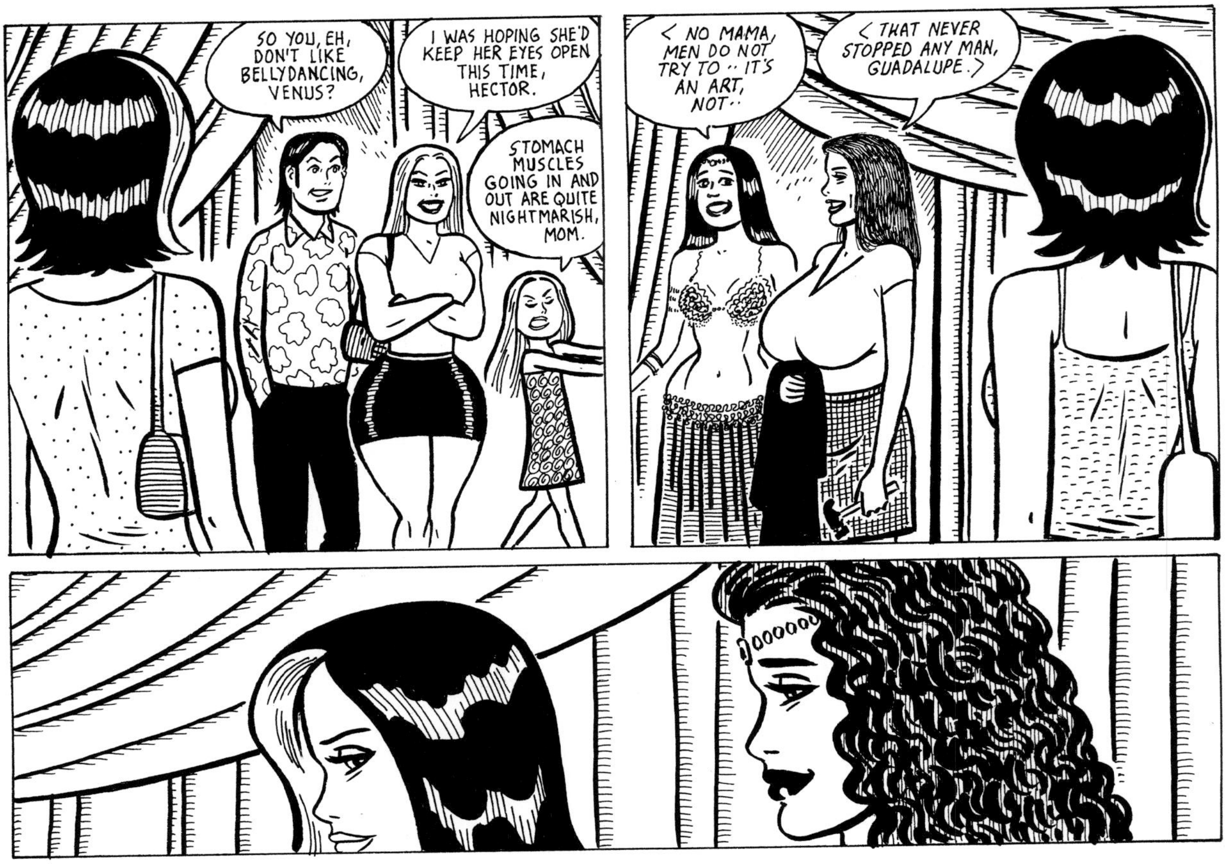
SO YOU, EH, DON'T LIKE BELLYDANCING, VENUS?
I WAS HOPING SHE'D KEEP HER EYES OPEN THIS TIME, HECTOR.
STOMACH MUSCLES GOING IN AND OUT ARE QUITE NIGHTMARISH, MOM.
< NO MAMA, MEN DO NOT TRY TO ·· IT'S AN ART, NOT··
< THAT NEVER STOPPED ANY MAN, GUADALUPE. >

SOMETHING ABOUT PIPO

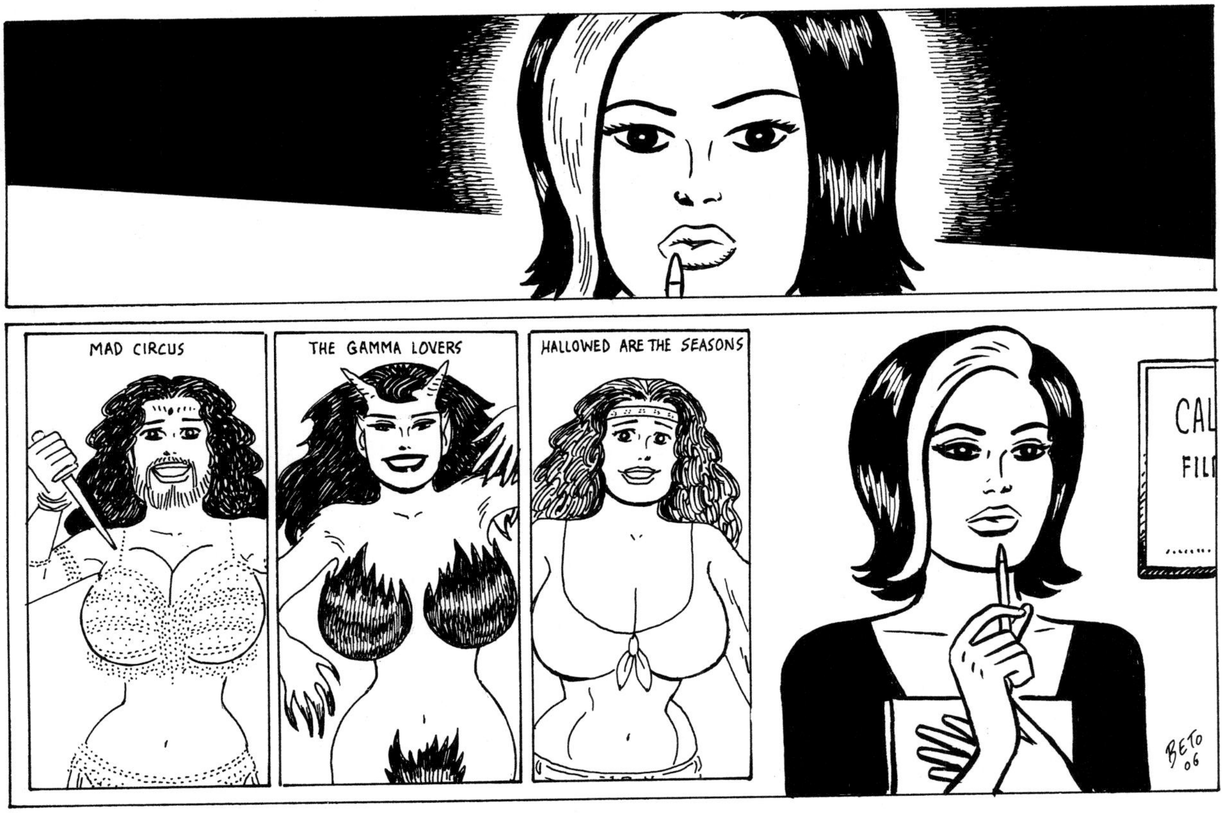
MAD CIRCUS
THE GAMMA LOVERS
HALLOWED ARE THE SEASONS
BETO 06

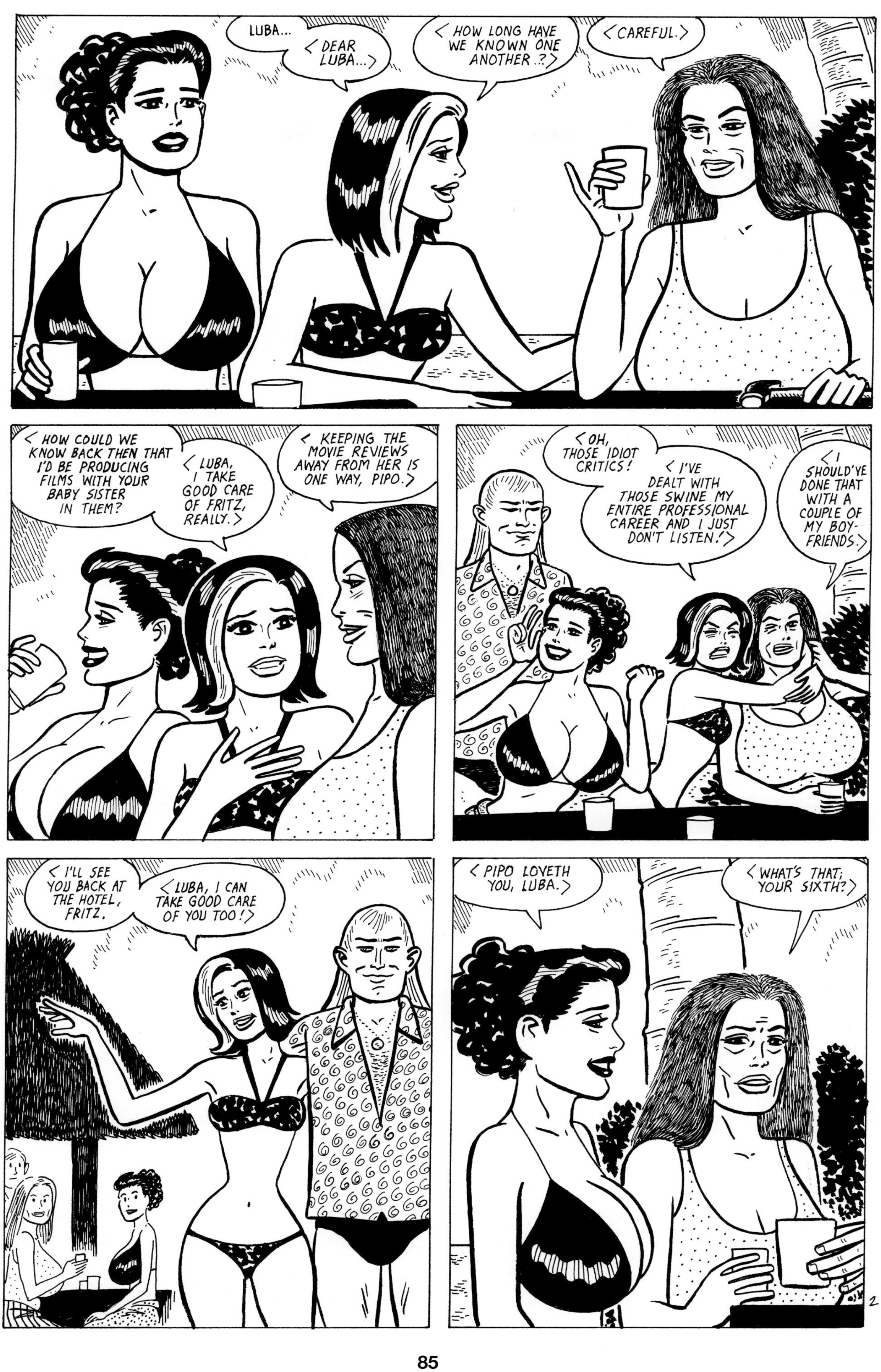
LUBA...
< DEAR LUBA...>
< HOW LONG HAVE WE KNOWN ONE ANOTHER..?>
< CAREFUL.>
< HOW COULD WE KNOW BACK THEN THAT I'D BE PRODUCING FILMS WITH YOUR BABY SISTER IN THEM?
< LUBA, I TAKE GOOD CARE OF FRITZ, REALLY.>
< KEEPING THE MOVIE REVIEWS AWAY FROM HER IS ONE WAY, PIPO.>
< OH, THOSE IDIOT CRITICS!
< I'VE DEALT WITH THOSE SWINE MY ENTIRE PROFESSIONAL CAREER AND I JUST DON'T LISTEN.>
< I SHOULD'VE DONE THAT WITH A COUPLE OF MY BOY-FRIENDS.>
< I'LL SEE YOU BACK AT THE HOTEL, FRITZ.
< LUBA, I CAN TAKE GOOD CARE OF YOU TOO!>
< PIPO LOVETH YOU, LUBA.>
< WHAT'S THAT; YOUR SIXTH?>

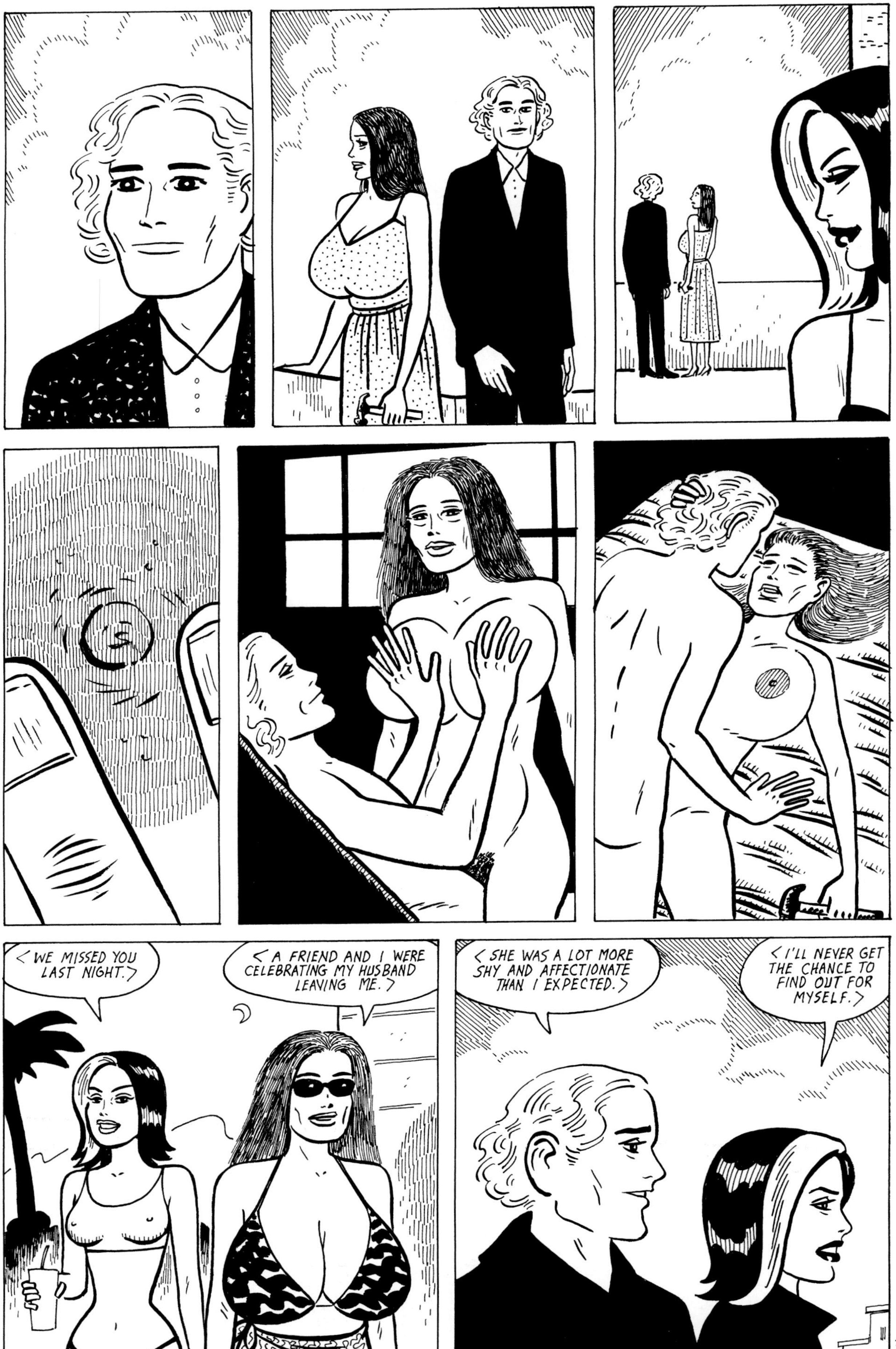

< WE MISSED YOU LAST NIGHT. >
< A FRIEND AND I WERE CELEBRATING MY HUSBAND LEAVING ME. >
< SHE WAS A LOT MORE SHY AND AFFECTIONATE THAN I EXPECTED. >
< I'LL NEVER GET THE CHANCE TO FIND OUT FOR MYSELF. >
3

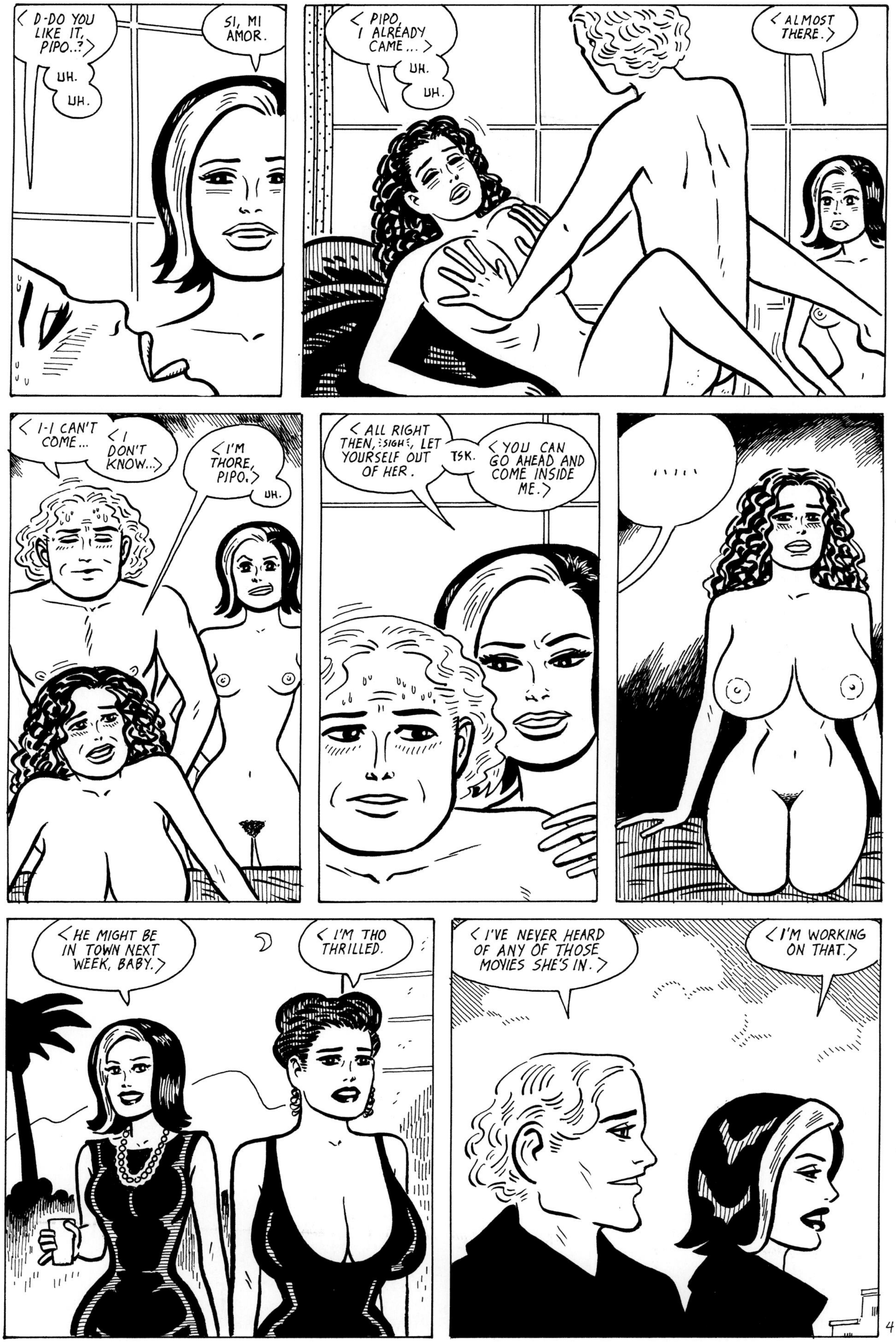

< D-DO YOU LIKE IT, PIPO..? >
UH.
UH.
SI, MI AMOR.
< PIPO, I ALREADY CAME... >
UH.
UH.
< ALMOST THERE. >
< I-I CAN'T COME...
< I DON'T KNOW... >
< I'M THORE, PIPO. >
UH.
< ALL RIGHT THEN, SIGH, LET YOURSELF OUT OF HER.
TSK.
< YOU CAN GO AHEAD AND COME INSIDE ME. >
. . . . .
< HE MIGHT BE IN TOWN NEXT WEEK, BABY. >
< I'M THO THRILLED.
< I'VE NEVER HEARD OF ANY OF THOSE MOVIES SHE'S IN. >
< I'M WORKING ON THAT. >
4

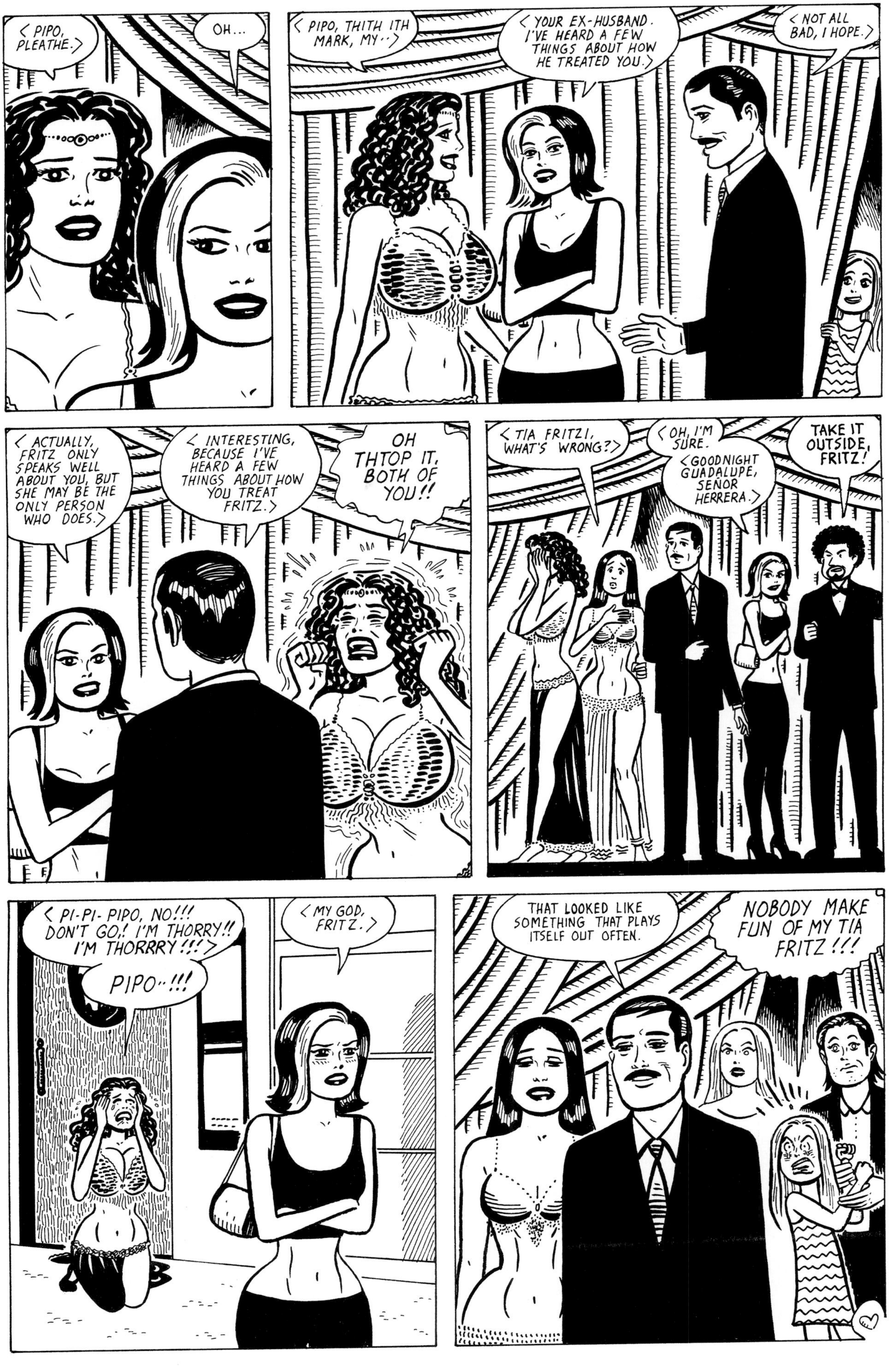

< PIPO, PLEATHE. >
OH...
< PIPO, THITH ITH MARK, MY.. >
< YOUR EX-HUSBAND. I'VE HEARD A FEW THINGS ABOUT HOW HE TREATED YOU. >
< NOT ALL BAD, I HOPE. >
< ACTUALLY, FRITZ ONLY SPEAKS WELL ABOUT YOU, BUT SHE MAY BE THE ONLY PERSON WHO DOES. >
< INTERESTING, BECAUSE I'VE HEARD A FEW THINGS ABOUT HOW YOU TREAT FRITZ. >
OH THTOP IT, BOTH OF YOU!!
< TIA FRITZI, WHAT'S WRONG? >
< OH, I'M SURE.
< GOODNIGHT GUADALUPE, SEÑOR HERRERA. >
TAKE IT OUTSIDE, FRITZ!
< PI-PI-PIPO, NO!!! DON'T GO!! I'M THORRY!! I'M THORRRY!!! >
PIPO..!!!
< MY GOD, FRITZ. >
THAT LOOKED LIKE SOMETHING THAT PLAYS ITSELF OUT OFTEN.
NOBODY MAKE FUN OF MY TIA FRITZ!!!

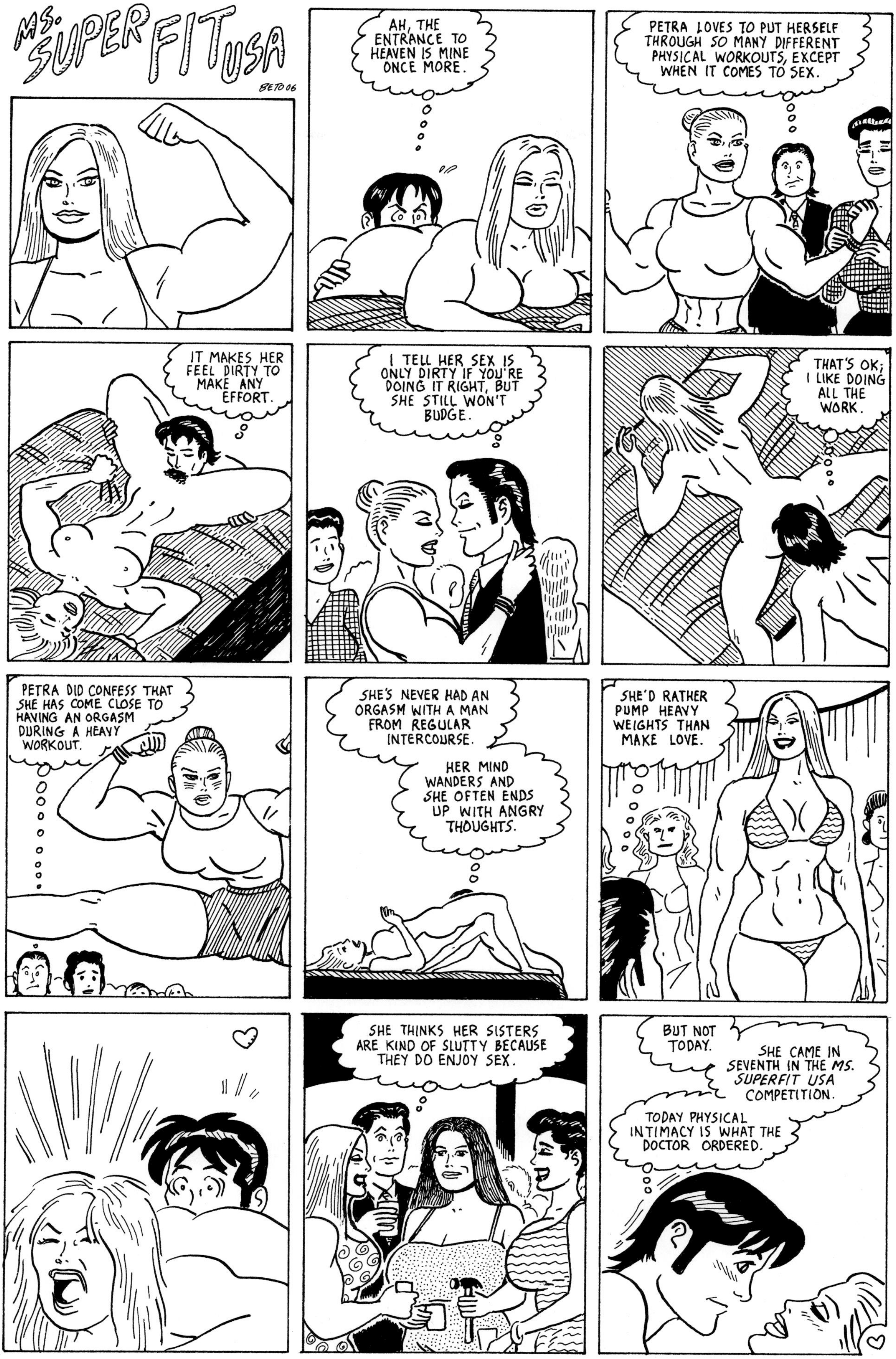
MS. SUPER FIT USA
BETO 06
AH, THE ENTRANCE TO HEAVEN IS MINE ONCE MORE.
PETRA LOVES TO PUT HERSELF THROUGH SO MANY DIFFERENT PHYSICAL WORKOUTS, EXCEPT WHEN IT COMES TO SEX.
IT MAKES HER FEEL DIRTY TO MAKE ANY EFFORT.
I TELL HER SEX IS ONLY DIRTY IF YOU'RE DOING IT RIGHT, BUT SHE STILL WON'T BUDGE.
THAT'S OK; I LIKE DOING ALL THE WORK.
PETRA DID CONFESS THAT SHE HAS COME CLOSE TO HAVING AN ORGASM DURING A HEAVY WORKOUT.
SHE'S NEVER HAD AN ORGASM WITH A MAN FROM REGULAR INTERCOURSE.
HER MIND WANDERS AND SHE OFTEN ENDS UP WITH ANGRY THOUGHTS.
SHE'D RATHER PUMP HEAVY WEIGHTS THAN MAKE LOVE.
SHE THINKS HER SISTERS ARE KIND OF SLUTTY BECAUSE THEY DO ENJOY SEX.
BUT NOT TODAY.
SHE CAME IN SEVENTH IN THE MS. SUPERFIT USA COMPETITION.
TODAY PHYSICAL INTIMACY IS WHAT THE DOCTOR ORDERED.

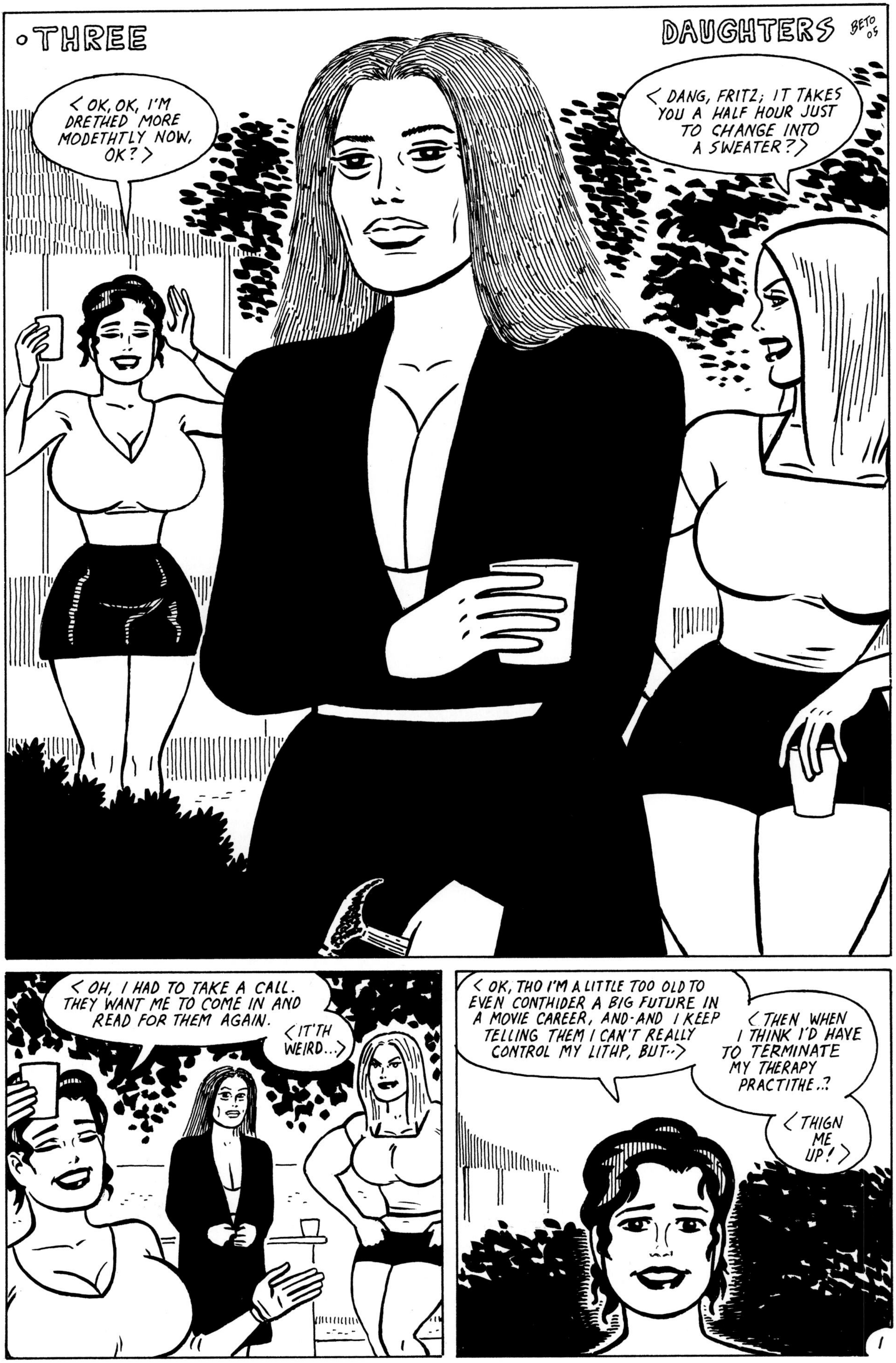
THREE DAUGHTERS
BETO 05
< OK, OK, I'M DRETHED MORE MODETHTLY NOW, OK? >
< DANG, FRITZ; IT TAKES YOU A HALF HOUR JUST TO CHANGE INTO A SWEATER? >
< OH, I HAD TO TAKE A CALL. THEY WANT ME TO COME IN AND READ FOR THEM AGAIN.
< IT'TH WEIRD...>
< OK, THO I'M A LITTLE TOO OLD TO EVEN CONTHIDER A BIG FUTURE IN A MOVIE CAREER, AND-AND I KEEP TELLING THEM I CAN'T REALLY CONTROL MY LITHP, BUT..>
< THEN WHEN I THINK I'D HAVE TO TERMINATE MY THERAPY PRACTITHE..?
< THIGN ME UP! >
1

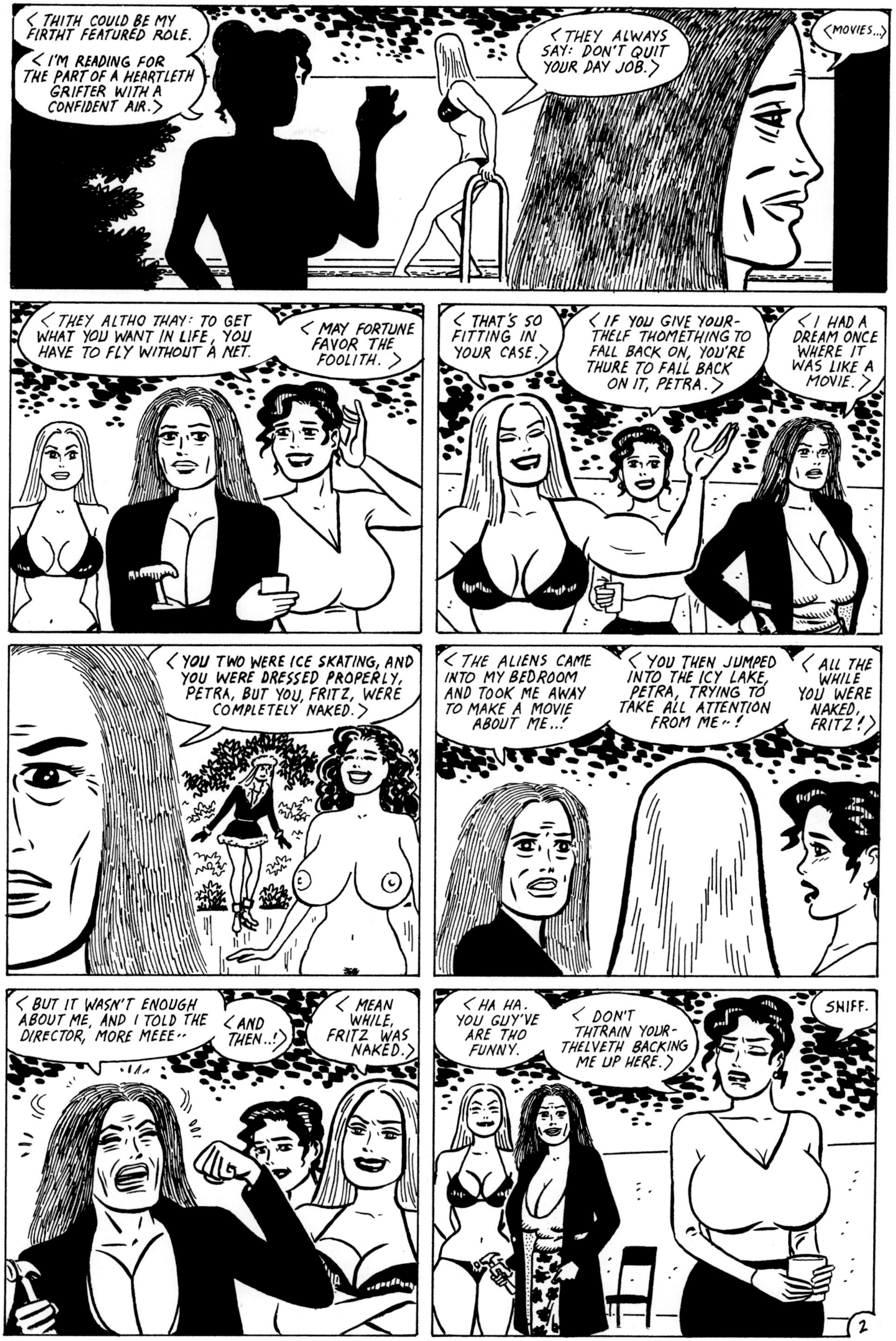
<THITH COULD BE MY FIRTHT FEATURED ROLE.
<I'M READING FOR THE PART OF A HEARTLETH GRIFTER WITH A CONFIDENT AIR.>
<THEY ALWAYS SAY: DON'T QUIT YOUR DAY JOB.>
<MOVIES...>
<THEY ALTHO THAY: TO GET WHAT YOU WANT IN LIFE, YOU HAVE TO FLY WITHOUT A NET.
<MAY FORTUNE FAVOR THE FOOLITH.>
<THAT'S SO FITTING IN YOUR CASE.>
<IF YOU GIVE YOURTHELF THOMETHING TO FALL BACK ON, YOU'RE THURE TO FALL BACK ON IT, PETRA.>
<I HAD A DREAM ONCE WHERE IT WAS LIKE A MOVIE.>
<YOU TWO WERE ICE SKATING, AND YOU WERE DRESSED PROPERLY, PETRA, BUT YOU, FRITZ, WERE COMPLETELY NAKED.>
<THE ALIENS CAME INTO MY BEDROOM AND TOOK ME AWAY TO MAKE A MOVIE ABOUT ME..!
<YOU THEN JUMPED INTO THE ICY LAKE, PETRA, TRYING TO TAKE ALL ATTENTION FROM ME..!
<ALL THE WHILE YOU WERE NAKED, FRITZ!>
<BUT IT WASN'T ENOUGH ABOUT ME, AND I TOLD THE DIRECTOR, MORE MEEE..
<AND THEN..!>
<MEANWHILE, FRITZ WAS NAKED.>
<HA HA. YOU GUY'VE ARE THO FUNNY.
<DON'T THTRAIN YOURTHELVETH BACKING ME UP HERE.>
SNIFF.
2

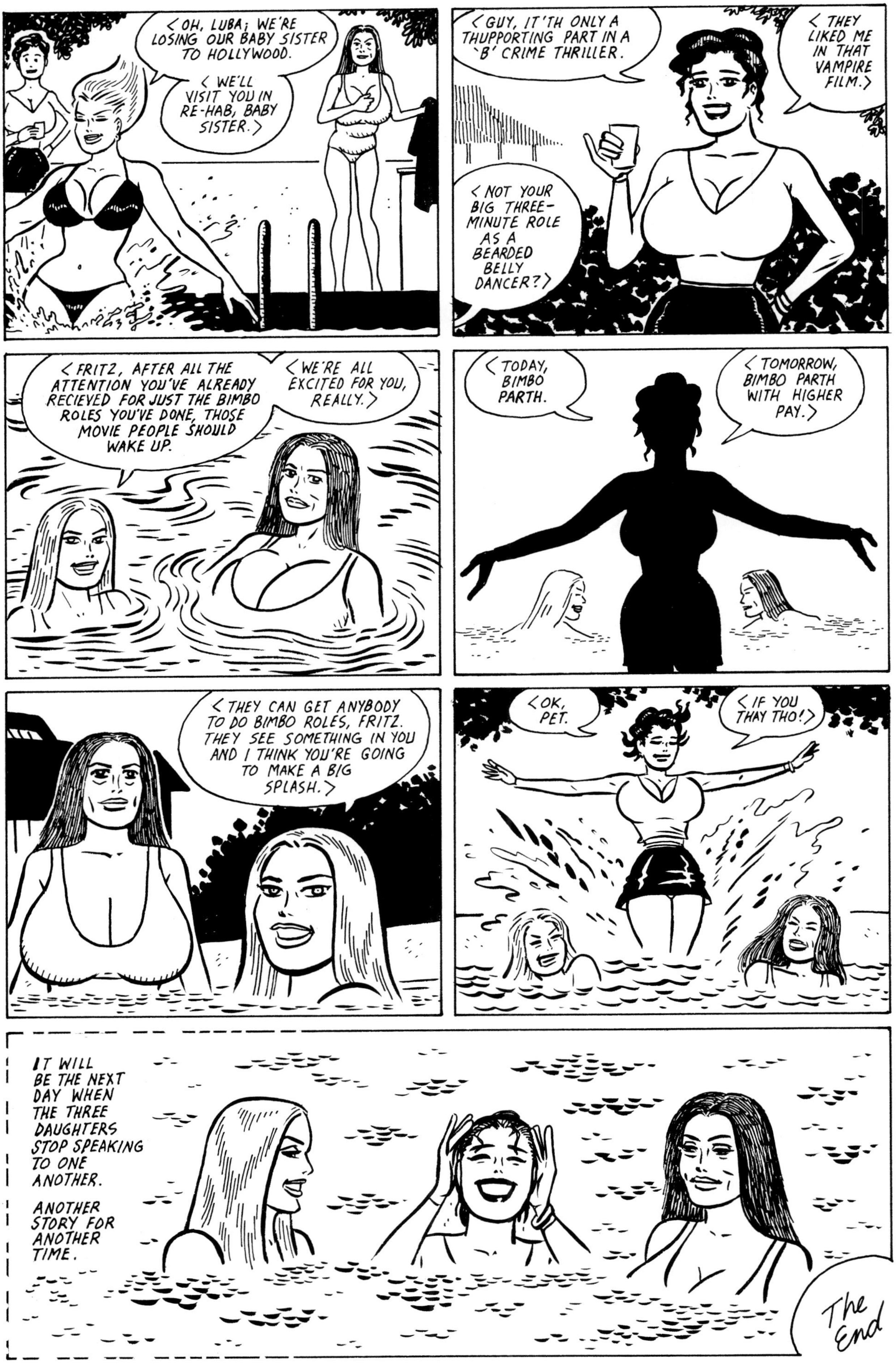
< OH, LUBA; WE'RE LOSING OUR BABY SISTER TO HOLLYWOOD.
< WE'LL VISIT YOU IN RE-HAB, BABY SISTER.>
< GUY, IT'TH ONLY A THUPPORTING PART IN A 'B' CRIME THRILLER.
< THEY LIKED ME IN THAT VAMPIRE FILM.>
< NOT YOUR BIG THREE-MINUTE ROLE AS A BEARDED BELLY DANCER?>
< FRITZ, AFTER ALL THE ATTENTION YOU'VE ALREADY RECIEVED FOR JUST THE BIMBO ROLES YOU'VE DONE, THOSE MOVIE PEOPLE SHOULD WAKE UP.
< WE'RE ALL EXCITED FOR YOU, REALLY.>
< TODAY, BIMBO PARTH.
< TOMORROW, BIMBO PARTH WITH HIGHER PAY.>
< THEY CAN GET ANYBODY TO DO BIMBO ROLES, FRITZ. THEY SEE SOMETHING IN YOU AND I THINK YOU'RE GOING TO MAKE A BIG SPLASH.>
< OK, PET.
< IF YOU THAY THO!>
IT WILL BE THE NEXT DAY WHEN THE THREE DAUGHTERS STOP SPEAKING TO ONE ANOTHER.
ANOTHER STORY FOR ANOTHER TIME.
The End

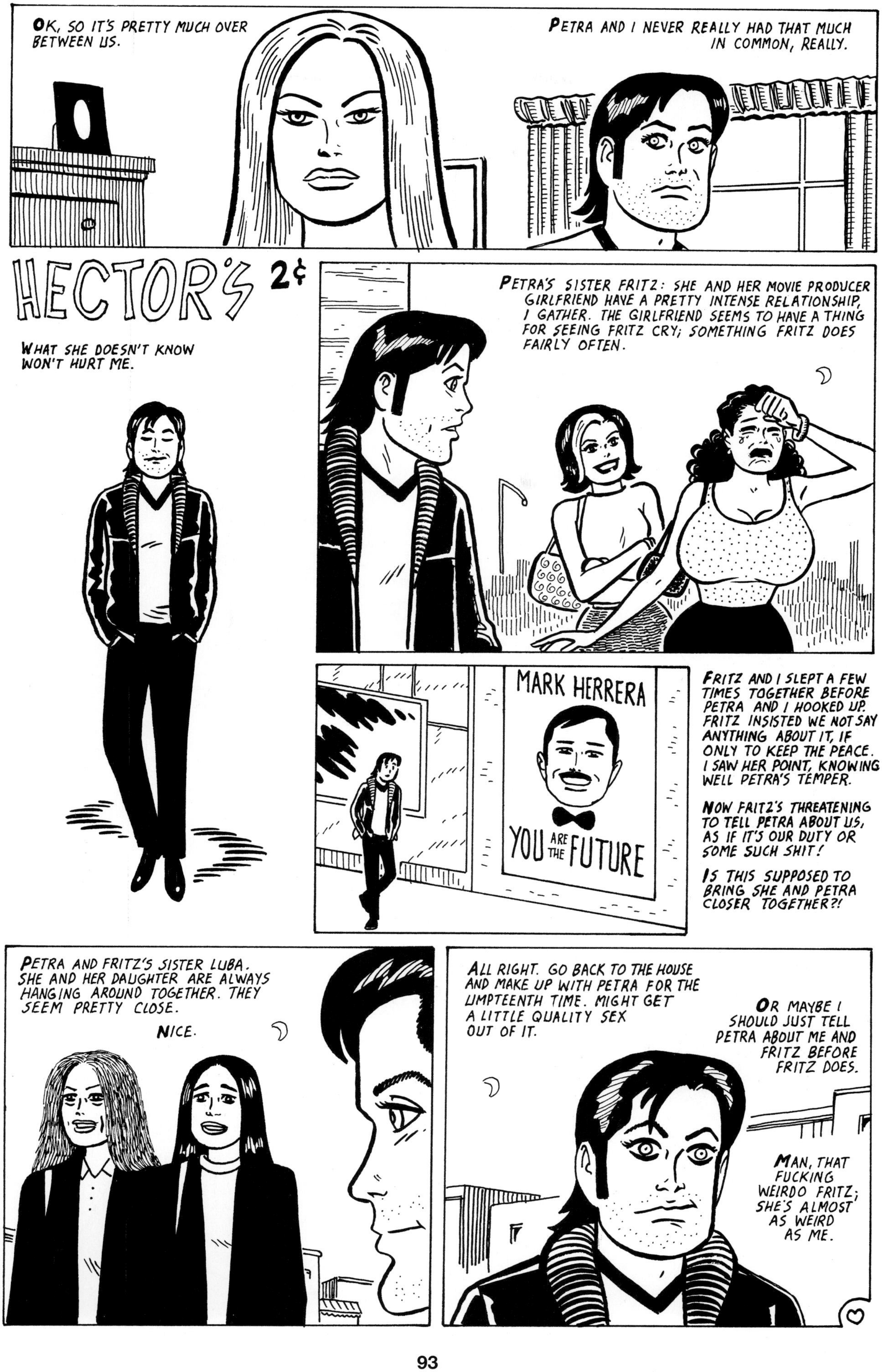
OK, SO IT'S PRETTY MUCH OVER BETWEEN US.
PETRA AND I NEVER REALLY HAD THAT MUCH IN COMMON, REALLY.
HECTOR'S 2¢
WHAT SHE DOESN'T KNOW WON'T HURT ME.
PETRA'S SISTER FRITZ: SHE AND HER MOVIE PRODUCER GIRLFRIEND HAVE A PRETTY INTENSE RELATIONSHIP, I GATHER. THE GIRLFRIEND SEEMS TO HAVE A THING FOR SEEING FRITZ CRY; SOMETHING FRITZ DOES FAIRLY OFTEN.
MARK HERRERA
YOU ARE THE FUTURE
FRITZ AND I SLEPT A FEW TIMES TOGETHER BEFORE PETRA AND I HOOKED UP. FRITZ INSISTED WE NOT SAY ANYTHING ABOUT IT, IF ONLY TO KEEP THE PEACE. I SAW HER POINT, KNOWING WELL PETRA'S TEMPER.
NOW FRITZ'S THREATENING TO TELL PETRA ABOUT US, AS IF IT'S OUR DUTY OR SOME SUCH SHIT!
IS THIS SUPPOSED TO BRING SHE AND PETRA CLOSER TOGETHER?!
PETRA AND FRITZ'S SISTER LUBA. SHE AND HER DAUGHTER ARE ALWAYS HANGING AROUND TOGETHER. THEY SEEM PRETTY CLOSE.
NICE.
ALL RIGHT. GO BACK TO THE HOUSE AND MAKE UP WITH PETRA FOR THE UMPTEENTH TIME. MIGHT GET A LITTLE QUALITY SEX OUT OF IT.
OR MAYBE I SHOULD JUST TELL PETRA ABOUT ME AND FRITZ BEFORE FRITZ DOES.
MAN, THAT FUCKING WEIRDO FRITZ; SHE'S ALMOST AS WEIRD AS ME.

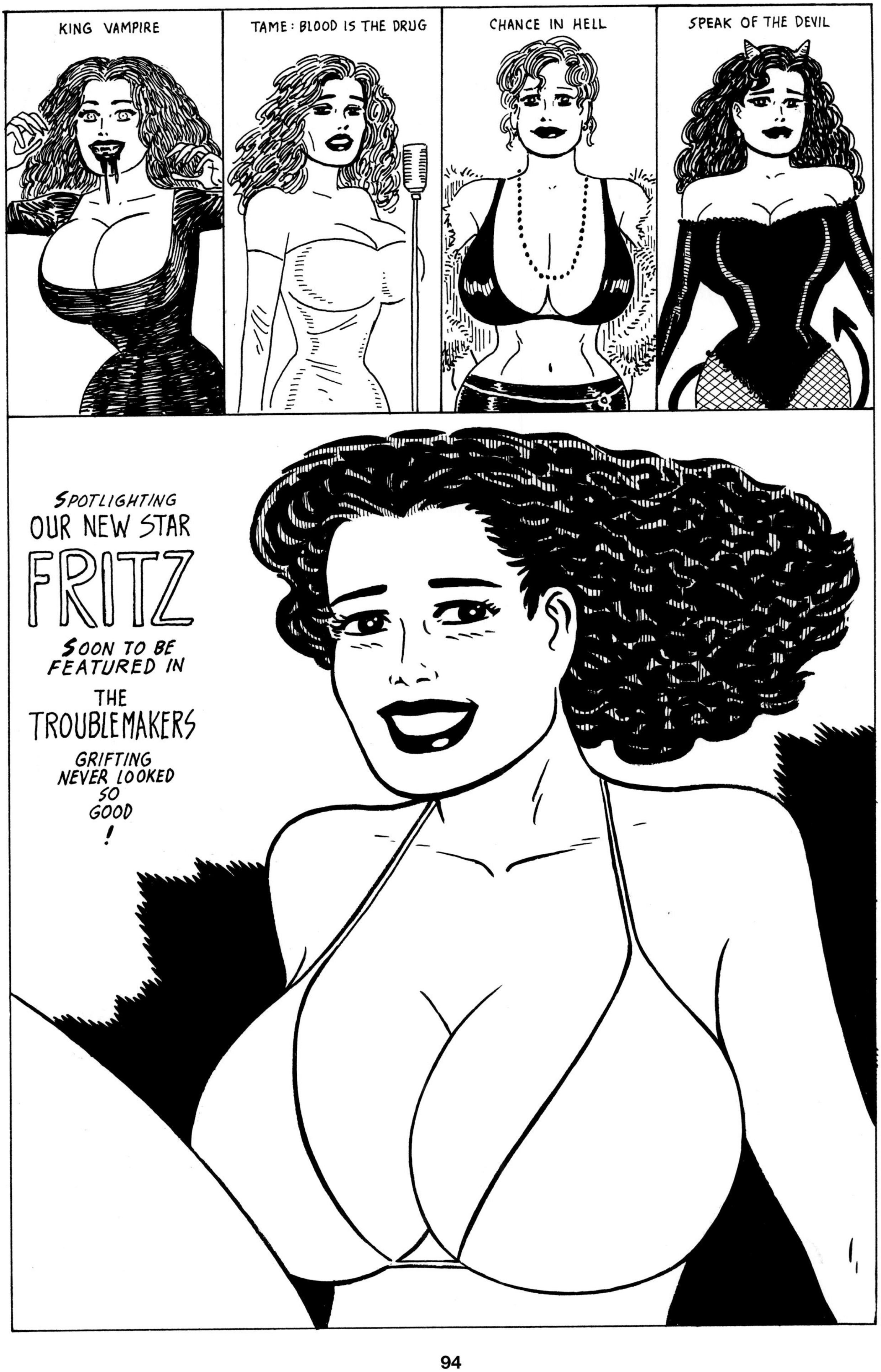
KING VAMPIRE
TAME: BLOOD IS THE DRUG
CHANCE IN HELL
SPEAK OF THE DEVIL
SPOTLIGHTING
OUR NEW STAR
FRITZ
SOON TO BE
FEATURED IN
THE
TROUBLEMAKERS
GRIFTING
NEVER LOOKED
SO
GOOD
!

DAY JOB

BETO
06

< I GUETH YOU BELIEVE IN ME A LITTLE. >

< OH, THE PROMOTIONAL? >

< WITH ALL I'VE GOT. >

< THEY'RE THAYING THAT A GIRL LIKE ME HATH NEVER MADE IT ATH A THTAR, THAT YOU'RE WATHTING YOUR TIME. >

< YOU DID QUIT, DIDN'T YOU? >

< YOUR THERAPY PRACTICE? >

< YEAH, BUT... >

< PIPO, I'M TOO OLD...>

< YOU'RE JUST RIGHT. >

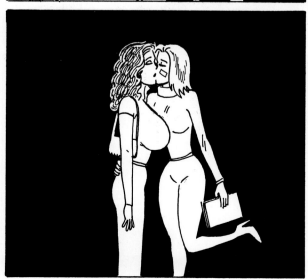

< I BELIEVE IN YOU, TOO. >

2

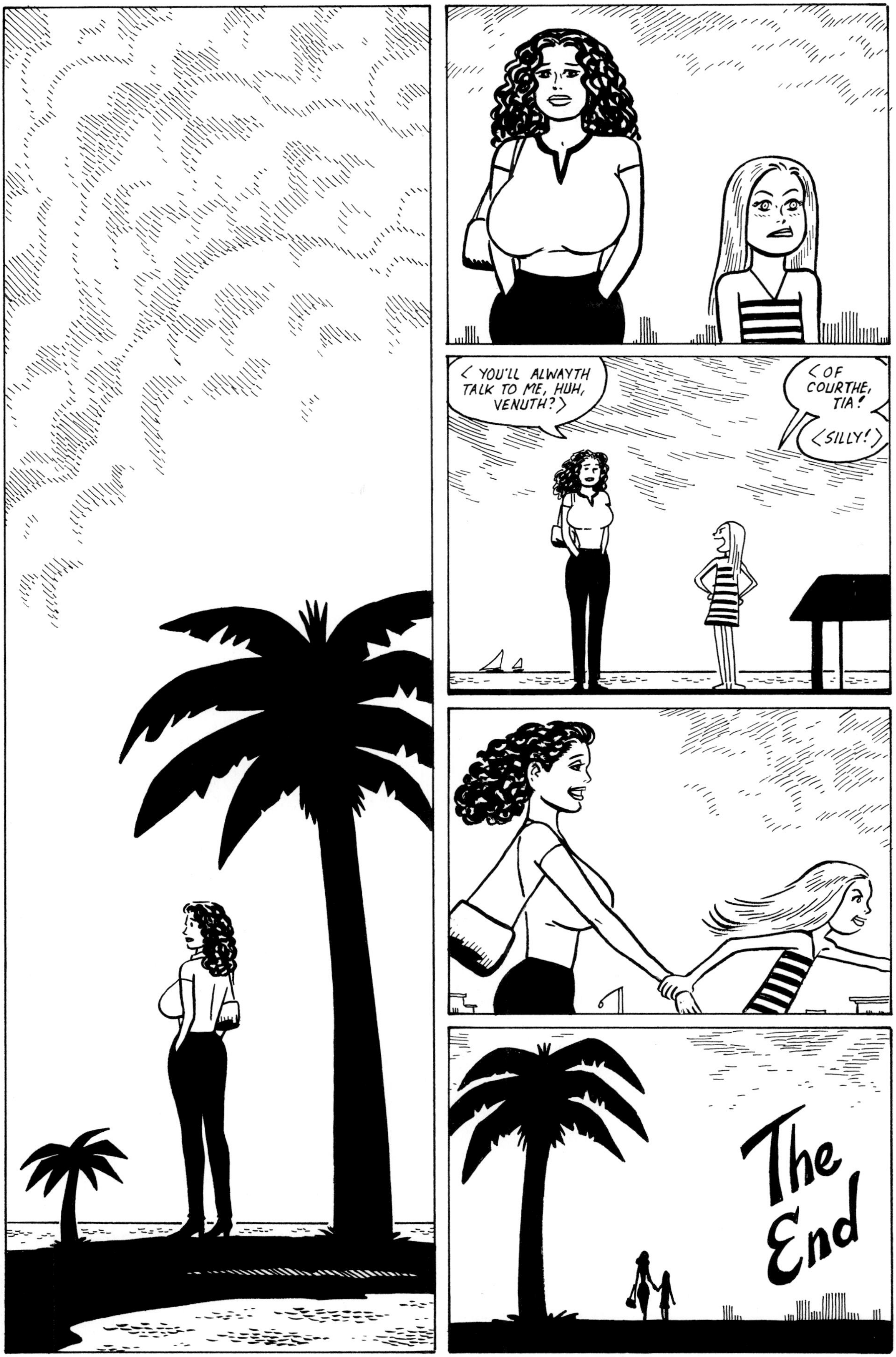
< YOU'LL ALWAYTH TALK TO ME, HUH, VENUTH? >
< OF COURTHE, TIA!
<SILLY!>
The End
3

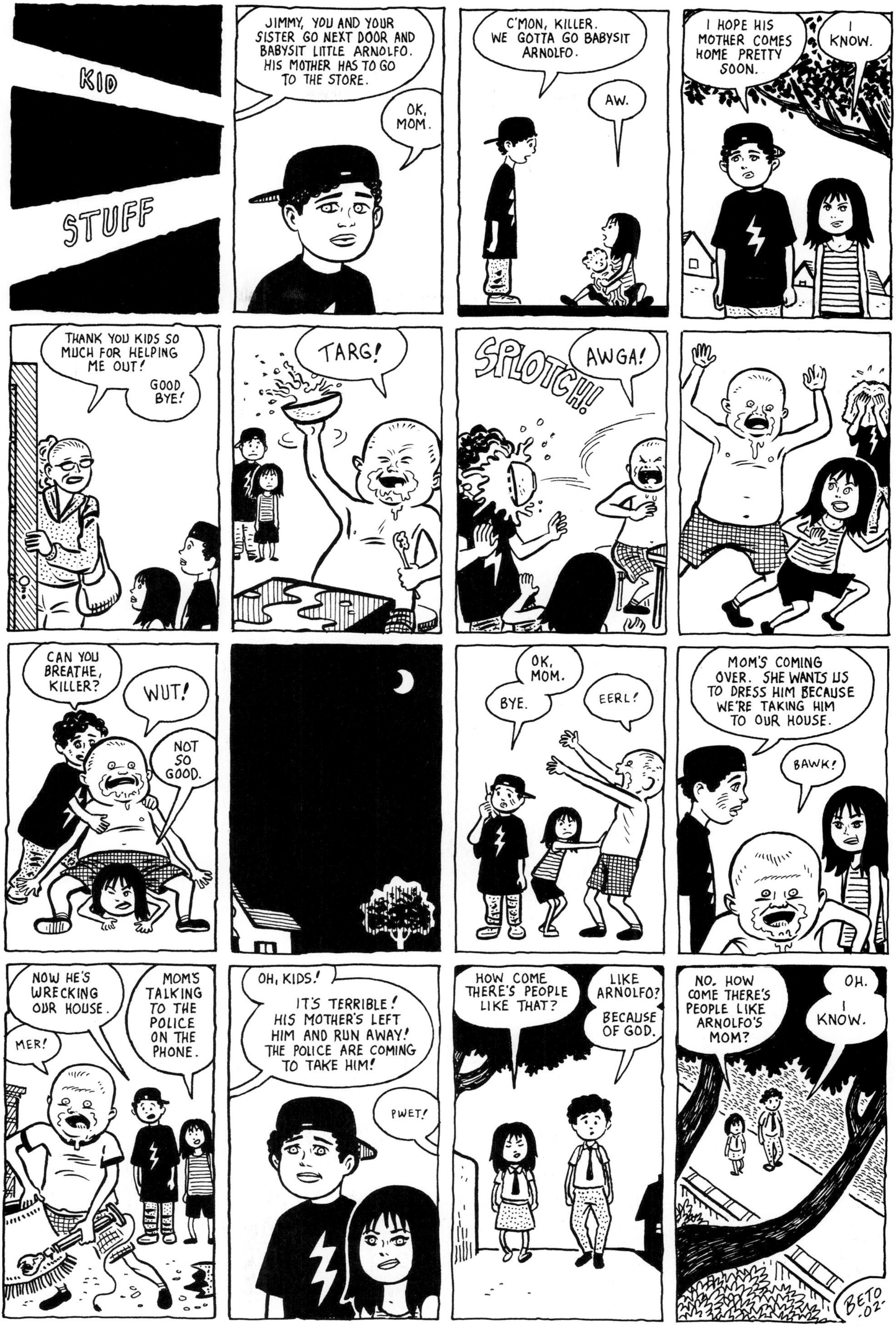
KID
STUFF
JIMMY, YOU AND YOUR SISTER GO NEXT DOOR AND BABYSIT LITTLE ARNOLFO. HIS MOTHER HAS TO GO TO THE STORE.
OK, MOM.
C'MON, KILLER. WE GOTTA GO BABYSIT ARNOLFO.
AW.
I HOPE HIS MOTHER COMES HOME PRETTY SOON.
I KNOW.
THANK YOU KIDS SO MUCH FOR HELPING ME OUT!
GOOD BYE!
TARG!
SPLOTCH!!
AWGA!
CAN YOU BREATHE, KILLER?
WUT!
NOT SO GOOD.
OK, MOM.
BYE.
EERL!
MOM'S COMING OVER. SHE WANTS US TO DRESS HIM BECAUSE WE'RE TAKING HIM TO OUR HOUSE.
BAWK!
NOW HE'S WRECKING OUR HOUSE.
MOM'S TALKING TO THE POLICE ON THE PHONE.
MER!
OH, KIDS!
IT'S TERRIBLE! HIS MOTHER'S LEFT HIM AND RUN AWAY! THE POLICE ARE COMING TO TAKE HIM!
PWET!
HOW COME THERE'S PEOPLE LIKE THAT?
LIKE ARNOLFO?
BECAUSE OF GOD.
NO. HOW COME THERE'S PEOPLE LIKE ARNOLFO'S MOM?
OH.
I KNOW.
BETO '02

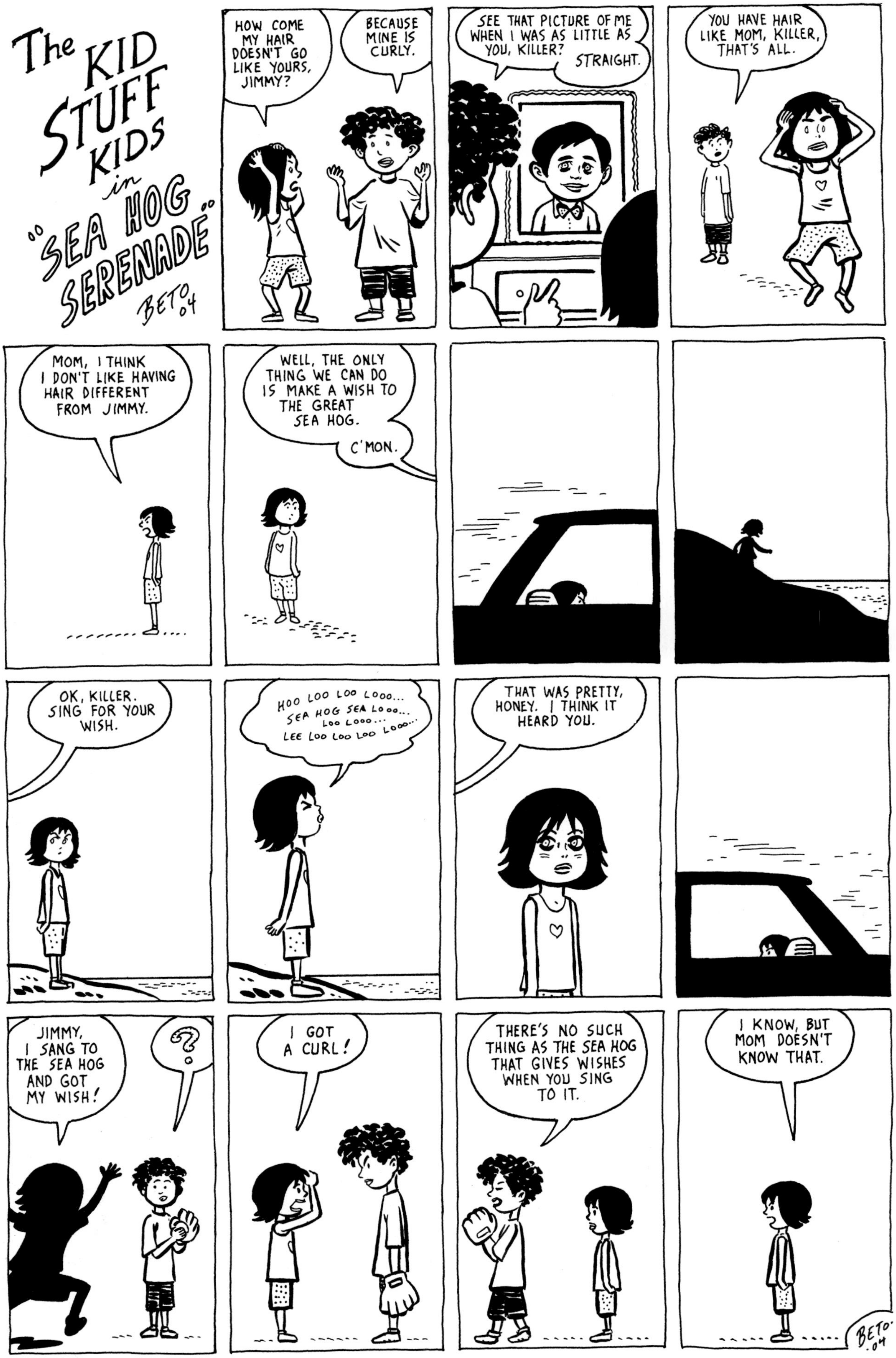

The KID STUFF KIDS in "SEA HOG SERENADE"
BETO 04
HOW COME MY HAIR DOESN'T GO LIKE YOURS, JIMMY?
BECAUSE MINE IS CURLY.
SEE THAT PICTURE OF ME WHEN I WAS AS LITTLE AS YOU, KILLER?
STRAIGHT.
YOU HAVE HAIR LIKE MOM, KILLER, THAT'S ALL.
MOM, I THINK I DON'T LIKE HAVING HAIR DIFFERENT FROM JIMMY.
WELL, THE ONLY THING WE CAN DO IS MAKE A WISH TO THE GREAT SEA HOG.
C'MON.
OK, KILLER. SING FOR YOUR WISH.
HOO LOO LOO LOOO... SEA HOG SEA LOOO... LOO LOOO... LEE LOO LOO LOO LOOO...
THAT WAS PRETTY, HONEY. I THINK IT HEARD YOU.
JIMMY, I SANG TO THE SEA HOG AND GOT MY WISH!
?
I GOT A CURL!
THERE'S NO SUCH THING AS THE SEA HOG THAT GIVES WISHES WHEN YOU SING TO IT.
I KNOW, BUT MOM DOESN'T KNOW THAT.
BETO. '04

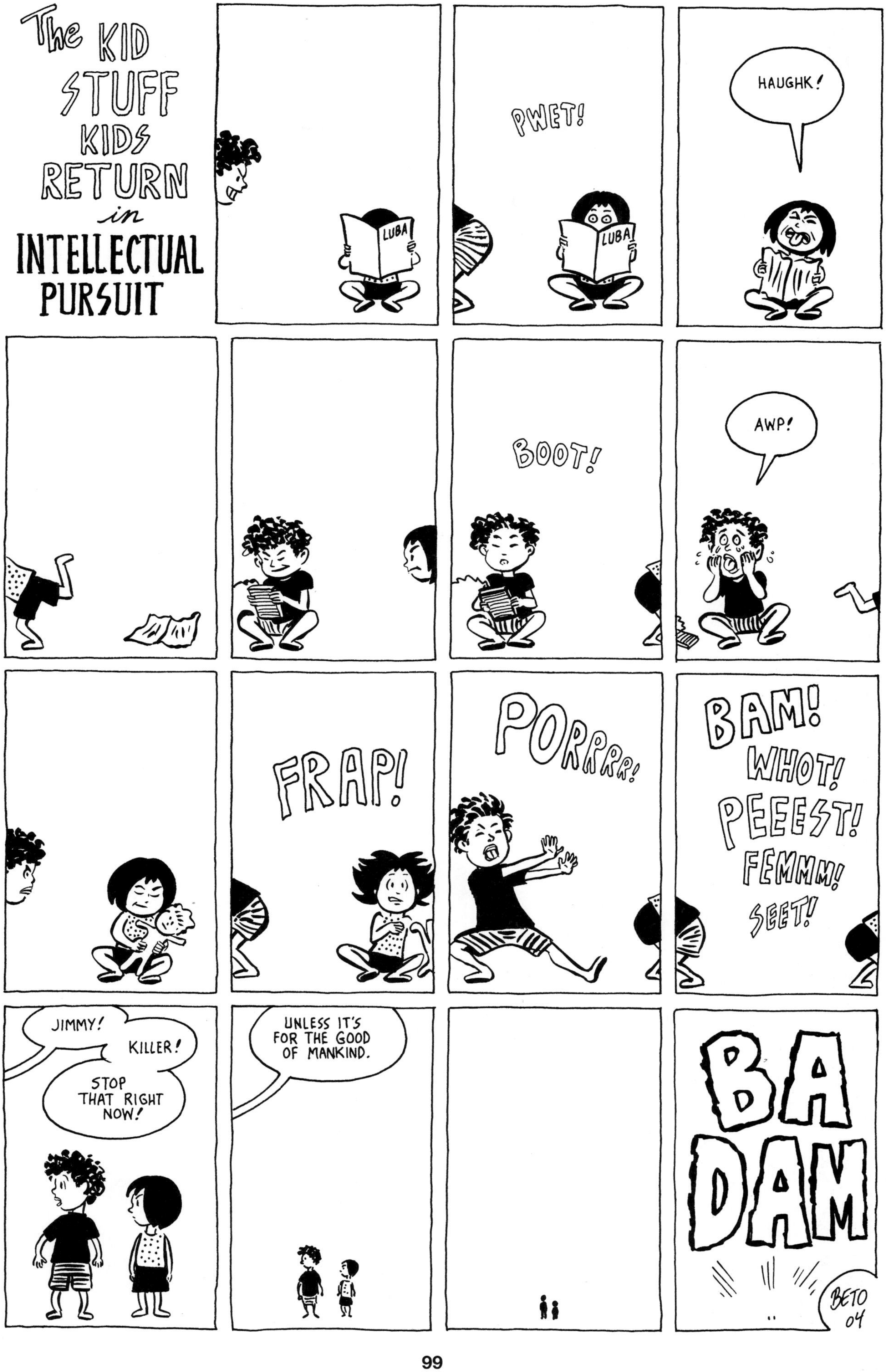
The KID STUFF KIDS RETURN in INTELLECTUAL PURSUIT
LUBA
PWET!
LUBA
HAUGHK!
BOOT!
AWP!
FRAP!
PORRRRR!
BAM!
WHOT!
PEEEST!
FEMMM!
SEET!
JIMMY!
KILLER!
STOP THAT RIGHT NOW!
UNLESS IT'S FOR THE GOOD OF MANKIND.
BA DAM
BETO 04

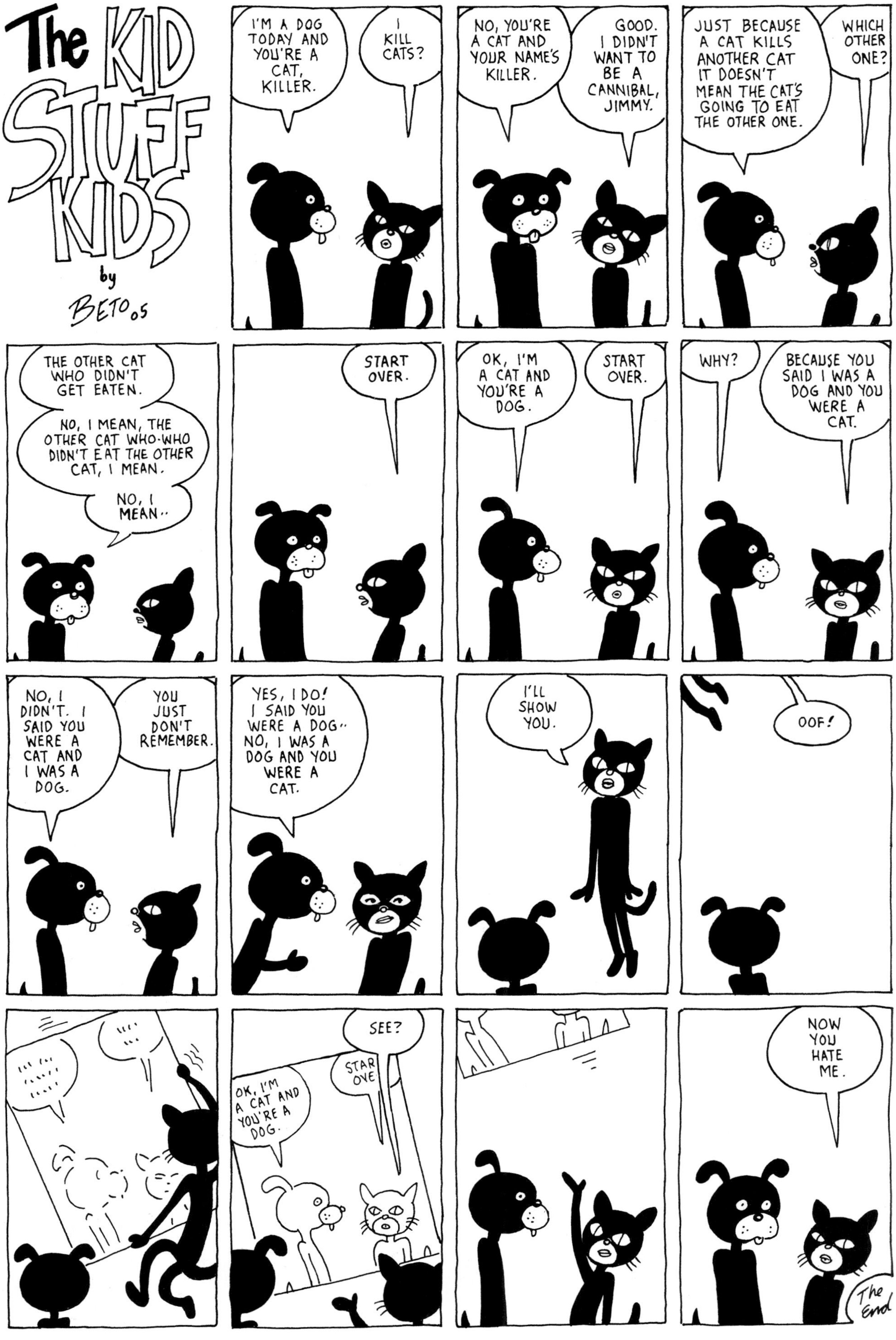

The KID STUFF KIDS
by
BETO 05
I'M A DOG TODAY AND YOU'RE A CAT, KILLER.
I KILL CATS?
NO, YOU'RE A CAT AND YOUR NAME'S KILLER.
GOOD. I DIDN'T WANT TO BE A CANNIBAL, JIMMY.
JUST BECAUSE A CAT KILLS ANOTHER CAT IT DOESN'T MEAN THE CAT'S GOING TO EAT THE OTHER ONE.
WHICH OTHER ONE?
THE OTHER CAT WHO DIDN'T GET EATEN.
NO, I MEAN, THE OTHER CAT WHO-WHO DIDN'T EAT THE OTHER CAT, I MEAN.
NO, I MEAN..
START OVER.
OK, I'M A CAT AND YOU'RE A DOG.
START OVER.
WHY?
BECAUSE YOU SAID I WAS A DOG AND YOU WERE A CAT.
NO, I DIDN'T. I SAID YOU WERE A CAT AND I WAS A DOG.
YOU JUST DON'T REMEMBER.
YES, I DO! I SAID YOU WERE A DOG.. NO, I WAS A DOG AND YOU WERE A CAT.
I'LL SHOW YOU.
OOF!
SEE?
OK, I'M A CAT AND YOU'RE A DOG.
STAR OVE
NOW YOU HATE ME.
The End

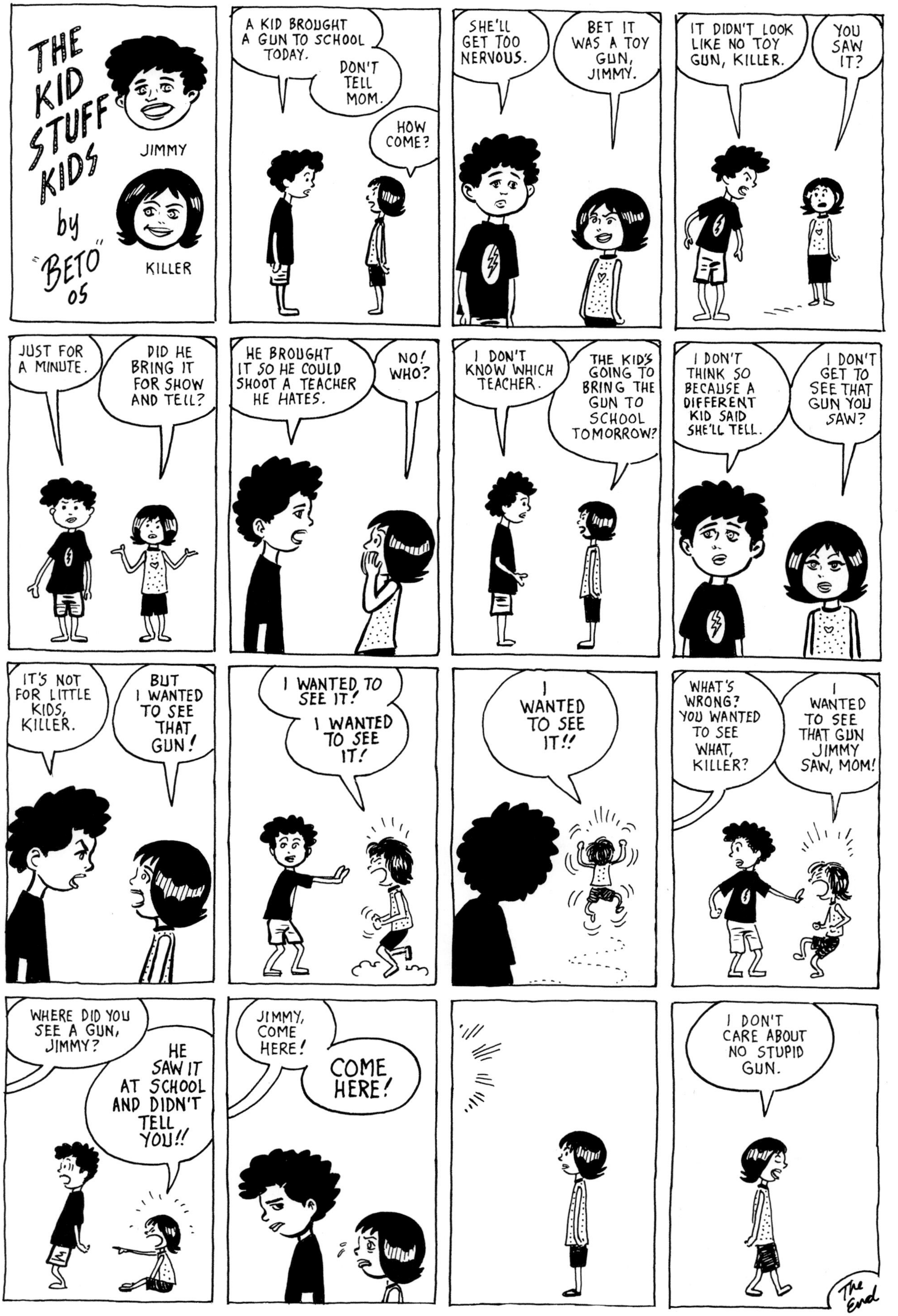
THE KID STUFF KIDS
by "BETO" 05
JIMMY
KILLER
A KID BROUGHT A GUN TO SCHOOL TODAY.
DON'T TELL MOM.
HOW COME?
SHE'LL GET TOO NERVOUS.
BET IT WAS A TOY GUN, JIMMY.
IT DIDN'T LOOK LIKE NO TOY GUN, KILLER.
YOU SAW IT?
JUST FOR A MINUTE.
DID HE BRING IT FOR SHOW AND TELL?
HE BROUGHT IT SO HE COULD SHOOT A TEACHER HE HATES.
NO! WHO?
I DON'T KNOW WHICH TEACHER.
THE KID'S GOING TO BRING THE GUN TO SCHOOL TOMORROW?
I DON'T THINK SO BECAUSE A DIFFERENT KID SAID SHE'LL TELL.
I DON'T GET TO SEE THAT GUN YOU SAW?
IT'S NOT FOR LITTLE KIDS, KILLER.
BUT I WANTED TO SEE THAT GUN!
I WANTED TO SEE IT!
I WANTED TO SEE IT!
I WANTED TO SEE IT!!
WHAT'S WRONG? YOU WANTED TO SEE WHAT, KILLER?
I WANTED TO SEE THAT GUN JIMMY SAW, MOM!
WHERE DID YOU SEE A GUN, JIMMY?
HE SAW IT AT SCHOOL AND DIDN'T TELL YOU!!
JIMMY, COME HERE!
COME HERE!
I DON'T CARE ABOUT NO STUPID GUN.
The End

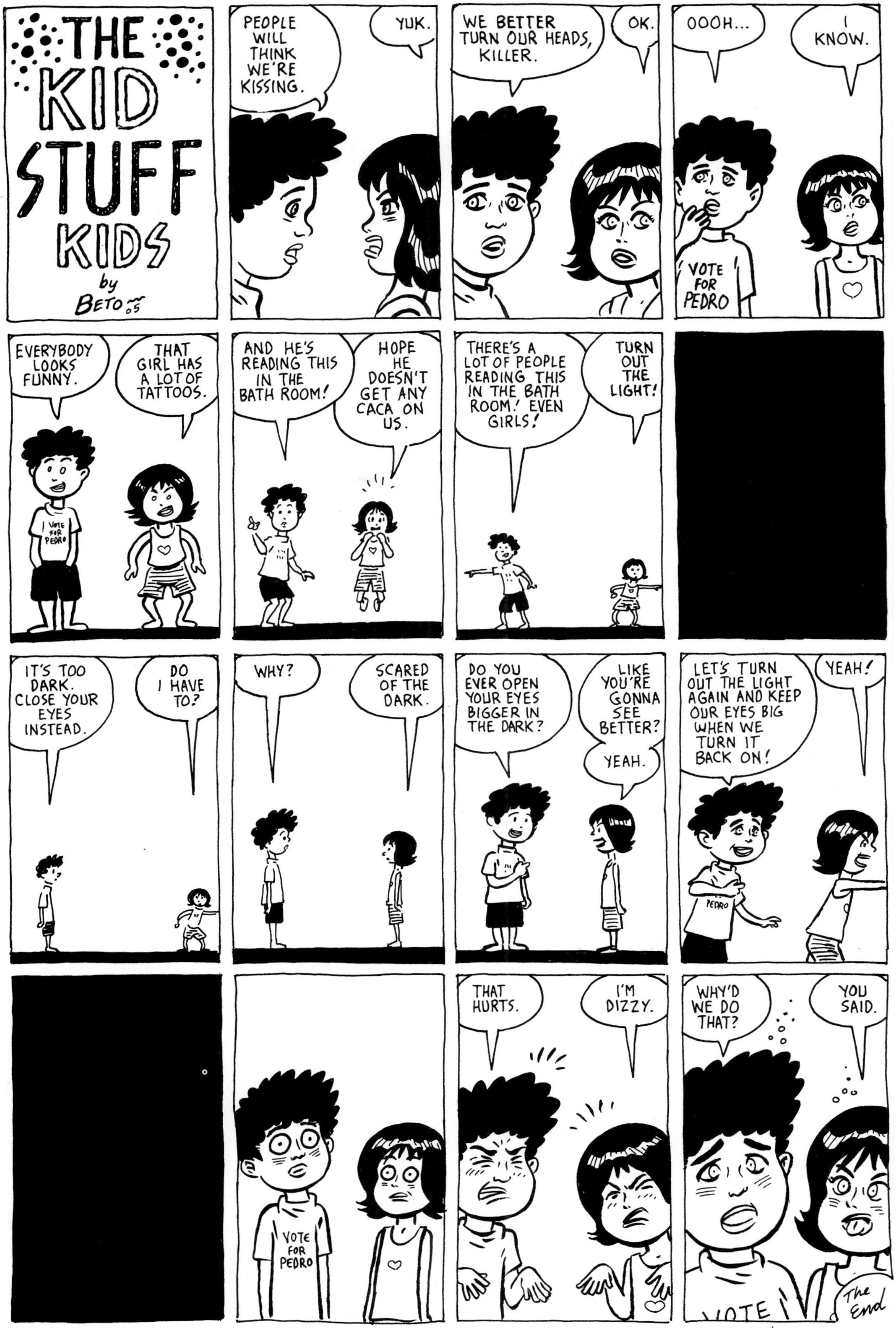
THE KID STUFF KIDS
by BETO 05
PEOPLE WILL THINK WE'RE KISSING.
YUK.
WE BETTER TURN OUR HEADS, KILLER.
OK.
OOOH...
I KNOW.
VOTE FOR PEDRO
EVERYBODY LOOKS FUNNY.
THAT GIRL HAS A LOT OF TATTOOS.
VOTE FOR PEDRO
AND HE'S READING THIS IN THE BATH ROOM!
HOPE HE DOESN'T GET ANY CACA ON US.
THERE'S A LOT OF PEOPLE READING THIS IN THE BATH ROOM! EVEN GIRLS!
TURN OUT THE LIGHT!
IT'S TOO DARK. CLOSE YOUR EYES INSTEAD.
DO I HAVE TO?
WHY?
SCARED OF THE DARK.
DO YOU EVER OPEN YOUR EYES BIGGER IN THE DARK?
LIKE YOU'RE GONNA SEE BETTER?
YEAH.
LET'S TURN OUT THE LIGHT AGAIN AND KEEP OUR EYES BIG WHEN WE TURN IT BACK ON!
YEAH!
PEDRO
VOTE FOR PEDRO
THAT HURTS.
I'M DIZZY.
WHY'D WE DO THAT?
YOU SAID.
VOTE
The End

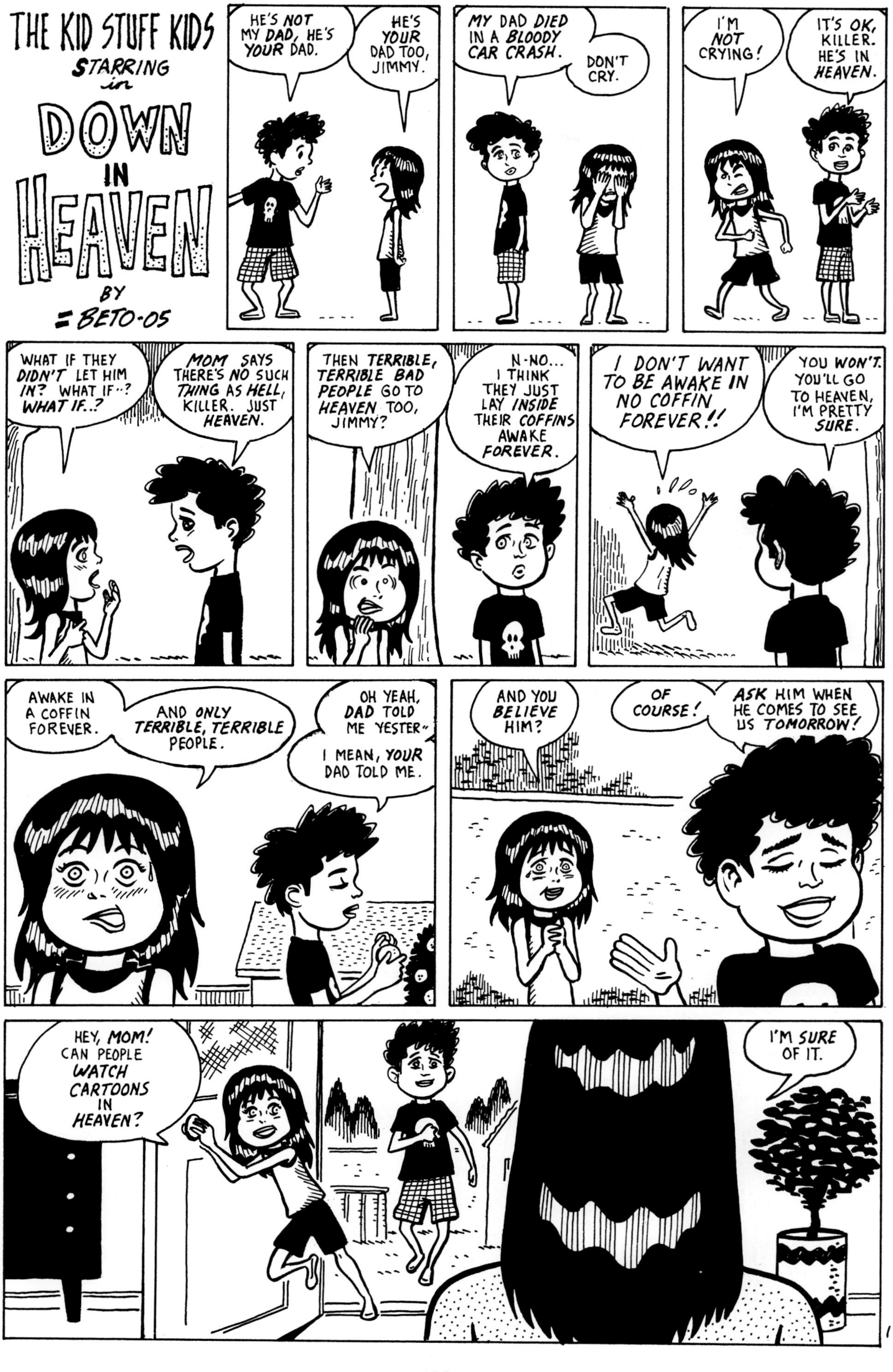
THE KID STUFF KIDS
STARRING in
DOWN IN HEAVEN
BY BETO·05
HE'S NOT MY DAD, HE'S YOUR DAD.
HE'S YOUR DAD TOO, JIMMY.
MY DAD DIED IN A BLOODY CAR CRASH.
DON'T CRY.
I'M NOT CRYING!
IT'S OK, KILLER. HE'S IN HEAVEN.
WHAT IF THEY DIDN'T LET HIM IN? WHAT IF..? WHAT IF..?
MOM SAYS THERE'S NO SUCH THING AS HELL, KILLER. JUST HEAVEN.
THEN TERRIBLE, TERRIBLE BAD PEOPLE GO TO HEAVEN TOO, JIMMY?
N-NO... I THINK THEY JUST LAY INSIDE THEIR COFFINS AWAKE FOREVER.
I DON'T WANT TO BE AWAKE IN NO COFFIN FOREVER!!
YOU WON'T. YOU'LL GO TO HEAVEN, I'M PRETTY SURE.
AWAKE IN A COFFIN FOREVER.
AND ONLY TERRIBLE, TERRIBLE PEOPLE.
OH YEAH, DAD TOLD ME YESTER--
I MEAN, YOUR DAD TOLD ME.
AND YOU BELIEVE HIM?
OF COURSE!
ASK HIM WHEN HE COMES TO SEE US TOMORROW!
HEY, MOM! CAN PEOPLE WATCH CARTOONS IN HEAVEN?
I'M SURE OF IT.

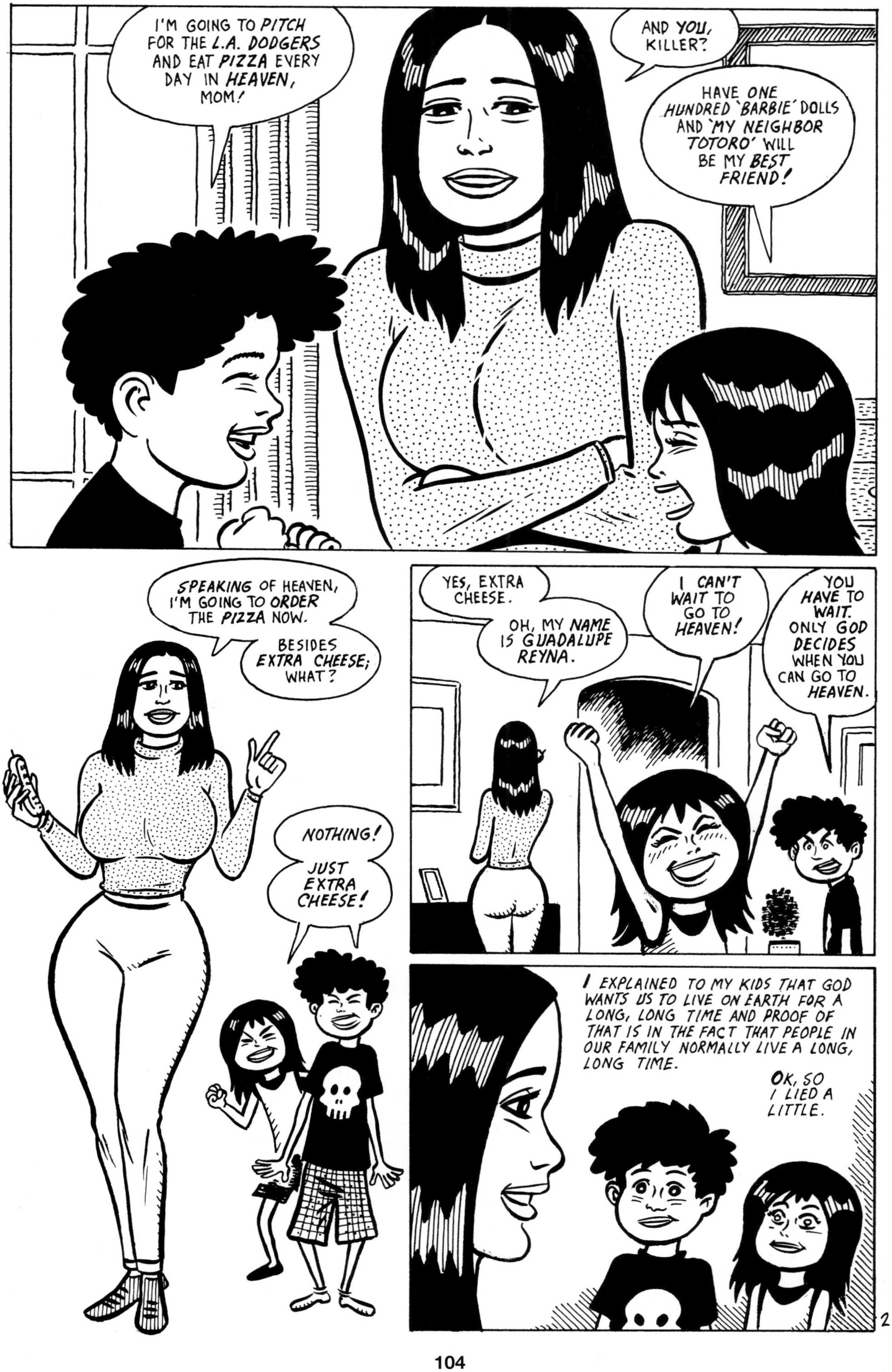
I'M GOING TO PITCH FOR THE L.A. DODGERS AND EAT PIZZA EVERY DAY IN HEAVEN, MOM!
AND YOU, KILLER?
HAVE ONE HUNDRED `BARBIE' DOLLS AND `MY NEIGHBOR TOTORO' WILL BE MY BEST FRIEND!
SPEAKING OF HEAVEN, I'M GOING TO ORDER THE PIZZA NOW.
BESIDES EXTRA CHEESE; WHAT?
NOTHING!
JUST EXTRA CHEESE!
YES, EXTRA CHEESE.
OH, MY NAME IS GUADALUPE REYNA.
I CAN'T WAIT TO GO TO HEAVEN!
YOU HAVE TO WAIT. ONLY GOD DECIDES WHEN YOU CAN GO TO HEAVEN.
I EXPLAINED TO MY KIDS THAT GOD WANTS US TO LIVE ON EARTH FOR A LONG, LONG TIME AND PROOF OF THAT IS IN THE FACT THAT PEOPLE IN OUR FAMILY NORMALLY LIVE A LONG, LONG TIME.
OK, SO I LIED A LITTLE.
2

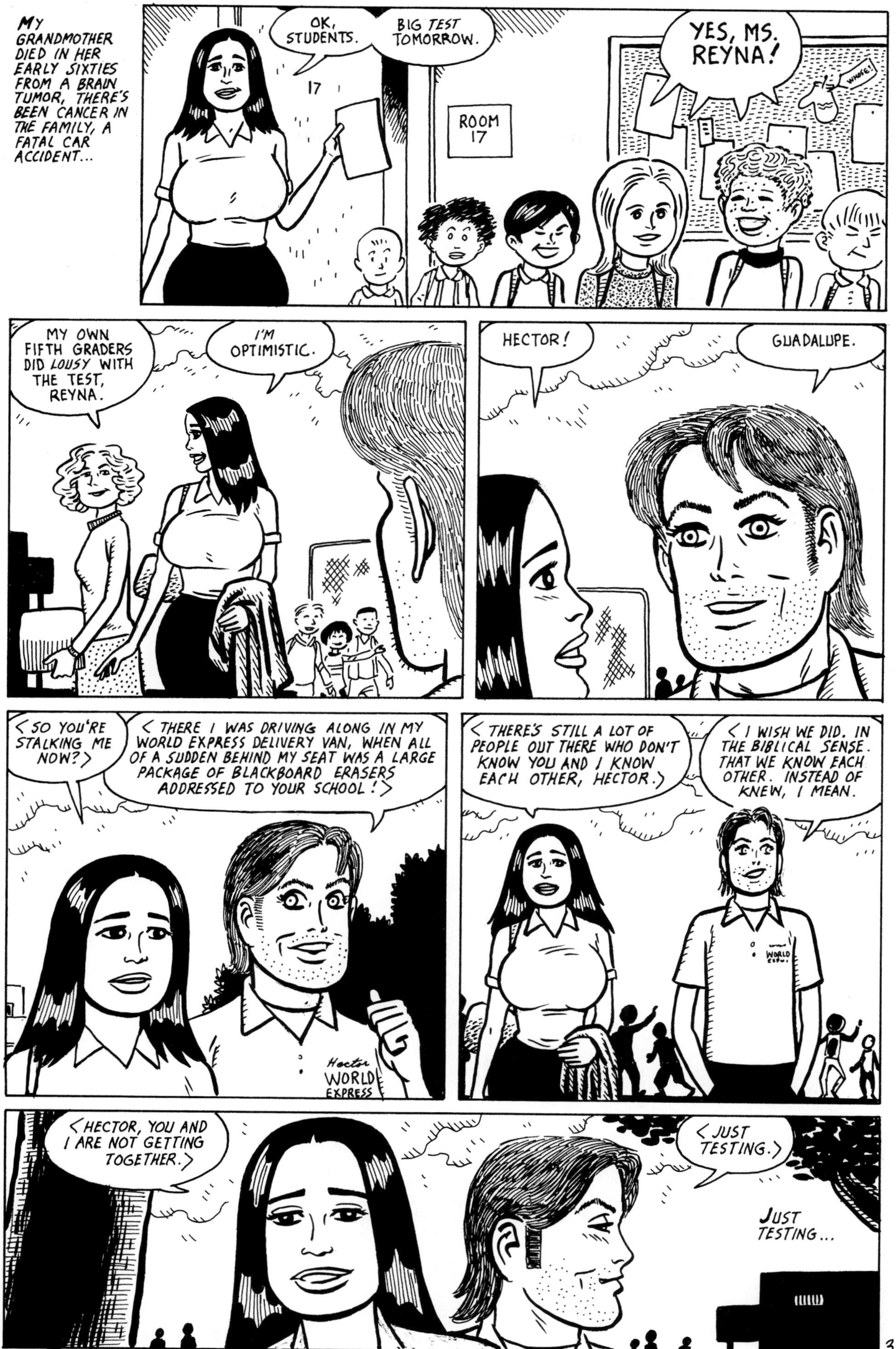
MY GRANDMOTHER DIED IN HER EARLY SIXTIES FROM A BRAIN TUMOR, THERE'S BEEN CANCER IN THE FAMILY, A FATAL CAR ACCIDENT...
OK, STUDENTS.
BIG *TEST* TOMORROW.
17
ROOM 17
YES, MS. REYNA!
WHOSE!
MY OWN FIFTH GRADERS DID *LOUSY* WITH THE TEST, REYNA.
I'M OPTIMISTIC.
HECTOR!
GUADALUPE.
<SO YOU'RE STALKING ME NOW?>
<THERE I WAS DRIVING ALONG IN MY WORLD EXPRESS DELIVERY VAN, WHEN ALL OF A SUDDEN BEHIND MY SEAT WAS A LARGE PACKAGE OF BLACKBOARD ERASERS ADDRESSED TO YOUR SCHOOL!>
Hector WORLD EXPRESS
<THERE'S STILL A LOT OF PEOPLE OUT THERE WHO DON'T KNOW YOU AND I KNOW EACH OTHER, HECTOR.>
<I WISH WE DID. IN THE BIBLICAL SENSE. THAT WE KNOW EACH OTHER. INSTEAD OF KNEW, I MEAN.
<HECTOR, YOU AND I ARE NOT GETTING TOGETHER.>
<JUST TESTING.>
JUST TESTING...
3
<SPANISH>

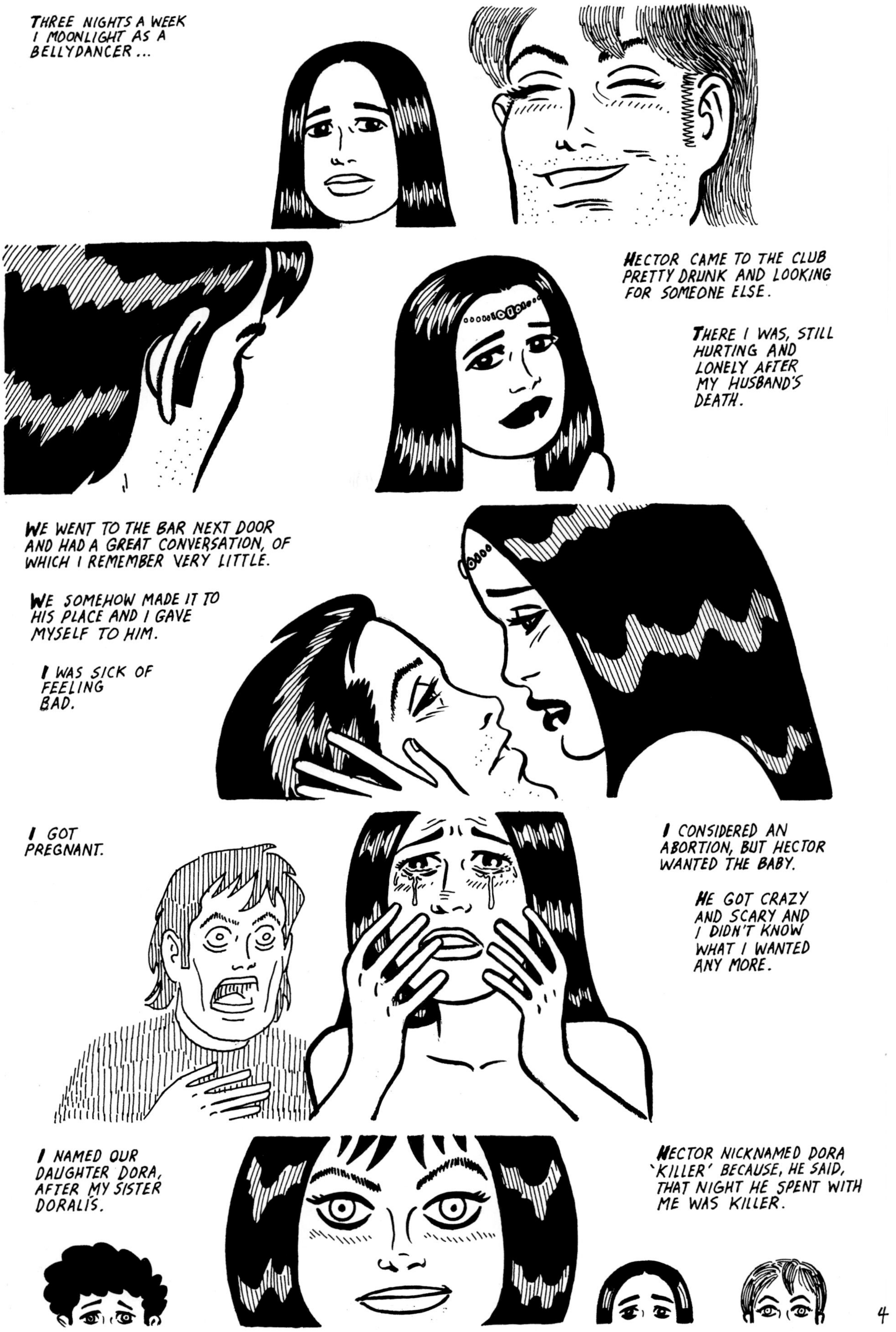
THREE NIGHTS A WEEK I MOONLIGHT AS A BELLYDANCER...
HECTOR CAME TO THE CLUB PRETTY DRUNK AND LOOKING FOR SOMEONE ELSE.
THERE I WAS, STILL HURTING AND LONELY AFTER MY HUSBAND'S DEATH.
WE WENT TO THE BAR NEXT DOOR AND HAD A GREAT CONVERSATION, OF WHICH I REMEMBER VERY LITTLE.
WE SOMEHOW MADE IT TO HIS PLACE AND I GAVE MYSELF TO HIM.
I WAS SICK OF FEELING BAD.
I GOT PREGNANT.
I CONSIDERED AN ABORTION, BUT HECTOR WANTED THE BABY.
HE GOT CRAZY AND SCARY AND I DIDN'T KNOW WHAT I WANTED ANY MORE.
I NAMED OUR DAUGHTER DORA, AFTER MY SISTER DORALÍS.
HECTOR NICKNAMED DORA 'KILLER' BECAUSE, HE SAID, THAT NIGHT HE SPENT WITH ME WAS KILLER.
4

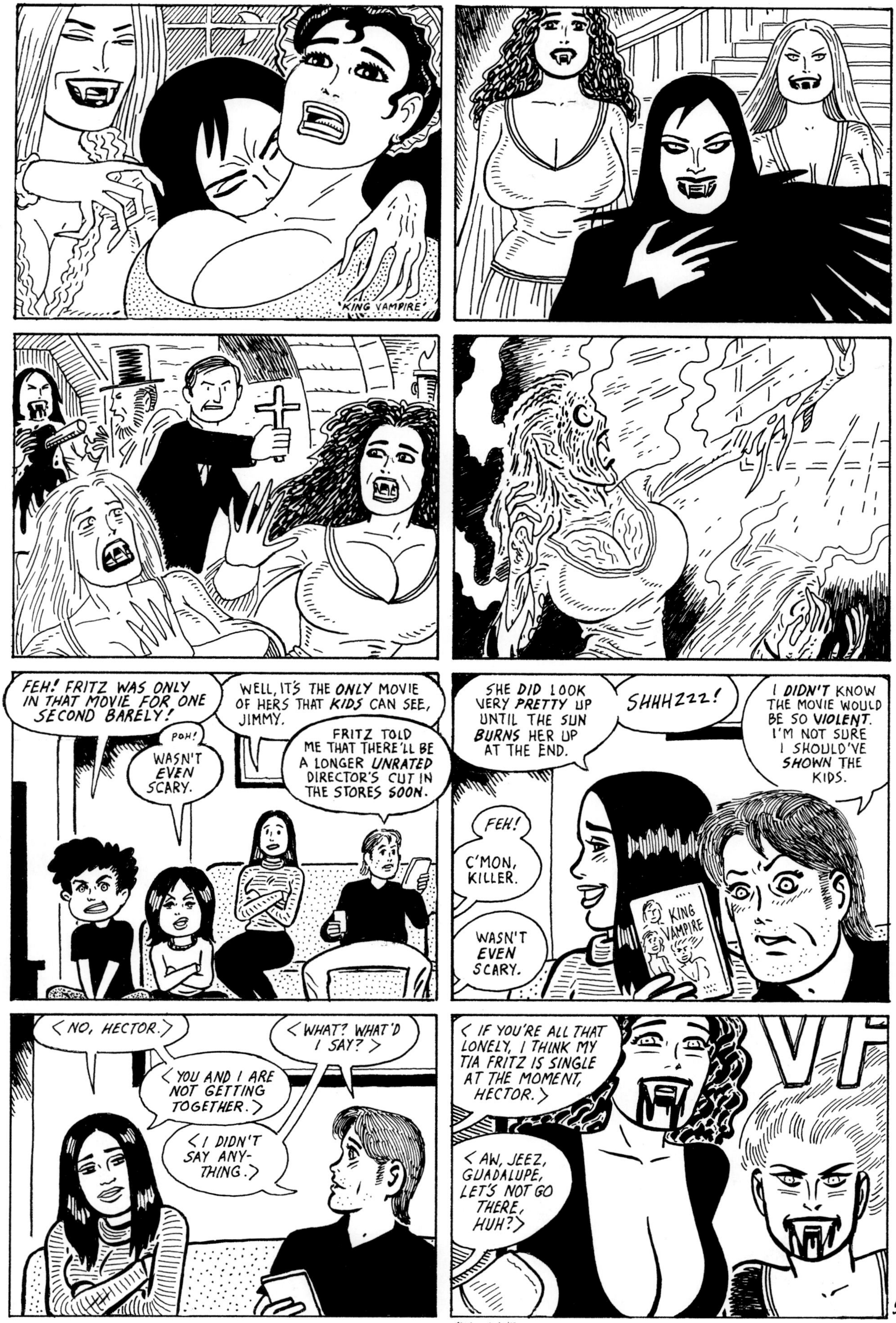
"KING VAMPIRE"
FEH! FRITZ WAS ONLY IN THAT MOVIE FOR ONE SECOND BARELY!
POH!
WASN'T EVEN SCARY.
WELL, IT'S THE ONLY MOVIE OF HERS THAT KIDS CAN SEE, JIMMY.
FRITZ TOLD ME THAT THERE'LL BE A LONGER UNRATED DIRECTOR'S CUT IN THE STORES SOON.
SHE DID LOOK VERY PRETTY UP UNTIL THE SUN BURNS HER UP AT THE END.
SHHHZZZ!
I DIDN'T KNOW THE MOVIE WOULD BE SO VIOLENT. I'M NOT SURE I SHOULD'VE SHOWN THE KIDS.
FEH!
C'MON, KILLER.
WASN'T EVEN SCARY.
KING VAMPIRE
< NO, HECTOR. >
< YOU AND I ARE NOT GETTING TOGETHER. >
< I DIDN'T SAY ANY-THING. >
< WHAT? WHAT'D I SAY? >
< IF YOU'RE ALL THAT LONELY, I THINK MY TIA FRITZ IS SINGLE AT THE MOMENT, HECTOR. >
< AW, JEEZ, GUADALUPE, LET'S NOT GO THERE, HUH? >
5

TIA - AUNT

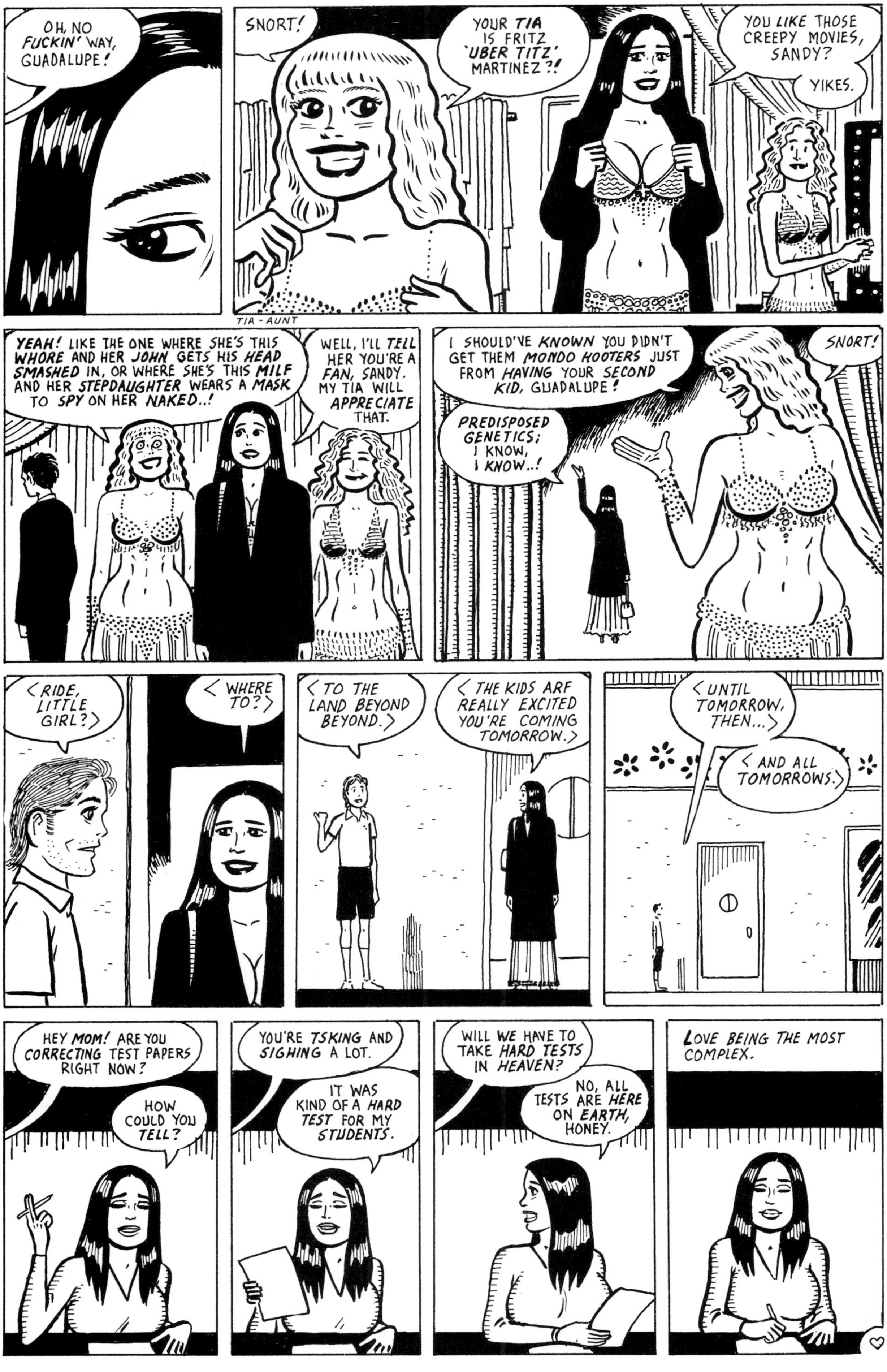
OH, NO FUCKIN' WAY, GUADALUPE!
SNORT!
YOUR TIA IS FRITZ 'UBER TITZ' MARTINEZ?!
YOU LIKE THOSE CREEPY MOVIES, SANDY?
YIKES.
TIA - AUNT
YEAH! LIKE THE ONE WHERE SHE'S THIS WHORE AND HER JOHN GETS HIS HEAD SMASHED IN, OR WHERE SHE'S THIS MILF AND HER STEPDAUGHTER WEARS A MASK TO SPY ON HER NAKED..!
WELL, I'LL TELL HER YOU'RE A FAN, SANDY. MY TIA WILL APPRECIATE THAT.
I SHOULD'VE KNOWN YOU DIDN'T GET THEM MONDO HOOTERS JUST FROM HAVING YOUR SECOND KID, GUADALUPE!
SNORT!
PREDISPOSED GENETICS; I KNOW, I KNOW..!
< RIDE, LITTLE GIRL? >
< WHERE TO? >
< TO THE LAND BEYOND BEYOND. >
< THE KIDS ARF REALLY EXCITED YOU'RE COMING TOMORROW. >
< UNTIL TOMORROW, THEN... >
< AND ALL TOMORROWS. >
HEY MOM! ARE YOU CORRECTING TEST PAPERS RIGHT NOW?
HOW COULD YOU TELL?
YOU'RE TSKING AND SIGHING A LOT.
IT WAS KIND OF A HARD TEST FOR MY STUDENTS.
WILL WE HAVE TO TAKE HARD TESTS IN HEAVEN?
NO, ALL TESTS ARE HERE ON EARTH, HONEY.
LOVE BEING THE MOST COMPLEX.

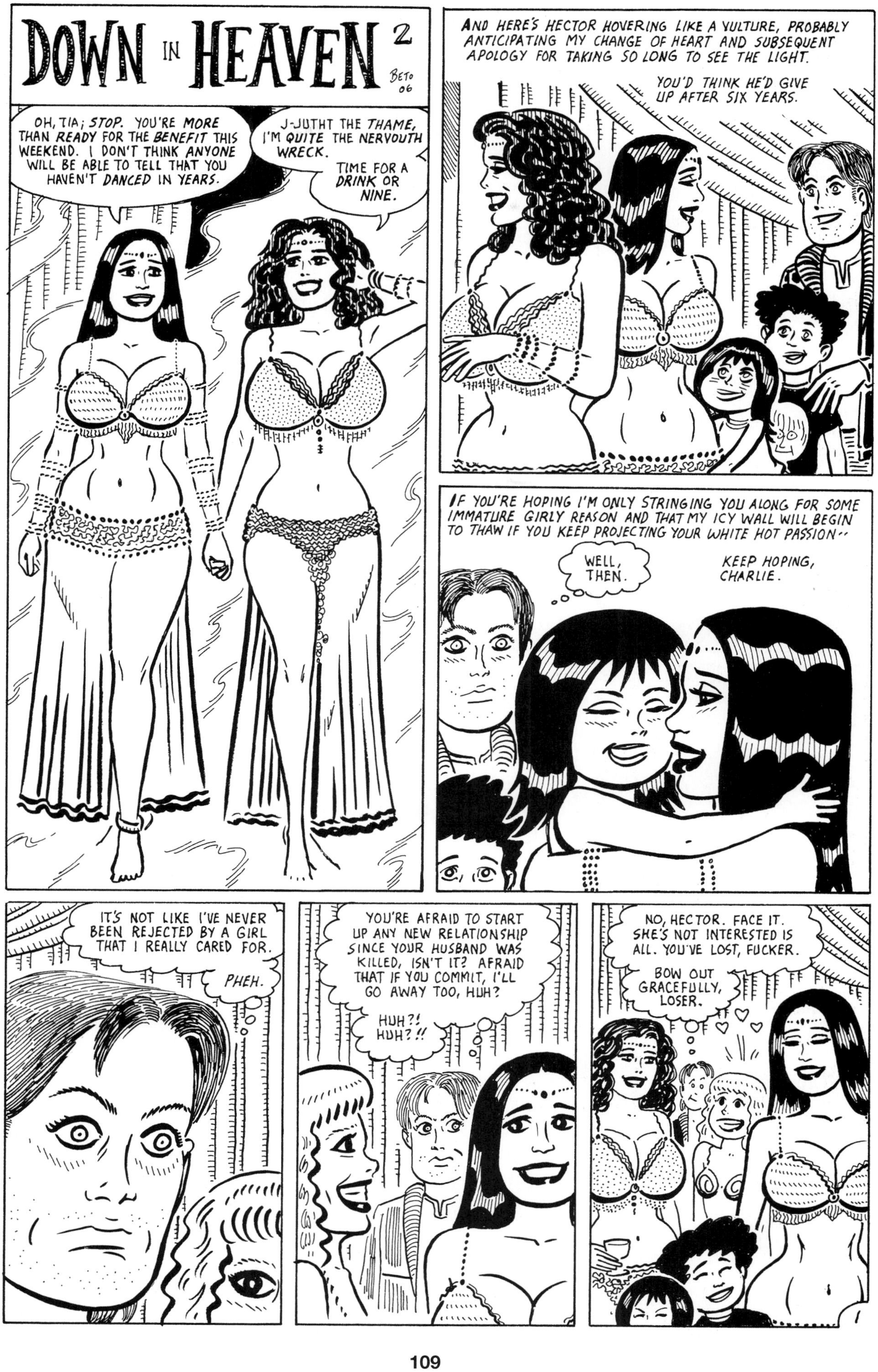
DOWN IN HEAVEN 2
BETO 06
OH, TIA; STOP. YOU'RE MORE THAN READY FOR THE BENEFIT THIS WEEKEND. I DON'T THINK ANYONE WILL BE ABLE TO TELL THAT YOU HAVEN'T DANCED IN YEARS.
J-JUTHT THE THAME, I'M QUITE THE NERVOUTH WRECK.
TIME FOR A DRINK OR NINE.
AND HERE'S HECTOR HOVERING LIKE A VULTURE, PROBABLY ANTICIPATING MY CHANGE OF HEART AND SUBSEQUENT APOLOGY FOR TAKING SO LONG TO SEE THE LIGHT.
YOU'D THINK HE'D GIVE UP AFTER SIX YEARS.
IF YOU'RE HOPING I'M ONLY STRINGING YOU ALONG FOR SOME IMMATURE GIRLY REASON AND THAT MY ICY WALL WILL BEGIN TO THAW IF YOU KEEP PROJECTING YOUR WHITE HOT PASSION--
WELL, THEN.
KEEP HOPING, CHARLIE.
IT'S NOT LIKE I'VE NEVER BEEN REJECTED BY A GIRL THAT I REALLY CARED FOR.
PHEH.
YOU'RE AFRAID TO START UP ANY NEW RELATIONSHIP SINCE YOUR HUSBAND WAS KILLED, ISN'T IT? AFRAID THAT IF YOU COMMIT, I'LL GO AWAY TOO, HUH?
HUH?! HUH?!!
NO, HECTOR. FACE IT. SHE'S NOT INTERESTED IS ALL. YOU'VE LOST, FUCKER.
BOW OUT GRACEFULLY, LOSER.

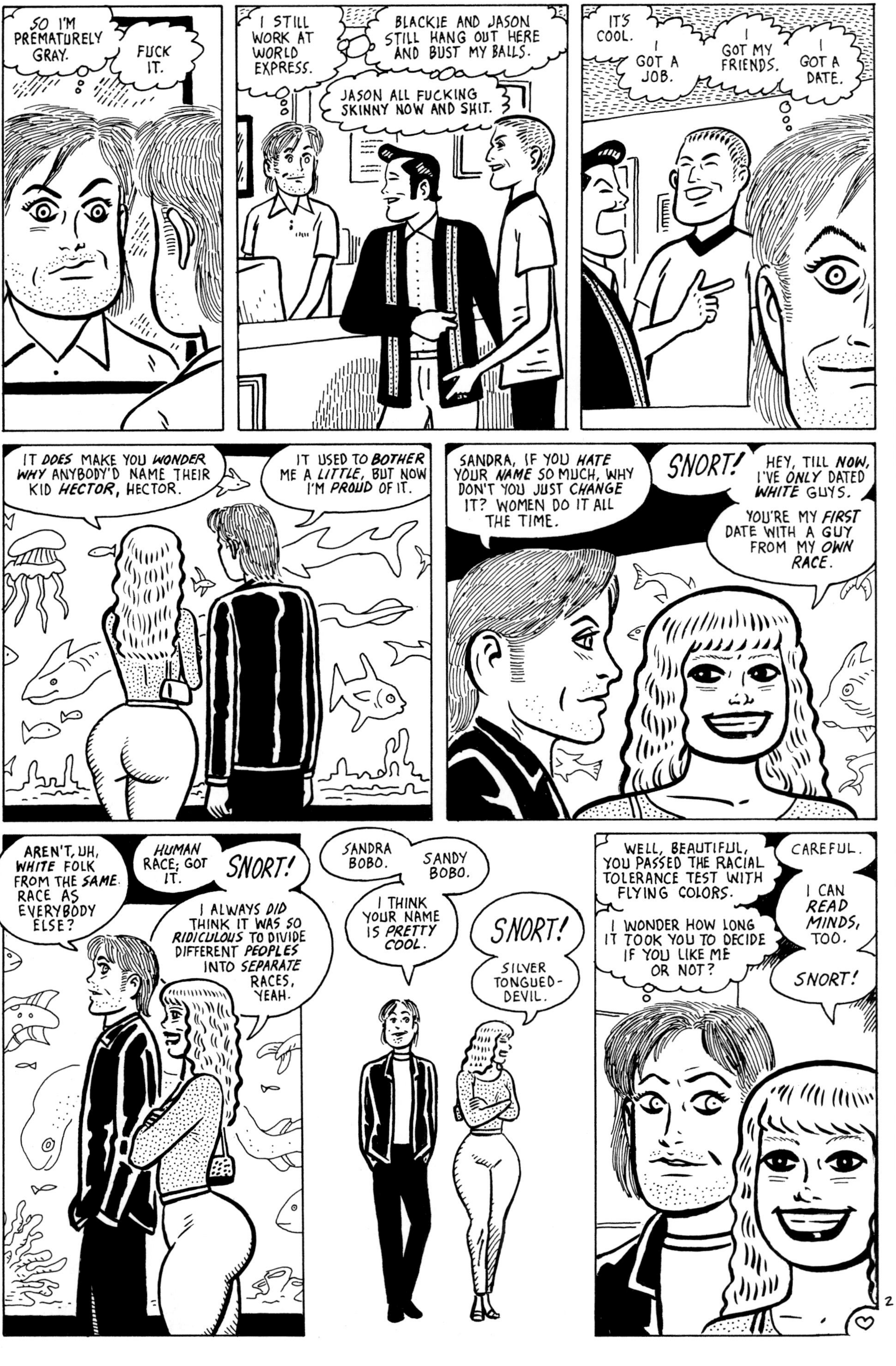
SO I'M PREMATURELY GRAY.
FUCK IT.
I STILL WORK AT WORLD EXPRESS.
BLACKIE AND JASON STILL HANG OUT HERE AND BUST MY BALLS.
JASON ALL FUCKING SKINNY NOW AND SHIT.
IT'S COOL.
I GOT A JOB.
I GOT MY FRIENDS.
I GOT A DATE.
IT DOES MAKE YOU WONDER WHY ANYBODY'D NAME THEIR KID HECTOR, HECTOR.
IT USED TO BOTHER ME A LITTLE, BUT NOW I'M PROUD OF IT.
SANDRA, IF YOU HATE YOUR NAME SO MUCH, WHY DON'T YOU JUST CHANGE IT? WOMEN DO IT ALL THE TIME.
SNORT!
HEY, TILL NOW, I'VE ONLY DATED WHITE GUYS.
YOU'RE MY FIRST DATE WITH A GUY FROM MY OWN RACE.
AREN'T, UH, WHITE FOLK FROM THE SAME RACE AS EVERYBODY ELSE?
HUMAN RACE; GOT IT.
SNORT!
I ALWAYS DID THINK IT WAS SO RIDICULOUS TO DIVIDE DIFFERENT PEOPLES INTO SEPARATE RACES, YEAH.
SANDRA BOBO.
SANDY BOBO.
I THINK YOUR NAME IS PRETTY COOL.
SNORT!
SILVER TONGUED-DEVIL.
WELL, BEAUTIFUL, YOU PASSED THE RACIAL TOLERANCE TEST WITH FLYING COLORS.
I WONDER HOW LONG IT TOOK YOU TO DECIDE IF YOU LIKE ME OR NOT?
CAREFUL.
I CAN READ MINDS, TOO.
SNORT!
2

DOWN IN HEAVEN 3

BETO '06

MOM, WHAT'S A NERD?

ANYONE WHO KNOWS MORE ABOUT ANY GIVEN SUBJECT THAN THE PERSON WHO BROUGHT UP SAID GIVEN SUBJECT.

WHAT YOU SAID, MOMMY.

NERD NERD NERD.

YEAH, THESE DAYS, THE MORE YOU KNOW, THE MORE YOU'RE DISMISSED AS CREEPY.

OF COURSE, UNLESS YOU'RE, LIKE, WAY TOTALLY 'HOT.'

THAT ONE NIGHT I SPENT WITH GUADALUPE SEEMS MOSTLY LIKE A DREAM NOW.

IT STARTED OUT WITH ME ON FOOT HITTING EVERY BAR I PASSED...

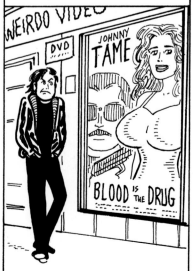

I'D JUST GONE THROUGH A NASTY BREAK-UP WITH MY GIRLFRIEND AND ALL I COULD THINK OF WAS REVENGE! THEN I HAPPENED BY A MOVIE POSTER WITH MY GIRLFRIEND'S SISTER ON IT.

WEIRDO VIDEO

DVD

JOHNNY TAME

BLOOD IS THE DRUG

MY GIRLFRIEND'S SISTER FRITZ SOMETIMES BELLYDANCED AT SOME EXOTIC RESTAURANT. I'D SPENT SOME QUALITY TIME WITH FRITZ BEFORE DATING HER SISTER, SO I FIGURED SINCE I AM PETTY AND VINDICTIVE...

GARDEN OF THE SUN

THAT NIGHT FRITZ WOULD BE SEDUCED INTO BEING MY UNWITTING SEX TOOL FOR VENGEANCE.

WELL, JUST AS ONE OF THE RESTAURANT GUYS WAS ABOUT TO THROW MY SORRY DRUNK ASS OUT, FRITZ'S LOVELY NIECE GUADALUPE CAME TO MY RESCUE.

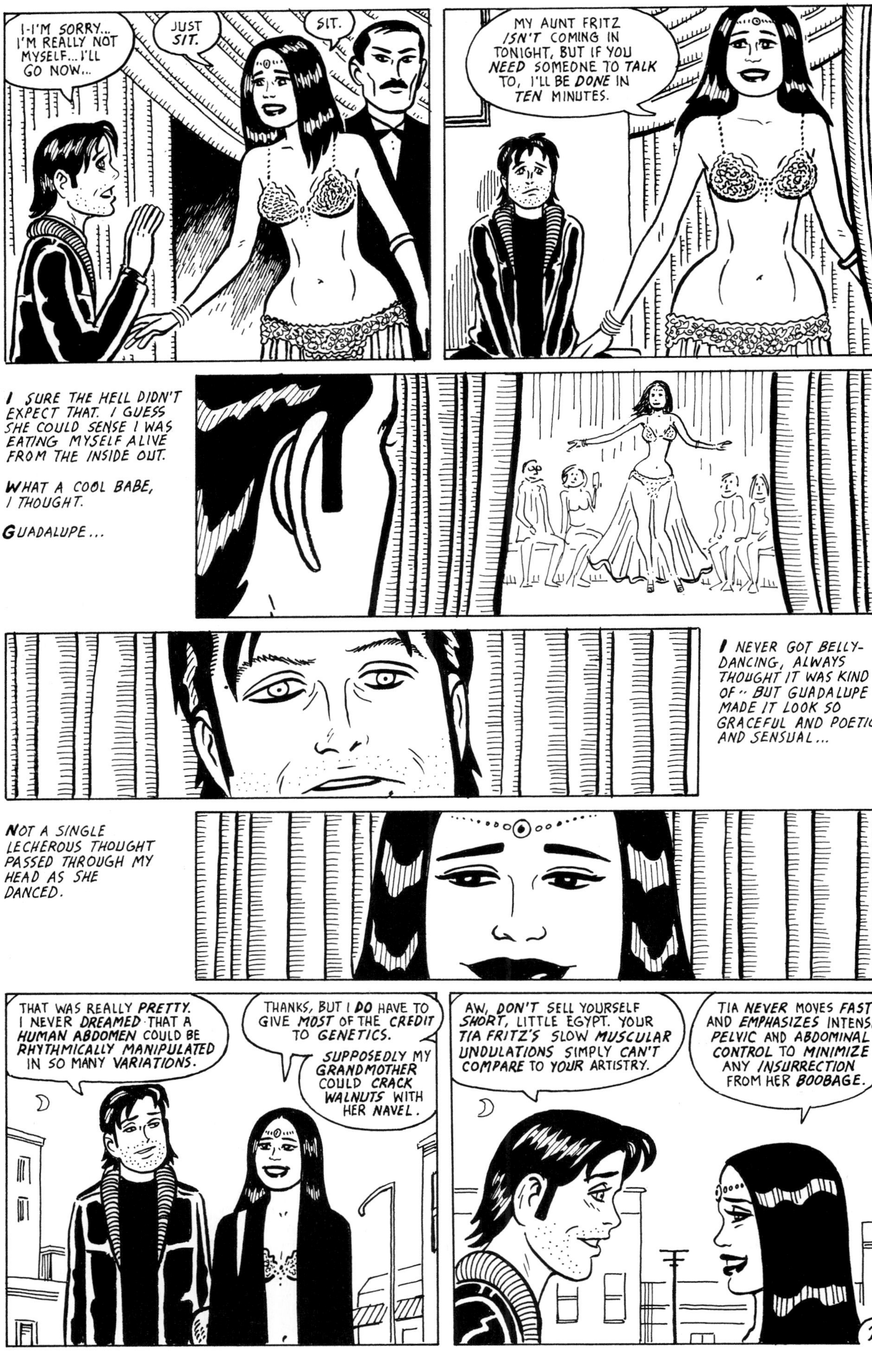
I-I'M SORRY... I'M REALLY NOT MYSELF... I'LL GO NOW...
JUST SIT.
SIT.
MY AUNT FRITZ ISN'T COMING IN TONIGHT, BUT IF YOU NEED SOMEONE TO TALK TO, I'LL BE DONE IN TEN MINUTES.
I SURE THE HELL DIDN'T EXPECT THAT. I GUESS SHE COULD SENSE I WAS EATING MYSELF ALIVE FROM THE INSIDE OUT.
WHAT A COOL BABE, I THOUGHT.
GUADALUPE...
I NEVER GOT BELLY-DANCING, ALWAYS THOUGHT IT WAS KIND OF.. BUT GUADALUPE MADE IT LOOK SO GRACEFUL AND POETIC AND SENSUAL...
NOT A SINGLE LECHEROUS THOUGHT PASSED THROUGH MY HEAD AS SHE DANCED.
THAT WAS REALLY PRETTY. I NEVER DREAMED THAT A HUMAN ABDOMEN COULD BE RHYTHMICALLY MANIPULATED IN SO MANY VARIATIONS.
THANKS, BUT I DO HAVE TO GIVE MOST OF THE CREDIT TO GENETICS.
SUPPOSEDLY MY GRANDMOTHER COULD CRACK WALNUTS WITH HER NAVEL.
AW, DON'T SELL YOURSELF SHORT, LITTLE EGYPT. YOUR TIA FRITZ'S SLOW MUSCULAR UNDULATIONS SIMPLY CAN'T COMPARE TO YOUR ARTISTRY.
TIA NEVER MOVES FAST AND EMPHASIZES INTENSE PELVIC AND ABDOMINAL CONTROL TO MINIMIZE ANY INSURRECTION FROM HER BOOBAGE.
2

WE DUCKED INTO THE BAR NEXT DOOR AND LET ME TELL YOU, SHE CAN PUT 'EM AWAY.

EXIT

WE WOKE UP AT MY PLACE AFTER CLEARLY HAVING DONE THE DEED.

I LOOKED AT HER, SHE LOOKED AT ME, AND, WELL...

WE WENT AT IT AGAIN, MORNING BREATH AND DIZZY HEADACHES AND ALL. AND AGAIN. AND AGAIN.

GUADALUPE SAID SHE WANTED TO THINK ABOUT IT AND TOLD ME NOT TO CALL HER.

SHE PROMISED SHE'D CALL ME IN A COUPLE OF DAYS.

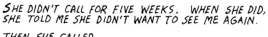

SHE DIDN'T CALL FOR FIVE WEEKS. WHEN SHE DID, SHE TOLD ME SHE DIDN'T WANT TO SEE ME AGAIN.

THEN SHE CALLED A MONTH LATER.

SHE WAS PREGNANT AND SAID SHE WANTED ME IN THE—OUR BABY'S LIFE BUT NOT IN HER OWN.

I WENT ALONG WITH HER DEMANDS.

MAYBE SHE'D CHANGE HER MIND ABOUT SEEING ME AGAIN.

SHE NEVER WILL, AS SURE AS THERE IS DEATH AND GENETIC PREDISPOSITION.

3

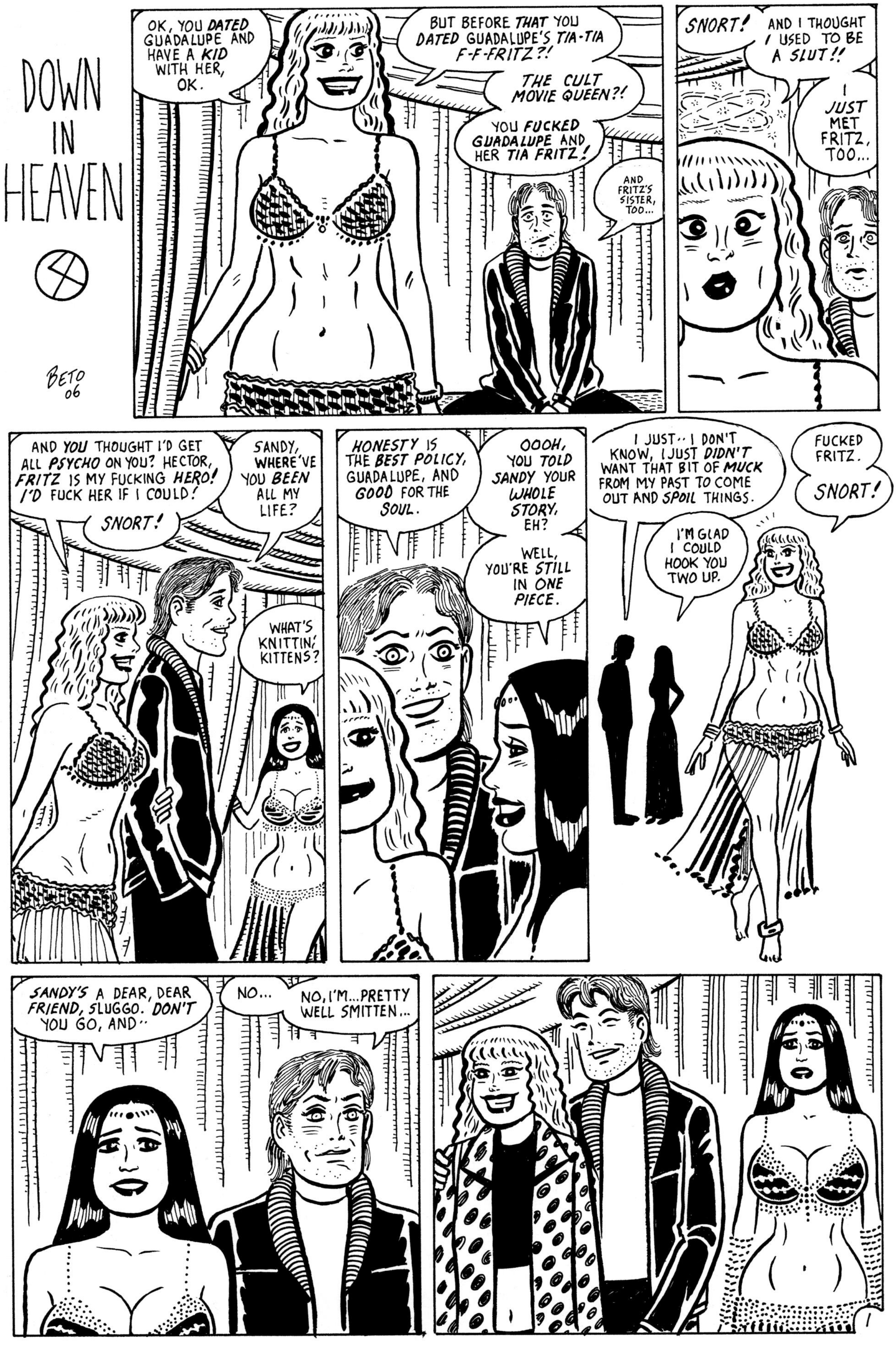
DOWN IN HEAVEN
4
BETO 06
OK, YOU DATED GUADALUPE AND HAVE A KID WITH HER, OK.
BUT BEFORE THAT YOU DATED GUADALUPE'S TIA-TIA F-F-FRITZ?!
THE CULT MOVIE QUEEN?!
YOU FUCKED GUADALUPE AND HER TIA FRITZ!
AND FRITZ'S SISTER, TOO...
SNORT!
AND I THOUGHT I USED TO BE A SLUT!!
I JUST MET FRITZ, TOO...
AND YOU THOUGHT I'D GET ALL PSYCHO ON YOU? HECTOR, FRITZ IS MY FUCKING HERO! I'D FUCK HER IF I COULD!
SNORT!
SANDY, WHERE'VE YOU BEEN ALL MY LIFE?
WHAT'S KNITTIN', KITTENS?
HONESTY IS THE BEST POLICY, GUADALUPE, AND GOOD FOR THE SOUL.
OOOH, YOU TOLD SANDY YOUR WHOLE STORY, EH?
WELL, YOU'RE STILL IN ONE PIECE.
I JUST.. I DON'T KNOW, I JUST DIDN'T WANT THAT BIT OF MUCK FROM MY PAST TO COME OUT AND SPOIL THINGS.
I'M GLAD I COULD HOOK YOU TWO UP.
FUCKED FRITZ.
SNORT!
SANDY'S A DEAR, DEAR FRIEND, SLUGGO. DON'T YOU GO, AND..
NO...
NO, I'M...PRETTY WELL SMITTEN...

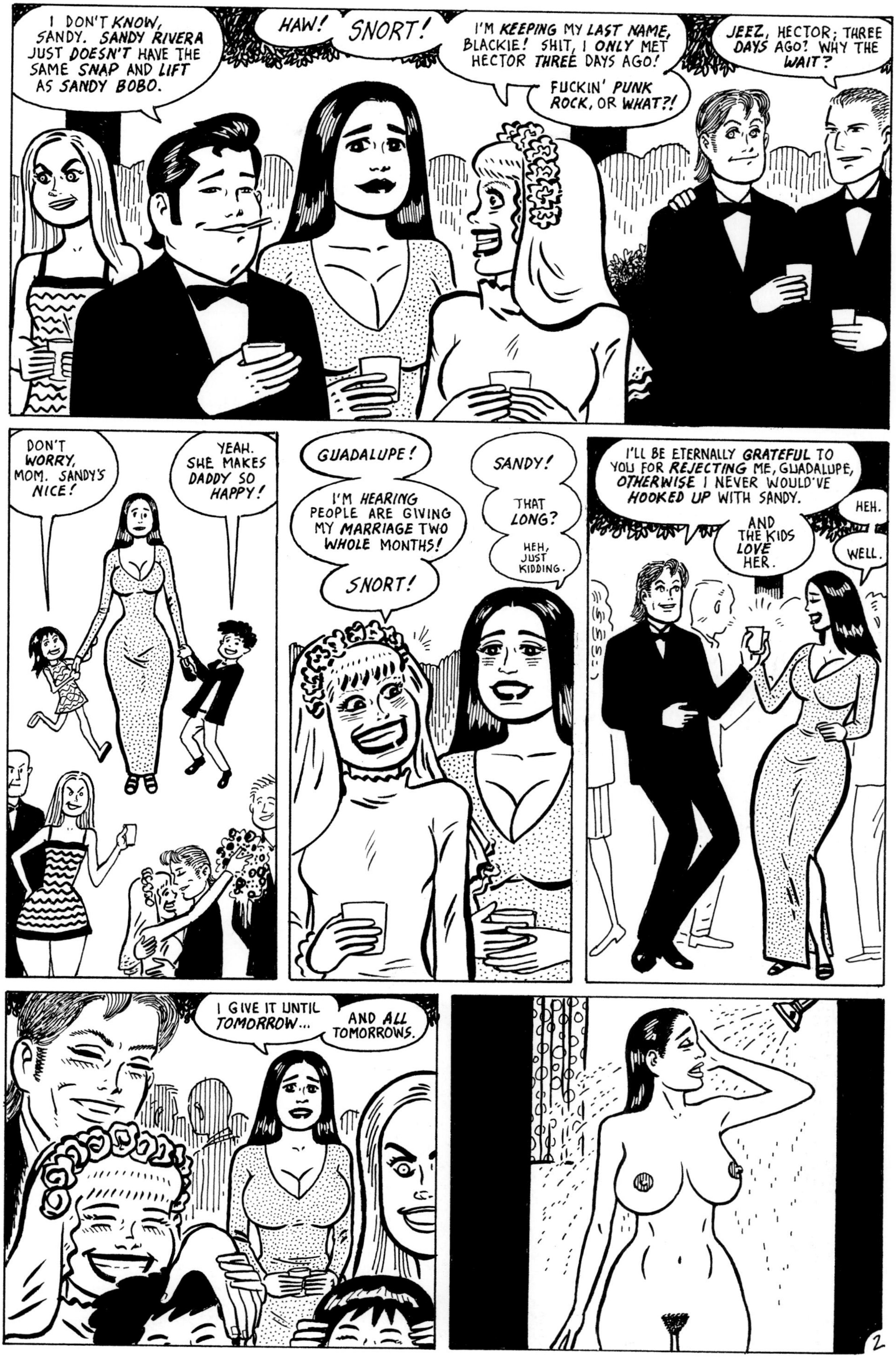

I DON'T KNOW, SANDY. SANDY RIVERA JUST DOESN'T HAVE THE SAME SNAP AND LIFT AS SANDY BOBO.
HAW!
SNORT!
I'M KEEPING MY LAST NAME, BLACKIE! SHIT, I ONLY MET HECTOR THREE DAYS AGO!
FUCKIN' PUNK ROCK, OR WHAT?!
JEEZ, HECTOR; THREE DAYS AGO? WHY THE WAIT?
DON'T WORRY, MOM. SANDY'S NICE!
YEAH. SHE MAKES DADDY SO HAPPY!
GUADALUPE!
I'M HEARING PEOPLE ARE GIVING MY MARRIAGE TWO WHOLE MONTHS!
SNORT!
SANDY!
THAT LONG?
HEH, JUST KIDDING.
I'LL BE ETERNALLY GRATEFUL TO YOU FOR REJECTING ME, GUADALUPE, OTHERWISE I NEVER WOULD'VE HOOKED UP WITH SANDY.
AND THE KIDS LOVE HER.
HEH.
WELL.
I GIVE IT UNTIL TOMORROW...
AND ALL TOMORROWS.
2

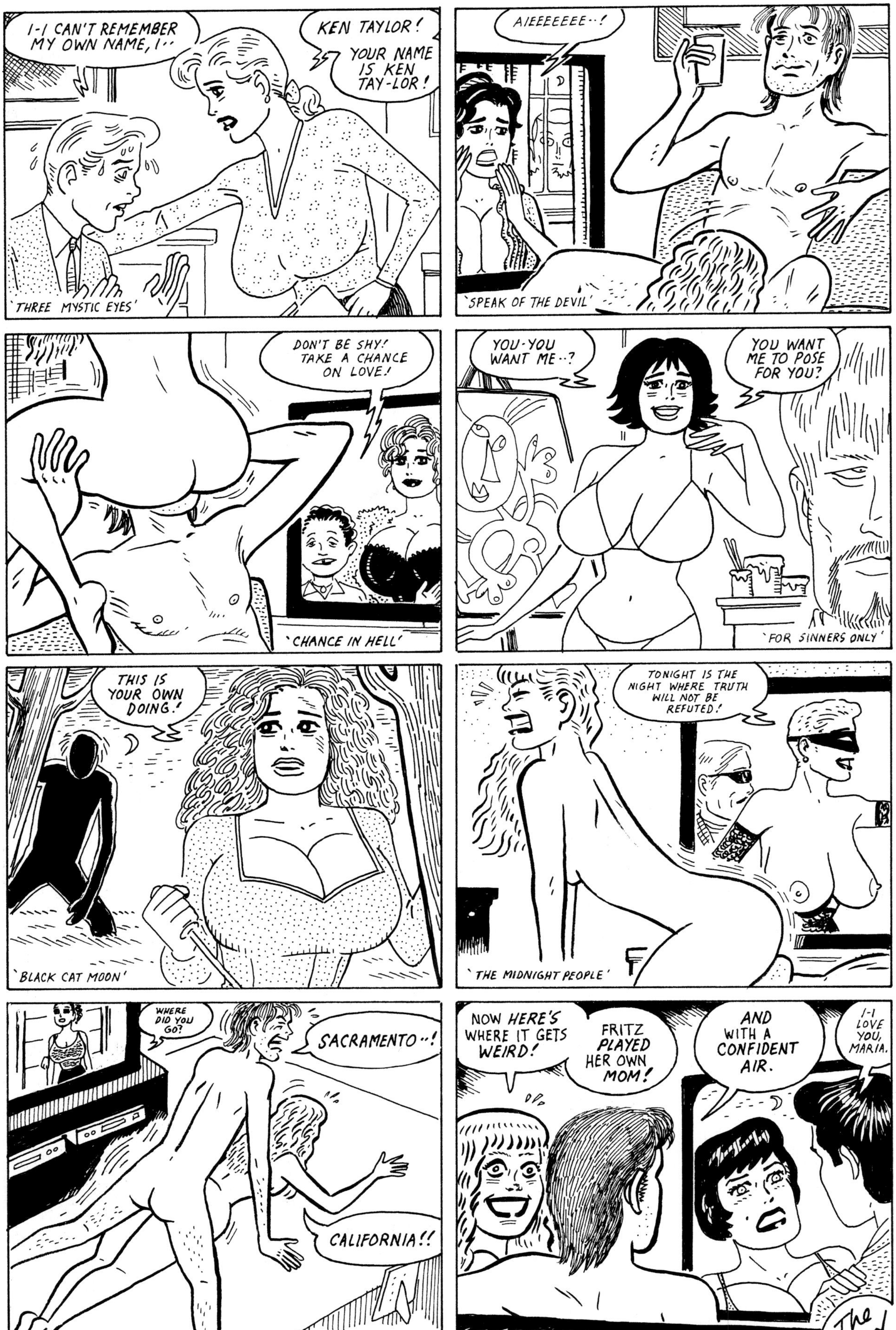
I-I CAN'T REMEMBER MY OWN NAME, I··
KEN TAYLOR!
YOUR NAME IS KEN TAY-LOR!
'THREE MYSTIC EYES'
AIEEEEEEE··!
'SPEAK OF THE DEVIL'
DON'T BE SHY! TAKE A CHANCE ON LOVE!
'CHANCE IN HELL'
YOU-YOU WANT ME··?
YOU WANT ME TO POSE FOR YOU?
'FOR SINNERS ONLY'
THIS IS YOUR OWN DOING!
'BLACK CAT MOON'
TONIGHT IS THE NIGHT WHERE TRUTH WILL NOT BE REFUTED!
'THE MIDNIGHT PEOPLE'
WHERE DID YOU GO?
SACRAMENTO··!
CALIFORNIA!!
'TROUBLEMAKERS'
NOW HERE'S WHERE IT GETS WEIRD!
FRITZ PLAYED HER OWN MOM!
AND WITH A CONFIDENT AIR.
I-I LOVE YOU, MARIA.
'MARIA M.'
3
The End

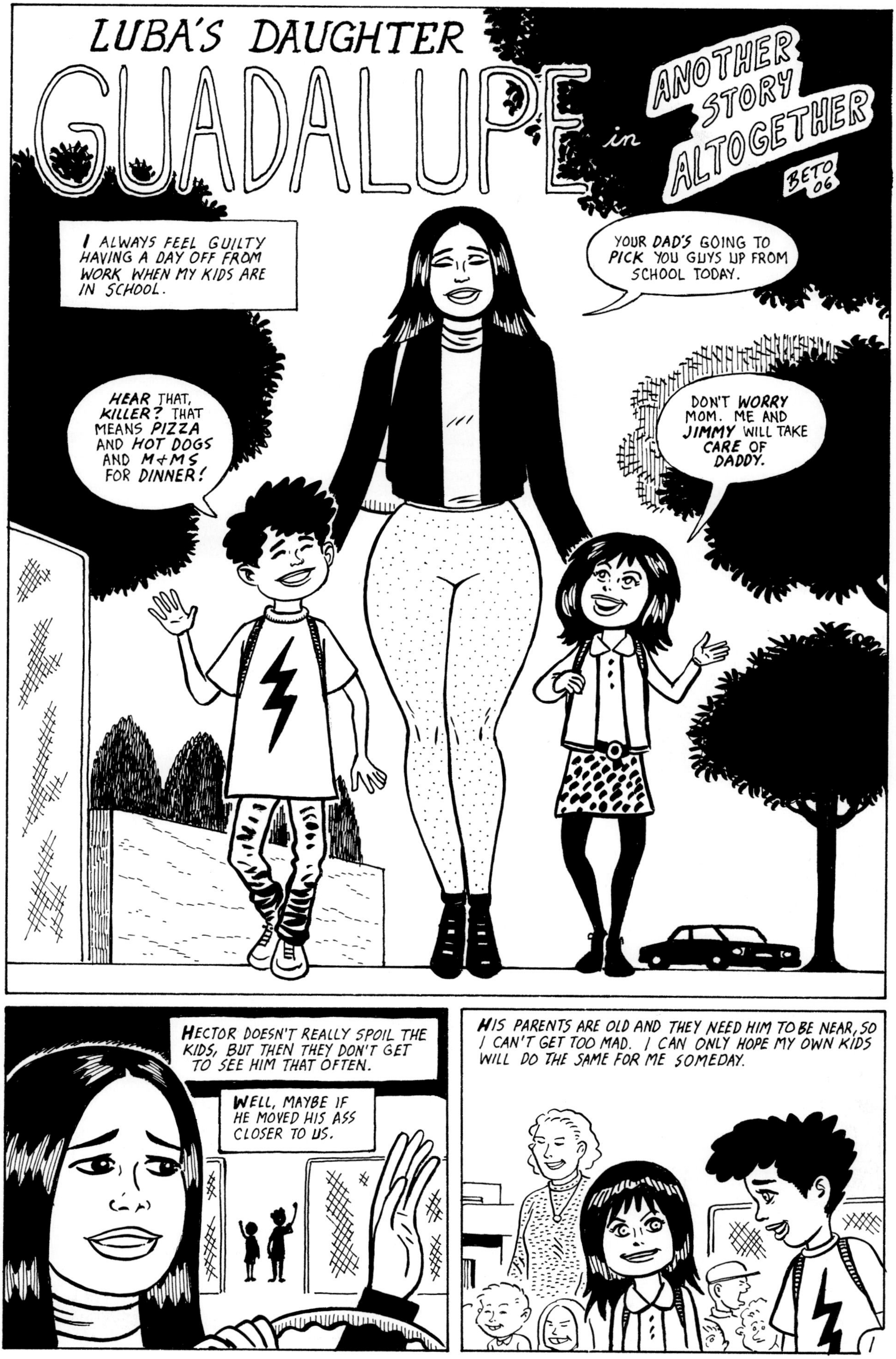
LUBA'S DAUGHTER
GUADALUPE in ANOTHER STORY ALTOGETHER
BETO 06
I ALWAYS FEEL GUILTY HAVING A DAY OFF FROM WORK WHEN MY KIDS ARE IN SCHOOL.
YOUR DAD'S GOING TO PICK YOU GUYS UP FROM SCHOOL TODAY.
HEAR THAT, KILLER? THAT MEANS PIZZA AND HOT DOGS AND M&MS FOR DINNER!
DON'T WORRY MOM. ME AND JIMMY WILL TAKE CARE OF DADDY.
HECTOR DOESN'T REALLY SPOIL THE KIDS, BUT THEN THEY DON'T GET TO SEE HIM THAT OFTEN.
WELL, MAYBE IF HE MOVED HIS ASS CLOSER TO US.
HIS PARENTS ARE OLD AND THEY NEED HIM TO BE NEAR, SO I CAN'T GET TOO MAD. I CAN ONLY HOPE MY OWN KIDS WILL DO THE SAME FOR ME SOMEDAY.
1

HECTOR'S A GOOD DAD TO THE KIDS, BUT HE AND I JUST WEREN'T MEANT TO BE. I DON'T REGRET THAT ONE NIGHT HE AND I SLEPT TOGETHER, BECAUSE IT GAVE ME A BEAUTIFUL DAUGHTER.

EVEN THOUGH PREPARATIONS FOR MY SISTER'S CANCER BENEFIT SHOW ARE GOING SMOOTHLY, MY NERVES ARE BEYOND RAGGED. IT'S ONLY A SMALL PRODUCTION, BUT IT'S A PRETTY BIG DEAL TO ME.

DORALIS

HECTOR'S SWEET. WHEN I HAPPENED TO MENTION MY GRANDMOTHER DIED OF A BRAIN TUMOR, HE WENT CRAZY AND TOLD ME IF I EVER GOT A HEADACHE TO GET MYSELF TO EMERGENCY IMMEDIATELY. HE'S ALWAYS INSISTING THAT THE KIDS AND I GET AN ANNUAL BRAIN SCAN.

IT WASN'T TOO HARD TO GET LOCAL ENTERTAINMENT FOR THE SHOW, BUT I NEEDED SOMETHING SPECIAL, A STAR, IF YOU WILL, TO GUARANTEE MORE THAN A FEW BUTTS IN THOSE THIRTY DOLLAR SEATS.

CALISTO STUDIOS

I HOOKED UP HECTOR WITH A FRIEND AND THEY HIT IT OFF GREAT. THEY GOT MARRIED THREE DAYS AFTER THEIR FIRST DATE! DO I HAVE THE TOUCH, OR WHAT?

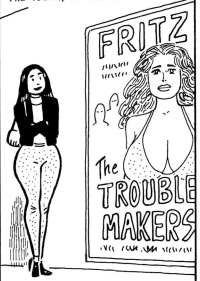

FRITZ

The TROUBLE MAKERS

I HOPE I HAVE THE TOUCH FOR SETTING UP A BENEFIT SHOW. I'M COUNTING ON MY STAR TO HELP ME MAKE IT A SUCCESS.

MIND SPURS

WHERE NO TELEVISION HAS GONE BEFORE

< PLEATH, PIPO! YOU KNOW I CAN'T THTAND TO WATCH MYTHELF ON THCREEN! >

< I JUST DON'T WANT YOU TO FINISH THE BOTTLE BEFORE I GET SOME, FRITZ! >

< WHAT I CAN'T STAND TO SEE IS YOU GUYS GETTING STARTED WITHOUT ME. >

2

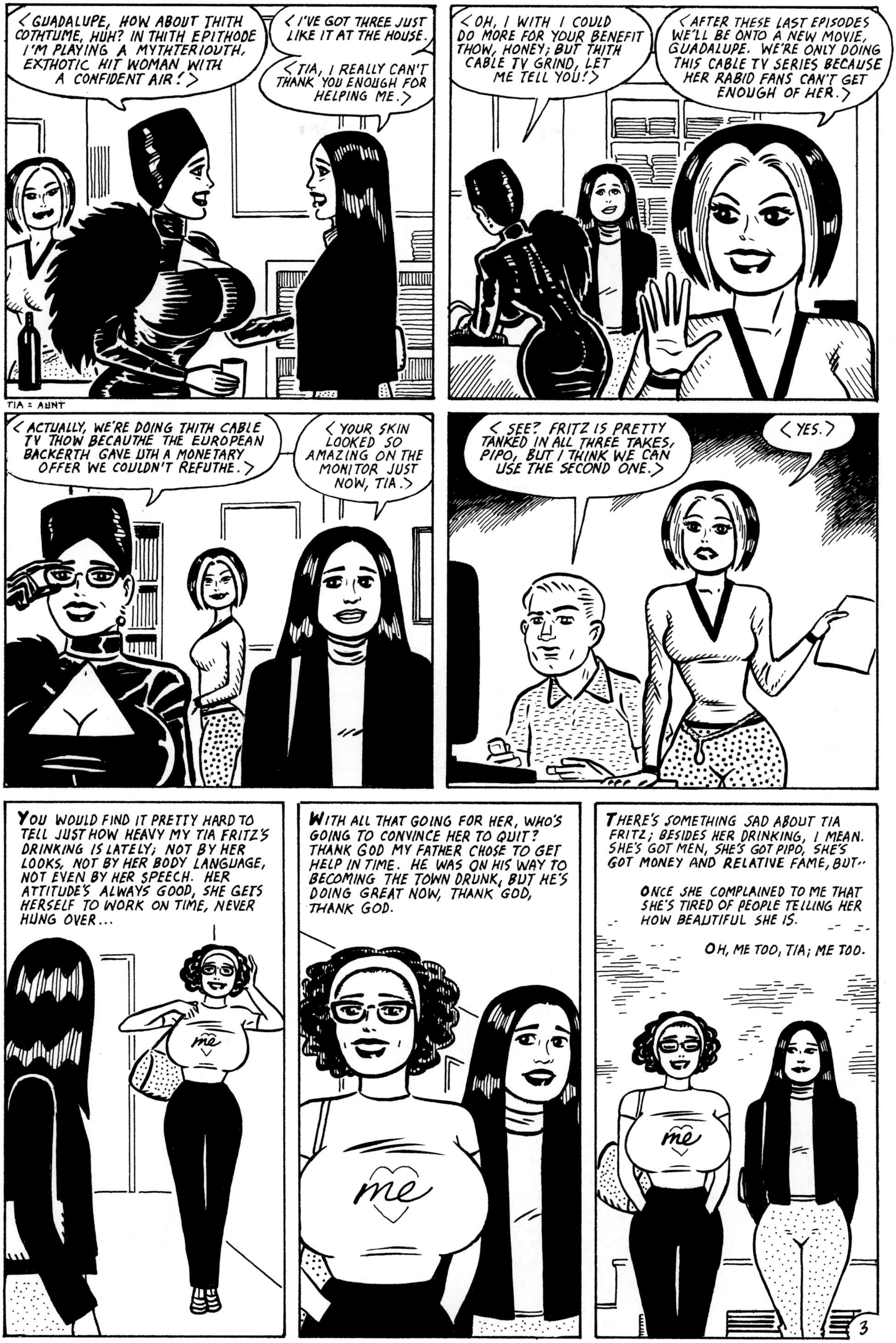

< GUADALUPE, HOW ABOUT THITH COTHTUME, HUH? IN THITH EPITHODE I'M PLAYING A MYTHTERIOUTH, EXTHOTIC HIT WOMAN WITH A CONFIDENT AIR! >
< I'VE GOT THREE JUST LIKE IT AT THE HOUSE. >
< TIA, I REALLY CAN'T THANK YOU ENOUGH FOR HELPING ME. >
TIA = AUNT
< OH, I WITH I COULD DO MORE FOR YOUR BENEFIT THOW, HONEY; BUT THITH CABLE TV GRIND, LET ME TELL YOU! >
< AFTER THESE LAST EPISODES WE'LL BE ONTO A NEW MOVIE, GUADALUPE. WE'RE ONLY DOING THIS CABLE TV SERIES BECAUSE HER RABID FANS CAN'T GET ENOUGH OF HER. >
< ACTUALLY, WE'RE DOING THITH CABLE TV THOW BECAUTHE THE EUROPEAN BACKERTH GAVE UTH A MONETARY OFFER WE COULDN'T REFUTHE. >
< YOUR SKIN LOOKED SO AMAZING ON THE MONITOR JUST NOW, TIA. >
< SEE? FRITZ IS PRETTY TANKED IN ALL THREE TAKES, PIPO, BUT I THINK WE CAN USE THE SECOND ONE. >
< YES. >
YOU WOULD FIND IT PRETTY HARD TO TELL JUST HOW HEAVY MY TIA FRITZ'S DRINKING IS LATELY; NOT BY HER LOOKS, NOT BY HER BODY LANGUAGE, NOT EVEN BY HER SPEECH. HER ATTITUDE'S ALWAYS GOOD, SHE GETS HERSELF TO WORK ON TIME, NEVER HUNG OVER...
me
WITH ALL THAT GOING FOR HER, WHO'S GOING TO CONVINCE HER TO QUIT? THANK GOD MY FATHER CHOSE TO GET HELP IN TIME. HE WAS ON HIS WAY TO BECOMING THE TOWN DRUNK, BUT HE'S DOING GREAT NOW, THANK GOD, THANK GOD.
me
THERE'S SOMETHING SAD ABOUT TIA FRITZ; BESIDES HER DRINKING, I MEAN. SHE'S GOT MEN, SHE'S GOT PIPO, SHE'S GOT MONEY AND RELATIVE FAME, BUT..
ONCE SHE COMPLAINED TO ME THAT SHE'S TIRED OF PEOPLE TELLING HER HOW BEAUTIFUL SHE IS.
OH, ME TOO, TIA; ME TOO.
me
3

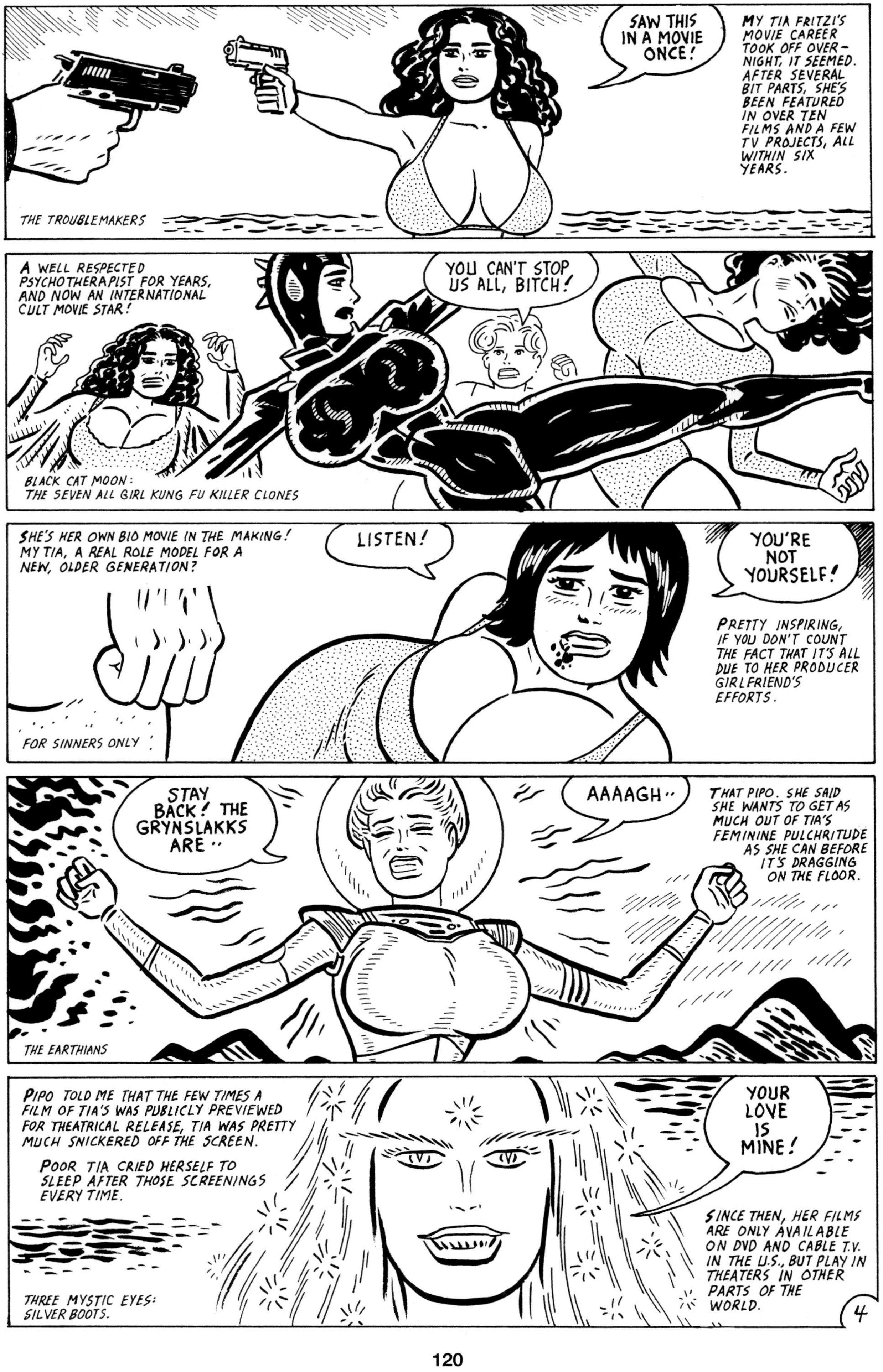
SAW THIS IN A MOVIE ONCE!
MY TIA FRITZI'S MOVIE CAREER TOOK OFF OVER-NIGHT, IT SEEMED. AFTER SEVERAL BIT PARTS, SHE'S BEEN FEATURED IN OVER TEN FILMS AND A FEW TV PROJECTS, ALL WITHIN SIX YEARS.
THE TROUBLEMAKERS
A WELL RESPECTED PSYCHOTHERAPIST FOR YEARS, AND NOW AN INTERNATIONAL CULT MOVIE STAR!
YOU CAN'T STOP US ALL, BITCH!
BLACK CAT MOON:
THE SEVEN ALL GIRL KUNG FU KILLER CLONES
SHE'S HER OWN BIO MOVIE IN THE MAKING! MY TIA, A REAL ROLE MODEL FOR A NEW, OLDER GENERATION?
LISTEN!
YOU'RE NOT YOURSELF!
PRETTY INSPIRING, IF YOU DON'T COUNT THE FACT THAT IT'S ALL DUE TO HER PRODUCER GIRLFRIEND'S EFFORTS.
FOR SINNERS ONLY
STAY BACK! THE GRYNSLAKKS ARE..
AAAAGH..
THAT PIPO. SHE SAID SHE WANTS TO GET AS MUCH OUT OF TIA'S FEMININE PULCHRITUDE AS SHE CAN BEFORE IT'S DRAGGING ON THE FLOOR.
THE EARTHIANS
PIPO TOLD ME THAT THE FEW TIMES A FILM OF TIA'S WAS PUBLICLY PREVIEWED FOR THEATRICAL RELEASE, TIA WAS PRETTY MUCH SNICKERED OFF THE SCREEN.
POOR TIA CRIED HERSELF TO SLEEP AFTER THOSE SCREENINGS EVERY TIME.
YOUR LOVE IS MINE!
SINCE THEN, HER FILMS ARE ONLY AVAILABLE ON DVD AND CABLE T.V. IN THE U.S., BUT PLAY IN THEATERS IN OTHER PARTS OF THE WORLD.
THREE MYSTIC EYES:
SILVER BOOTS.
4

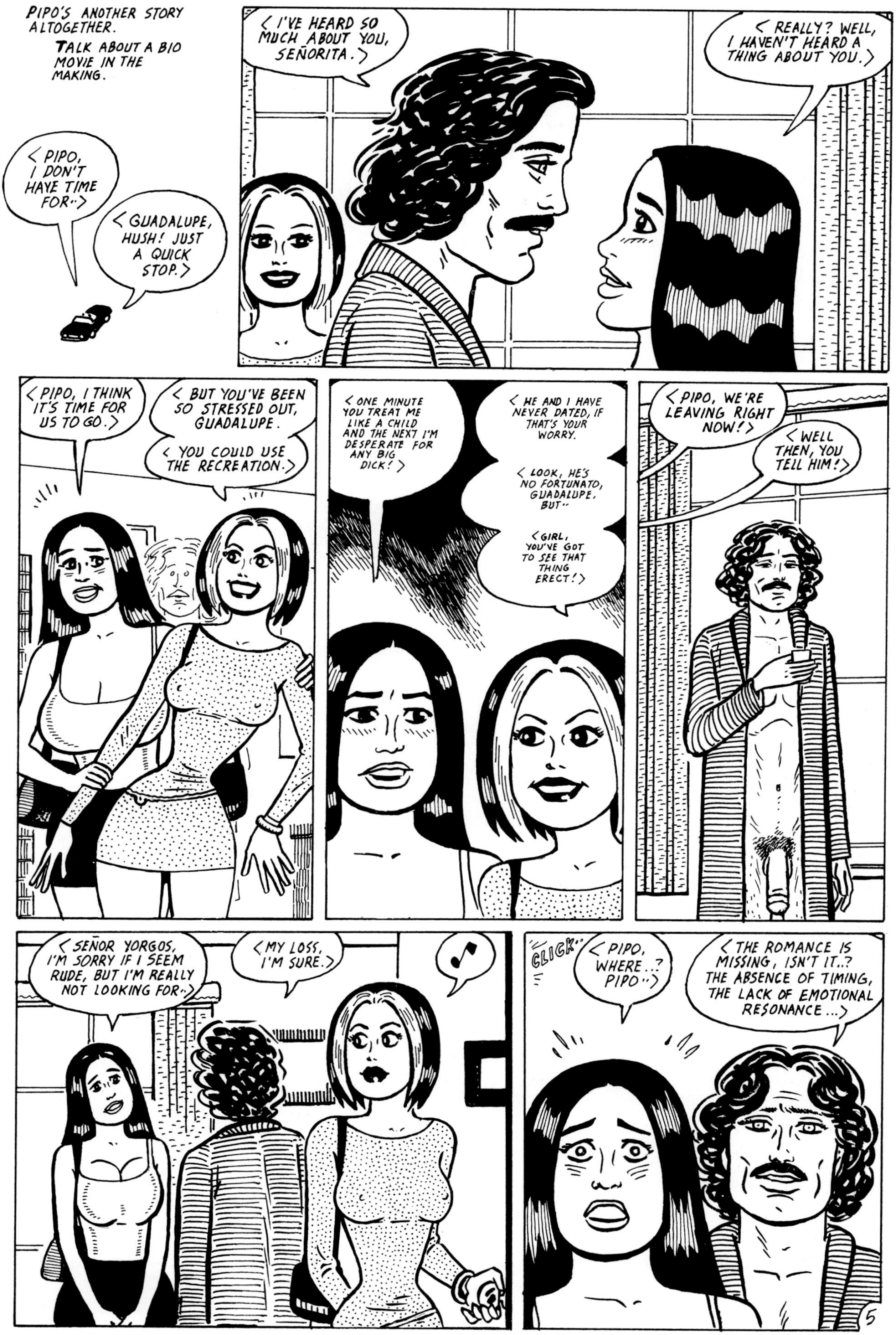
PIPO'S ANOTHER STORY ALTOGETHER.
TALK ABOUT A BIO MOVIE IN THE MAKING.
< PIPO, I DON'T HAVE TIME FOR..>
< GUADALUPE, HUSH! JUST A QUICK STOP.>
< I'VE HEARD SO MUCH ABOUT YOU, SEÑORITA.>
< REALLY? WELL, I HAVEN'T HEARD A THING ABOUT YOU.>
< PIPO, I THINK IT'S TIME FOR US TO GO.>
< BUT YOU'VE BEEN SO STRESSED OUT, GUADALUPE.
< YOU COULD USE THE RECREATION.>
< ONE MINUTE YOU TREAT ME LIKE A CHILD AND THE NEXT I'M DESPERATE FOR ANY BIG DICK! >
< HE AND I HAVE NEVER DATED, IF THAT'S YOUR WORRY.
< LOOK, HE'S NO FORTUNATO, GUADALUPE, BUT..
< GIRL, YOU'VE GOT TO SEE THAT THING ERECT! >
< PIPO, WE'RE LEAVING RIGHT NOW! >
< WELL THEN, YOU TELL HIM! >
< SEÑOR YORGOS, I'M SORRY IF I SEEM RUDE, BUT I'M REALLY NOT LOOKING FOR..>
< MY LOSS, I'M SURE.>
CLICK
< PIPO, WHERE..? PIPO..>
< THE ROMANCE IS MISSING, ISN'T IT..? THE ABSENCE OF TIMING, THE LACK OF EMOTIONAL RESONANCE...>
5

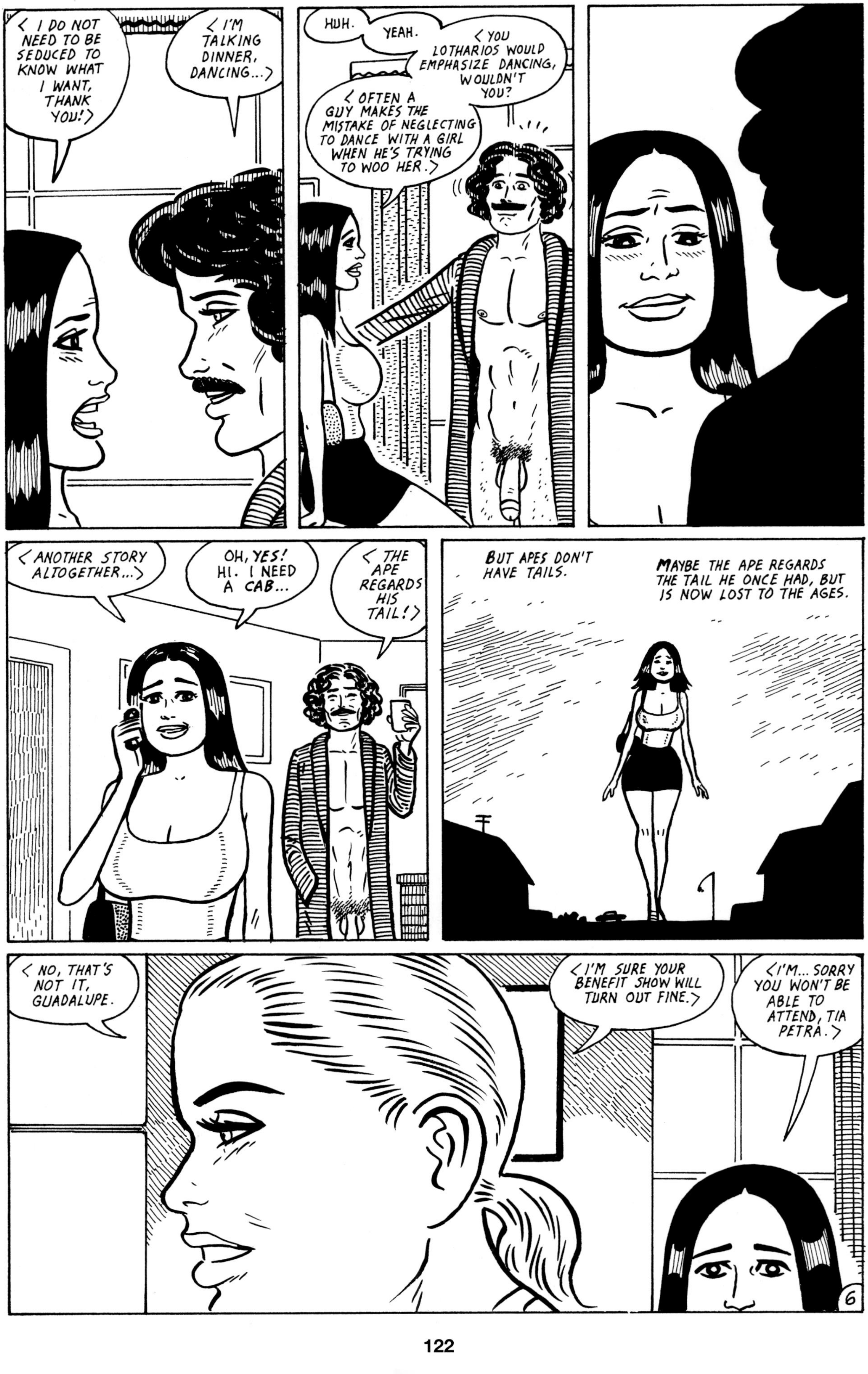
< I DO NOT NEED TO BE SEDUCED TO KNOW WHAT I WANT, THANK YOU!>
< I'M TALKING DINNER, DANCING...>
HUH.
YEAH.
< YOU LOTHARIOS WOULD EMPHASIZE DANCING, WOULDN'T YOU?
< OFTEN A GUY MAKES THE MISTAKE OF NEGLECTING TO DANCE WITH A GIRL WHEN HE'S TRYING TO WOO HER.>
< ANOTHER STORY ALTOGETHER...>
OH, YES! HI. I NEED A CAB...
< THE APE REGARDS HIS TAIL!>
BUT APES DON'T HAVE TAILS.
MAYBE THE APE REGARDS THE TAIL HE ONCE HAD, BUT IS NOW LOST TO THE AGES.
< NO, THAT'S NOT IT, GUADALUPE.
< I'M SURE YOUR BENEFIT SHOW WILL TURN OUT FINE.>
< I'M... SORRY YOU WON'T BE ABLE TO ATTEND, TIA PETRA.>
6

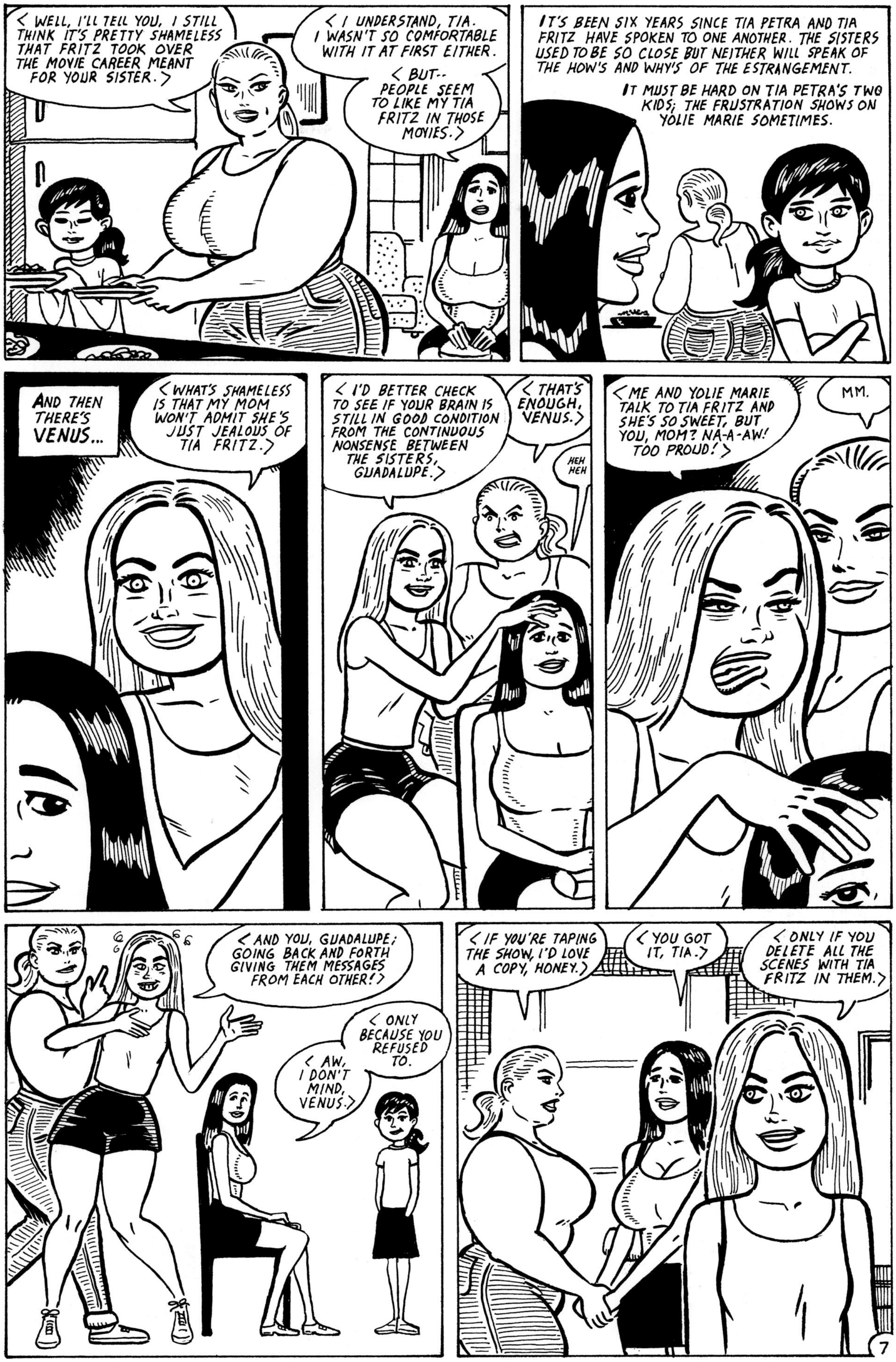
< WELL, I'LL TELL YOU, I STILL THINK IT'S PRETTY SHAMELESS THAT FRITZ TOOK OVER THE MOVIE CAREER MEANT FOR YOUR SISTER. >
< I UNDERSTAND, TIA. I WASN'T SO COMFORTABLE WITH IT AT FIRST EITHER.
< BUT-- PEOPLE SEEM TO LIKE MY TIA FRITZ IN THOSE MOVIES. >
IT'S BEEN SIX YEARS SINCE TIA PETRA AND TIA FRITZ HAVE SPOKEN TO ONE ANOTHER. THE SISTERS USED TO BE SO CLOSE BUT NEITHER WILL SPEAK OF THE HOW'S AND WHY'S OF THE ESTRANGEMENT.
IT MUST BE HARD ON TIA PETRA'S TWO KIDS; THE FRUSTRATION SHOWS ON YOLIE MARIE SOMETIMES.
AND THEN THERE'S VENUS...
< WHAT'S SHAMELESS IS THAT MY MOM WON'T ADMIT SHE'S JUST JEALOUS OF TIA FRITZ. >
< I'D BETTER CHECK TO SEE IF YOUR BRAIN IS STILL IN GOOD CONDITION FROM THE CONTINUOUS NONSENSE BETWEEN THE SISTERS, GUADALUPE. >
< THAT'S ENOUGH, VENUS. >
HEH HEH
< ME AND YOLIE MARIE TALK TO TIA FRITZ AND SHE'S SO SWEET, BUT YOU, MOM? NA-A-AW! TOO PROUD! >
MM.
< AND YOU, GUADALUPE; GOING BACK AND FORTH GIVING THEM MESSAGES FROM EACH OTHER! >
< ONLY BECAUSE YOU REFUSED TO.
< AW, I DON'T MIND, VENUS. >
< IF YOU'RE TAPING THE SHOW, I'D LOVE A COPY, HONEY. >
< YOU GOT IT, TIA. >
< ONLY IF YOU DELETE ALL THE SCENES WITH TIA FRITZ IN THEM. >
7

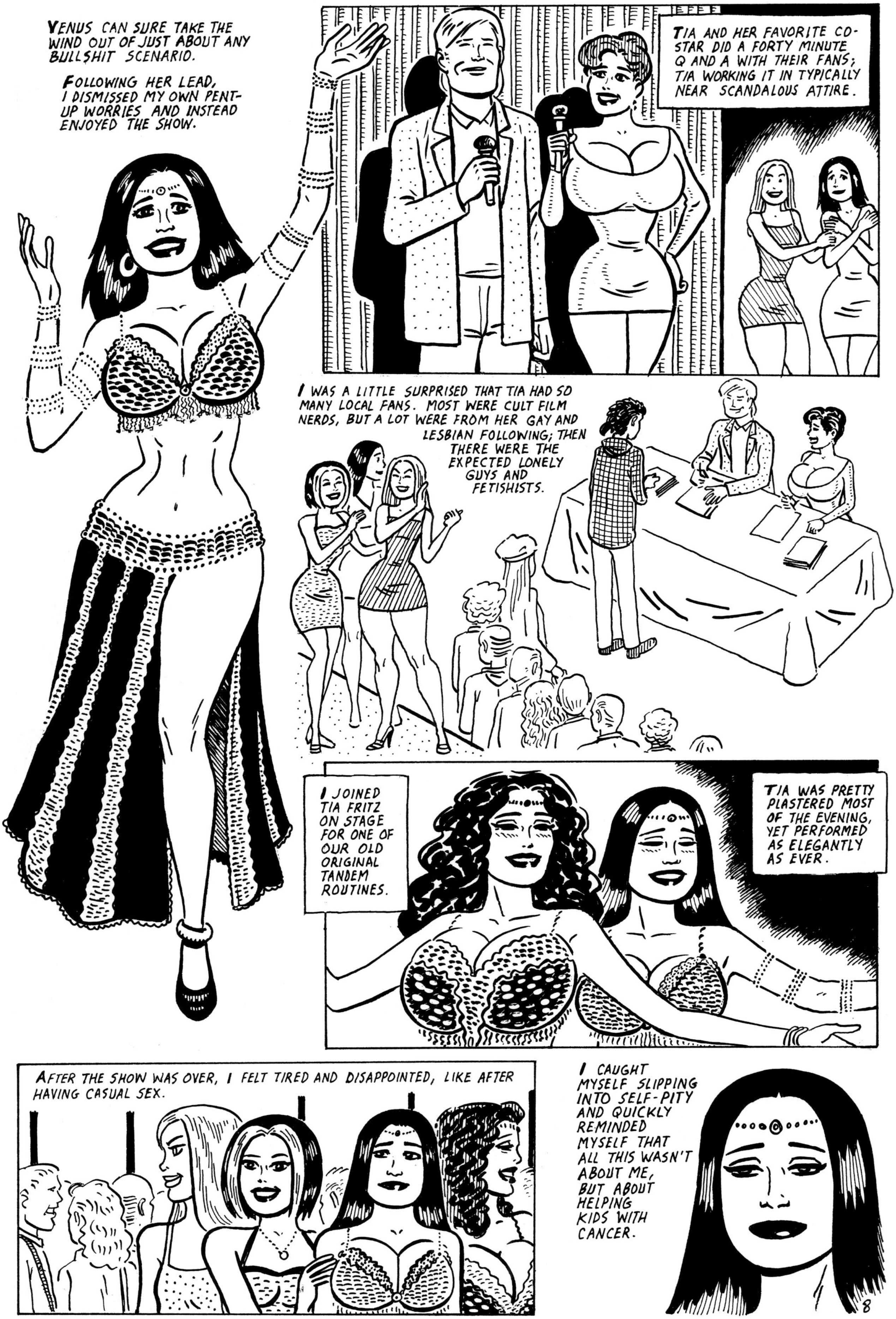
VENUS CAN SURE TAKE THE WIND OUT OF JUST ABOUT ANY BULLSHIT SCENARIO.
FOLLOWING HER LEAD, I DISMISSED MY OWN PENT-UP WORRIES AND INSTEAD ENJOYED THE SHOW.
TIA AND HER FAVORITE CO-STAR DID A FORTY MINUTE Q AND A WITH THEIR FANS; TIA WORKING IT IN TYPICALLY NEAR SCANDALOUS ATTIRE.
I WAS A LITTLE SURPRISED THAT TIA HAD SO MANY LOCAL FANS. MOST WERE CULT FILM NERDS, BUT A LOT WERE FROM HER GAY AND LESBIAN FOLLOWING; THEN THERE WERE THE EXPECTED LONELY GUYS AND FETISHISTS.
I JOINED TIA FRITZ ON STAGE FOR ONE OF OUR OLD ORIGINAL TANDEM ROUTINES.
TIA WAS PRETTY PLASTERED MOST OF THE EVENING, YET PERFORMED AS ELEGANTLY AS EVER.
AFTER THE SHOW WAS OVER, I FELT TIRED AND DISAPPOINTED, LIKE AFTER HAVING CASUAL SEX.
I CAUGHT MYSELF SLIPPING INTO SELF-PITY AND QUICKLY REMINDED MYSELF THAT ALL THIS WASN'T ABOUT ME, BUT ABOUT HELPING KIDS WITH CANCER.
8

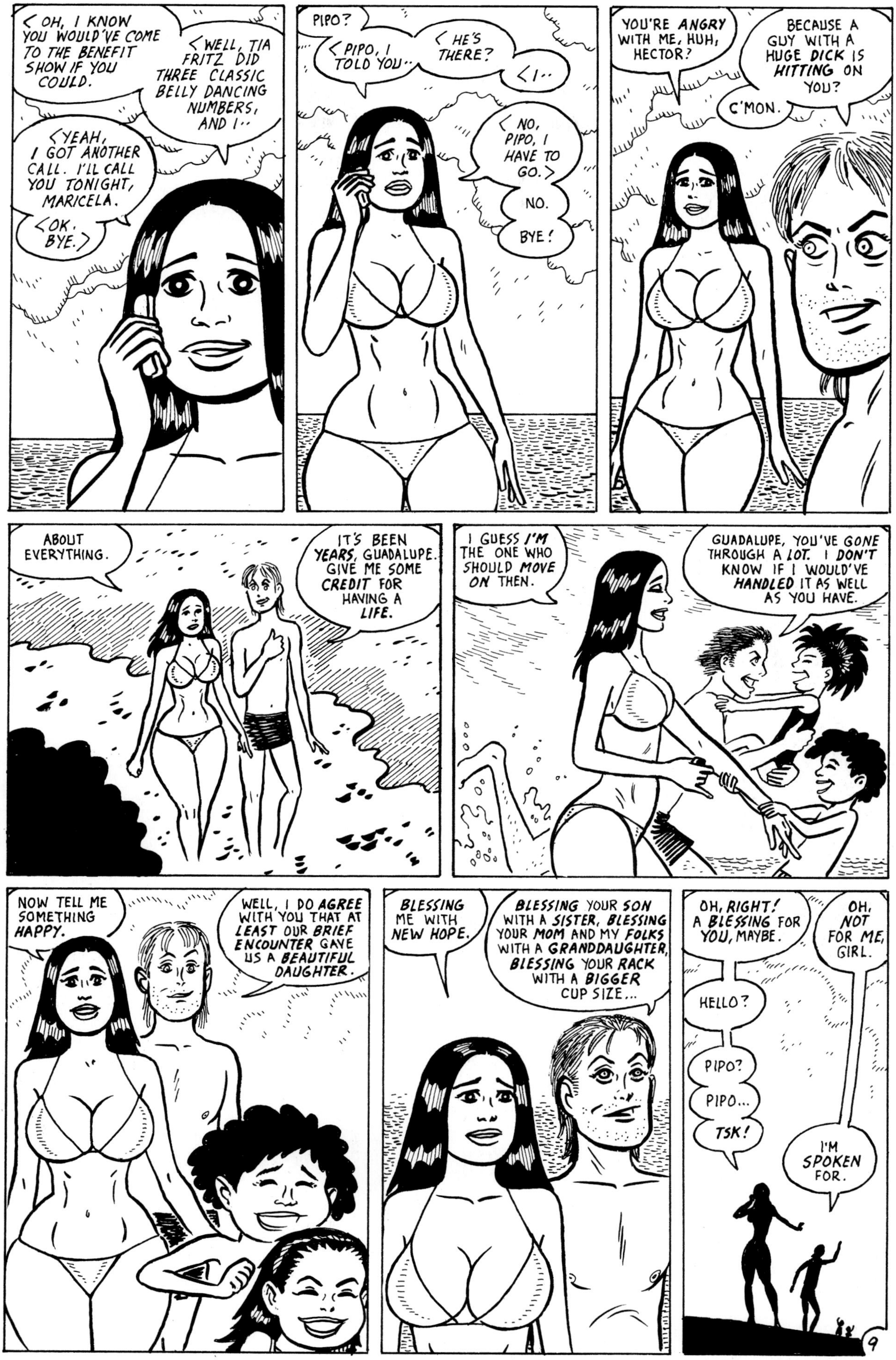

< OH, I KNOW YOU WOULD'VE COME TO THE BENEFIT SHOW IF YOU COULD.
< WELL, TIA FRITZ DID THREE CLASSIC BELLY DANCING NUMBERS, AND I...
< YEAH, I GOT ANOTHER CALL. I'LL CALL YOU TONIGHT, MARICELA.
< OK. BYE. >
PIPO?
< PIPO, I TOLD YOU...
< HE'S THERE?
< I...
< NO, PIPO, I HAVE TO GO. >
NO.
BYE!
YOU'RE ANGRY WITH ME, HUH, HECTOR?
BECAUSE A GUY WITH A HUGE DICK IS HITTING ON YOU?
C'MON.
ABOUT EVERYTHING.
IT'S BEEN YEARS, GUADALUPE. GIVE ME SOME CREDIT FOR HAVING A LIFE.
I GUESS I'M THE ONE WHO SHOULD MOVE ON THEN.
GUADALUPE, YOU'VE GONE THROUGH A LOT. I DON'T KNOW IF I WOULD'VE HANDLED IT AS WELL AS YOU HAVE.
NOW TELL ME SOMETHING HAPPY.
WELL, I DO AGREE WITH YOU THAT AT LEAST OUR BRIEF ENCOUNTER GAVE US A BEAUTIFUL DAUGHTER.
BLESSING ME WITH NEW HOPE.
BLESSING YOUR SON WITH A SISTER, BLESSING YOUR MOM AND MY FOLKS WITH A GRANDDAUGHTER, BLESSING YOUR RACK WITH A BIGGER CUP SIZE...
OH, RIGHT! A BLESSING FOR YOU, MAYBE.
OH, NOT FOR ME, GIRL.
HELLO?
PIPO?
PIPO...
TSK!
I'M SPOKEN FOR.
9

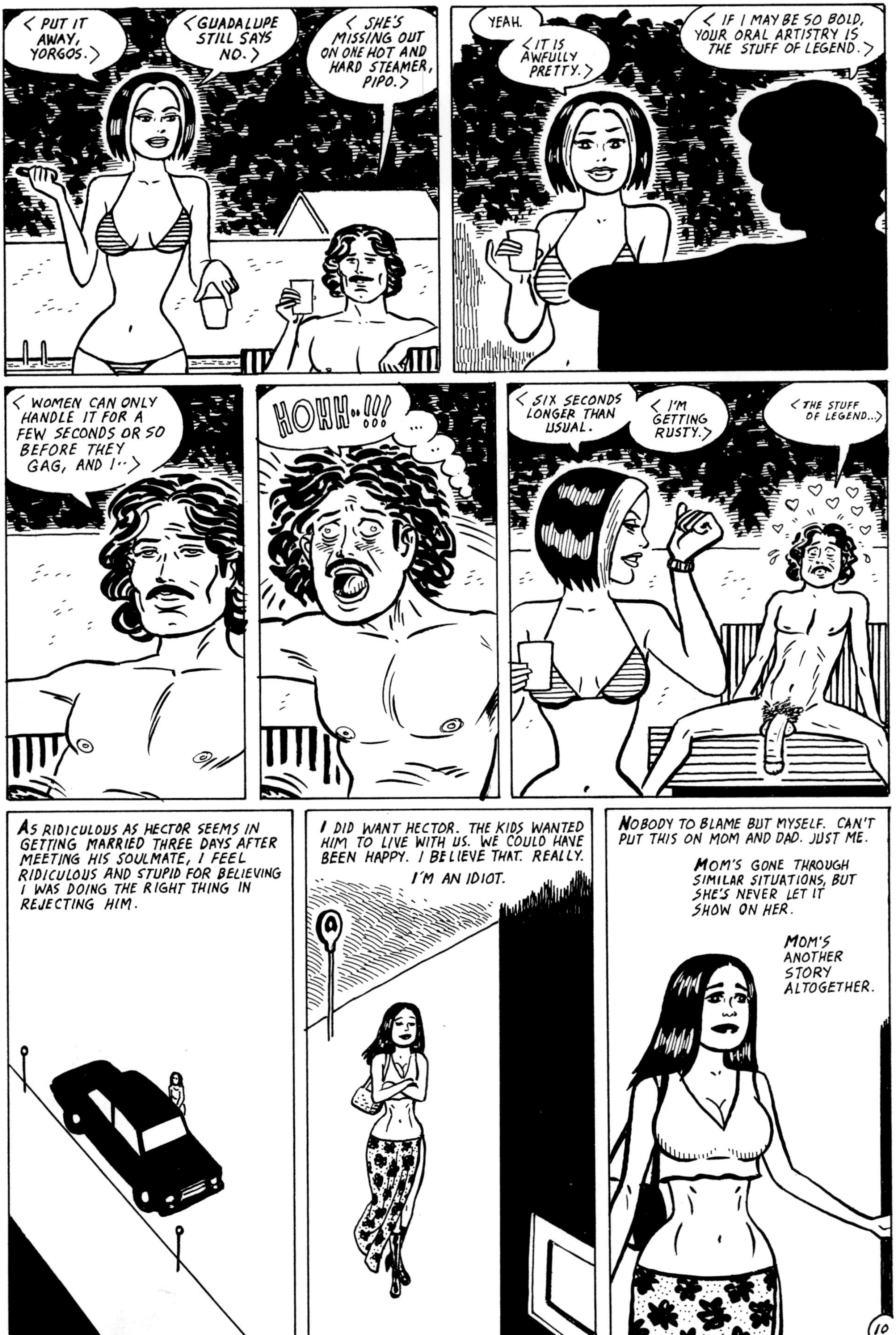

< PUT IT AWAY, YORGOS. >
< GUADALUPE STILL SAYS NO. >
< SHE'S MISSING OUT ON ONE HOT AND HARD STEAMER, PIPO. >
YEAH.
< IT IS AWFULLY PRETTY. >
< IF I MAY BE SO BOLD, YOUR ORAL ARTISTRY IS THE STUFF OF LEGEND. >
< WOMEN CAN ONLY HANDLE IT FOR A FEW SECONDS OR SO BEFORE THEY GAG, AND I.. >
HOHH..!!!
...
< SIX SECONDS LONGER THAN USUAL. >
< I'M GETTING RUSTY. >
< THE STUFF OF LEGEND... >
AS RIDICULOUS AS HECTOR SEEMS IN GETTING MARRIED THREE DAYS AFTER MEETING HIS SOULMATE, I FEEL RIDICULOUS AND STUPID FOR BELIEVING I WAS DOING THE RIGHT THING IN REJECTING HIM.
I DID WANT HECTOR. THE KIDS WANTED HIM TO LIVE WITH US. WE COULD HAVE BEEN HAPPY. I BELIEVE THAT. REALLY.
I'M AN IDIOT.
NOBODY TO BLAME BUT MYSELF. CAN'T PUT THIS ON MOM AND DAD. JUST ME.
MOM'S GONE THROUGH SIMILAR SITUATIONS, BUT SHE'S NEVER LET IT SHOW ON HER.
MOM'S ANOTHER STORY ALTOGETHER.
10

Panel 1:
< THE SHOW WAS GREAT, GUADALUPE. GOOD MUSIC, EVERYTHING. >

< THANKS, PAULO. I'M GLAD YOU COULD BRING YOUR FAMILY. >

TSK, OH!

< GUADALUPE, I THOUGHT YOUR SHOW WAS NEXT WEEK, HONEY. >

TAXES

Panel 2:
< YOU USED TO BE BETTER AT LYING, MAMA. YOU'RE OUT OF PRACTICE. >

< THE THINGS KIDS SAY TO THEIR PARENTS THESE DAYS! >

IMMIGRATION

Panel 3:
MOM'S NOT SPEAKING TO HER HALF-SISTERS ANY MORE. TIA FRITZ AND TIA PETRA REFUSE TO TALK ABOUT IT.

IT MUST HAVE BEEN ONE SERIOUS NUCLEAR BLOWOUT FOR THE AGES.

TAXES

Panel 4:
< I LOST THAT BIG JACKPOT LOTTERY BY FIVE NUMBERS. >

< I QUIT PLAYING. THE DISAPPOINTMENT WAS WEARING ME OUT. >

Panel 5:
MY GRANDMOTHER ABANDONED MOM WHEN SHE WAS A BABY. MOM AND HER HALF SISTERS DIDN'T EVEN KNOW ABOUT EACH OTHER UNTIL A FEW YEARS AGO.

MOM NEVER WARMED UP TO HAVING LONG LOST SIBLINGS AND NOW ACTS LIKE SHE NEVER KNEW THEM.

SHE DOES SEEM HAPPIER WITH HER SIMPLER LIFE THESE DAYS.

Panel 6:
< WELL, I BETTER GET HOME, MAMA. I HAVE TO CORRECT A TON OF TEST PAPERS. >

< PIPO CAME TO SEE ME YESTERDAY. WE HAD A GOOD CRY TOGETHER. >

CELL PHONES

BEEPERS

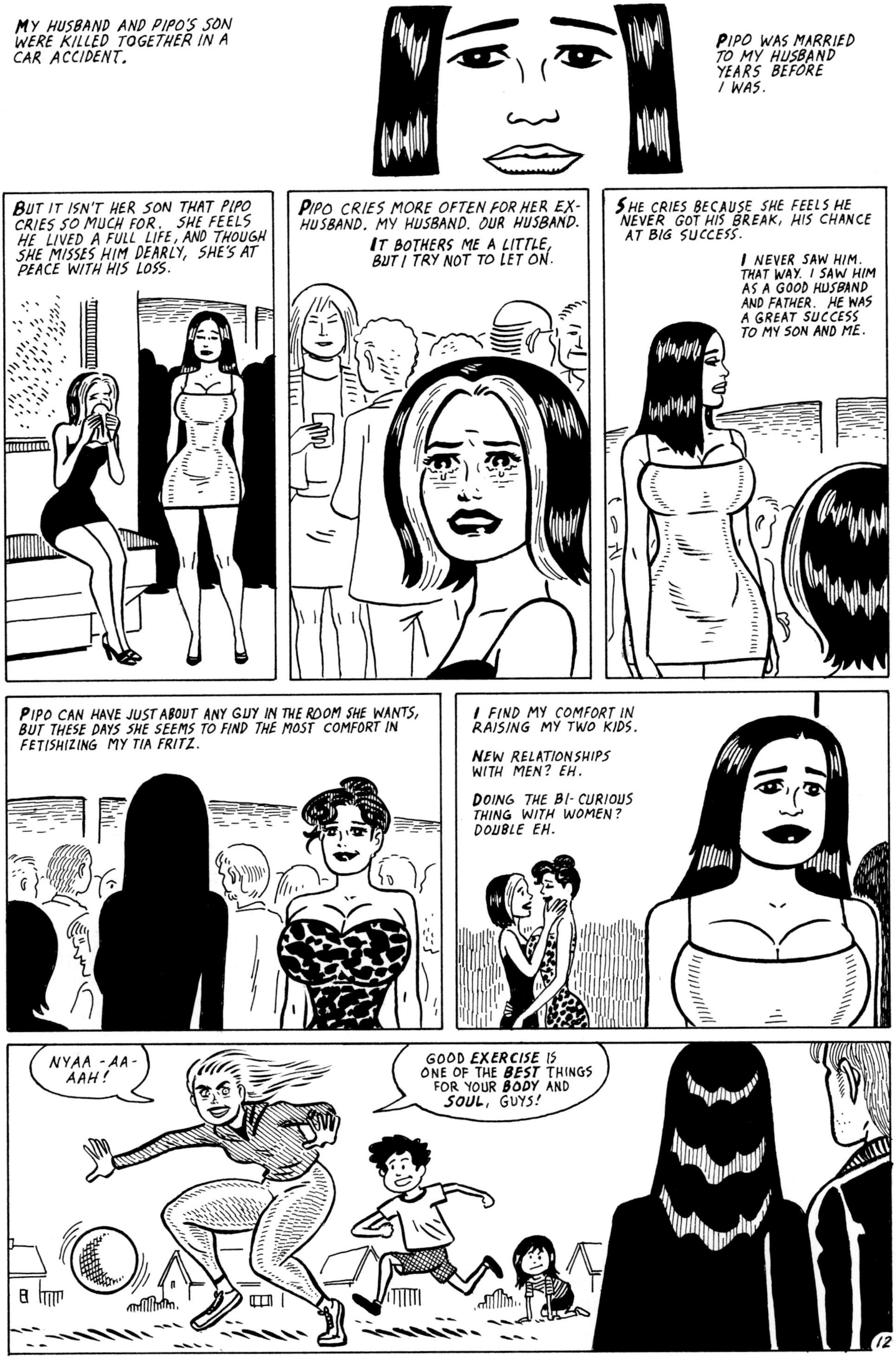
MY HUSBAND AND PIPO'S SON WERE KILLED TOGETHER IN A CAR ACCIDENT.
PIPO WAS MARRIED TO MY HUSBAND YEARS BEFORE I WAS.
BUT IT ISN'T HER SON THAT PIPO CRIES SO MUCH FOR. SHE FEELS HE LIVED A FULL LIFE, AND THOUGH SHE MISSES HIM DEARLY, SHE'S AT PEACE WITH HIS LOSS.
PIPO CRIES MORE OFTEN FOR HER EX-HUSBAND. MY HUSBAND. OUR HUSBAND.
IT BOTHERS ME A LITTLE, BUT I TRY NOT TO LET ON.
SHE CRIES BECAUSE SHE FEELS HE NEVER GOT HIS BREAK, HIS CHANCE AT BIG SUCCESS.
I NEVER SAW HIM. THAT WAY. I SAW HIM AS A GOOD HUSBAND AND FATHER. HE WAS A GREAT SUCCESS TO MY SON AND ME.
PIPO CAN HAVE JUST ABOUT ANY GUY IN THE ROOM SHE WANTS, BUT THESE DAYS SHE SEEMS TO FIND THE MOST COMFORT IN FETISHIZING MY TIA FRITZ.
I FIND MY COMFORT IN RAISING MY TWO KIDS.
NEW RELATIONSHIPS WITH MEN? EH.
DOING THE BI-CURIOUS THING WITH WOMEN? DOUBLE EH.
NYAA-AA-AAH!
GOOD EXERCISE IS ONE OF THE BEST THINGS FOR YOUR BODY AND SOUL, GUYS!
12

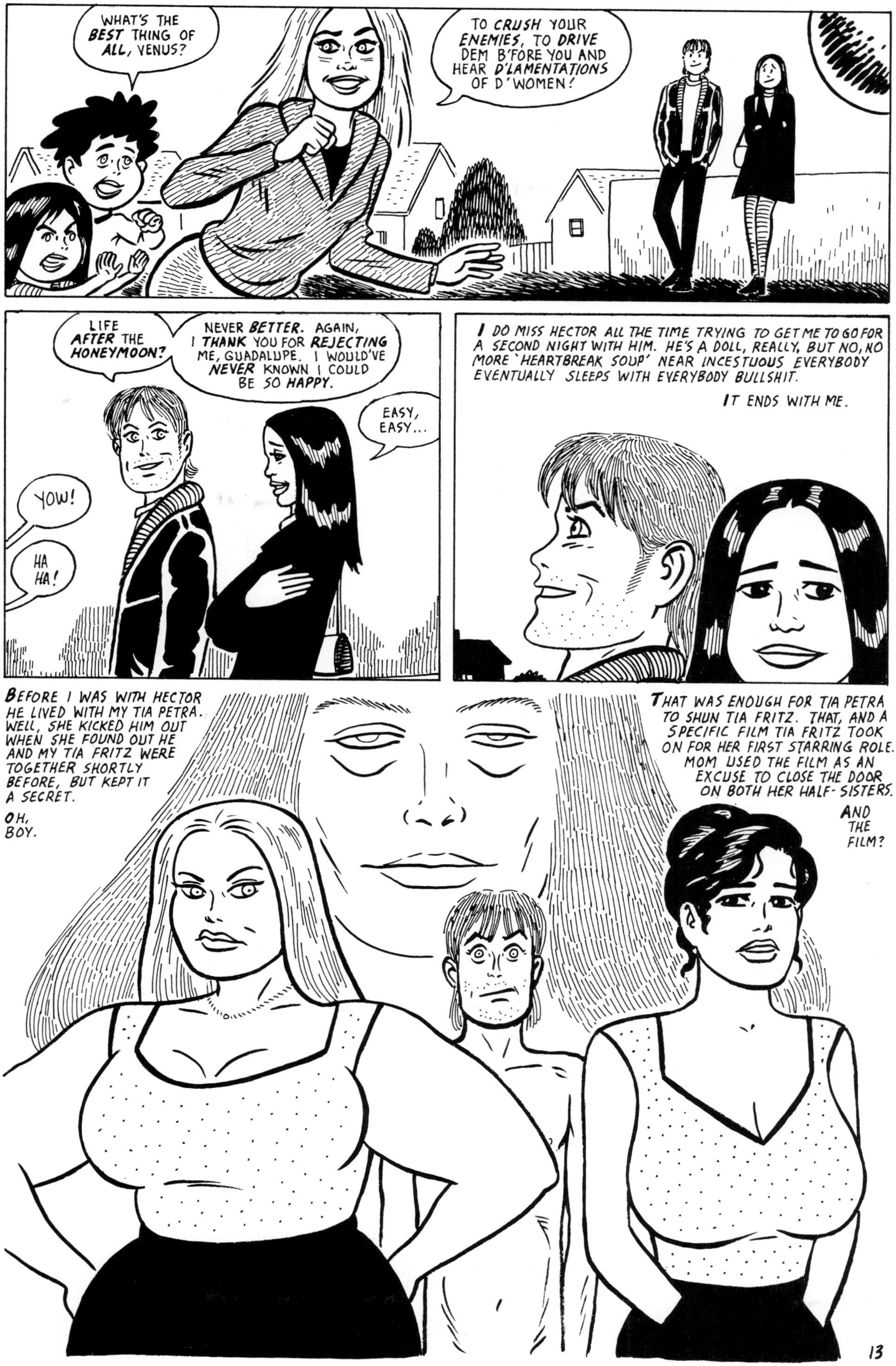

WHAT'S THE BEST THING OF ALL, VENUS?
TO CRUSH YOUR ENEMIES, TO DRIVE DEM B'FORE YOU AND HEAR D'LAMENTATIONS OF D'WOMEN!
LIFE AFTER THE HONEYMOON?
NEVER BETTER. AGAIN, I THANK YOU FOR REJECTING ME, GUADALUPE. I WOULD'VE NEVER KNOWN I COULD BE SO HAPPY.
EASY, EASY...
YOW!
HA HA!
I DO MISS HECTOR ALL THE TIME TRYING TO GET ME TO GO FOR A SECOND NIGHT WITH HIM. HE'S A DOLL, REALLY, BUT NO, NO MORE 'HEARTBREAK SOUP' NEAR INCESTUOUS EVERYBODY EVENTUALLY SLEEPS WITH EVERYBODY BULLSHIT.
IT ENDS WITH ME.
BEFORE I WAS WITH HECTOR HE LIVED WITH MY TIA PETRA. WELL, SHE KICKED HIM OUT WHEN SHE FOUND OUT HE AND MY TIA FRITZ WERE TOGETHER SHORTLY BEFORE, BUT KEPT IT A SECRET.
OH, BOY.
THAT WAS ENOUGH FOR TIA PETRA TO SHUN TIA FRITZ. THAT, AND A SPECIFIC FILM TIA FRITZ TOOK ON FOR HER FIRST STARRING ROLE. MOM USED THE FILM AS AN EXCUSE TO CLOSE THE DOOR ON BOTH HER HALF-SISTERS.
AND THE FILM?
13

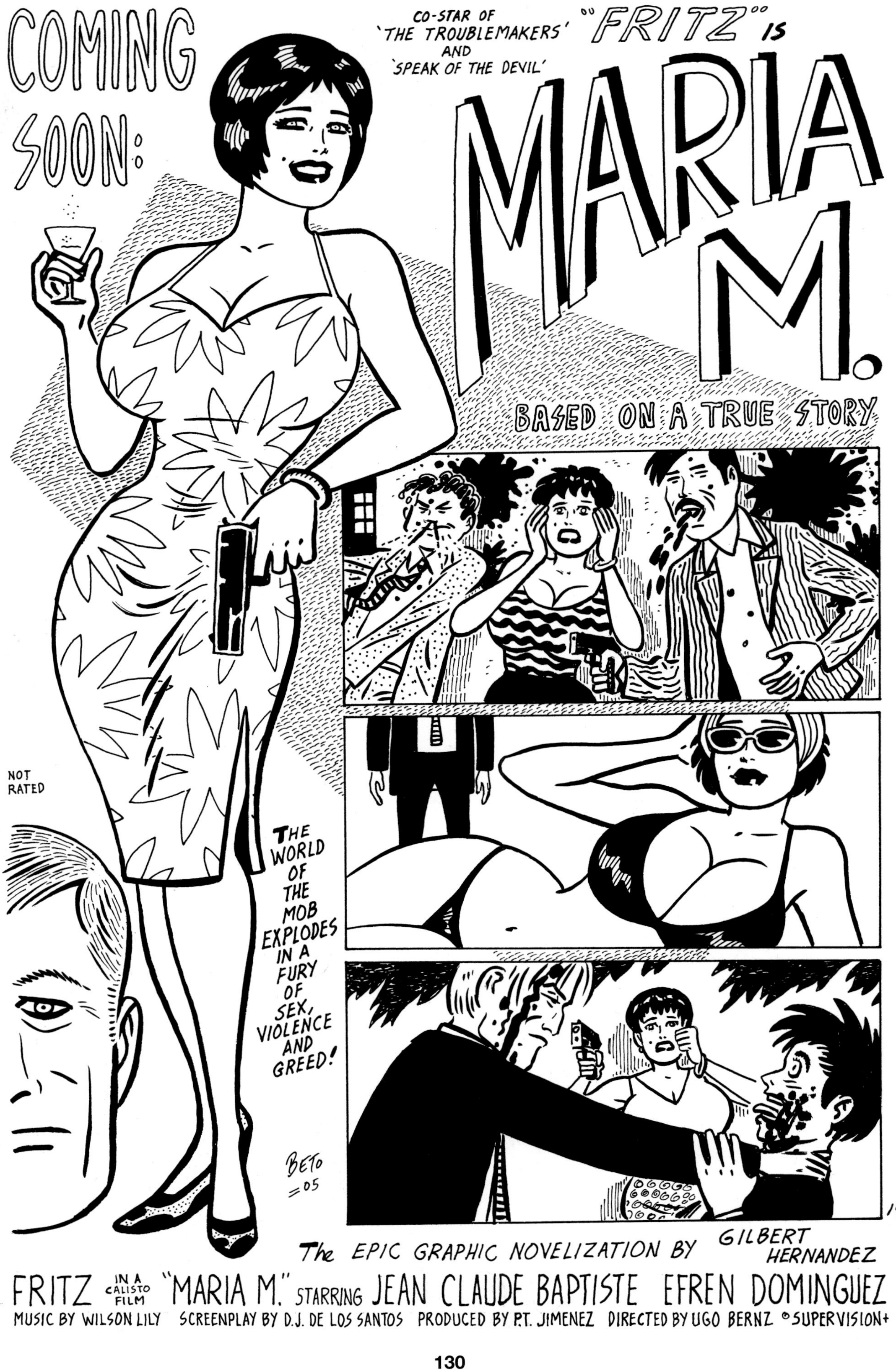
COMING SOON:
CO-STAR OF 'THE TROUBLEMAKERS' AND 'SPEAK OF THE DEVIL'
"FRITZ" IS
MARIA M.
BASED ON A TRUE STORY
NOT RATED
THE WORLD OF THE MOB EXPLODES IN A FURY OF SEX, VIOLENCE AND GREED!
BETO =05
14
The EPIC GRAPHIC NOVELIZATION BY GILBERT HERNANDEZ
FRITZ IN A CALISTO FILM "MARIA M." STARRING JEAN CLAUDE BAPTISTE EFREN DOMINGUEZ
MUSIC BY WILSON LILY SCREENPLAY BY D.J. DE LOS SANTOS PRODUCED BY P.T. JIMENEZ DIRECTED BY UGO BERNZ ©SUPERVISION+

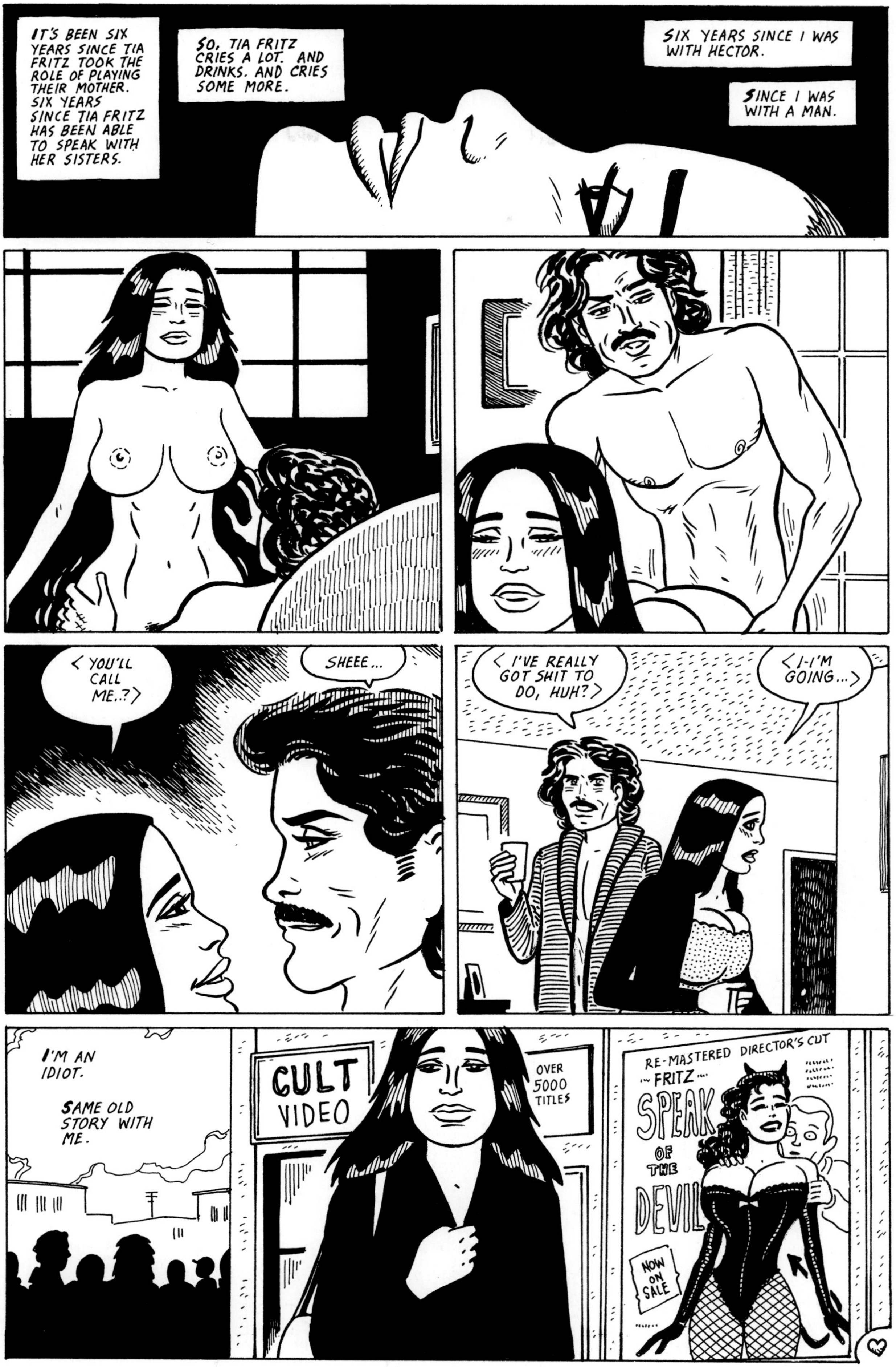
IT'S BEEN SIX YEARS SINCE TIA FRITZ TOOK THE ROLE OF PLAYING THEIR MOTHER. SIX YEARS SINCE TIA FRITZ HAS BEEN ABLE TO SPEAK WITH HER SISTERS.
SO, TIA FRITZ CRIES A LOT. AND DRINKS. AND CRIES SOME MORE.
SIX YEARS SINCE I WAS WITH HECTOR.
SINCE I WAS WITH A MAN.
< YOU'LL CALL ME..? >
SHEEE...
< I'VE REALLY GOT SHIT TO DO, HUH? >
< I-I'M GOING... >
I'M AN IDIOT.
SAME OLD STORY WITH ME.
CULT VIDEO
OVER 5000 TITLES
RE-MASTERED DIRECTOR'S CUT
FRITZ
SPEAK OF THE DEVIL
NOW ON SALE
15

GENETICALLY
PREDISPOSED

BETO/06

WHAT DO YOU MEAN? SCARED OF WHAT?

IF YOU'RE SCARED BECAUSE YOU DON'T REALLY KNOW ME.

BECAUSE WE GOT MARRIED THREE DAYS AFTER WE MET.

ARE YOU SCARED?

NO,.. I WAS JUST, Y'KNOW, WONDERING...

YOU ARE! YOU ARE SCARED!

YOU'RE SCARED BECAUSE YOU WON'T ANSWER THE QUESTION!

WE'RE HAVING OUR FIRST FIGHT.

OH.

I'M GENETICALLY PREDISPOSED TO SAY THE FIRST THING THAT COMES TO MIND; WHATEVER THE SITUATION.

MY DAD'S GOTTEN HIMSELF IN DEEP SHIT FROM THINGS HE'S SAID; MY GRANDMA TOO...

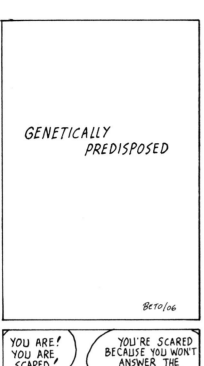

GUADALUPE'S NOT TOO SHY ABOUT THE EXTRA ATTENTION SHE GETS FROM HER GENETICALLY PREPISPOSED BIG TITS!

AY, SANDY; YOU AND HECTOR WITH MY BOOBS!

DO YOU THINK I SHOULD BE WEARING A MORE REVEALING TOP?

I'M GENETICALLY PREDISPOSED TO BE SECOND GUESSING EVERYTHING TO THE NTH DEGREE.

JUST LIKE MY MOM, MY UNCLES...

IT SCARES ME BECAUSE NONE OF THEM HAVE EVER BEEN TRULY HAPPY.

WELL, SINCE WE'VE HAD OUR FIRST FIGHT, WE'RE ENTITLED TO OUR FIRST 'MAKING UP' LOVE SESSION, Y'KNOW.

SNORT.

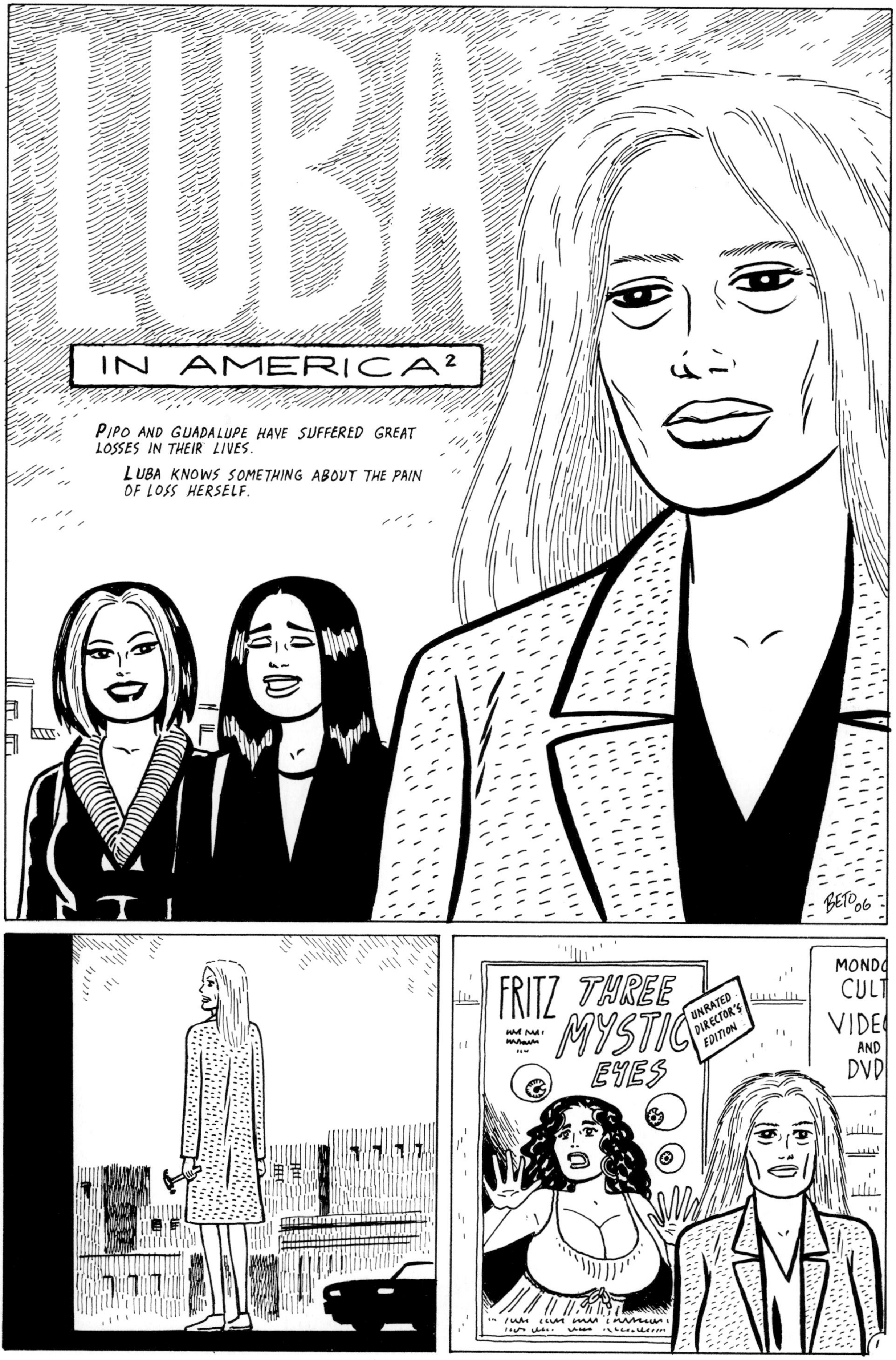
LUBA
IN AMERICA²
PIPO AND GUADALUPE HAVE SUFFERED GREAT LOSSES IN THEIR LIVES.
LUBA KNOWS SOMETHING ABOUT THE PAIN OF LOSS HERSELF.
BETO 06
FRITZ
THREE MYSTIC EYES
UNRATED DIRECTOR'S EDITION
MONDO CULT VIDEO AND DVD

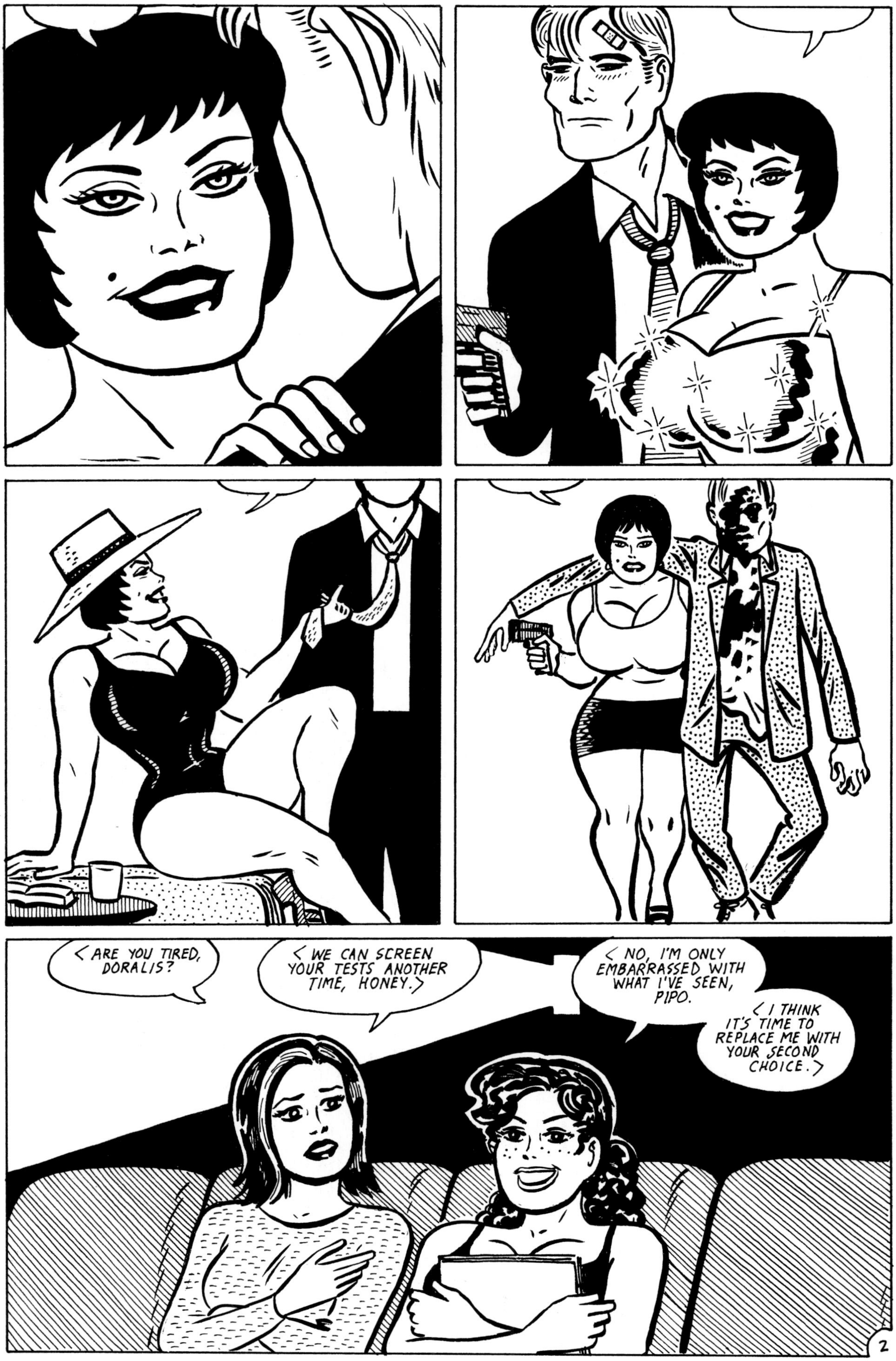

< ARE YOU TIRED, DORALIS?
< WE CAN SCREEN YOUR TESTS ANOTHER TIME, HONEY.>
< NO, I'M ONLY EMBARRASSED WITH WHAT I'VE SEEN, PIPO.
< I THINK IT'S TIME TO REPLACE ME WITH YOUR SECOND CHOICE.>
2

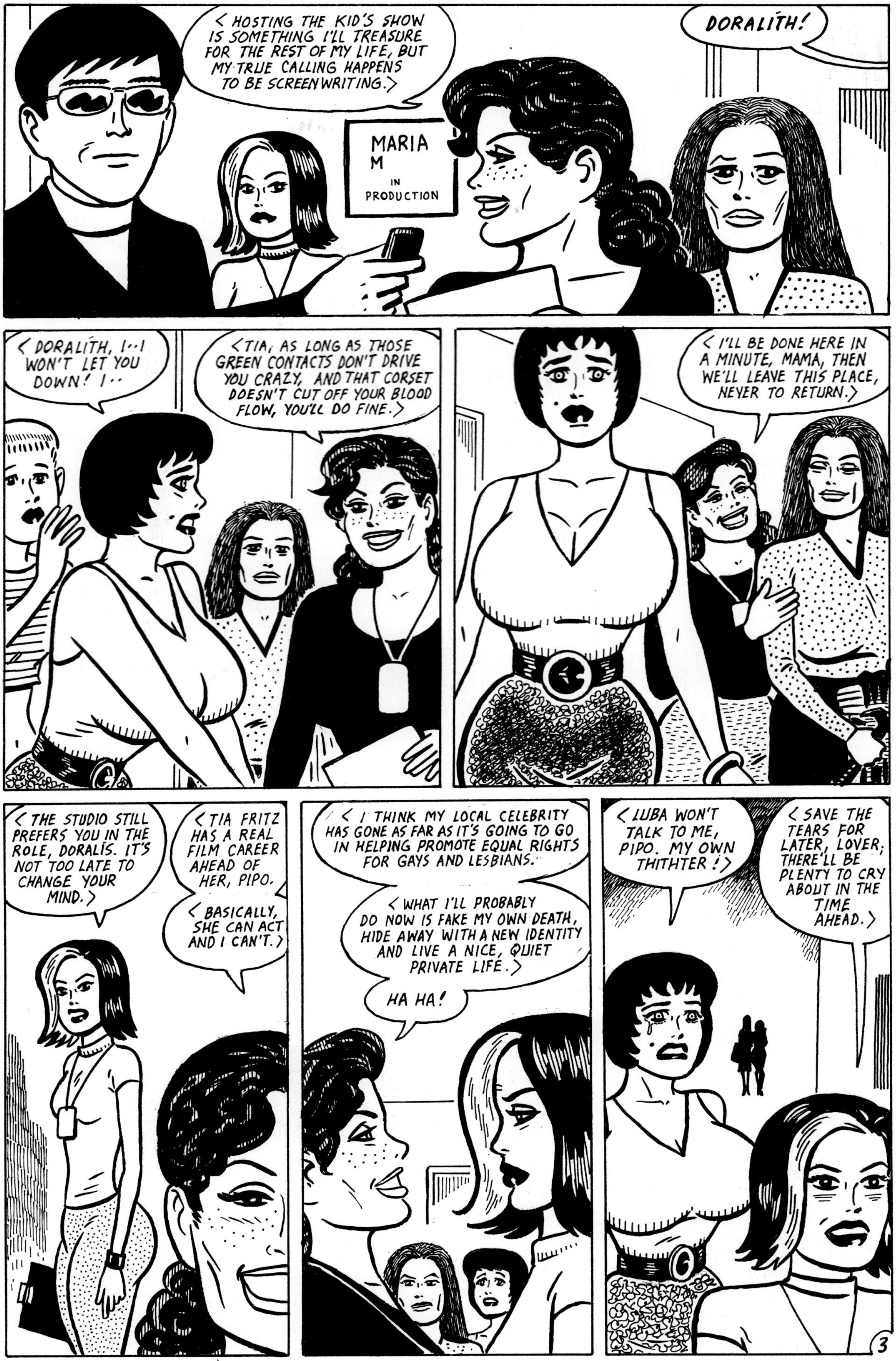

< HOSTING THE KID'S SHOW IS SOMETHING I'LL TREASURE FOR THE REST OF MY LIFE, BUT MY TRUE CALLING HAPPENS TO BE SCREENWRITING. >
MARIA M IN PRODUCTION
DORALITH!
< DORALITH, I.. I WON'T LET YOU DOWN! I.. >
< TIA, AS LONG AS THOSE GREEN CONTACTS DON'T DRIVE YOU CRAZY, AND THAT CORSET DOESN'T CUT OFF YOUR BLOOD FLOW, YOU'LL DO FINE. >
< I'LL BE DONE HERE IN A MINUTE, MAMA, THEN WE'LL LEAVE THIS PLACE, NEVER TO RETURN. >
< THE STUDIO STILL PREFERS YOU IN THE ROLE, DORALÍS. IT'S NOT TOO LATE TO CHANGE YOUR MIND. >
< TIA FRITZ HAS A REAL FILM CAREER AHEAD OF HER, PIPO.
< BASICALLY, SHE CAN ACT AND I CAN'T. >
< I THINK MY LOCAL CELEBRITY HAS GONE AS FAR AS IT'S GOING TO GO IN HELPING PROMOTE EQUAL RIGHTS FOR GAYS AND LESBIANS.
< WHAT I'LL PROBABLY DO NOW IS FAKE MY OWN DEATH, HIDE AWAY WITH A NEW IDENTITY AND LIVE A NICE, QUIET PRIVATE LIFE. >
HA HA!
< LUBA WON'T TALK TO ME, PIPO. MY OWN THITHTER! >
< SAVE THE TEARS FOR LATER, LOVER; THERE'LL BE PLENTY TO CRY ABOUT IN THE TIME AHEAD. >
3

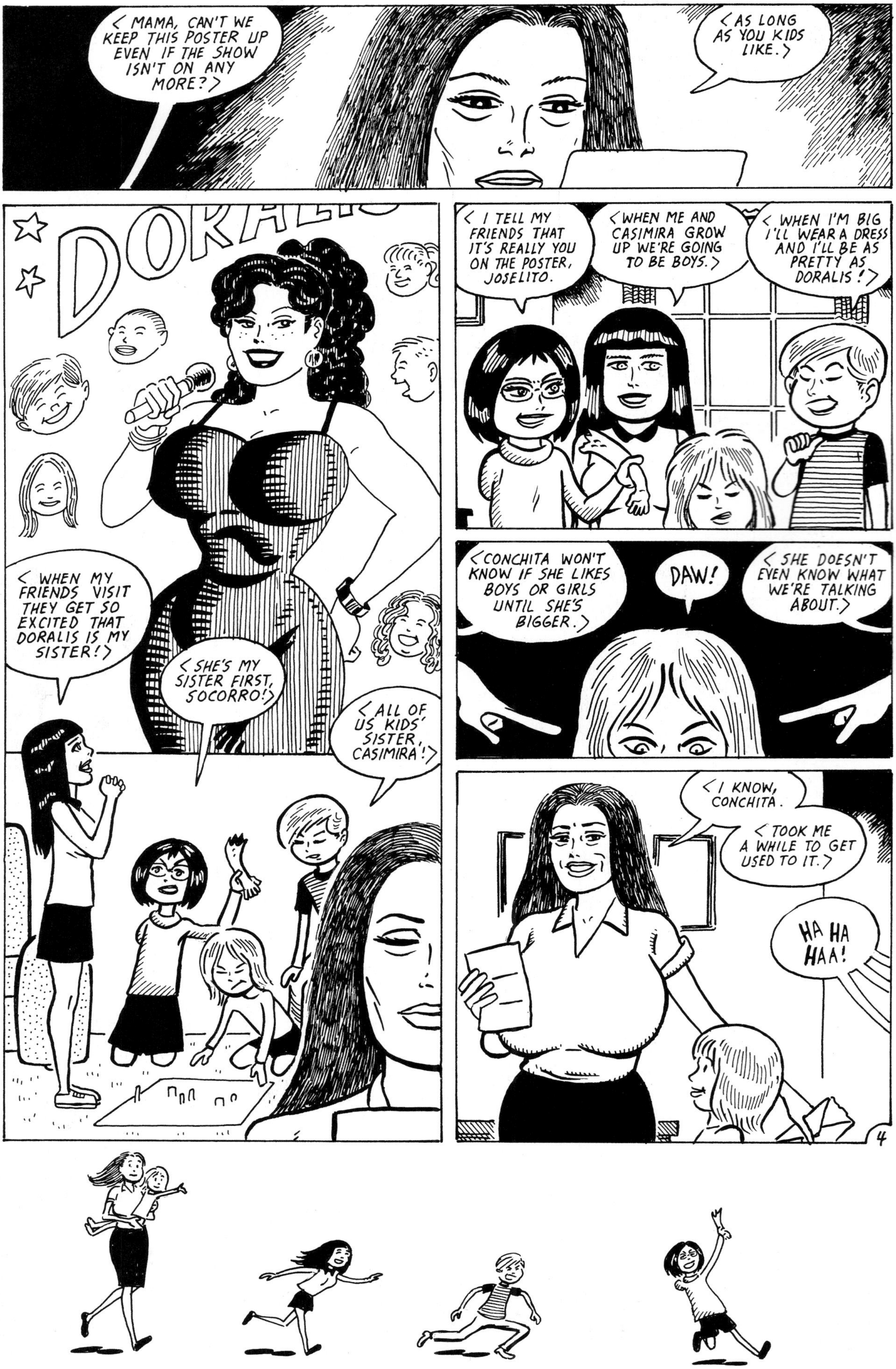

< MAMA, CAN'T WE KEEP THIS POSTER UP EVEN IF THE SHOW ISN'T ON ANY MORE? >
< AS LONG AS YOU KIDS LIKE. >
DORALIS
< WHEN MY FRIENDS VISIT THEY GET SO EXCITED THAT DORALIS IS MY SISTER! >
< SHE'S MY SISTER FIRST, SOCORRO! >
< ALL OF US KIDS' SISTER, CASIMIRA! >
< I TELL MY FRIENDS THAT IT'S REALLY YOU ON THE POSTER, JOSELITO.
< WHEN ME AND CASIMIRA GROW UP WE'RE GOING TO BE BOYS. >
< WHEN I'M BIG I'LL WEAR A DRESS AND I'LL BE AS PRETTY AS DORALIS! >
< CONCHITA WON'T KNOW IF SHE LIKES BOYS OR GIRLS UNTIL SHE'S BIGGER. >
DAW!
< SHE DOESN'T EVEN KNOW WHAT WE'RE TALKING ABOUT. >
< I KNOW, CONCHITA.
< TOOK ME A WHILE TO GET USED TO IT. >
HA HA HAA!
4

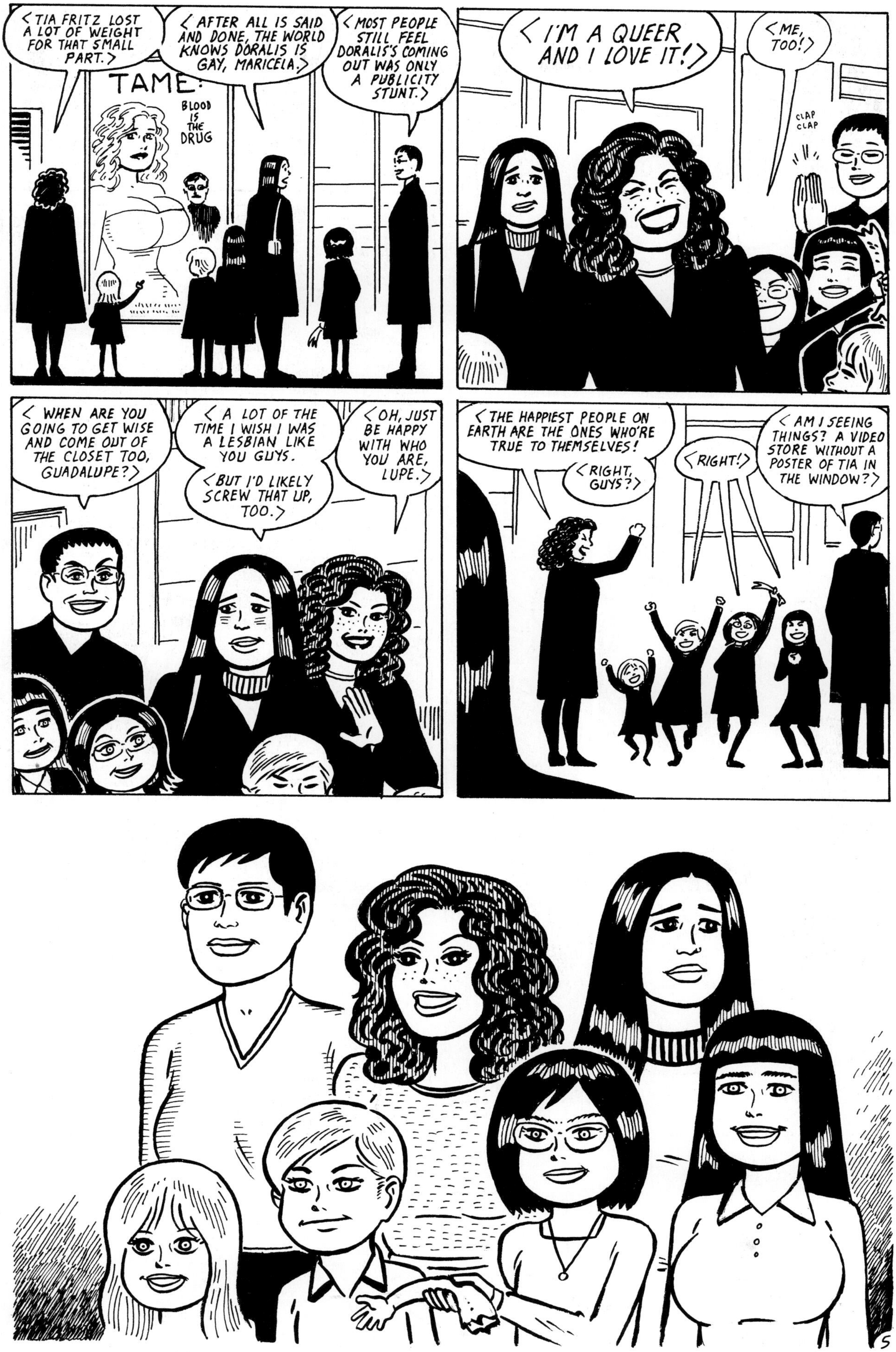
<TIA FRITZ LOST A LOT OF WEIGHT FOR THAT SMALL PART.>
TAME: BLOOD IS THE DRUG
<AFTER ALL IS SAID AND DONE, THE WORLD KNOWS DORALIS IS GAY, MARICELA.>
<MOST PEOPLE STILL FEEL DORALIS'S COMING OUT WAS ONLY A PUBLICITY STUNT.>
<I'M A QUEER AND I LOVE IT!>
<ME, TOO!>
CLAP CLAP
<WHEN ARE YOU GOING TO GET WISE AND COME OUT OF THE CLOSET TOO, GUADALUPE?>
<A LOT OF THE TIME I WISH I WAS A LESBIAN LIKE YOU GUYS.
<BUT I'D LIKELY SCREW THAT UP, TOO.>
<OH, JUST BE HAPPY WITH WHO YOU ARE, LUPE.>
<THE HAPPIEST PEOPLE ON EARTH ARE THE ONES WHO'RE TRUE TO THEMSELVES!
<RIGHT, GUYS?>
<RIGHT!>
<AM I SEEING THINGS? A VIDEO STORE WITHOUT A POSTER OF TIA IN THE WINDOW?>

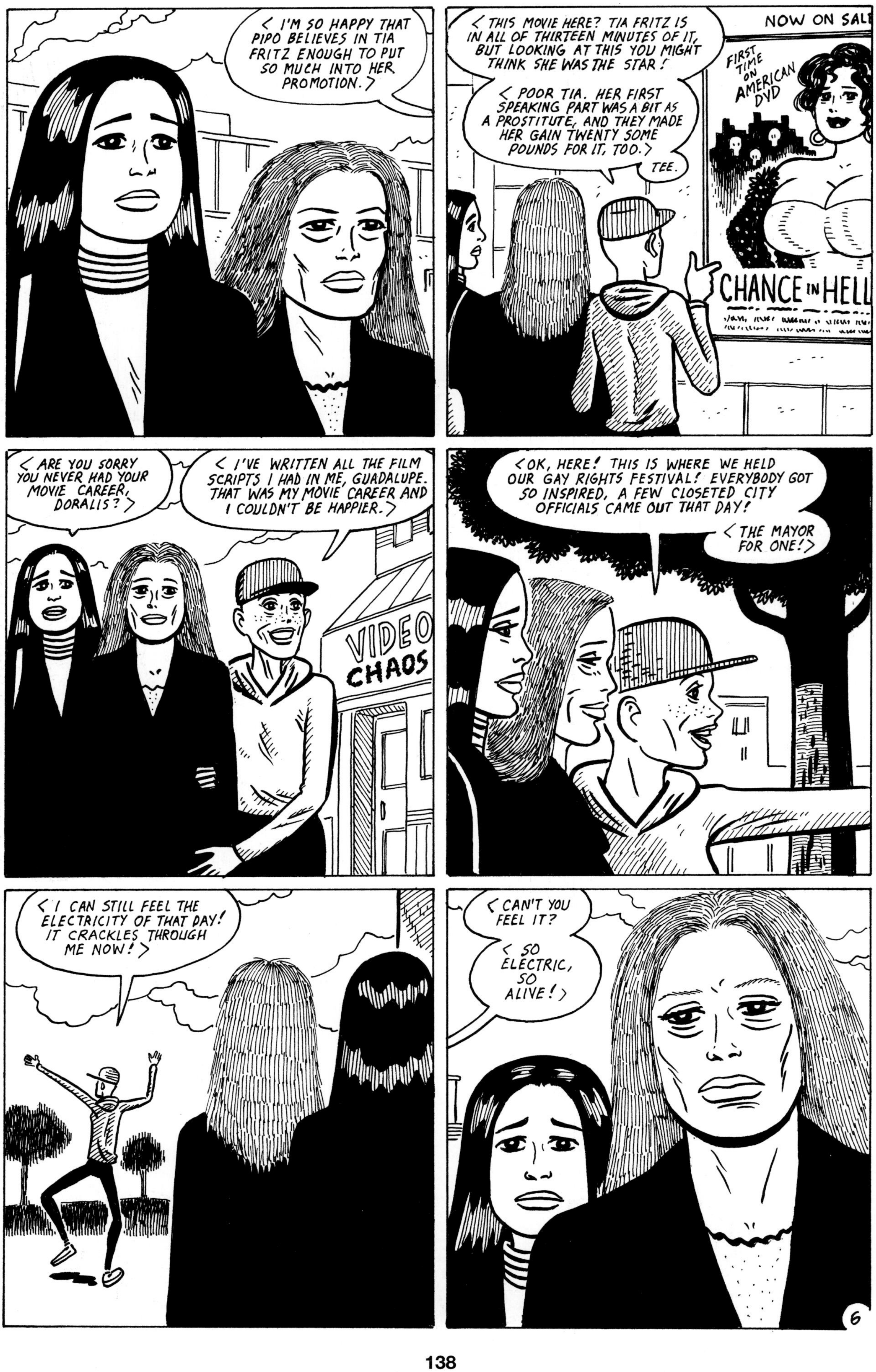
< I'M SO HAPPY THAT PIPO BELIEVES IN TIA FRITZ ENOUGH TO PUT SO MUCH INTO HER PROMOTION. >
< THIS MOVIE HERE? TIA FRITZ IS IN ALL OF THIRTEEN MINUTES OF IT, BUT LOOKING AT THIS YOU MIGHT THINK SHE WAS THE STAR!
< POOR TIA. HER FIRST SPEAKING PART WAS A BIT AS A PROSTITUTE, AND THEY MADE HER GAIN TWENTY SOME POUNDS FOR IT, TOO. >
TEE.
NOW ON SAL
FIRST TIME ON AMERICAN DVD
CHANCE IN HELL
< ARE YOU SORRY YOU NEVER HAD YOUR MOVIE CAREER, DORALIS? >
< I'VE WRITTEN ALL THE FILM SCRIPTS I HAD IN ME, GUADALUPE. THAT WAS MY MOVIE CAREER AND I COULDN'T BE HAPPIER. >
VIDEO CHAOS
< OK, HERE! THIS IS WHERE WE HELD OUR GAY RIGHTS FESTIVAL! EVERYBODY GOT SO INSPIRED, A FEW CLOSETED CITY OFFICIALS CAME OUT THAT DAY!
< THE MAYOR FOR ONE! >
< I CAN STILL FEEL THE ELECTRICITY OF THAT DAY! IT CRACKLES THROUGH ME NOW! >
< CAN'T YOU FEEL IT?
< SO ELECTRIC, SO ALIVE! >
6

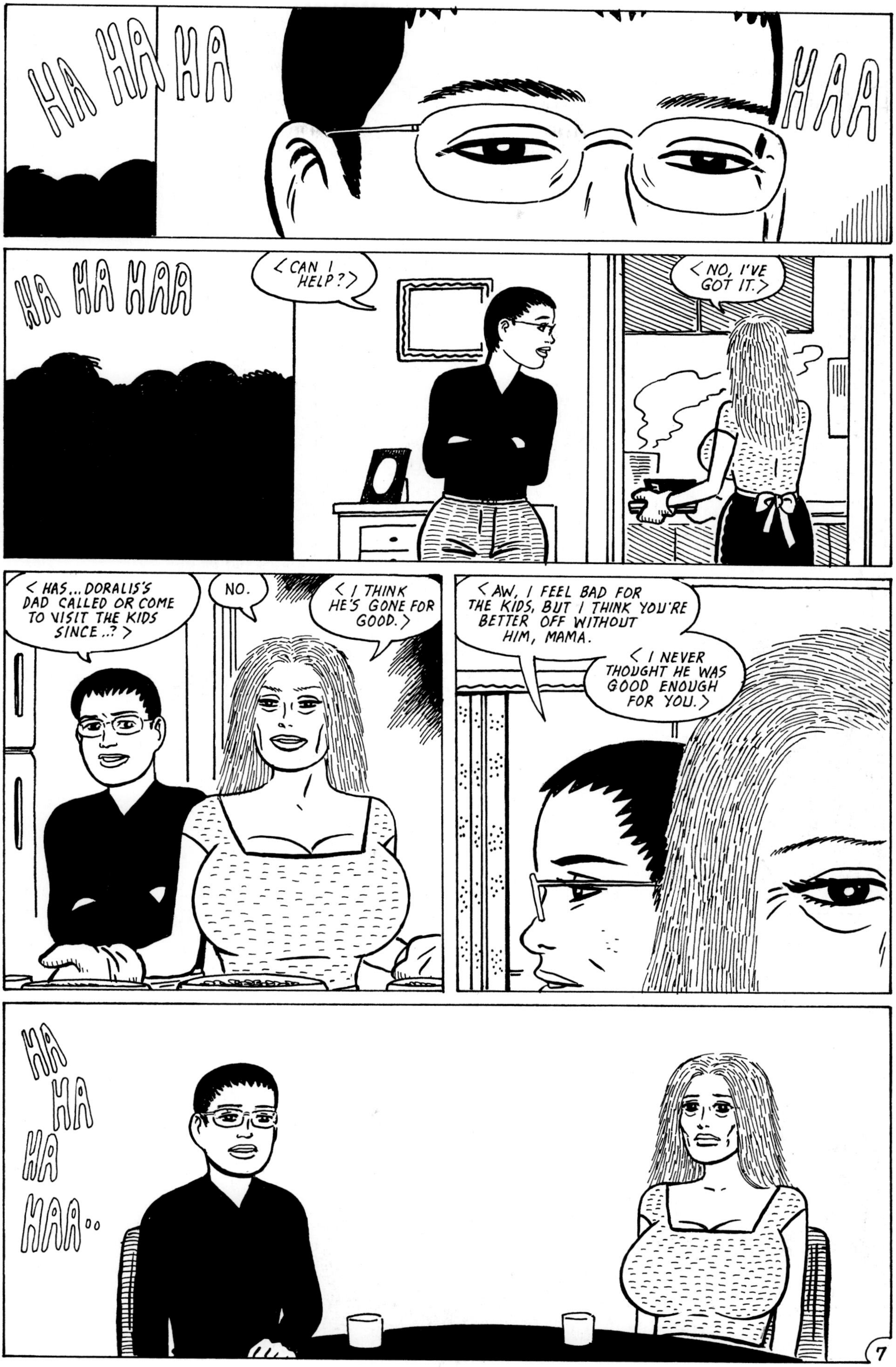
HA HA HA
HAA
HA HA HAA
< CAN I HELP? >
< NO, I'VE GOT IT. >
< HAS... DORALIS'S DAD CALLED OR COME TO VISIT THE KIDS SINCE..? >
NO.
< I THINK HE'S GONE FOR GOOD. >
< AW, I FEEL BAD FOR THE KIDS, BUT I THINK YOU'RE BETTER OFF WITHOUT HIM, MAMA.
< I NEVER THOUGHT HE WAS GOOD ENOUGH FOR YOU. >
HA HA HA HAA..
7

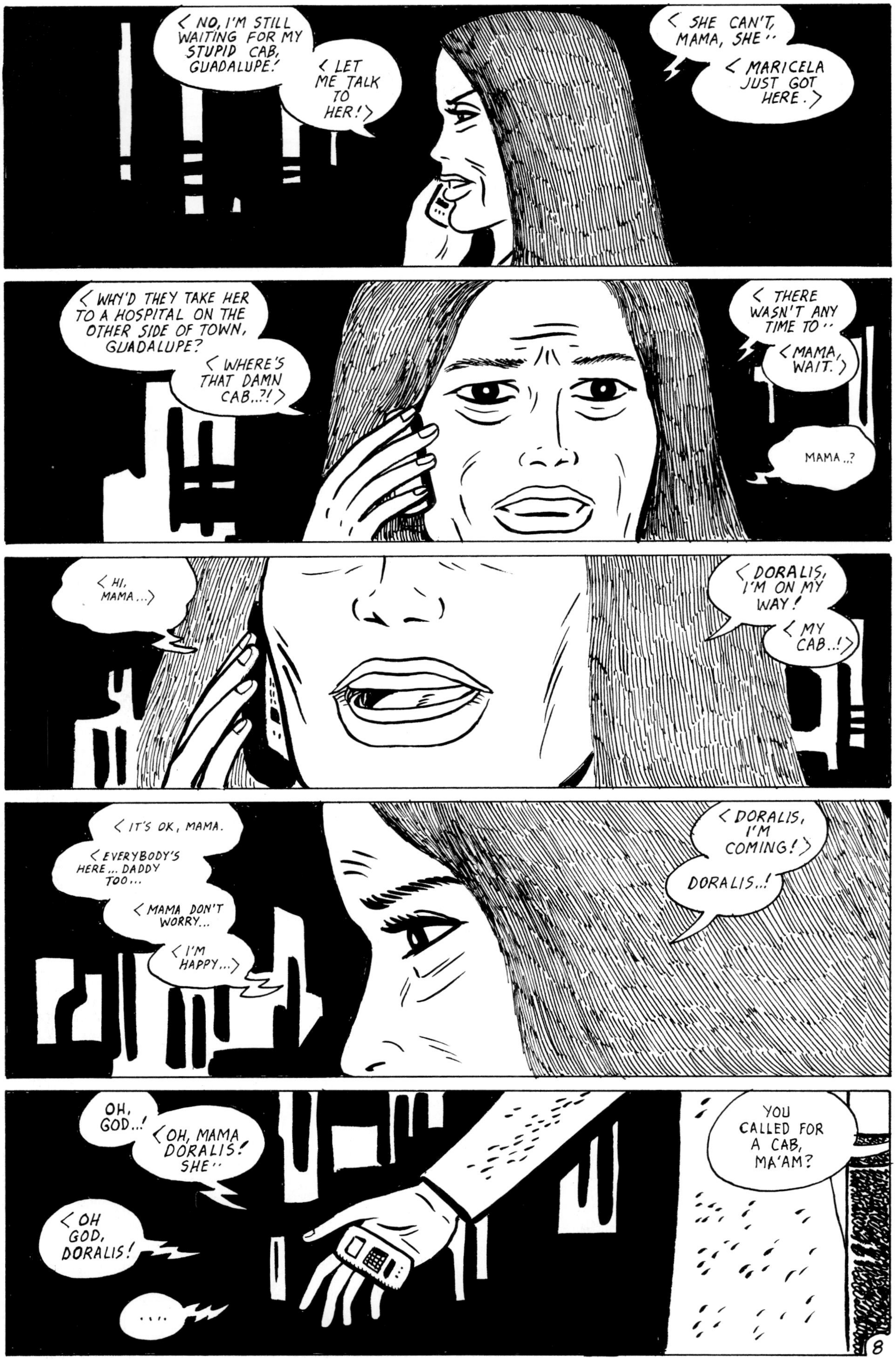

< NO, I'M STILL WAITING FOR MY STUPID CAB, GUADALUPE!
< LET ME TALK TO HER! >
< SHE CAN'T, MAMA, SHE ··
< MARICELA JUST GOT HERE. >
< WHY'D THEY TAKE HER TO A HOSPITAL ON THE OTHER SIDE OF TOWN, GUADALUPE?
< WHERE'S THAT DAMN CAB..?! >
< THERE WASN'T ANY TIME TO ··
< MAMA, WAIT. >
MAMA..?
< HI, MAMA... >
< DORALIS, I'M ON MY WAY!
< MY CAB..! >
< IT'S OK, MAMA.
< EVERYBODY'S HERE... DADDY TOO...
< MAMA DON'T WORRY...
< I'M HAPPY... >
< DORALIS, I'M COMING! >
DORALIS..!
OH, GOD..!
< OH, MAMA DORALIS! SHE ··
< OH GOD, DORALIS!
....
YOU CALLED FOR A CAB, MA'AM?
8

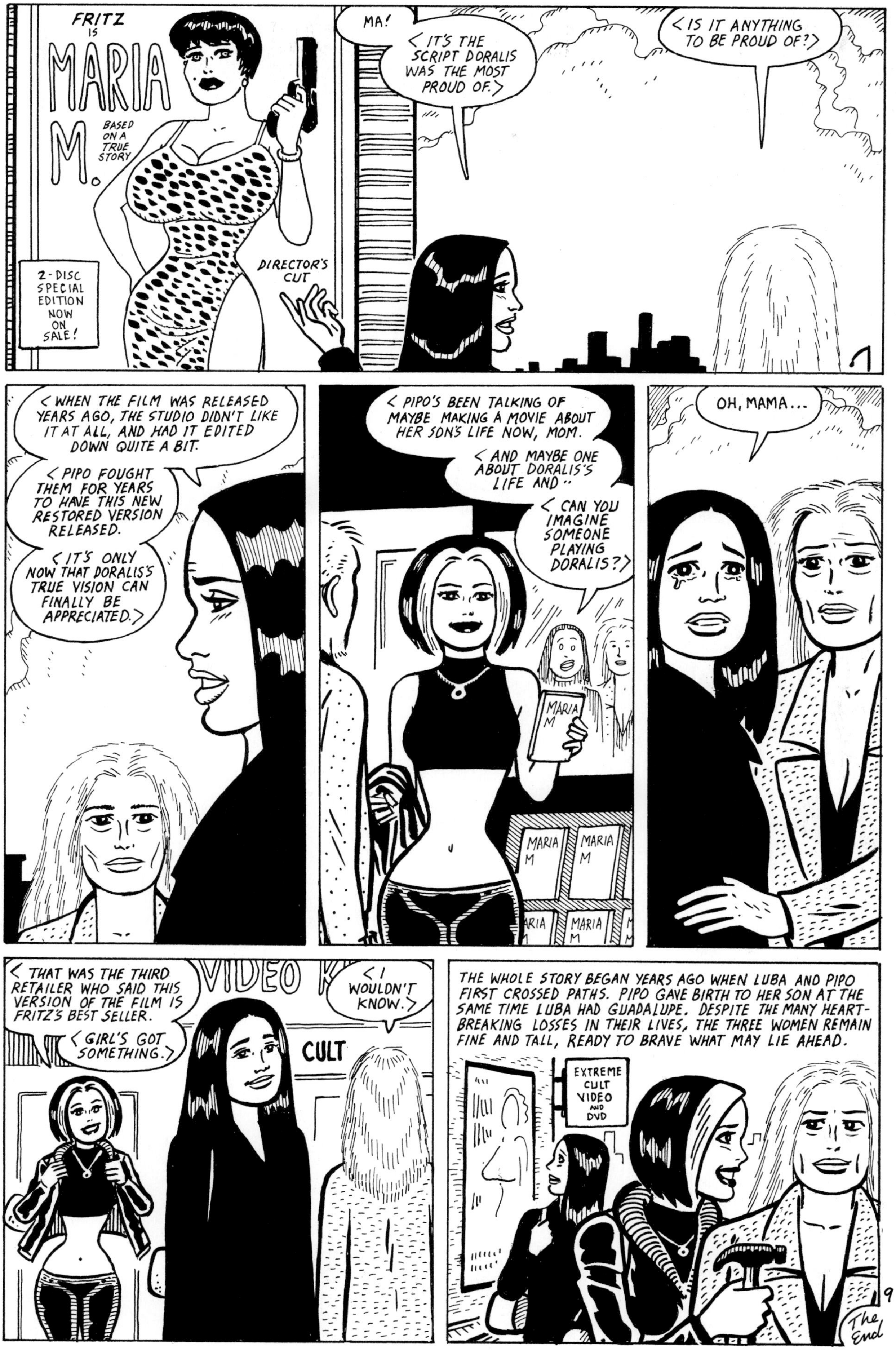
FRITZ IS MARIA M.
BASED ON A TRUE STORY
2-DISC SPECIAL EDITION NOW ON SALE!
DIRECTOR'S CUT
MA!
< IT'S THE SCRIPT DORALIS WAS THE MOST PROUD OF.>
< IS IT ANYTHING TO BE PROUD OF?>
< WHEN THE FILM WAS RELEASED YEARS AGO, THE STUDIO DIDN'T LIKE IT AT ALL, AND HAD IT EDITED DOWN QUITE A BIT.
< PIPO FOUGHT THEM FOR YEARS TO HAVE THIS NEW RESTORED VERSION RELEASED.
< IT'S ONLY NOW THAT DORALIS'S TRUE VISION CAN FINALLY BE APPRECIATED.>
< PIPO'S BEEN TALKING OF MAYBE MAKING A MOVIE ABOUT HER SON'S LIFE NOW, MOM.
< AND MAYBE ONE ABOUT DORALIS'S LIFE AND "
< CAN YOU IMAGINE SOMEONE PLAYING DORALIS?>
MARIA M
OH, MAMA...
< THAT WAS THE THIRD RETAILER WHO SAID THIS VERSION OF THE FILM IS FRITZ'S BEST SELLER.
< GIRL'S GOT SOMETHING.>
< I WOULDN'T KNOW.>
VIDEO
CULT
THE WHOLE STORY BEGAN YEARS AGO WHEN LUBA AND PIPO FIRST CROSSED PATHS. PIPO GAVE BIRTH TO HER SON AT THE SAME TIME LUBA HAD GUADALUPE. DESPITE THE MANY HEART-BREAKING LOSSES IN THEIR LIVES, THE THREE WOMEN REMAIN FINE AND TALL, READY TO BRAVE WHAT MAY LIE AHEAD.
EXTREME CULT VIDEO AND DVD
9
The End

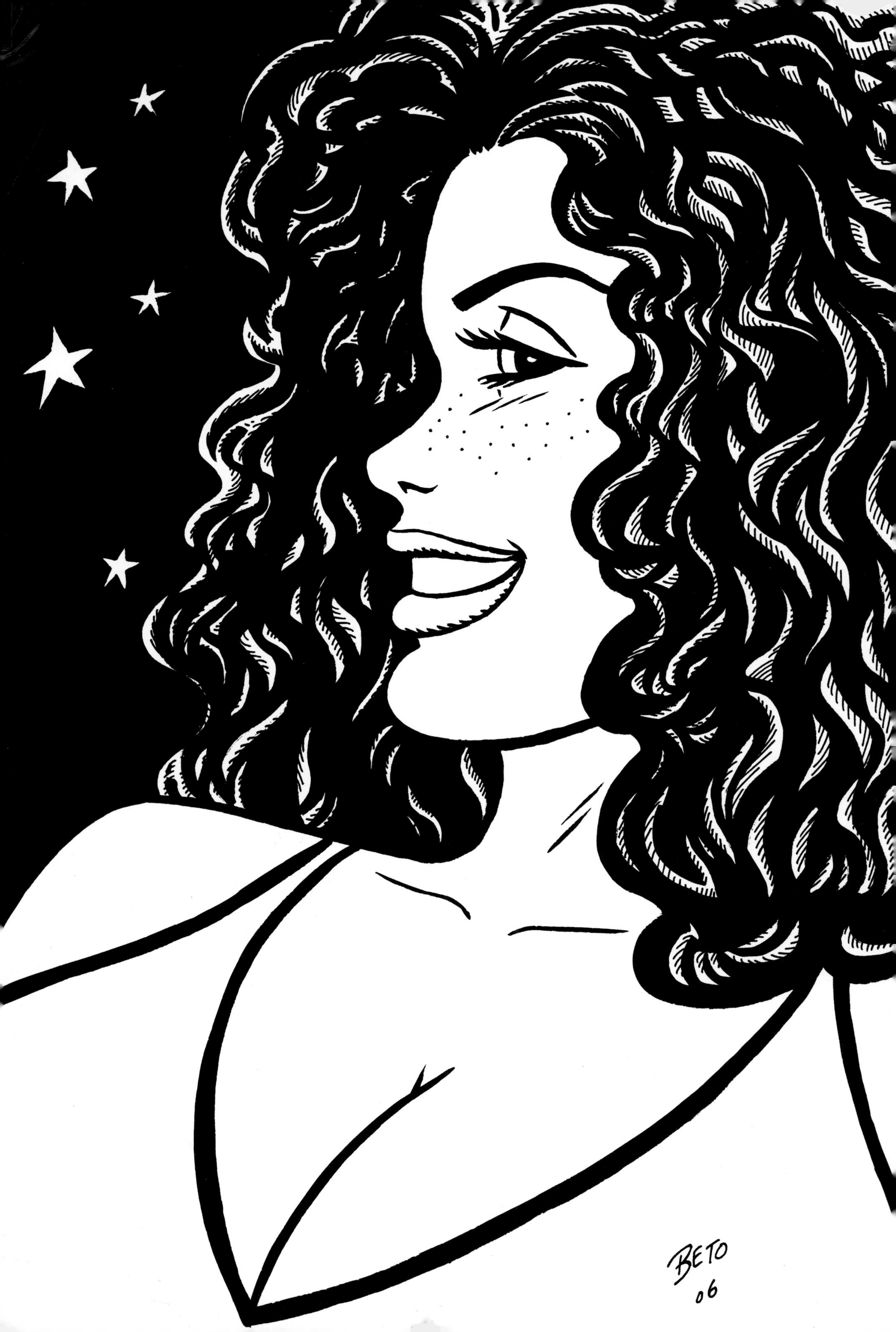
BETO
06

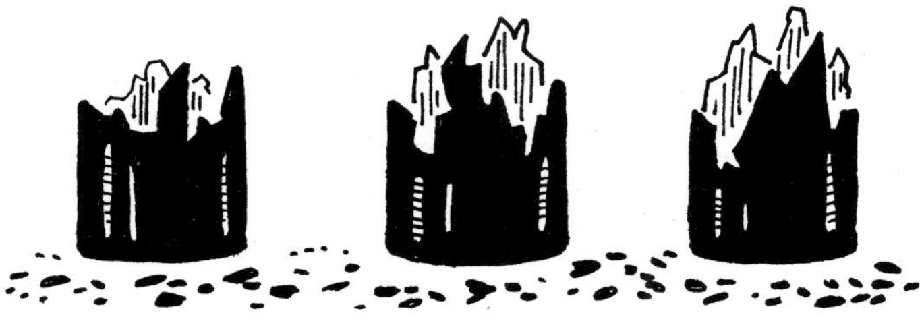

THE COMPLETE LOVE & ROCKETS LIBRARY
from Fantagraphics Books

Love & Rockets Book 1
MUSIC FOR MECHANICS
Short stories by Los Bros.; collects LR #1-2

Love & Rockets Book 2
CHELO'S BURDEN
Short stories by Los Bros.; collects LR #3-4

Love & Rockets Book 3
LAS MUJERES PERDIDAS
Graphic novel by Jaime plus short stories by Gilbert

Love & Rockets Book 4
TEARS FROM HEAVEN
Short stories by Gilbert & Jaime

Love & Rockets Book 5
HOUSE OF RAGING WOMEN
Short stories by Gilbert & Jaime

Love & Rockets Book 6
DUCK FEET
Short stories by Gilbert & Jaime

Love & Rockets Book 7
THE DEATH OF SPEEDY
Graphic novella and short stories by Jaime

Love & Rockets Book 8
BLOOD OF PALOMAR
Graphic novel by Gilbert

Love & Rockets Book 9
FLIES ON THE CEILING
Short stories by Gilbert & Jaime

Love & Rockets Book 10
LOVE & ROCKETS X
Graphic novel by Gilbert

Love & Rockets Book 11
WIGWAM BAM
Graphic novel by Jaime

Love & Rockets Book 12
POISON RIVER
Graphic novel by Gilbert

Love & Rockets Book 13
CHESTER SQUARE
Graphic novel by Jaime

Love & Rockets Book 14
LUBA CONQUERS THE WORLD
Short stories by Gilbert

Love & Rockets Book 15
HERNANDEZ SATYRICON
Short stories by Los Bros.

Love & Rockets Book 16
WHOA, NELLIE!
Graphic novel by Jaime

Love & Rockets Book 17
FEAR OF COMICS
Short stories by Gilbert

Love & Rockets Book 18
LOCAS IN LOVE
Short stories by Jaime

Love & Rockets Book 19
LUBA IN AMERICA
Short stories by Gilbert

Love & Rockets Book 20
DICKS AND DEEDEES
Short stories by Jaime

Love & Rockets Book 21
THE BOOK OF OFELIA
Short stories by Gilbert

Love & Rockets Book 22
GHOST OF HOPPERS
Short stories by Jaime

Love & Rockets Book 23
THREE DAUGHTERS
Short stories by Gilbert

Volume 1 and Volume 2
LOVE & ROCKETS SKETCHBOOKS
By Gilbert & Jaime